BLOOD RED, SNOW WHITE

Also by Nicholas Horrock

THE CORSICAN CONTRACT

BLOOD RED, SNOW WHITE

A NOVEL

DIANE HENRY AND NICHOLAS HORROCK

LITTLE, BROWN AND COMPANY
Boston   Toronto   London

ACKNOWLEDGMENTS

WE are grateful to Alice Martell, who was the first to have faith in this book.

We owe special thanks to William D. Phillips, an editor with an incisive eye and an elegant touch. He saw the scenes as they might be played out onstage, providing a looking glass through which his suggestions were vivid and compelling.

And, of course, we are in debt to all the prosecutors, defenders, judges, cops, bailiffs, narcs, court clerks, FBI agents, probation officers, customs agents, and crooks who filled our heads with such stories.

BLOOD RED, SNOW WHITE

1

THE July heat shimmered off the water, giving the sails at the horizon line a wavy appearance. His binoculars had picked up the Lightning out by Peach Island as the woman tacked toward the channel. Where other boats lay lifeless, she had found breeze, skillfully working the jib sheet to keep forward movement. The Lightning had no outboard. Other sailors used their outboards to get back across the busy channel. Once, on a totally windless day, he had seen her paddle in around the channel buoy. She had seemed embarrassed when he walked down to help her pull the boat in. "I've never had to use the paddle before," she had said.

Today the tiny wisp of air she had found seemed to carry her on a collision course with a giant cabin cruiser. A fat bald man at the wheel was gesturing angrily. He had a beer in one hand and he had let go of the wheel. The cabin cruiser gave a sickening lurch, but the Lightning seemed almost to dance away from the oncoming prow. The woman in the sailboat never looked up. The fat man's fat wife was now standing up in the cockpit waving. It was too far for him to hear the yells.

She tacked again, now catching the cross breeze that came around the Wilton Point power plant. She might make it on this tack, he thought, skirt the rocks, slide inside the buoy, but it would not be neat. That would land her by the clubhouse and she would have to wade to her house and pull her boat along. Somehow he knew she wouldn't wade in dragging the boat behind her, shattering her image as a superior sailor. She would come about just past the buoy, tack just short of the channel, and sail to her mooring.

Almost as he framed the thought, the Lightning came about, beginning the final tack. She was facing him, her features clear. Her dark blond hair was pulled tight away from her face in a ponytail that accentuated the oval shape of her head, her high cheekbones. She was looking right at him now, her blue eyes highlighting the dark tan of her face.

He felt a sharp pang of guilt. Could she see him watching her? Maybe the binocular lenses were reflecting the sun? He was inside his sun porch, back against the house wall, and the late-morning sun wouldn't pick up reflections. His fear was silly. From that distance, the shore was a row of houses; there were probably people looking at her from all of them.

At that moment her head turned back to face the bow as the Lightning entered the cove formed by the channel island. It seemed effortless the way she landed, the jib sheet dropping, the mainsail coming free, and the Lightning stopping, as though it had brakes, right at her mooring.

She stood up now, a big woman, her breasts heavy as she bent over the bow to attach the line to the mooring buoy. He watched her as she busied herself securing the boat, standing, legs braced against the rocking swells. She had full thighs, not flabby, but full, and large calves. She had told him she'd been captain of the lacrosse team at school, and he could almost imagine her then, trimmer of course, but the big legs running and jumping.

She bent to tie the sail to the mast and her shorts pulled up tight, the binoculars picking up the white skin above her tan line.

Edith Piaf had stopped her throaty "I Shouldn't Care," and the record was making a whooshy, whooshy sound. He got up and went inside. He turned the record over and started it again, this time with "Autumn Leaves."

When he came back out the blonde was gone and the Lightning rocked slowly, empty in the sun. He made a new drink, pouring the Stolichnaya over fresh ice and cutting a new twist of lemon. He remembered his father telling him that when they didn't drink the vodka in the war they used it for fuel to cook because it burned so hot and clean.

The *Times* said the Mujahadeen were unable to down Soviet helicopters with machine guns, Ronald Reagan had talked to Senate leaders about the tax cut, and social programs did not deal with rising food prices in Harlem. He began his dutiful trip through the Sunday paper.

He had always loved Sundays with Karen. He would awaken first and then gently try to arouse her without arousing her anger. They would finally entwine, enveloping one another with moist kisses. Unwilling to break even for birth control, they would make love like bullfighters, relying on timing to end without danger.

"We'll have children later," she would say. "This is our part of our lives. Once we know each other and ourselves, we'll be better able to care for someone else." He had not demurred. Life was so perfect he had been afraid to change it, afraid it would disappear. It had been like sailing in a light wind, afraid any movement of the tiller would becalm the boat.

On Sundays, he would come down and make coffee, warm a baguette of French bread, and get the *Times*. They would sit in bed looking out across the Sound and divide up the sections, hopelessly tangling the pages, leaving jelly and crumbs from the bread on the sheets. He could remember making love with a crisp piece of French bread digging into his back, head half buried in newspapers.

Now she was gone and he couldn't bear to use the front room as a bedroom. Anyway, she'd taken the big four-poster. So he slept in a back bedroom, which was cozy and overlooked the roses.

On Sunday mornings he ran now, long, slow loping runs, five and six miles along the road to Westport or down through Rowayton and up to the posh estate area of Darien and then back over the causeway to the island, passing the Catholics heading for seven o'clock mass at St. Timothy's.

He was reading the inside stories now, turning the pages, half digesting the headlines when he saw it. Shit! He sat bolt upright, letting his feet drop from the coffee table. "Indictments in Freezetemp Case Expected.

"The U.S. attorney is expected shortly to ask for indictments of executives of Freezetemp on charges they looted millions of dollars from the Brooklyn maritime refrigeration firm, according to sources who asked not to be identified."

Fucking A, they didn't want to be identified. The story had Benny Stein's byline. Stein was the *Times* federal court reporter. Benny never dug anything up. This was a message. Vincent Xavier Santorini was sending him a message. Gee, Vinny, you should have called.

The unnamed sources said that yearlong negotiations between prosecutors and Freezetemp executives had broken down and unnamed prosecutors were under pressure from unnamed superiors to indict Felix Schwartzberg and James Gallagher. You bet the negotiations had broken down, he thought. The fucking U.S. attorney wanted Felix and Jimmy to plead to enough crimes to keep them in jail until the next century, abandon a firm they had built over thirty years, and give the IRS the rest.

He was shaking with anger as he read. The story was a nasty little hit designed to do several things. It would frighten his clients, who were already scared, suggest to them they ought to get a lawyer who would have negotiations that don't break down. It was a cheap way to bolster the government's witnesses, the bookkeeper, Valery Vennuzio, that Felix had been balling on the side, and the supervisor in the Baltimore plant; and last but not least it would signal to his law partners that he wasn't such an insider at the U.S. attorney's office because he didn't know the story was coming.

That fucking Stein should have called him. Six hundred words into this little hate-gram, Stein had adroitly noted that "Alec Anton, who represents Schwartzberg and Gallagher, could not be reached for comment late Friday." Late Friday! Stein didn't use phones on Saturday? Even if he was Orthodox and disappeared at sundown, the *Times* should have had somebody else call.

He had to move fast. He ran upstairs to the front room. He'd put his desk there so he could look out over the Sound when he worked.

He opened a black personal telephone book and began dialing. He started with Felix, punching in the Northport number with angry jabs at the telephone. Almost as he did it, an inner voice said "Calm down. Be cool."

The FBI had wiretapped Felix for 180 days during the investigation, and even though a conversation with a lawyer was privileged, he knew the bureau liked to spook a suspect and then listen to the calls he made when he was excited.

Could they have gotten a warrant for a new tap? Maybe they were getting anxious about whether Felix and Jimmy were going to plead. Maybe they were going to push them a little with new surveillance, with the *Times* story?

Sophie answered, her coarse Long Island accent made harsher

with cigarettes and booze. Sophie was Felix's fourth wife, a buxom dyed blonde he met at Club Med, where she'd gone after shedding her second husband. They deserve each other, Alec often thought. "Hiya, beautiful. Is Felix around?" He made his voice sound light, assured. When he first entered private practice Connie Callaghan had told him "As a prosecutor, a big part of your job was intimidating white-collar crooks into pleading guilty. Well this is the other side of the coin. A big part of this job is holding their hands, so they don't start to cry. Never show fear to a client."

"He's out by the pool," Sophie answered. "So what's this story in the *Times?* Everybody's calling and Felix is very upset. He didn't eat any breakfast."

God, Alec thought, that's serious. Felix could inhale a tray of prune danishes and never stop talking.

"That's just why I called, sweetheart. I don't want the big guy to worry. It's all in the game. They planted that story to push Felix and Jimmy. I know I don't have to tell you that. You've been around this town. You know how it plays. So I'm depending on you to keep him cool." He suddenly had a vision of Sophie, who probably weighed in at a generous 160 pounds, stroking Felix's hairy 250-pound body and murmuring soothing words.

Sophie loved to be flattered. From the beginning she'd enjoyed the notion that Alec recognized she was more worldly than her husband. Hadn't her second husband been a stockbroker? She liked the role of nurse, with Alec the doctor who gave her private instructions on how to care for her patient.

Another thing Callaghan had told him. "It's the wives. The wives sit there and they nod and they nod and on the way home they say 'Get another lawyer. Get that friend of my cousin's. This schmuck isn't doing anything for you.' Yeh, it's the wives."

Sophie had already made a big adjustment. She didn't need a map to figure that Miss Vennuzio hadn't acquired enough information to be a government witness from just doing books. Sophie had never said a word to him, but Alec bet she'd said a word to Felix.

"I'll do my best, Alec. I want him to get away. Just the two of us. No phones. Maybe take the boat up to Maine," Sophie said. Schwartzberg had a boat that made the *Queen Mary* look small. Sail it while you can, thought Alec, the government has its eye on that boat.

"I'll back your play, doll. Now you better get Felix. Otherwise he'll think you and I are doing more than talking law."

Sophie erupted in a guffaw. "That'll be the day." She sang it like the song. Felix came on almost at once. Either he'd been listening for his cue or the electronic marvel of his home had scored again. Felix loved the gadgets of the late twentieth century. He had cordless phones, cellular phones, a security system that could scan every room in the house, built-in television sets in every room except the dining and kitchen areas, a television grounds-monitoring system, a computer-regulated water system, and another that drained, filtered, and recycled the pool.

"Do I need a lawyer who lets me have Sunday-morning surprises? Do I need such a lawyer?" Felix was warming up, the wonderful rich accents of Poland, Israel, and Brooklyn flavoring his speech like a good East European ragout.

Alec cut in hard. "Remember our friends," he said, reminding Felix of the FBI, the unannounced ears on the telephone.

"Okay. Okay, but what's going on? How come on Thursday you say everything's percolating and on Sunday I'm reading in the *New York Times* that percolating it isn't?" Felix asked, the anger still in his voice.

"Games. Felix, they're playing games. It's the kind of games you know far more about than I do, games of terror, games of fear. This is to remind the victim they can destroy him. This is to get your attention. To push you into a bad decision." Alec was talking soothingly, the way you talk to somebody who has just been in an accident.

"All through this, I've known that these games wouldn't work on you, that your life would be a shield."

He could see Felix in his mind's eye sitting hunched over the phone, the giant forearms and enormous shoulders. When Alec was growing up, the Jews he had met were mostly rich, often delicate, the children of the first German Jewish migration to New York, whose parents were wealthy, cultured. Families like the Sulzbergers, the Schlesingers.

Felix was different. He was a peasant, a child of peasants. Thick arms and legs. His neck, even in the late years of what had become too good a life, corded with muscles. His strength had preserved his life. It had preserved him as a wild runaway in the Carpathian forest, running with a band of child-adults orphaned by the war. It had saved him at Belsen, where instead of being one he had been chosen to load the bodies onto carts.

Alec could remember the first time they'd met with the FBI agents; Felix had been perfect. He volunteered nothing, said nothing unless prompted by Alec. He never made eye contact with the agents; instead he watched their hands.

Later Alec had told him, "You know, for a guy who has no criminal record, no experience dealing with the bureau, you really were very good."

Felix had gazed at him a long time, the way you look at a fool. "I have been in that room before, kiddling. Oh yes, I have been in that room before. In the rooms I was in there were no right answers. No right answers." His voice had trailed off. Alec had not known much about Felix then, and he felt mystified by the strange demeanor of this giant, richly attired businessman with hands so rough touching them was like touching iron.

"Why did you watch the agents' hands all the time?" Alec asked.

"In the rooms where I sat," Felix murmured, "the hands held truncheons."

Now on the telephone, on this summer Sunday more than a year later, Felix seemed weary.

"I want to see you tomorrow. We have to talk. Time is too short in life to do this," Felix said.

Alec winced. If the bureau was listening, it got what it wanted. It was wearing Felix down.

"Sure, Felix. Why don't you and Jimmy come downtown after lunch. Meanwhile I'll try to get to Santorini and find out why he's playing this game. You know games work both ways, and I'm not sure the real story here isn't that Mr. Santorini and company are having a little trouble. This case has had three FBI agents, the wiretap technicians, two IRS agents, six enforcement types from the SEC, two lawyers in the U.S. attorney's office, and a guy from the Defense Investigative Service. The recovery zone for them is the conviction of two guys with no prior record, recovery of maybe ten to fifteen million dollars, tops, when every day the newspapers are talking about defense companies and stockbrokers stealing billions."

"Should I do anything now?" Felix asked. His voice had calmed. "Yeh. Don't talk to the newspapers, turn your phone off, and get laid." Alec chuckled.

"Listen, counselor, that's my advice to you. Why don't I fix you up with this nice little girl we got down in purchasing. She's a Sephardi who looks like a spic and fucks like an Arab."

Jesus, Alec thought. Felix had managed to violate seven equal opportunity laws in one sentence.

"See you tomorrow, big guy, maybe two-thirty or three. Okay?" Felix grunted and hung up.

Jimmy Gallagher worried Alec more. He was a slimy little bum. Alec knew Santorini had spotted that early and had tried twice to pry Jimmy and Felix apart. If the case went to indictment, Alec knew, the government's first move would be to try to force Jimmy to get a separate lawyer. If he got a new counsel, Santorini figured he might be able to get a deal with Jimmy against Felix.

Alec's strongest card, which he had just turned the corner up on once, was that even if the government got a conviction, it was trying to lock up the American dream. Two working stiffs, one a survivor of the death camps, no prior record, was not an attractive conviction anywhere and particularly not in the Southern District.

The Southern District of New York was the Super Bowl of white-collar crime, home base of the Mafia, all in a city where every day's television news brought forth a nun raped in a church or a Son of Sam case. By comparison Felix and Jimmy were the proverbial choirboys.

Felix was true tough and he could work this through. He knew what real bad was. But Jimmy only looked tough and talked tough. He was Red Hook, son of a city bus driver from Cork. Jimmy had shipped out in the merchant marine just after World War II as an electrician.

But when he got married his wife hadn't liked him gone that long, so he got a job at the repair docks in Hoboken.

Jimmy was a professional Irishman. He and his wife flew to Dublin half a dozen times a year. If you got a gift from them it was Waterford. He wore tweeds even when the weather was too warm and talked incessantly of "getting out of the rat race" and retiring to Ireland.

From the beginning Gallagher had misunderstood his plight. In the first meeting with Alec he had brought his wife, a birdlike woman who clearly had an alcohol problem. They both drank heavily, but Gallagher held it well and its effects had not ravaged his face as they had his wife's.

"You get in touch with Tip O'Neill," the wife, Kerry Gallagher, had said. "We go to the races with him every year. And then we'll call Cardinal Connor and the nice man who works for Ted Kennedy."

How stupid can they get? Alec remembered reacting. She thinks this is fixing a ticket. "Mrs. Gallagher, you're right, those are important allies for us. But this is a Republican administration and a case that has been developed by professional government enforcement officers. Let's learn more about this before we use up your contacts."

From that first meeting, the Gallaghers had fluctuated between arrogance and despair. Jimmy Gallagher showed no guilt or remorse.

He was, he seemed to feel, the victim of perverse regulations. "I don't understand why America has turned against people who want to work and make something of themselves. It's okay to be a nigger on welfare shooting heroin, but God help you if you want to work and pay taxes."

Once, when Alec had grown weary of the tirades, he dryly noted that the IRS was claiming Jimmy hadn't exactly paid taxes either.

The Gallaghers lived in a cooperative apartment off Sutton Place, and the number rang three times when Alec called before it switched to the front desk. "The Gallagher residence," came a Jamaican voice. Alec left his name and his New York number, relieved that he had not had to talk to Jimmy.

The vodka was now taking its effect. He felt weary and his right leg ached from his morning run. He went into the bedroom and lay down, hoping to ease the cramp.

Karen was screaming at him, her hair disheveled, and he could not make out what she was saying. He saw her throw the coffee and then watched it drip down the wall, and then he realized he was in Judge Kelsey's chambers and the coffee was dripping down the wall there.

Karen had no clothes on and he felt it was very important to cover her body so the judge wouldn't see. I'm sorry, your honor, he kept saying. I'm sorry, your honor. He found his face close to the tiny hairs that grew from the areolae. The old quip he teased her with kept running through his mind: "I always wanted a girl with hair on her chest." The judge was looking at her breasts as well. But try as he might, Alec couldn't cover them.

When he awoke the room was dark and he was covered with cold perspiration. His mouth tasted awful and the vodka had left him feeling puffy and bloated.

He looked at his watch. It was nearly 9 P.M. He had missed the best New York train. He sat up and put his legs over the edge of the bed. His stomach turned. He realized that he had not eaten since Saturday night and all he'd had all day was coffee and vodka.

What a strange dream. He had seldom had dreams before, or at least he could seldom remember them, and now he had them all the time. Why Judge Kelsey's chambers? He probably hadn't been in Kelsey's chambers twice in his life, and he'd never been there with Karen.

He hated to go back to New York on Monday mornings. The trains were packed, and from that moment on the week seemed cluttered and confused. But now the only train was the 11 P.M., which didn't get into Grand Central until nearly two. If he didn't take the train, he would have to drive. He wasn't sure the old VW would make it to a garage space worth ten times what the car was.

His mind seemed clouded. He went downstairs shakily. The morning's run had left his legs weak, and when he didn't eat his blood sugar dropped.

In the midevening rush, the harbor and the Sound looked like a field of multicolored jewels on blue velvet, the running lights of the boats, tracing little designs, set off by the red and green lights of the channel markers. Way in the far distance, like a star, the New Haven lighthouse beam sparkled.

He went out on the porch and lit the storm lamp on the table. The air was filled with the sound of crickets and the soft lapping of the water against the seawall. Wearily he realized he didn't have enough energy to go to New York.

He foraged in the refrigerator, but it was bleak: some eggs, butter, and milk. A feast, Karen would have said, a feast. He walked back through the darkened house to the garden, picking up a flashlight in the tool room. The far corner, seventy-five feet from the house, where the vegetables had been laid out, was a tangle of weeds, but he found two small zucchini and an onion.

They had set out the garden every year feeling like pioneers, bringing their produce back to New York with the pride of the self-reliant. Once as they were buying yet another tool at the hardware store, they calculated that these were some of the most expensive vegetables in the New York area, farmed by two lawyers who made $300,000 a year, using tools from Darien, seeds from New Canaan, and enough books and accoutrements to start an agribusiness.

After Karen left he planted each spring, filled with the energy of April and May, but by midsummer the garden was abandoned to the animals and weeds. He was surprised the zucchini had survived the slugs and mice.

In the kitchen he made a fresh vodka and put on Ray Price. It was his signal that he was going to feel sorry for himself.

It was his inheritance. His father had left him little else but a strange, Slavic melancholy. It did not come at moments of grief or crisis, but arose unheralded by an event, sometimes even when the events around him were joyful.

He whisked the eggs into froth as Ray Price remembered the "good times." He steamed the zucchini quickly over boiling water and sautéed the onion until the pieces were clear and soft.

Using the same pan in which he cooked the onion, adding just a small dollop of new butter, he began the omelet, gently folding in the sides until the bottom had firmed. His mother had taught him to cook, standing in a kitchenette that was part of the living-room wall and telling him stories of the Montana mountains. She could transport a child from a cramped New York apartment and the vicissitudes of genteel poverty to a land of prairies and mountains, cowboys, and the Blackfoot Indians.

Cooking was a wonderful device for seducing women. He wondered if his mother knew how he had used this skill. The way to a woman's vagina is through her stomach, Karen would joke as she ate some late-night concoction.

When the egg had firmed into a saucer on the bottom of the pan, he spooned in the onion and steamed zucchini, folding the sides in to make a yellow envelope.

He noted with pleasure that the omelet had not browned on the bottom, the true test of the fine chef — no burning butter.

When he sat down at the porch table, he realized he had been talking to himself. Self-consciously, he looked through the darkened screen to see if anyone was walking along the seawall path.

The vodka had made him feel better, and he wolfed down the food, pausing only to sip from his drink.

He was glad he had fallen asleep, not called Vinny, not reached Jimmy, and, thank God, not called the *Times*. Those would have been signs of panic. Being a criminal lawyer, Connie Callaghan always said, is better than going on the stage, you're acting all the time.

He got up from the table and walked out across the lawn to the seawall. A cool onshore breeze shook the rigging of the sailboats, creating that familiar urgent rattle of lines and masts in the darkness. Suddenly, impulsively, he waded out to the Windmill. The tide was in and he was up to his chest in the cool salt water before he reached the mooring. He clumsily hauled himself over the side and began to rig for sailing.

He didn't sail at night often. Two of the Windmill's running lights were out, and he never seemed to have time to go down and get new bulbs. But the bow and masthead lights were working and he could set the flashlight on the bench by the tiller. The harbor was quieter now, the only traffic the steady stream of powerboats coming up the channel to Cove Marine after their Sunday outings.

He fitted the jib sheet first, then the mainsail, and took the 1.5 horsepower and set it on the outboard panel, putting his finger in the gas tank to see how much fuel was left. He hadn't used the flashlight yet; the light from the houses on shore was enough to rig by. For a moment he watched Lee, the big blonde, in her living room. He could only see the upper half of her body, a white halter sharp against dark tan skin. She was talking to somebody he could not see, gesturing angrily.

The small vessel was like a rambunctious horse under him in the onshore breeze. As soon as the sails were rigged it began pulling at the mooring, swinging wildly back and forth on the line.

He crawled to the bow, unhooked the line from the mooring buoy, and let the boat drift until he set his place in the stern. When he raised the jib, the sharp night breeze picked up the Windmill and it was off.

He tacked toward the channel island on the wind in the jib and waited to raise the mainsail until he'd passed the island's dark form. He didn't want to drop the centerboard until he was outside the cove for fear it would snag on the marsh tangle near the island.

Suddenly, like an animal who has been let to pasture, the Windmill was in open harbor, already zipping along as he pulled the mainsail up.

He came about once, to wait for a pause in the line of powerboats so he could sail across the channel. From the Windmill, the houses on Harborview, frame cottages mainly, looked warm and inviting.

He had been in California when Karen found the cottage, and he could remember her excited description of its view of the water. "You can hear Gershwin in every room," she had said, "and Gatsby lives right across the harbor."

The cant of Harborview Island left it facing a row of sixty-year-old mansions on the Westport shoreline, great wooded pieces of land with docks often hosting long yachts.

Once he crossed the channel and headed for the open Sound, he was virtually alone. The summer weekend was over, the water was clear of pleasure boats, and the workboats of the weekdays would not be out until Monday. In the darkness, with no cockpit light and only the flashlight next to him, the water provided splendid isolation. The breeze was brisk and steady, and soon the old Windmill was heeled over, with Alec hanging hard out on the port. The flashlight had slid off the seat and was trailing in the water on its lanyard, the beam making strange contortions in the wake.

For Alec, the flighty Windmill had been pure exhilaration, and he sailed with the joy of the speed, the wind and excitement of a boat dancing on the edge of floundering.

But Alec realized though Karen loved the wind, and the beauty of a race across the water, speed had always frightened her. As a child, she had told him, she could never grant the faith that going fast on a bicycle gave her better control. She liked things where she was in control. That was her final indictment: "You're reckless, Alec, reckless and out of control."

He found himself letting the Windmill's sail out, slowing the boat without even the realization he was doing so.

He was in mid-Sound now, the vastness of big water more sensed than seen in the darkness, Rowayton, Wilton, Norwalk, and Westport now clusters of sparkling lights divided by the inky black of woods and open country and covered by a glow of accumulated light.

Way out in the darkness of the Sound he could see a string of running lights stretched behind a large oceangoing tugboat. The tug would never see him, he thought, until it was too late. On the tug's radar the Windmill would appear as a large piece of driftwood, something the crew would not, even if they could, change course to avoid. It would be the perfect suicide. Double indemnity with a chance to recover negligence from the tug's insurance carrier.

A windfall for his heirs. But of course he had no heirs. He brought the Windmill about, pointing the bow toward the Norwalk lights.

2

As he turned off of City Hall Plaza, the buildings afforded little shade. The granite caverns were as hot as a pizza oven, radiating the sun. He realized his head hurt and he wished he could postpone the lunch with Vinny. He wanted to go lie down somewhere. The vodka he'd drunk the night before wasn't helping. Could you call in sick to life? Hello, I'd like to report that I'm sick and I plan to stay home for a couple of years, then I'll be back.

At the India House he went right into a washroom, soaked a towel, and cooled his face. He tried to pull his wrinkled shirt into shape and adjusted his tie.

"You know why you have to be a dresser?" Connie Callaghan would start defensively, dusting imaginary flint from his thousand-dollar Savile Row suit. "Because the clients figure if you look shabby you're not doing too well, and if you're not doing well you're not going to do well for them."

The water made Alec feel better and he buttoned his jacket, which hid the view of his rumpled clothes. He looked at himself a long time in the mirror. He had been looking at his face for forty-one years and suddenly he saw what others must see. He looked tired. There were lines where he had not noticed them before and his eyes seemed lifeless. He shook his head as though clearing a cobweb, fluffed up the starched white handkerchief in his breast pocket, and entered the foyer.

Above him rose the grand stairway to the club's first level of tables. Maurice, the maître d', looked diffident and frozen, as though he was one of the statues next to a giant oil of the *Dewitt Clinton* on its trial run along the Hudson.

If the Communists could crystallize a single vision of capitalism, the India House would be it.

Maurice moved past an oil of Cornelius Vanderbilt, who clearly had never worried about cholesterol, to the second-tier dining room. "Mr. Santorini is already here, Mr. Anton." Maurice took the lead across the room with the purpose of a destroyer escorting a convoy through a mine field.

But Alec wove in and out. "Hey, Charlie." A wave. That was Charles Duckett, clerk of the federal court in Brooklyn. "Hey, Tony." Tony DeLuga. He'd defended Tony's brother in the Marston fraud matter, found out well into the case and to his dismay that the DeLuga's had a branch of the family that was a branch of the family.

Mayor Koch looked up as he passed. "Hello, counselor." Alec stopped. "Mr. Mayor." It was amazing what $20,000 in Democratic contributions would do. "Do you know Abe Rosenthal?" The mayor gestured toward the *New York Times* editor, who had just put a shrimp in his mouth. That was okay because Koch wasn't going to let him talk anyway.

"This young man was a constituent of mine when I was in Congress and he had just come back from Vietnam. One day — do you remember that day, Alec?" Alec smiled. He could remember it. "One day he went out in his marine officer's uniform with some young kids who were demonstrating against the war and just stood there to keep a bunch of hooligans from beating them up."

It had been a silly gesture. But it had enraged Alec the day before to read construction workers had beat up kids in front of NYU. He hadn't carried a sign or banner, just stood among them in his greens staring down a bunch of hard hats who gathered across the street. Koch, who represented Greenwich Village in those days, had come by at almost the same time with the local police precinct commander to make sure the cops protected the kids.

"So what's your big case today, counselor?" the mayor asked.

"My big case today is to get at some of those shrimps." Alec nodded toward Rosenthal's plate, smiling at the others who crowded the table. He knew most by sight; two were *Times* editors, one the owner of the *Village Voice*, and one was Bobby Wagner, the son of a former New York mayor. He now worked on Koch's staff.

The encounter hadn't hurt. Alec could see Vinny out of the corner of his eye looking ignored.

Vinny had already ordered a Perrier; it stood pristine, without ice, a lime cartwheel floating near the top. His hands placed and replaced the silverware. He repositioned the fish knife, lined it up precisely with the dessert spoon, unconsciously reset the salad fork, and put the butter knife in a new position so it dissected the butter plate.

They were long, thin white hands, manicured and set off with white cuffs, coming a perfect quarter inch below the cuff of the perfectly cut gray jacket. Vinny had studied to be a priest. Alec could see those fingers placing the wafer on the tongue, making the sign of the cross like a wand.

They exchanged the pleasantries of a business lunch. How were things? Did you read Waverly has been nominated to the Fifth Circuit? Do you and Karen ever see each other?

Alec hardly listened. He was struggling with a conundrum. It had bothered him from the beginning. Why was Vinny handling Freezetemp himself? In the preliminary meetings, Vinny had said it was the press of business. "You remember how it is. Too many cases, too few lawyers." Sure. But U.S. attorneys didn't horse around with medium-size white-collar cases.

Other things bothered him today. Nothing was wasted with Vinny, no gesture, no word, no action. Why lunch?

Why not just sit in his office and listen to Alec rail about the *Times* story? He watched Vinny's face. It gave no hint. Vinny was talking past Alec to some other audience, like he was already running for governor.

A decade ago they had been friends. Young prosecutors without wealth or political connections trying to make it in the Southern District. Vinny the cautious had stayed and worked up. Alec had taken the risk, gone private. Now he had wealth and Vinny had connections.

Finally with the fish came the meat. "Vinny, how come I read in the Sunday *New York Times* that my negotiations with you have broken down? You don't own a telephone? You have to reach me through the *Times?*"

Vinny seemed intent on avoiding eye contact when he spoke, addressing his hands at first, then a sliver of lower Manhattan skyline that was caught by the window to his right.

"Alec, I resent the suggestion that I try my cases in the papers.

Benjamin Stein is a good reporter; he has dug out some facts and published them. I don't agree with such stories, but I will defend the *Times*'s right to publish them."

"Benny Stein is a lazy schmuck, Vinny. Schmuck in case your Yiddish is weak means prick. He hasn't dug out a story since Christ was a corporal. In fact even if it were handed to him, Benjamin's natural instinct would be to hold it until the trial. You know that, I know that."

Alec's voice was gaining volume with indignation. His finger stabbed the air in Vinny's direction as rapidly as a jackhammer. Two men at a nearby table looked up.

Connie Callaghan had once warned him against anger. "Anger, Alec, is your worst enemy. You let go too often. When you get truly angry, truly mad, you're lost. That means you can be provoked, and if you can be provoked you will say or do injudicious things and you give your opponent an opening."

Alec tried to guard himself. He chose his words carefully so that he would only appear to be out of control.

"Vinny, you told me by telephone early last week that our discussions were fruitful and we could make a deal. You told me that yourself. From your office. By phone. That was really you, right?

"Four days later I read in the *New York Times* that our negotiations are breaking down. What the fuck is going on?"

"You and your clients were holding out on us, that's what the fuck is going on," Vinny answered. Vinny had grown up in a working-class home. Fuck was unheard there. Your mother strapped you if you said fuck. Fuck was for the streets. Now when Vinny said it, it sounded strained, like he expected his mother to appear, strap in hand.

Incredulity must have shown on Alec's face.

"My clients have had every record they possess gone over by the IRS, the FBI, and the SEC. You have tapped their telephones and had them followed. They have sat through interminable interviews, and dozens of their employees have been questioned. What could they be holding out?" Alec's voice was growing louder.

Vinny put his hand on Alec's, a long white hand on a short thick hand. It was a strange gesture. Alec pulled his hand away uncomfortably. He wasn't tactile.

"We can't discuss this here." Vinny's voice was without anger. "You're getting upset. Finish and we'll go back."

Vinny had scored. Alec appeared the confused and angry one, Vinny the priest. Let me help you, my son.

Outside the Mercury Monarch sat cool and black. A government chauffeur with dark glasses was reading the *Daily News*. The taxpayers had paid for Vinny to be driven ten blocks to lunch. A cab round-trip would have cost ten dollars, even with a hefty tip.

In his office Vinny opened a file with the gestures of a surgeon about to operate and drew out a tissuelike paper. There was a silence. A silence in which Alec had a chill of fear. He hoped his face didn't show it. But the old lawyers' adage was always true: Never ask a question you don't know the answer to.

Vinny studied the paper with an expression that fell just short of a smirk. "Has Mr. Gallagher ever discussed with you a bank account he has in Zurich?"

Uncontrollably Alec's mind shifted to Zurich. He could see the canal and the bridges into the lake. They had eaten near the canal one evening, he and Karen, in a funny little walled garden with a fountain. They'd had an Austrian Riesling and had sat outside until the sun went down and the unexpected chill of a spring evening had settled over the garden.

With difficulty he brought himself back to Vinny's office. He knew he must freeze. The way they would freeze in Vietnam when they thought a path was mined. No one moved either forward or back. No one breathed. They just stood stock-still and tried to figure a way out. Alec froze.

The feds would never tell a defense lawyer about a discovery like a Swiss bank account. They would use that to surprise the victim. They would want to scare Gallagher first, hoping to get an admission. It was wasted on Alec. Unless. Unless they had already surprised Gallagher.

Jimmy had never called him, not Sunday night or Monday. He wasn't on the recorder at the apartment and he hadn't called the answering service at the office.

"Vinny, I wouldn't want to engage you on this without Mr. Gallagher and Mr. Schwartzberg being present. I think they would believe I was going beyond my authority as their counsel, don't you think?"

Vinny smiled. It was the smile of a man who had won several races and tried for the daily double with no real expectation he would win that too. "I think you should get in touch with your clients, see what's going on, and get back to me. I have been told the case is moving very swiftly. The agents told me that. Very swiftly," Vinny said.

He pressed forward. "The train is leaving the station for them, Alec. We have made an offer. But we can't wait forever. I don't know where Benny got his information, but the truth is I am under pressure to take this case to trial. You've worked here. You know there are other forces at work. The investigative agencies think they have a strong case and they want to go to trial and get this manpower back on the street . . . on to something else.

"The attorney general wants more trials. No matter how good for the government, plea-bargains don't look good. He thinks it makes us look like we aren't doing our job."

Vinny reached over the desk, palm upward. It was the gesture of a supplicant.

"You and I go back a ways, Alec. Let me tell you something, as a friend. Plead these guys! I have made a good offer. Your clients should take it. It would be better for everybody."

Whatever Vinny had on a Swiss bank account, it had made him more confident. He was visibly more assured than he had been a week ago. Alec moved cautiously.

"Vinny, one of these men is in his late fifties, the other in his sixties. If they are convicted at trial of the charges you're talking about, no federal judge in this district is going to send them to jail. They have no prior record. These are paper crimes; there is no charge of violence, no charge of intimidation. A judge is going to set a fine. He is going to punish them from the view of taking back what he will call ill-gotten gains. You and I know that's going to be his sentencing theory. That means the government is going to the extraordinary expense of a trial without the expectation of imprisoning the culprits!"

Alec paused to let his argument sink in.

"I can't recommend your offer to my clients because it calls for them to go to jail. Take jail out of the deal! I can't discuss an arrangement that's going to send a man who survived Belsen back behind bars." Alec was warming to his task.

His voice was low, which had forced Vinny to lean slightly forward to hear. It was the voice of one veteran assistant U.S. attorney trying to get another to resist the wrongful pressures of his boss and the FBI.

"What I said last week still goes. Please try to work out an offer that serves us both. They believe they were doing business, tough, sharp business. They don't want to spend the latter years of their lives in trials and appeals. If they were younger I suspect they would be saying to me 'Take it to trial. We did nothing wrong.' But they are getting along. They want to be spending time with their grand-children, traveling. . . ."

Suddenly the mood was broken. Vinny cut in sharply. "That reminds me. We want their passports. The indication of new unre-ported foreign bank accounts, I think, raises the danger of their fleeing. I can ask for their passports after indictment, but in the interval I want you to deliver them to us voluntarily. Otherwise indictment and immediate arrest would be our only protection."

Alec kept a strong grip on his voice. "Vinny, I've got limitations. These are two American citizens. They're businessmen. They know their rights. They're not going to flee. I can assure you of that. Whether they will sit still for the indignity of surrendering their passports is another matter."

Alec knew he had to get out now. Withdraw like a rifle squad, always facing the enemy, not running, giving up ground tree by tree, rock by rock. The longer he stayed in this office, the more dangerous it became.

He had avoided letting Vinny know the Swiss account was a big deal. Vinny would be unsure. He would call in the IRS guy and the FBI agents and report that Gallagher's lawyer didn't seem at all surprised. Every other word he uttered, Alec knew, was going to cost him.

He feigned surprise at his watch. "Jesus, look at the time. I've got a heavy deposition." His face wrinkled in worry. "Let me leave it at this: We've got to get something on the table I can work with. My offer has been a single felony count. They both want me to press for misdemeanors, because their corporate counsel has made a major issue of loss of civil rights. But I may be able to persuade them to consider a single felony count, no joint time, and fines in some realistic relation to their crime. No RICO. Vinny, we've got to get closer together. You think on it and I will."

Alec had risen and was closing his leather portfolio as he talked, limiting Vinny's answer. "I'll call you Tuesday or Wednesday."

Vinny was clearly annoyed that he had been virtually dismissed in his own office. "Get me those passports," he said as Alec headed down the hall.

The federal courthouse at Foley Square was one of those marble edifices to Franklin Delano Roosevelt's Work Projects Administration. It had wide open hallways and as years went on the U.S. attorney's offices had blocked these graceful layouts with a rabbit warren of partitions.

Even though Alec had worked there, he was soon lost, following empty winding corridors stacked with files.

He came around a corner and almost stumbled over a woman bent down before him. She was picking up a file that had broken and the position had pulled her navy blue skirt tight across her bottom. Each bottom cheek was clearly delineated through the material.

He said her name, "Karen," before he saw her face. The woman turned to look up at him. "That's all you were ever interested in, wasn't it?" She looked into his eyes knowingly.

"I don't know what you're talking about," he lied, extending his hand to help her up. Her beauty still took his breath away. She had a long, oval face with a strong nose and full lips. Her black hair, touched by gray since her twenties, had always set off her pink and white skin and her fair complexion. But it was her eyes that drew the attention. They were saucy in repose, promising sensuality, or warning of anger, yet wide and open as though she viewed the world as a wonderful game she was about to play. He had never tired of gazing into those eyes.

Karen had turned back to the papers on the floor. "You came at just the right time. Give me a hand and be careful. This is a transcript, so try to pick it up in order," she said.

Busily, they picked up the papers. He felt comfortable in the closeness. "How ya doing?" Alec asked. He knew, as he had known at other meetings, that he wanted her to answer "awful," to turn and tell him how miserable she was, how her life was terrible without him.

He met her occasionally now, in a hall or courtroom, on the street near federal court. He could never adjust to the realization that their intimacy was destroyed, that if he reached out to stroke her cheek, or rub her shoulder as he used to do, it would be as though he touched a perfect stranger.

He had known her since she was in law school, a long-legged girl in a miniskirt working as an intern in the U.S. attorney's office during the days, going to antiwar demonstrations at night.

Karen was talking now, bringing his mind back to the shabby hallway. "Oh God, I'm tired of prosecuting unending lines of Mexican boat captains, Colombian fishermen. 'Meeeese, I deeed not know we had mary warner, I thought it was the feeeshes.'" She put on an exaggerated Spanish accent. "'Meeese, I thought theeese white powder was sugar, meeese. The coast guard knows theeese, meeeese.'"

He started to reminisce about his drug cases, but she cut him off. "I've got to hustle. Rod and I are going to Maine Friday. I've got to get a vacation, and I've got a million things to clear on this case so I can get out. Call me for lunch in August, okay?" Karen was backing away down the hall, giving a funny little-girl wave as she turned a corner.

Alec ran after her. "Let me ask one thing — off the record. Who planted the Freezetemp story Sunday?"

Karen looked around nervously. "You know I can't discuss cases with you," she whispered.

"All I know is it wasn't Vinny for a change. At the staff meeting this morning, Vinny said we would be looking at affidavits and polygraphs if he saw any more stories like that. It may have been the SEC guys. I heard they think Vinny is dragging his Guccis."

Karen loved gossip. She had always understood, better than he had, that she lived in a small town — the federal criminal law system — that happened to be located in a big city. Everybody knew everybody, and enemies you made, or friends you made, could change your whole life. Gossip was information and information was power, she always said.

She was leaning close now and he could smell her body, the wonderful mixture of soap and very faint cologne.

"I've really got to go. Call me in August." She pecked him on the cheek. "And cheer up. You look awful — sort of down in the mouth."

3

TROWBRIDGE, Wilton, Pogue and Callaghan had not accepted Jewish partners until 1948. It was sixty years old then. The Irish, like Callaghan, had only climbed into the boat after World War I when they were getting firm footing in construction, unions, and the U.S. attorney's office.

It was twenty years after the first Jew came into the firm that the first black entered who wasn't delivering a deli lunch or cleaning the floor.

Trowbridge had started as a maritime insurance law firm, defending shipping firms and maritime insurance companies against claims for cargoes lost at sea. Now its main "profit center," as the management consultants like to call them, was the civil needs of vast international casualty companies.

After Connie Callaghan had joined the firm straight from working as a prosecutor for John Dewey, it had always maintained a small criminal law department. When white-collar crime prosecutions surged, Trowbridge had begun to take large fraud and tax cases.

Things had gone so well the partners hung a painting of Connie in the reception area of the criminal law wing. "A law office," Connie would explain defensively, "should be designed to reassure the client, but also to warn him about what the fees are likely to be. For some reason people feel reassured when there are oil paintings of partners."

Alec led Felix and Jimmy, subdued and perspiring, past the painting and down the west wing. He had not told them anything.

"Shirley, would you show these two gentlemen to the west conference room," Alec told his secretary. All the way back to his office he had been thinking of Karen, not Felix and Jimmy, thinking of the way water would glisten on her shoulders after a shower, or the way she would turn to have him towel her back.

"Alec, a woman named Hastings has called six times. Says its urgent. The number's on the pad," Shirley said as she walked away.

"Hastings?"

"She says she's your neighbor."

The blonde. He could see her stretching to pull sail. He felt his pulse quicken. His own eagerness amazed him; Karen had gone out of his mind.

He dialed hurriedly.

"Lee? This is Alec Anton. You called —"

"I need your help." She had one of those Colleen Dewhurst voices, throaty and rich. The words were tumbling out.

"My son is in trouble. He's missing. He disappeared on a trip to Europe. I need to talk to you."

"Whoa! Slow down!" Alec tried to bring her son to mind. College kid, fancy dresser. Karen said he was the kind of kid thirty-five-year-old women wanted to seduce.

"Give it to me again slowly."

"Noah — that's my son — disappeared and I'm frightened. I need somebody to tell me how to handle this."

"Are you sure he just hasn't forgotten to call you?"

"Yes! Yes!" she said impatiently.

"How old is Noah now?"

"He's twenty-two."

"Lee, he's grown. I suspect he's just off doing something and didn't tell you."

"No. It's not that way! Something's wrong. I know it! You've got to help me!"

Unconsciously, his voice took on a lawyer's bedside tone.

"Look, I'll be glad to help you any way I can," he said patiently.

She started to speak again, but Alec cut in. "But you may not need a lawyer."

"Yes. Yes I do. He's in trouble."

"Lee, he's an adult. You don't have to tell anyone what you're doing when you're twenty-two, especially your mother. Besides his not calling, what makes you think there's something wrong?"

"That's what I want to talk to you about. I found something last night. . . ."

She paused as though catching her breath.

"Can I come and see you?" she asked.

Alec suddenly felt anxious. "I don't think I'm the right person at all. I'm in a firm that does nothing but corporate Wall Street stuff, and I haven't handled a private law matter in years. Maybe I can suggest someone —"

She interrupted again. "I realize that. This isn't what you think. There are things involved I can't deal with. Please."

"Can you tell me more about this, and maybe," he said, "I can find some way to help you."

"I'd rather not tell you on the phone. Could I come to your office?"

"Jeez, I hate to see you come all the way to New York for me to tell you to get a lawyer in Norwalk."

For reasons not clear to himself, he wanted to keep Lee in Connecticut. He wanted her to be separate from his New York life. "Look, we're old friends. Let me help you as a neighbor. We could have dinner Friday, say the Silvermine Tavern, and you can tell me all about it then. If you still need a lawyer —"

"It can't wait." Her voice was urgent. "He left on June third and I haven't see him . . . haven't heard from him, and what's worse . . ." There was a pause. She was changing course. "He's not in any of the places he was supposed to be."

Alec sighed. The whole fucking day had been like this. The U.S. attorney said Alec's clients were lying to him. His ex-wife said he looked awful, and now this very sexy lady who lived down the block wanted him to take a missing persons case. He could see the faces of his partners when they got her client profile.

As she talked Alec was cataloging her in his mind. Divorced. Seemed well-heeled. Three kids. Two girls and a boy. Succession of men friends. Arnold Palmer sweater guys with Oldsmobile Cutlasses and New Canaan golf club stickers.

He had danced with her once, two years ago, at the marina party, danced so long Karen had teased him all the way home. He remembered her dress. It had no back. The feel of her returned, and he rubbed his right hand against his thigh without thinking.

"I am very frightened for him. Please . . ." Lee's voice trailed off.

"Lee, have you gone to the police about Noah?" Alec asked. "I mean they're the experts."

"They can't do anything, they said. He's not a minor and he hasn't been missing long enough."

"Well, maybe that's the best anyone can do. I don't see how I can help. I —"

"I need to talk to someone." Lee was begging now and it embarrassed Alec.

"Of course. If you don't mind coming all the way to New York, then come tomorrow afternoon." He glanced at Shirley's schedule. "Maybe about four?"

"I'll be there." She hung up.

Felix and Jimmy had been arguing. They sat in cold, drawn-back positions, like a married couple caught in a heated exchange by an unexpected guest.

Alec ostentatiously settled himself, taking off his jacket, loosening his tie, placing a blank yellow legal pad and a half dozen pencils on the surface of the polished mahogany.

Life, he realized at these moments, had made him very tough appearing, very ugly. Karen had always said his ugly side frightened her, and she did not frighten easily.

Today he felt more ugly than most days. These guys were guilty. They had gotten a big contract, sold stock against its earnings, looted the proceeds, and stuck the money in Caribbean banks. Simple! Except until today nobody had mentioned a Swiss bank account!

"You two gents have been holding out on me." He said it very low, but not as a whisper. "When I get up from this table I better know everything material to defending you in the case, or when I get up you need a new lawyer."

"What the fuck are you talking about?" Felix glared at him.

"You tell me. Or maybe Jimmy here can tell us."

"What'ya mean, material to defending us?" Jimmy asked weakly.

"Don't shit around with me, Jimmy. I'm not some goddamn uptown lawyer. You got about ten seconds or I'm going to forgo the pleasure and take a walk." Alec gritted the words out.

Felix turned his whole body to look at Jimmy; it was like a turret on a battleship swinging around.

Jimmy's hands quivered. "I have a bank account in Switzerland, in Zurich. I never mentioned it because I didn't think it was going to become part of anything; it was private.

"Last week the feds waylaid me coming out of a bank. They said 'What's this?' They wanted me to make a deal. I didn't go for it."

Alec put his head in his hands. "Do you read anything besides the *Irish Times*, Jimmy? Where have you been? The U.S. government has been dislodging Swiss bank accounts for five years. Robert Vesco and a lot of other guys started hopping around because Uncle Sam cannot only count their money, there is a good chance he can seize it."

"I swear to God I didn't know about the account." Felix put his hand on Alec's forearm.

"He didn't know," Jimmy agreed. "It's my account, with my money."

Alec had the same feeling of fear he had felt in Vinny's office. This was to have been an easy case, a fat, high-fee, summer case. Plead a couple of greedy businessmen guilty to a little evasion, a little looting. No jail time. They pay, you play. That's what their lawyer, an old friend of Connie's, had said when he brought them in. "These guys are better than a couple of dentists from Scarsdale."

He couldn't put his finger on it yet, but it was like somebody had opened a trapdoor to a basement filled with snakes. Felix was trying to slam it shut, sucking in his breath and glaring at Gallagher.

Alec spoke in the same low, toneless voice.

"Let me tell you what this means. This means Vincent Xavier Santorini, the FBI, the IRS, and the SEC think you guys have been lying to them throughout. Feds don't like that!"

Both men were shaking their heads.

"You both are very likely to go to prison. For you, Felix, this will not be even in the cosmos of what you have suffered, but at your age it will not be pleasant. If we hit the wrong judge it could mean real time — five years behind bars. . . ."

Jimmy again started to speak, but Alec held up one hand, and the Irishman sunk back, his eyes filled with raw hatred, so clear that Alec paused for a moment seeing it.

"Jimmy, prison will probably dry you out. They still make hooch and smuggle booze, but it is my guess you won't be able to get any until weeks after the orientation and admission process, and by that time you'll have gone cold turkey and seen all the dreams of snakes and pits you'll ever want."

Jimmy again tried to speak, but again Alec's manner silenced him.

Alec could feel the heat of their anger. It was so strong it was physical.

"Don't get me wrong, I don't take pleasure in your predicament. You came to me because I'm a winner and your lawyer told you I delivered, and now I'm going to take a bad fall because you held out on me, so this isn't going to be pleasant for any of us."

Felix was half out of his seat. Even at fifty-six his physical power and presence were impressive. "Fuck you! You won't ever practice law again. You fucked this up and now you're trying to cover it up by blaming us."

He was roaring now and Jimmy was grabbing his sleeve. Alec was gripping the table edge to keep still. The force of Felix's anger had stunned him.

It was literally minutes before Felix calmed, settling like a volcano, his face florid, his eyes filled with the same weariness Alec had heard in his voice the day before.

Jimmy spoke first. "What can we do?"

"I don't know," said Alec. "I really don't. Lawyers know when they tell a client to reveal everything that the information is as sacrosanct as a confessional and all that crap — that most clients don't level.

"I hoped, however, that you were respectful enough of the power of the federal government, that I had persuaded you of this power, so that you wouldn't try to hide things.

"If you want me to continue representing you, you tell me everything that can be discovered. Not simply what you think the feds already know, but what really went down here."

The two businessmen sat in silence. Alec guessed that five minutes went by before anyone spoke.

"You know Trumbull Oakes?" said Felix.

"Sure. His firm took you public."

Alec pictured Trumbull Oakes on the *MacNeil-Lehrer* show explaining that the fundamental economy is sound, periodically reminding the audience that's what he just told the President.

"Let me tell you a little story about Mr. Oakes." Felix had pushed his chair back from the table and loosened his tie.

"I don't know about the account the U.S. attorney found. But it don't mean shit by itself! Jimmy shouldn't have done it!" Felix glared again at Jimmy. " 'Cause it could lead to things."

Felix brushed by the Swiss account, fixing Alec with his gaze.

"You thought we won the Interglobal contract, nice and clean. Just send in your plans, contract in the mail for six hundred million in refrigeration? On the most modern natural gas tanker fleet in the world?"

Alec started to answer.

"Uh-uh.

"Do you think we got the Interglobal contract because we are such nice fellows, because we went to Harvard and we belong to the Fifth Avenue Club?

"I'm a Yid with a number on my arm, so I don't belong to the Fifth Avenue Club.

"Shit! When we first read of the tankers, we didn't even think of bidding. There is no way in hell that a firm our size should have gotten that contract. There is a refrigeration company in Norway that could deliver on those vessels without even retooling."

Felix leaned forward as though pointing to a piece of paper. "Did you notice the name Spanos Canosous in the files?"

Alec nodded. It rang a vague bell.

"Early in the planning stage, this guy calls me. He's a vice president at Interglobal. We'd met maybe ten years ago. I bid a little freighter job at a yard he ran in Halifax. We gave Spanos and his yard manager some gifts, little schmittle gifts, and we'd won the contract.

"Now! Mr. Canosous comes out of the blue and says he thought I ought to bid the Interglobal natural gas project.

"I said no way — the cost of the estimation, the workup, the bid-bond, and all the travel would be a couple hundred thousand and we wouldn't get it in the end.

"We go back and forth for maybe two, three weeks. Then he comes to New York and we go out to dinner. Just me and him. And we eat and it is all old times, Felix and Spanos, what good times we had, what a great guy I am, what a great deal this would be working together again.

"Spanos knows all about us. He knows cash flow, he knows Jimmy's personal problems." Gallagher bristled. "He knows my divorce settlements, he knows our labor problems, he knows our books. He lets little details drop all evening that tell me he has really been reading our mail.

"So Spanos is eating and he is bullshitting and eating and bull-shitting. Finally, like it was dessert, he leans over to me and he says 'You do what I say — just like I say — and you get the biggest job you ever had.'

"Spanos tells us to work up a straight bid, the best price we can offer, one that gives us a decent profit.

"The bid goes in and we don't hear nothing from Spanos for weeks. Then a trade magazine calls us for comment. They heard we have been selected for a six-hundred-million-dollar project to refrig-erate twenty-first-century vessels!

"Six hundred million." Felix's voice rises in awe. "That's more than we grossed in the last ten years!

"This is so big a job, Jimmy and I realize we'll need a new plant where the hulls can be brought in to refrigerate. Maybe double our work force. We work day and night to put together an expansion plan."

Felix begins to chuckle at an unseen joke.

"We fly to London to give Interglobal the plan. During the day everybody is smiling and saying that's great. But that night Spanos told us to go to Oakes, Ames and Dumont. They would make up our plan, they would take us public, and they would tell us what to do."

Jimmy is picking up the narrative, as though he had finally gotten the floor from a boring political speaker.

"What Felix is saying is that we didn't choose Oakes, Ames and Dumont. Interglobal made that part of the price of our getting the contract. This is not so strange. Oakes is on the board of Interglobal.

"So we went to Trumbull Oakes. It was an office just like this. His staff is expecting us. They want us to raise half the contract price, three hundred million, in one public stock offering.

"We said, we don't need that much at first. They all laughed. Yes you do!

"Oakes joins us for lunch. He has just come from Washington, he said. Even Carter is interested in this project. He said he is so glad we won, like it was really a bid."

"It all meant bubkus," Felix guffawed. "The real story came from two guys sitting in my driveway in a rented car at seven A.M. They only mentioned Oakes's name once and Oakes has never mentioned them. Never has Oakes ever let on he knows what's going on. Never!"

"Who were these men?" Alec asked.

"Don't let me get ahead. Wait. Wait."

They are tumbling over each other to tell the story now. Gallagher took it up.

"Over maybe five months, these guys put us in touch with lawyers in Panama and the Netherlands Antilles. The lawyers are coming up with corporations — dummy corporations — that can sell us material or services it would appear we need.

"How much of that do you think we really needed?"

Alec shook his head. "I don't know."

"Very damn little."

"How much do your friends in the U.S. attorney's office estimate is missing from Freezetemp?" asked Felix.

"Maybe twenty-five to thirty million," Alec answered.

"That ain't the half of it," Felix said wryly.

"You know what is so funny? So funny is that the Greek and Jew are not the big crooks. No sir. Not the big crooks. It turns out that the big crook is a Mr. Trumbull Oakes. Mr. Oakes told me that there is a town in Connecticut named after his forebears. I should wonder? He is a master."

Alec felt a burst of anger. These two guys are shitting me. They've been sitting in here trying to decide who they can dump on, so they pick the investment banker.

Alec found his voice shaking with anger. "Felix, Felix. Don't start a fairy tale. You aren't going to be able to pin this on Oakes. Stop this."

Gallagher cut in almost crying. "As God is my witness, Alec. Listen to him."

"Let me finish, Mr. Counselor. Let me finish." Felix held up his hand.

Gallagher paused, smiling at Alec.

"When we first came to you, you thought it was a two-way split. Some goes for the refrigeration, and some for Jimmy and Felix. Right?"

Alec nodded.

"Wrong! It is a three-way split. Some goes for the refrigeration. Some goes for Jimmy and Felix, and a lot goes to somewhere. Spanos? Interglobal? Oakes? Who knows? It was just gone."

"They deducted their cut before you got it?" Alec interjected.

"Effectively! Our books, Miss Valery Vennuzio's books, will show transfers to us and payouts for materials. But in the Caymans, for instance — we don't know who some of those companies are.

"You told us, to make a deal we would have to tell the feds where the money went. That's what you said.

"Shit! We couldn't tell the feds where two thirds of that money went if we wanted to."

Felix picks up the numbers.

"Look, there is sixty million of give — ten percent — written over the life of our contract alone! Out of that we only know what we've got."

Alec looked incredulous.

Felix goes on now. He is comfortable with numbers.

"There's more, counselor. Something even bigger than us, bigger than Freezetemp.

"Interglobal has raised capital around the world for twenty super-tankers at two hundred million apiece. That's something over four billion dollars. How many tankers have actually been built?" He paused so Alec could answer his question.

"One," Alec said softly.

"And it hasn't passed sea trials," Felix interjected with a gruff laugh.

"Interglobal is indemnified against loss" — his voice is rising again — "indemnified against loss by the treasuries of the United States, Holland, Great Britain, and France." He ticked them off on his fingers.

"So four billion dollars have been raised. Four billion smack-eroos!" Felix says the figure very slowly for emphasis.

"It took Jimmy and I a while to figure it out. Didn't it, Jimmy?" Gallagher is furiously nodding in agreement.

"You know what?"

Alec shook his head.

"Interglobal never gave a shit if we could refrigerate tankers! But we did attract three hundred million in capital!"

"You know what else?"

Alec silently shook his head again.

"No more tankers will ever be built. This is a honey pot. Interglobal is going to divvy it up. They know it will be years before the investors catch on, maybe even a decade before the lawsuits came to trial."

Alec sat dumbfounded. Felix and Jimmy rested as though weary from a great race.

"Why didn't you tell me this when you retained me?"

"They told us we probably wouldn't have to," Jimmy answered weakly. "They told us to tell you the Caribbean deal. They said you were wired with the U.S. attorney. Everything would go smooth!"

Felix went on.

"They said they knew the Netherlands Antilles and some of the Cayman transactions could be spotted, but they design deals so that one level doesn't link to another. They said the feds would only find one level."

"So what has Vinny found in Switzerland?" Alec looked at Jimmy.

"You know what's funny?"

Alec said he didn't, like maybe nothing was funny.

"What they found's got nothing to do with this. It was some cash we kept to one side." Jimmy smiled weakly. "I shouldn't have done it." Jimmy wore the same look that he must have worn in confession. Father, forgive me, for I have sinned.

Felix didn't look like anything was funny either. "But it could make them look for other things, things in Switzerland." He said it almost under his breath.

For a time the three men neither moved nor spoke.

Alec wondered how much more his clients were hiding from him. Whatever the answer, they were in a new league. These little jerks from Brooklyn were in a new league.

He could see the trial. It would be bigger than Vesco. Trumbull Oakes was a big deal. He wasn't Watergate, but he was a big deal. Alec could see television cameras all over Foley Square and Ted Koppel examining whether it led to Reagan or Carter. Maybe this was why Vinny had taken Freezetemp himself. Maybe he smelled something.

Alec looked at his clients. They were not an impressive pair. He could see Trumbull Oakes on the stand. He knew, almost instinctively, the tack Oakes would take. The sadness he would show that these two men should be so desperate as to involve him.

Why should a jury believe them? Why would anybody believe them? They had already held out on him. Jesus, if you stumbled in a case implicating Trumbull Oakes you'd never get up again.

"Are you willing to testify against Oakes?"

"There is another problem." Jimmy's voice sounded suddenly very tense.

"Yeah, tell him the problem," Felix growled.

Here it comes, Alec thought, the dodge.

"When we first came under investigation, the two men who had been in Felix's driveway came back. They told us in the end we would plead, but that any deal we made must never be based on delivering anybody else. That sounded okay, until" — Jimmy's voice became shrill — "you said the feds wanted us to do jail time.

"So we talked to them again. We told them what you said. This time they were not so nice." Gallagher's voice was taking on the nervous twinge again. Felix cut in.

"One hour by the clock after they left our office, Sophie got a package. It was news clippings from all over the world; stories about businessmen who had been in deadly accidents over the past few years. This wasn't a joke."

"Let's get a drink." Alec stood up abruptly, picking up the pad and grabbing his coat off the back of the chair. His mind was on the trial that would be bigger than Vesco.

Jimmy went into the men's room and Alec and Felix walked down the hall.

The law firm was deserted now. Summer dusk was settling over

New York and the windows of Trowbridge gave varying vistas as the city began to twinkle with evening lights.

Felix was silent as Alec made the drinks. He seemed mesmerized by the beauty of the harbor. The sun was ocher over Hoboken, its rays filtered through the earth's gasses had painted gold leaf on the Statue of Liberty.

"I cannot go behind bars, Alec." Felix looked older sitting there than Alec could remember him having ever looked. "I wouldn't live through it." He said it as though it was decided.

"Any deal I can make now could be tough." Alec didn't say what could be tough.

"Do it! I can't go behind bars."

They sipped their drinks, the sharp vodka numbing Alec's tongue.

Jimmy came in and sat down. No one spoke for some time, time enough for the sun to disappear behind Hoboken and leave the harbor in darkness.

Finally Alec said: "Trumbull Oakes is one of the most powerful Republicans in New York. He's a personal friend of Reagan, Bush, Ford, and Nixon. He's on the board of every charity and do-gooder agency in the city. Why didn't you implicate the pope, or Santa Claus?"

He was almost talking to himself. "This is going to be a very tricky business. Very tricky."

Alec looked at Felix. "You guys have a lot more money?" Even though he phrased it as a question, his tone did not require an answer.

The two men sat in silence. Finally Felix nodded.

"That's good. You're gonna need it. Now go home and try to stay away from federal agents."

4

WHEN she entered he was struck with how beautiful she was and how handsomely turned out. She wore a loose-fitting cream-colored raw silk suit, the nub of the cloth and European cut giving it an almost sporty look. Her blouse, a dark navy blue with a high neck, was also cut full, but it could not hide the swell of her breasts.

She had done her hair in a French knot that drew attention to her sculptured features. He guessed she wore almost no makeup, and her dark tan framed her bright blue eyes and full lips painted with a muted lipstick.

She crossed Alec's office with the grace they learn at finishing schools by balancing books on their heads, and took a chair that bathed her in the afternoon sunlight.

Shirley had clearly been impressed, announcing her with a flourish suitable for Princess Diana, "Leland Hastings is here, Alec," and following Lee's stunning legs across the carpet with her eyes.

An hour before Lee arrived he had Shirley order coffee served in some of the firm's best German silver, the set they reserved for their most important clients. He found himself getting more and more excited at the thought of her visit.

"I'm sorry if I sounded like I was trying to put you off last night" — Alec poured Lee a cup, fussing with sugar and cream — "but lawyers know that people often come to them when they need a different service entirely."

"I probably seemed hysterical." She was looking out over the water and avoiding eye contact with him. "I find myself fluctuating in and out of hysteria. He's just disappeared and I've . . ."

Alec interrupted. He wanted her to calm down.

"Why don't you sort of take it slowly from the top," he said softly, "and I'll take notes. Okay?"

There was a long pause as though she was trying to decide where to begin.

"Well, Noah graduated in the last week of May. It was really his day," she said proudly. "He paid his own tuition, clothes, everything. Graduation day was a big triumph.

"John — his father — came with his wife. I guess that was the first time Noah and his father had been together in years."

"Where does his father live?" Alec interrupted her.

"In New Canaan. Not far away, but Noah and his father have not gotten along. . . ."

"Go ahead. I didn't mean to break your train of thought."

"The next day Noah announced he was going to Europe. This surprised me. Only in April he told me he had lined up a position with an investment firm here in New York, and he had already turned down chances to take graduation trips with his friends."

"Where was he going to work? Have you called them?" Alec had gotten up and walked to a window.

"I know you'll think this is odd, but I don't know where he was going to work. I know he'd been going down to the offices and had known the people for a couple of years. He said it was a securities house here in the city. If he told me the name I can't remember it. But Noah doesn't tell you a lot. Or maybe I wasn't listening. I was preoccupied this spring. I'm trying to put together a complicated real estate swap with three properties.

"Anyway, a week after graduation, he came home, drove his car down with everything in it, and parked it at my house.

"The girls and I . . . my daughters. You know my daughters?" For the first time her eyes locked on his, but, to his distress, she turned away again. "The girls and I had a good time helping him pick out some hotels and pensions to stay at.

"He was home about a week, quite happy and cheerful. Kept talking about a girl he knew at school, who he was going to try to get back together with. I guess they'd had a falling out."

"When did he leave for Europe?"

"We drove him down to Kennedy on June third. He seemed excited about going places he'd visited before."

"He'd been there before?" Alec interjected.

"Yes, John . . . my husband, was in the army and we were there when Noah was small."

"Is Kennedy where you last saw Noah?" Alec asked.

"The last time I saw him, he was walking through the sliding doors. He turned and waved. . . ." Lee paused as though recreating the scene in her mind.

Her eyes had filled with tears, forming watery lenses that made them seem larger and more blue.

Alec, who had been perched on his desk in front of her, reached out and touched her shoulder. He sensed her closeness, a fresh smell with the odor of some kind of flower, too light to be perfume.

"Then what happened?"

"A few hours after he left, I got a call for him. It was a man. He said it was urgent he talk to Noah. I said he was on his way to Europe. He became very upset. He started screaming to somebody else. 'He's left . . .' Something like that. He hung up before I could get his name.

"A week later I got another call. It was a man with a Spanish accent. He asked if I owned a silver Porsche. I said it was my son's. He also hung up abruptly. Then I began getting calls all the time. The person wouldn't say anything. When I'd say hello, they'd hang up.

"Finally, I knew I had to reach Noah. I bought a Fodor's guide and tried to remember where he had made reservations. He was supposed to have spent the night of June eleventh at a pension in Munich, so I called there.

"The woman who ran it said he had not checked in or called to cancel. She was a mother too, and she said she had been worried because when the rooms are prepaid she usually gets a call.

"Then I tried the hotel in Zurich where he was supposed to have stayed when he got there. At first they wouldn't look up the record, but I became very excited and said I would call the police. Their records showed he hadn't arrived and they had billed his American Express card for the price of the room. . . ."

"That's when I started to panic. I called John right away. He was very unpleasant."

"Unpleasant?"

"John has a great hatred for me. Our lives were very . . . diffi-cult."

"Wasn't he worried about his son?" Alec asked.

"Not at all. He said that was what we could always expect from Noah and he was sure Noah would call when he wanted something. We had a terrible argument. It was like we were married again. He was awful."

"What did you do then?"

"I was so upset I started calling people I know, asking for advice. I called your house but there was no answer.

"Finally . . . finally I got hold of myself. I think I scared Veronica and Mindy so badly it made me realize how hysterical I had been. That night I went over to the Norwalk police department, the station on Route One. They were very nice. I have the detective's card, Rich or Reich or something.

"He said there wasn't much they could do about missing adults unless there is evidence they were kidnapped or they were incapaci-tated, you know, diabetes or mental illness. But he looked through flyers from other departments to see if there was some report of Noah. He didn't find anything.

"He suggested I call the airlines and the State Department. Oh, God, they both gave me a runaround. Pan Am said its records didn't show a Noah Hastings took the Zurich flight on June third, but he could have changed to another airline or another connection.

"The State Department said it wasn't their job to keep track of everybody's kid who goes to Europe.

"Of course then I was desperately afraid. I mean then I knew that Noah had really disappeared. There wasn't any trace or any-thing. At first I thought, this can't be happening. No one just disappears.

"I've called the State Department every other day, and the police. Reich or whatever his name is has notified the FBI and the Immigra-tion Department, but there's been no report."

"Have you spoken to the FBI?" Alec asked.

"I tried. They said it had to be handled through my local police department and I should check back with the person I filed the report with.

"So last Sunday while I was out sailing, trying to think, I

suddenly realized that I should go through Noah's things and see if there wasn't a clue as to where he was. Maybe he had decided to go someplace I didn't know about or had a reservation I didn't know about. I went through his car and his room from top to bottom and that was when I found . . ."

She had begun to fuss in a clutch purse as she talked and handed Alec a business envelope wrapped with a rubber band.

He opened it as she watched.

In it was a U.S. passport, worn and well traveled, visa entries for the Caribbean and several for Colombia. Noah's handsome face and intense gaze looked out from the passport picture. The name on the line underneath was John Grant.

Lee was silent as he examined the document, the way a patient sits in a doctor's office, expecting a diagnosis.

"You ever heard of John Grant?" Alec didn't look up as he asked the question.

"No," she answered.

"Is it a family name of any sort, or combination of family names?" he said.

"No."

She stood up, walked over to where Alec sat, and leaned over his shoulder. One breast brushed against him, soft and warm. "You see there." She pointed. "The birth date is also wrong. It's the right year but the wrong month and day.

"There is something else," she said, turning wordlessly and taking another brown manila envelope out of her purse.

He opened it. The bills were old and worn, all one hundreds. He guessed there was $20,000 or $30,000 there. Alec whistled soundlessly.

"This envelope was taped to the wall behind a picture in Noah's room. I only found it because I accidentally knocked the picture down."

"Where would Noah get this kind of money?" Alec asked.

"I don't know." She looked down at him.

They sat in silence while Alec stared at the money and the passport.

"Do you think Noah's all right?

"He's not . . ." She paused, her voice shaky. "He's not hurt?"

"I think if he was hurt you'd have heard about it right away. Police or hospitals would have it reported to you."

"What could all this mean?" Her hand swept over his desk.

"Your guess is as good as mine. There could be benign answers; college jobs, savings accounts." His voice didn't sound convincing to him and it probably wasn't to her. "But if you don't know how he got this much money and you've never heard of the name John Grant, then it's more than likely your son's involved in something. . . ." He put no name to it.

"Did you check to see if he flew under the name Grant?" Alec asked.

She nodded. "The airline wouldn't tell me anything, and I . . . I didn't want to ask too many questions about Grant. That's why I need you. I don't know how to proceed or what to do now."

"Maybe he has another passport in another name?" Alec speculated to himself.

Lee didn't answer.

He sensed that she was having difficulty controlling herself; her hands and the muscles on her neck seemed strained and her body seemed taut.

"Is there something else? Is there something you're not . . ." Alec never finished.

She whirled around, her face flushed, her eyes blazing. "What have I done that's so wrong? What was I supposed to do? He is twenty-two years old. What was I supposed to do?"

"Whoa, whoa, slow down." Alec was talking gently, as though to a small child. "You came to me, remember? You're frightened and worried about your son. What I'm asking is whether there's something you're reluctant to tell me. If I'm going to help you, you have to tell me as much as you can."

Lee was silent.

"Let's say that as of right this minute you're my client. Okay? When you leave" — he used an old lawyer's gimmick — "you give me a dollar as a retainer.

"From now on what you tell me will be in complete confidence. I cannot confide it to a law enforcement officer or anyone else. Does that make it easier?"

She was quiet for a long time before she answered.

"Money has made me suspicious of Noah."

"Money?"

"Money. He has lots of it. This envelope didn't surprise me. He seems to have all he wants. His clothes! Everything is from the best shops. He has three dozen cashmere sweaters! Two dozen pairs of shoes! He bought a Porsche a year ago! Once he said he could . . ." Her voice trailed off.

"Where does he get it?"

"That's what I'm trying to tell you! I don't know! He won't tell me."

"What do you mean you don't know? You're his mother." Alec tried to keep exasperation out of his voice. "Did you ask him?"

"I've asked him a thousand times!"

"What does he say?"

"At first, when I first noticed how much he had, he would say it was his job."

"What job?"

"Flowers."

"Flowers?"

Suddenly Lee sat down, pulling a chair directly in front of Alec and riveting him with her gaze.

"I have never told anyone this. Do you know why?"

Alec shook his head.

"Because now, when I think of it, it sounds ridiculous. But it wasn't when it started. It seemed normal. . . ." Lee took a deep breath as though preparing to dive.

"Eight years ago when Noah was in boarding school he was assigned a roommate named Philip. Nice kid from a rich family in Colombia."

"Colombia?"

Lee nodded, seeming miserable at the implications of the country's name.

"That spring, just before summer vacation, I got a call from Bogotá. It was Philip's father. His English was very good and he was very gracious. Mr. Ochoa said Philip was really looking forward to bringing his friend home, and would I allow him to pay for the trip.

"I said I couldn't do that and I was also anxious about Noah traveling that far alone. I tried to be very nice, but I didn't know them and I didn't want to give my permission.

"So Marco said he understood and we had a long talk about the boys and he hung up.

"But Noah wouldn't give in. The whole thing went on for weeks. My saying no, I couldn't do that, and Noah saying he couldn't live without going. I finally gave up."

"He went?" Alec asked.

"And every summer from then on."

"Every summer! You let him?" Alec was incredulous.

"It seemed so great. The Ochoas are flower growers, carnations, roses, mums, everything. Noah said they had field after field all around Bogotá. He loved it. He always looked great when he came back. He enjoyed each summer more than the last. He and Philip got to be better and better friends."

Lee was running out of breath with all the superlatives. It seemed important to establish how right this was.

"They let him work with Philip preparing the flowers for shipping. He made spending money and he even became fluent in Spanish! I remember wishing somebody would arrange wonderful summers like that for the girls!"

"When did the big money show up?"

"The year he graduated from boarding school."

"What did he say then?"

Lee took another deep breath.

"Then he told me he was making money investing the money he made in the summers."

"You believed that?"

"I know you think it is crazy. But he said he was investing with Philip, and Philip's father was helping them. It all seemed so plausible. I realize now I never saw any account statements, receipts, but he would talk a lot about particular stocks and bonds; it was all very believable. He even had me get the *Wall Street Journal* at home."

She took Alec's stunned silence for a signal she should continue.

"He was doing so well. He told me just at Christmas that he wanted to get into investments and securities as a career. Noah is really very smart about numbers, and I didn't find that so hard to believe."

"Where'd he get the job he told you about?"

"I think he found his new job through the Ochoas." Her voice fell as though this was the final evidence of her gullibility.

For a moment Alec thought he was going to laugh. If this woman were not so forlorn he probably would have.

"Why didn't you just sit him down and ask him what the hell he was doing?" It seemed so simple to Alec that his impatience showed again.

She looked at him with a gaze of wonderment, as though he reported the earth was round.

"It was always easier not to get to the bottom of it. Don't you see? Because it has been perfect. Noah flowed smoothly through school, graduating, paying fifty thousand dollars in tuition for college. I didn't have fifty thousand dollars. His father wouldn't give it to him. Where in God's name did he get fifty thousand dollars? The problem is, I didn't care. Things were working. Life was working! Can you understand that?"

She started walking around the room, avoiding Alec's eyes as though she were all by herself.

"Let me tell you about Noah. You don't have children. Do you? I mean, from before you and Karen were married?"

Being childless engendered a sense of guilt, Alec thought. People who have them, even people who don't deserve them, always ask that in an accusing way.

"No. I don't have any children. Tell me about children." He said it very softly.

"What do I tell you about Noah? Do I tell you he was my favorite? Mothers are not supposed to have favorites. But he was so beautiful. People would come up on the street or in the park and say 'Is that your little boy? He's a treasure.'"

She was talking rapidly now, her strides in the cage of his office growing longer and faster as her story poured out. The long steps pulled her skirt tight over her buttocks, the flesh wobbling sensually with her movements. Alec tried not to be distracted.

"You don't want to hear things about your children. You go to a school meeting, you don't want the teacher to say he has a reading disability. You don't want the pediatrician to tell you one leg is shorter than the other. If things are going along, you want desperately for them to get along."

"Leland!" He went back to her formal name because this had become preposterous. "You've had every indication here that your son is involved in drugs. Jesus! Fake passport! Money! Clothes! Cars!"

She had walked back to the window, hands clenched.

"But he didn't use drugs!" Her voice was rising. "How could he have maintained his grades, gotten through college, if he was using drugs? For four years I don't think he's even been sick one day. All the things they tell you to look for: unexplained illness, loss of energy, ups and downs in behavior. None!"

So the kid didn't use it, he carried it. Alec's eyes rolled to the ceiling. She missed the gesture. What he had here was a smart-ass rich kid who went down to Colombia and carried for the gang back at college. He was probably down there right now trying to load up for the summer.

Alec stood up, wordlessly, and moved to her. He put his arms around her, awkwardly; he was not a tender person, but she seemed so alone that the gesture came naturally.

They stood there in the middle of the office, rocking back and forth, and Lee was gulping, not crying but sobbing in large gulps of air. There were no tears.

"There's not much I can do." He said it very softly. "I think your son is involved in narcotics smuggling. He's probably doing something right now. If he doesn't get arrested crossing a border, he'll be back. Then sit him down, get him a lawyer, and try to get him to quit this."

"I thought that too." She was leaning against his shoulder. "But I tell you it's worse. Call it mother's intuition, call it what you like. Why did Noah have to set up a whole trip to Europe? I would have been far less suspicious if he said he was going to Colombia. Who are these people calling him?"

He drew back from her. "If you thought of that why didn't you tell me that first, last night on the telephone? Why didn't you just say 'I think my son's in drugs and he's in danger'?"

She was standing very close now, not touching him, but very close. "Would you have seen me?"

Alec didn't say anything for a time. "Did you call the Ochoas?"

"Yes. Right away. I thought the person with the Spanish accent might be connected to them. Both Marco and Philip said they hadn't seen Noah. Philip seemed worried."

He looked at her a long time. Her eyes were deep. The kind of eyes that had a story. He wondered if he'd heard it.

5

"YOU know, I don't know why I come here." Eddie Doherty was talking with his mouth half full. "The fucking Irish can't cook, so it follows that an Irish restaurant is an oxy-oxy —"

Alec finished for him. "Oxymoron."

"Yeah," Eddie agreed.

Despite his distaste for the food, Alec noted, Eddie was putting away a prodigious lunch. On his plate lay only the scant remains of a steak, French fries, coleslaw, and green beans — luncheon special at the Bit o' Ireland Pub.

In front of Alec a cheeseburger remained, undisturbed.

"You don't look so good, counselor," Eddie observed. "You got a hangover?"

"As a matter of fact, yes. It's funny, when I was in the U.S. attorney's office I started almost every day with a hangover. I'd forgotten how it feels."

Alec had gotten up just after nine, stumbling through his Manhattan apartment trying to find the Alka-Seltzer. Lee had been on his mind all evening, at a party for a client, at the apartment. She hung there in his consciousness, even putting Felix, Jimmy, and Trumbull Oakes momentarily aside.

The phone rang in the midst of his waking up.

"Will you help me?" No "Good morning." No "How are you?"

"I need you."

"You need somebody."

"Then you'll do it?"

"I don't know . . ."

"Please. I have no one else."

He could not say no. Her voice had frozen all explanations or excuses on his lips.

"Thank you." Her voice was very husky.

He realized he had begun to be aroused.

Shirley asked no questions when he called saying he would be late. She shifted a meeting with insurance officials to the afternoon and scratched a lunch with a woman who was going to be an expert witness on depreciation of vessels. "Reach out for Eddie Doherty, will you? See if he can have lunch."

Eddie was talking again, but now his mouth was empty.

"The owner of this joint is in the IRA. Scout's honor." Eddie mistook the impatience in Alec's eyes for disbelief.

"So the Guardia is tapping these calls from America that are coming into a house in Dublin, right? And I'm reading these reports and I'm reading and reading and something is bothering me. Then I realize that it's the fucking phone number. This is where a lot of Irish cops I know hang out so I'm calling here all the time, and I recognized the phone number." Eddie's infectious laugh rumbles forth.

"Anyway, we never have enough to take him out, but that phone over there" — Eddie gestures with his fork — "that little phone is memorialized in thirty thousand pages of transcripts."

Alec leaned forward. "Listen, I need a favor. Off the books. Okay?"

Eddie's look is cautious. He's a federal customs investigator, Alec a private lawyer. The camaraderie, the friendship, and the promises when they made cases together, that's history.

"If I can, counselor. If I can."

"Take a look at this." Alec handed over Noah's passport in the name of Grant.

Eddie's thick fingers ruffled the papers with the practiced gesture of a policeman who has scanned a lot of credentials.

"What'ya want to know?" he asked.

"First, is it genuine?" Alec answered.

"Yeah. This is genuine. Right dates, right paper and issuing office. Also, take here. The Bahamas stamp. They don't stamp American passports anymore, but they did on the dates of that trip.

That kind of detail wouldn't come in the kind of fakes we get. This is the real thing or a U.S. intelligence agency produced it."

"How easy is it to get a real passport in a fake name?" Alec asked.

"It's not easy anymore. A lot more records are computerized than they once were, and so setting it up can be risky." Doherty is lecturing.

"How would a young kid like that get one?" Alec nodded toward Noah's pictu. e.

"My bet is not by himself. First you have to find a person born about the time you were born, same gender and hopefully the same race, who died when he was very young. Then you write to the state health department, signing that person's name, and request a notarized copy of your birth certificate.

"At any point someone can get suspicious. But if you get the birth certificate you use that birth certificate to obtain other I.D., Social Security card, that sort of thing, then you go for a passport. You become the dead person."

"So there is a John Grant?"

"There was."

"How do you find the dead person?" Alec asked.

"Newspaper death announcements, cemetery plots, church records. I've heard of them all. But the person has to have died before he or she created written records, because if they have a signature on file, health offices can match handwriting, signatures."

"Have you ever heard of this John Grant?" Alec asked.

"Naww. I hear twenty thousand names a year. But you saw the visa stamps and his age.

"If he comes through the line, he fits our drug profile. We'd go over him hard. Point of embarkation in a narcotics transfer country, sure."

"What about a Colombian flower dealer named Marco Ochoa?"

"Not the name — 'Ochoa' is like 'Smith' in Colombia — but the business, sure."

"What do you mean sure?"

"Colombia's the biggest exporter of flowers to the U.S. We go over every shipment hard because it's a coke cover. The week before

Valentine's Day or Easter is bananas. Every narcotrafficante in the business is hiding his stuff in the flower boxes."

"But the name Marco Ochoa doesn't mean anything?"

"Not to me, but remember, I don't work narcotics anymore. Financial crimes."

Alec had drawn back as if the conversation was coming to a close. "Now comes the favor."

"You mean that wasn't the favor." Eddie is teasing. "What'ya think a lunch at the Bit o' Ireland buys?"

"Check Soundex on these names." Alec wrote down 'Philip Ochoa, Marco Ochoa, John Grant, Noah Hastings, Leland Hastings.' Alec's face was serious. "If they come up I'll tell you what I know about them. If they don't, they don't. Okay?"

"Okay." Eddie's face showed relief. Alec realized he bid too low. Eddie was ready to go into the files and pull jackets. What the hell; save Eddie for next time.

He took a cab back downtown, riding with a Jamaican who smelled like he never took a bath, but he had a fiercely worded note warning the passengers not to smoke. The thick smell of cigarette smoke would have been a defense.

When he settled in behind his desk, he found a thick report and documents on Trumbull Oakes, accompanied by an eager young associate. She was a leggy kid and she reminded him for a moment of Karen as a young law intern.

"I hope that's what you need. It's all public records, clippings, and there was no contact with any Oakes entity or his office," she said.

"There'll have to be several addenda because of time delay on some material from abroad. I'll let Shirley know when they're ready."

Alec smiled and the young woman turned down the hall with a swift flash of calf.

Taking off his jacket, he settled down to read. The associate had found a cover photo of Oakes from *Forbes* magazine and had mounted it onto the front of her report.

His face was round and fleshy, heading fast, despite health clubs and workout salons, to full jowls. His eyes were pale blue and had a flat "gunfighter" quality that must have made it hard to gauge his feelings. His hair was a wispy blond, touched only by gray at the temples.

Oakes came from wealth; from the American aristocracy such as it was in the early twentieth century. The Oakeses and the Trumbulls had made money in weapons and brass. They had made guns for the Revolutionary War, the Civil War, and all wars since, including some in which they had no stake.

By the time the names were linked in the Oakes baby in 1925, the Oakes side was out of weapons and into brass. Though they made brass artillery-shell casings in the two world wars and that added to their fortune, the business mainly concentrated on brass for electrical and industrial use.

Oakes had never strayed from the path of advantage. St. Paul's School, Yale, the secret societies, the debutantes, the whole ball of wax.

Alec looked again into the pale eyes in the picture. He had gone to boarding school with the Trumbull Oakeses of the world, and to college. The dances, the lacrosse games, and the late-night study sessions. Yet he was as foreign to them as he was to the aborigines in Borneo.

They were so assured, so confident. It was like playing musical chairs with somebody who has an assigned seat. God he had wanted to be like them when he was fourteen! He laughed out loud. But he had ended up like himself.

This establishment was finished now. Oakes was in the last generation that could assume it would run the country. Power had shifted. Now Texas and California and the South would produce competing or interlocking aristocracies.

According to the report, Oakes had inherited some $5 million as a young man, eschewing the brass business for Wall Street as his father had. By 1960 he was the managing partner of his firm.

The intern, using careful citations, had spotted that Trumbull, Trum, as he was known in the trade, had been quietly shifting the firm from handling the personal fortunes of wealthy industrialists to the new and more lucrative business of pension funds, municipal financing programs, and leading firms from private to public ownership.

Oakes had built his business in the classic manner. He had

nurtured every school connection, every family friend, every social contact. He was on the board at the Guggenheim, chairman of the St. Paul's School annual fund-raising, a big money man for the Republicans. He had raised funds for Lincoln Center and the restoration of Bryant Park, for Vietnamese orphans and the hungry of Bangladesh.

Alec had a half memory of meeting him. It had been with Karen at the Guggenheim. Chardonnay. Tiny canapés so quickly gone you had to go out to dinner afterward. He could remember a warm, moist, fleshy hand and a conversation in which Oakes had turned Karen aside as though Alec didn't exist. The memory was fleeting and then gone.

The file was filled with news and magazine photos of Oakes and his wife in evening clothes, shaking hands and holding plaques. The law associate had found the original *New York Times* wedding story, which had a two-column head and list of guests at the reception in New Canaan that included Senator Prescott Bush, Vice President Bush's father, as well as half of the moneyed white Protestant crust of the Northeast.

His wife, the former Helen Van Wagnen, stared hard into the camera with haughty eyes under a traditional wedding veil. She came of more modest Hudson Valley wealth, sprung from a family that went as far back in the old colonial Dutch heritage as Oakes did among the English.

It was like breeding dogs, Alec thought, Helen Van Wagnen out of Strongheart of King's Farm.

Oakes's Republican work had twice brought him into government — once as an assistant secretary of commerce under Eisenhower and later as deputy secretary of the Treasury under Nixon. He was credited with giving Reagan a strong vote in New York and with being one of the authors of the trickle-down theory. "Oakes is the Republican king maker in New York," said *Newsday*. "If a candidate is heading for Albany or Washington, the first stop is Trum Oakes."

But the research associate had found nothing that suggested Oakes, Ames and Dumont had ever, even indirectly, been associated with a criminal venture. There were no SEC cases, not even warnings from regulatory agencies, and the personal lives of the principals suggested nothing.

Strangely there was no indication Oakes sat on Interglobal's board or any sign that he drew income from that project.

What wasn't at all clear was how much money Oakes was making. The law associate had pulled a Dun and Bradstreet, but the estimate as to the investment house's financial position seemed vague and imprecise.

In the latest year covered, D&B estimated the firm handled over $4 billion in investments with earnings of $32 million. Financial stories about the firm talked mainly of "slow, steady growth" and "firm, hardheaded management."

When Alec stood up an hour later he was no closer to finding support for Felix and Jimmy's charges.

He went back through the clippings, searching for clues about the connection with Freezetemp or Interglobal. No client mentioned in any story was as small a firm or from the maritime industry. Alec guessed that when newspaper reporters called, Oakes and his associates probably didn't tick off the unglamorous meat-and-potatoes business of the firm.

The only other thing that caught his eye was a clipping on the death of Vernon Dumont, the youngest partner. He had died when his car hit a bridge abutment near his home in the Hamptons. Of Dumont, Oakes had said: "He had the vision to see our fortunes lay abroad and it is Vernon who deserves the credit for the development of our international department. We will miss him as a human being and a brilliant colleague."

Alec rang up Shirley. "What was the associate's name who did this report? She was just in here."

"Moira. Moira Moran."

"Could you ask her to come in, if she's still in the office?" Alec asked.

The kid was so fast Alec suspected she had been waiting in the hall. She sat down with a cross-her-legs motion that gave a burst of white nylon, drawn tight over her long legs. She knew her legs were good and, like Karen at her age, she knew the moves.

"This is a very good workup," Alec said.

"Thank you," Moira answered.

"Let me tell you a little more about our interest in the firm and see if you have some suggestions for further research. Okay?"

"Right," Moira answered. She was all cool efficiency.

"One of our clients has suggested to us that the firm may be implicated in money laundering and international maritime fraud. This seems on the face of it unlikely, and certainly we do not perpetuate idle criminal charges even in preparing a defense." Alec was choosing his words carefully.

Connie Callaghan used to caution, "Young lawyers are leaping to make a name for themselves. So they're reading your manner and your attitude as well as listening to your words. If you imply that shoddy tactics are okay, they'll follow that lead."

"It is suggested that Oakes, Ames and Dumont has assisted some selected clients in setting up foreign firms to create false billings and to siphon the money into accounts beyond the reach of the IRS. These clients also claim that Oakes may be helping Interglobal, a fuel tanker consortium, to defraud it's investors."

Alec leaned back, like a teacher before a class.

"This, of course, may not be true. Or sometimes there can simply be a bad apple in a firm that, when it discovered what was going on, quietly fired the offender."

Moira interrupted. "I think we ought to look more into Vernon Dumont's death." She had caught up with Alec's thinking. "If you look at the obit clip, Oakes credits Dumont with their foreign operations, but I couldn't find any indication in print that they had special foreign operations. You can see where their bigger clients had overseas interests, but nothing special."

"Exactly." Alec smiled.

"I could go out to the Hamptons," Moira suggested.

"Whoa." Alec put his hand up in caution.

"Let's not have some local calling the widow just yet to tell them a pretty New York lawyer is asking questions."

Moira blushed and sank back a little in her chair.

"First let's use our own strengths. See if one of our insurance clients can discreetly get us the insurance settlement on the accident. Don't make waves if it can be done easily. Okay?"

"Okay."

"Then instead of going to the Hamptons, go to Suffolk county court. Get any case that might have arisen from the accident. Suits. Countersuits. By the way, what index searches have you made?" Alec asked.

"Southern District civil and criminal, tax court, and New York State civil."

"Did you search all officers as individuals?"

"No."

"Let's do that. The whole ball of wax. Marriages, divorces, unpaid grocery bills. I'm especially looking for cases that might lay out financial information. Also for disgruntled employee cases. Another thing. Take Oakes, Ames, and Vernon." Alec was gesturing toward Moira's report. "Let's run their real estate. New York apartments, summer houses, the whole gamut. Hire a legal search firm where you need it."

"Okay." She was taking notes on a yellow legal pad.

"What makes me doubt this skimming–money laundering stuff," Alec said, "is that usually that's the practice of marginal outfits. Some lawyer or investment guy who wasn't doing too well who has a client who wants special service. There are overseas firms who specialize in this. But it's pretty unlikely for a mainline firm that has a lot to lose."

Alec nodded at Moira.

She seemed unconvinced.

"You know what struck me, Mr. Anton?" she asked.

"Shoot," Alec answered.

"I checked Oakes, Ames and Dumont against the clips of Goldman, Sachs and a couple of other well-known firms. Admittedly these were far more publicized investment houses, but the clippings all had fairly detailed stories about their profitability. Usually about every two years the *Wall Street Journal* or the *Times* or *Business Week* would write about how much money they were making. What you see is what I could find on Oakes, Ames."

"Maybe that's what you get when you go to Oakes, Ames," Alec mused. "You get discretion."

She returned his gaze. "When do you need this?"

"Yesterday," he said.

She started out, then turned back, holding onto the door jamb.

"I'm really grateful for the chance to work with you. I've read several of your cases here and when you were in the Southern District. Everyone says you're the best. It's a great chance for me."

Alec found himself blushing. When he recovered she was gone.

He realized he had been hurrying all day. He had half consciously been thinking of Lee, wanting to see her. He started to put on his coat. The ringing phone filled him with impatience.

"You know who this is?"

"Yep."

"You know that picture you showed me?"

"Sure."

"He's in heavy shit."

"What?"

"You remember the Jamaican massacre?"

"The what?"

"In Queens." Eddie's voice was impatient. "Nine people last summer."

"Yeh, vaguely."

"Your friend Mr. Ochoa."

"Marco?"

"We can't make him, but that's what intelligence says. His organization took them out to get control of Queens.

"Three of the victims were children. Drilled one little three-year-old in her eye with a nine millimeter. Shot two other kids under six.

"I don't know what's going on, counselor, but get out of it. This ain't your kind of case."

The line went dead.

6

"YOU'RE sure?" Pain was written on her face. Pain and fear.

"Sure I'm sure. You asked me to check, remember?"

"Your friend said what?"

"He said the Ochoas were major narcotics traffickers and they killed a whole family, including the children, to take over a territory in Queens."

"I don't believe it! It's not the same Ochoas."

"Don't practice any more denial." Alec's voice was angry. "You came to me already filled with suspicion about your son. You knew he was in deep trouble. But you keep playing games with yourself."

He had driven a good deal of the way at eighty miles an hour, weaving in and out of the traffic in a rental car and nearly getting killed on the Sawmill Turnpike. It had taken him an hour to find Lee, another hour to round up her daughters and put them on a train to her sister's.

Now this woman was standing on his porch arguing with him, like he made the whole thing up. He could see past her head the masts of two sailboats tacking up along the channel to Cove Marine. He wished he was sailing. He wished it was a week ago. He wished he had never heard of any of this.

"I know this sounds stupid, but go over it for me again, what you said."

She seemed like a child concentrating on the rules of a new game, staring not at him but at a silk lamp shade, as though its surface were a screen upon which information would appear.

He tried to pace his voice, to hide impatience and anger.

"Your son abruptly and mysteriously disappeared a few weeks after graduating from college. Right?"

It did not need an answer.

"You find a false passport and a lot of money. Right?

"You ask a lawyer to check. He checks with a federal agent. The federal agent says that one of your son's friends is involved in a major narcotics operation and a brutal massacre."

"But how do we know this?" Lee pleaded again.

"Shit! I'm not taking this to trial. I came out here to tell you this is very dangerous. You need to go to the police. You need to protect yourself and your daughters. I don't have to prove anything!"

"Stop screaming at me!"

"I'm sorry." He got his voice under control again.

He realized how forlorn she looked, still staring into the lamp.

"Can I get you something. A drink?"

"Please."

"What sort of drink?"

"Do you have any whiskey?"

He got a bottle of Jack Daniels from the bar in the living room, glasses and ice from the kitchen.

When he got back she was staring at the harbor, watching the lights come up.

"When we first came here, Noah was fourteen. It was before he went away to school. He would camp out there on Peach Island. All night I would watch that little tent light. As long as it was lit I knew he was all right."

They drank in silence. The whiskey warmed him and he felt better, as though he had new energy.

Alec was finding it difficult to concentrate on Lee's face. She had turned slightly in her chair so that the material of her blouse pulled tight over her breasts and they were clearly outlined. She wore no bra. He could see the tiny button of one nipple showing through the material.

He wanted desperately to touch her, even just a hand or a cheek, just lightly, to make connection. He didn't.

Suddenly she caught his gaze and blushed as though they had had the same thought at the same moment.

She poured herself another Jack Daniels, adding no ice and letting the whiskey half fill the glass.

"Are you hungry?" he asked. She shook her head. She had drawn her knees up close to her body and was balancing the whiskey glass on them with both hands.

"Did you ever really confront Noah about what was going on?" Alec asked.

"No. Not really."

"Why not?"

"It was always easier not to get to the bottom of it. I told you that. Don't you see. Because . . ." She laughed bitterly. "Because, I couldn't have managed without him.

"Oh, I know I look prosperous — my own agency, big, expensive house, Jaguar, lots of clothes. It all looks good, but the fact is, I'm in hock to every bank in Fairfield county. I'm not a fool. I've got several good deals working, and I'm pretty sure I'm going to end up a fairly wealthy woman. But it has taken a lot of capital. . . ."

"Did Noah give you capital?"

Lee grimaced. It was as though she had bitten into something bitter.

"It was a couple of years ago. I was agent for an office building. It was the biggest thing I had ever done. I'd put my own money in it, but no matter how I tried, I couldn't move it. I was going down the drain." She stopped for a second. "And Noah made a call to someone."

"And?"

"And a firm in New York bought it."

"Marco?"

"I guess so. I don't know. Noah wouldn't say anything else. He just said 'Go with it!' "

"Where was your husband in all this? Doesn't he pay anything?"

"He makes a big deal out of paying child support. But nothing in the league we're talking about. Besides, I would never ask him for money. You don't ask John for help. John can be very dangerous."

"Dangerous?"

She nodded absentmindedly as though Alec wasn't there. She took a big slug of the whiskey, wrinkling her face in response to the taste. She was talking rapidly now.

"You know, I've been away from John eight years. Yet, almost every day I still have a great feeling of relief, of life and independence. I seldom see him anymore. But when we met at Noah's graduation, I felt the old fear again. Do you know what it was like to live with somebody who terrorized you?"

Alec shook his head wordlessly.

"You spend every waking moment being very careful, careful of everything you say or do because anything might set him off."

"You mean physically violent?" Alec felt his pulse racing. It was irrational, he knew. She was speaking of events long past. Yet, he felt this urgent need to protect her.

"John used to say that pain was instructive. That was the word he used. Instructive. He said people learned from pain. I certainly did." She did not elaborate.

"After Vietnam, I tried to get him to see army doctors because I think he is ill, very ill, but he wouldn't.

"He said I was trying to destroy him. He . . . he . . ." She stopped, apparently unwilling to continue that course.

"In many ways Noah is like his father." Her eyes filled with tears. "He has his father's brown eyes, so dark and piercing that it amazes you.

"From the start Noah also had his father's charm. John was charming. Oh, that's not the right word. But he was very charming when he wanted to be. When John talked to you, really talked to you, he could make you believe you were the most important person in the world to him.

"Well, Noah is the same. You want to believe anything Noah tells you. When he was a little boy, children would give him things. I mean valuable things. I'd ask him where he got this or that. And he'd say 'Oh, Johnny gave it to me.' So I would take it back. I thought maybe he took it from them, you know? But the other little kid would always say 'I gave that to Noah.' "

"So it didn't surprise you that the Ochoas wanted to give him a lucrative job and trips to Colombia?" Alec prodded.

"Maybe it should have. But it didn't. Dammit! It didn't."

"Why didn't Noah get along with his father?" Alec found himself wanting to know about every moment of her life, and Noah's.

"When Noah was little they were inseparable." She was pacing the porch with one hand on her hip and the other rubbing her neck. Alec's mind was fixed on her neck. Somehow what Eddie had told him, the tension, the fear, had made her all the more desirable. He found he was literally sweating.

"Noah adored John. He would watch everything his father did and mimic it, like a little tiny John."

The whiskey seemed to warm her to the task of telling.

"But from the moment John came back from Vietnam the second time, it was different. Noah and John were at each other's throats. Noah had started dressing like a hippy. I didn't think much of it, but John couldn't abide it.

"Then one day the police came. We were living in Fayetteville. That awful little town. All it is, is Fort Bragg. Oh, God, how I hated it. I hated it so badly I wouldn't go out of the house.

"John was at Bragg, teaching. He virtually never came home. He would get up at four-thirty in the morning and I wouldn't see him until midnight."

Lee paused as though calculating.

"You know, it was the worst year of my life. Definitely! It was so bad I cannot to this day even bear to recall much of it."

The conclusion hung in the air.

"One day the police picked up Noah and two other little boys in a trailer park with a bag of marijuana. They said the boys were selling it to some other kids who had run away.

"Noah was fourteen and the only officer's child. The police had told the military police on the base, and they had agreed that since all three children were military dependents and had no record of arrests, they wouldn't charge them in juvenile court."

"Where did Noah get the marijuana?" Alec asked.

"He said they bought it from some soldiers. I don't think he and his friends knew what to do with it. It was just the intrigue, just the sneaking around.

"John was in a rage. He wouldn't hear Noah's side at all. He never once even seemed worried about whether Noah was using drugs or needed help. But when the military police were brought in, the story spread all over the base. John went around the house saying he was 'ruined.' "

"What did he mean, 'ruined'?" Alec asked.

"John acted like Noah had gotten himself arrested on purpose, as an affront, to hurt his career.

"Anyway, he said he was 'taking Noah over.' I wasn't to have anything to do with the boy. He shaved Noah's head like a paratrooper, burned all of Noah's clothes, and bought him new ones. He took to inspecting Noah every morning and every evening as if he were a soldier.

"By that time I knew something had happened to John." She was crying.

"He never touched me, never said a single word that was affectionate or even civil. We were treated like a platoon, a platoon full of misfits.

"I wasn't the only one who was having trouble. Other wives had the same story. Half the Green Berets returning from Vietnam were having serious emotional problems. God! Drinking was at an alltime high. The officers club was a cesspool. There were fights between husbands and wives every night and fights between the men."

"Did you have fights?"

"Sometimes . . ." Her voice caught. "Sometimes he taught me a lesson. It was all very controlled. He said I had to learn a lesson." She shifted direction, like a sailboat seeking the wind.

She downed the rest of the whiskey in one shot, throwing back her head and closing her eyes for a moment.

"You realize, don't you . . . you know John was West Point. He wasn't a brawler. It had never been like that before. When he was first commissioned he used to say 'A career soldier is a leader on duty and off duty.' He was very correct, correct in everything."

She found the Jack Daniels and poured again. Alec put his hand forward in a gesture of restraint, but she ignored it.

"You know why the wives were so terrified?" She stopped near Alec's chair, leaned against the table edge, and was looking very intently, very directly into his face. "Because we were married to murderers."

"What do you mean murderers?" Alec put his hand on her arm, steadied her.

"Killers. John killed people."

"I was in Vietnam." He said it very softly. "Some of us had to kill people."

"The Green Berets were different," she said stubbornly. "They killed with their bare hands. Just read his citation for the Silver Star. Just read the citation."

She recited as though from memory. "Killed fourteen of the enemy in hand-to-hand combat armed only with his pistol and a trench knife."

The story mesmerized Alec. So that was what they thought back in the world. He could see Sergeant Burns's old-young face in his mind. "You know lieutenant until I got to V-i-e-t N-a-m I didn't give a flying fuck for the M1911 Colt. It was extra weight. But you hang on to yours because close up in these bunkers it's the best little gook killer in the world."

Lee started pacing again.

"One night I was sound asleep. Mindy was heavy inside me, big enough to be uncomfortable. When I finally dropped off, I was dead to the world. Noah was in his room and Veronica was asleep, and John hadn't come home.

"Suddenly I heard this god-awful screaming. It was a wailing like an animal. I didn't know what it was, and I lay in bed for a few seconds trying to place the sound. Then I got up and ran into Veronica's room, but she was still asleep and I realized it was coming from the garage.

"I went in . . ." She stopped. "Went in and he was beating Noah. Beating him with an army belt. Noah was naked and there was blood dripping from little cuts all over his body. He must have beaten him for a long time before the child started to scream.

"I grabbed John and he pushed me down. I landed right on my stomach, right on the baby. It hurt awfully and I began to scream as well."

Her face was tangled in the painful memory, contorted and not beautiful at all.

"Suddenly our next-door neighbor came through the garage's side door. He wasn't army, about the only person in the development who wasn't army.

"When John saw him, he stopped cold for a minute. And then he just walked into the house without a word.

"And Mr. Wright, that was his name, Weldon Wright. If there ever was a 'Mr. Right.'

"He picked me up and he and his wife put me and Noah in the car. Then he went into the house and got Veronica.

"They took us all to the base hospital."

She stopped the tale as though this was the end, the final chapter. Alec waited, aware that they had gone far astray and not caring.

Her account seemed to have exhausted her, and her breath came in gasps as though she had been running.

"What happened then?" He finally spurred her memory.

"The doctors were worried about the baby for a while, but finally they agreed Mindy was all right.

"John's commanding officer came by later and said he would talk to John. But to them, you know, it was just a family fight. He kept saying things like 'It can get rough when boys and their dads get to arguing' — like it was out of *Field and Stream* magazine or *Boy's Life.*"

Both she and Alec were standing now, in the middle of the porch, facing each other. She had her feet planted wide apart, a pose of determination. Her voice had it too: determination.

"I never went back to that house. None of us did. I called my father and he wired money to set us up in a motel until he could get there. And that was the end of John and me."

"What happened to Noah?"

"John put him in a boarding school."

"Why?"

"John made it a condition of our divorce that we place Noah in a boarding school. His lawyer gave me a list of schools they found."

"Because he was using drugs?"

"John didn't know that."

"Then why the boarding school?"

"John wanted to take Noah away from me. Don't you see? He couldn't get him. The court would block that. But he could hurt me."

"Why did you go along with it?" Alec asked.

"I realize now I never should have agreed, but then . . ." Her voice trailed off. "I couldn't live without alimony and child support, and it seemed worthwhile for Noah. But you see what it did?" Lee looked at Alec as though the answer were clear.

"I don't think I do," he said.

"It hid Noah. So John didn't have to think of him or hear from him or be embarrassed by him."

He knew then that they would make love. He wanted to enter the mysteries of her body. She had undressed her life and her body would come next. He was sure.

They had been talking in the dark, and now they stripped, whirling and tearing off their clothing by the light of a full moon reflecting on the water.

It was the most violent lovemaking he could ever recall. She was a big woman and as strong as he was; she used him more than he used her, slamming his body again and again against the floor, forcing, kneading, pushing at him.

They wrestled hard, moaning wordlessly, urging one another with sounds. Her body was tight and looking for release. Alec could not remember how long it went on. His body hurt and he was tired, he knew, but she would not let him rest. When he had seemed to understand her demands, seemed to follow her directions, seemed to carry out her wishes, she would spur him on.

"Yes. Yes. Yesss. Yesss. YESSSS."

He would remember that single word from the night, that one word whispered and screamed.

He did not remember falling asleep.

7

THEY had pulled an Indian blanket from the couch for warmth and he could feel her body close and warm.

He lay in the darkness listening to her breathing and trying to think. He felt a strange sense of anxiety. The conquest had been too easy; could the prize be tainted?

"Can I ask you something without making you mad?"

"When anyone asks that question they know they are going to make somebody mad," Lee answered, her voice muffled by her shoulder.

"How can you make such fantastic love when all this is going on?" Alec had consciously avoided any reference to the danger to her son, the son she said was a favorite.

She leapt up to her knees and whirled to face him, her face flushed with anger, the blanket a tangle around her bare legs.

"I didn't see you refusing it," she hissed.

The question was a gratuitous cruelty. As soon as he uttered it he knew that. He wanted to take it back. He realized he was angry at himself, not her. He had fallen prey to her. He had been the conquest.

"You want to know the truth, you egoistical shit?" Lee's question was rhetorical. Alec knew she planned to answer it.

"I've watched you for years. You and Karen. How nice! How perfect! How I wanted you! Do you realize what it is like for a woman living years with children and no man.

"I've sat on that porch" — she swept her hand across the half-moon harbor toward her house — "a hundred nights alone and wondered what it would be like with you."

He was trying to stop her tirade, but she had drawn the blanket up as a wall between them and her pain was tumbling out.

"Do you know what it was like to be alone? For years if I wanted to be able to go out and stay all night with a man I had to find a place where the children would be safe.

"I couldn't take a man home. Oh no! I was single and God knows over twenty-one, but if I took a man to bed in my own home, I could lose custody of the children. John had people watching to make sure of that.

"I had to risk my children to do a simple goddamn thing like getting laid!

"But that was John's plan." She shifted her anger from Alec to John. "That was his plan."

"What plan? What are you talking about?" Her outburst dazed Alec.

"I'll tell you what plan! Every time I've thought I could find someone or be with someone, John has found a way to mess it up. He's spread stories about me. He's even threatened me."

She continued, now in a low voice, almost to herself, as though Alec wasn't there, unleashing pent-up anguish about John, about her life, and about her children and about Noah.

She began dressing in a whirlwind; tears for the first time now sparkled in her eyes.

Very slowly, very gently, he tried to take her in his arms, but she arched away from him.

"I'm going home."

Alec reached out again, but Lee still pulled back. "Don't touch me, you shit! Your penis will drop off on the ground before you ever touch me again!"

She stood for a moment by the door, looking down with the superiority of the clothed over the naked.

"Did it ever occur to your masculine superiority that being with a man might have helped me bear what's going on?

"I sought comfort from you — you bastard. Sex! How much caring or affection would you have for me without sex? I'd still be sitting in your secretary's office if I was old and haggard."

She marched out to the seawall without a word, taking great long strides as though she were alone. He pulled on his pants and loafers and stumbled after her.

Lee's house jutted out from a point of the island so that the expanse of large windows in the living room looked at both Norwalk Harbor and Long Island Sound. It was a large house, oddly shaped, and the white clapboard glowed in the moonlight.

She was almost at her door when he noticed the things on the driveway, clothes, a car seat.

Lee looked wildly about.

"These things are from Noah's car!" she cried in a hoarse whisper.

She ran to the Porsche, which was hidden from view by a hedge. Both doors and the trunk were open, seat ticking, wires, bags strewn all around.

Alec felt fear immediately. Whoever had entered the Porsche had slashed every seat cushion, torn up floor and trunk rugs.

He ran to the door of the house and motioned to Lee to stay outside.

The kitchen seemed undisturbed, messy, but not in an unnatural way. But the living room had been ransacked, seat cushions overturned, drawers pulled out, furniture moved.

"Don't touch anything," Alec warned. "We'll get the police to take fingerprints and we don't want to smudge any. Okay?" He found the phone in the kitchen, holding it midhandle with two fingers and punching in the numbers.

Moonlight lit the living room like a stage.

The expensive soft leather furniture was now in shreds. The strips of leather looked like snakes on the floor.

All drawers and cabinets in the dining room had been emptied, and there was not a single book left on the shelf in the study.

The second floor had also been ransacked: drawers open, beds overturned, closets undone, and the ladder to the attic was down. Someone had been there, too.

As Lee and the police officers walked through the rooms, they discovered that though the house was a shambles, nothing was missing. In her bedroom the burglars had passed up jewelry and an envelope for the maid with nearly a hundred dollars in it. On the first floor they'd ignored all the electrical appliances and credit cards they found in a desk.

It was full daylight before the policemen decided it was late enough to survey the neighbors.

"The only person who saw anything important," the young beefy cop said, "was Mrs. Long over in number twenty-eight. She says she saw the same car here about four or five times in the last week.

"She didn't get the license number, but she said the car was black with orange old-style New York plates and she thought it was a Trans Am. She said the drivers were foreign or Puerto Rican. What she noticed was they never went to anyone's house, just cruised the streets."

"Would strangers be normal?" Alec interjected. He knew the answer, but he wanted the officers to spell it out to Lee.

"Hell no!" The young cop laughed. "When they took down the old bridge, there's only one way on or off Harborview.

"Most of the locals know that there are people home here at all times of the day or night and any unusual car is spotted at once. Jesus, I don't think we've had a police report outta here except for a stray dog in six months. Right Charley?"

Charley only nodded. He looked sleepy.

"Does it make sense that they would only enter Mrs. Hastings's house?" Alec asked.

"It doesn't make sense they'd be here at all except if they're from New York. But if you were going to rob here, this house would be the best. It's one of the biggest on the island and its close to the causeway. I gotta tell you, though, it don't look to me like these guys were cruisin' for open doors. These guys knew where they were going."

"Why would they be coming to my house?" Lee's face looked weary and afraid.

"I don't know," the young cop answered. "You know, there are a lot of expensive homes around here. And we get two kinda burglaries. One is usually kids, who are hittin' on something and decide to break into a house. They'd have gone staggering outta here with everything you got.

"Then because this area is so rich we get professional burglars. These guys already know what the house has got in it. They get their information from insurance agents who talk too much or delivery boys or repairmen who come into your home.

"Last year, remember, Charley?" The second cop nodded to his partner. "Darien police broke up a ring that worked with an interior decorator. She was getting her ticket punched by one of the . . ." He stopped, embarrassed by his crudeness. "She was going with one of the burglars. She did your house in more ways than one." He laughed.

"Since you don't see nothing missing, Mrs. Hastings, maybe these guys came for something they thought was here, didn't find it, and decided to split. Professionals don't take knickknacks. They don't want to be carrying anything more from a bust than they have to. The most dangerous time for them out here is in the hour or so after a robbery. Getting stopped on the highway. They know that holding them on descriptions is hard, but if they have anything from the victim's house — boom — they're over."

He smacked his fist into his hand for emphasis.

Finally the two seemed to realize Lee was weary and bundled their clipboards, flashlights, and bulky bodies into the cruiser.

"Nice to meet you, Mrs. Hastings." The young cop was admiring Lee's breasts, which were level with his gaze from the car window. "We'll keep an eye out for your house and we'll put it on the day log."

Lee called the girls and told them the house had been burglarized. They wanted to come home, but she convinced them to stay at her sister's house.

"I can't stay here." She looked at the mess. "I can't deal with this now."

Alec took her hand and led her back up the beach. As they walked, he put his arm around her and she leaned hard into him.

Alec started to speak but she cut him off.

"I need help. I can't deal with this alone. I've needed help for a long time. Long before Noah disappeared. I knew something was desperately wrong. Men don't want to buy into despair." She shook her head back and forth.

"I can't hold my life together anymore. Noah running away like this was just the last straw. I was so hoping he would move back. Just for a while. Work in New York, help me." Her voice rose at the end.

"I would run away too if I could. Believe me. I would just go. But I can't. Then there would be no one to find Noah. No one to try to hang on to Veronica. No one" — she was crying now — "no one to comb Mindy's hair or be the Pumpkin Lady at the school fair. I'm caught. I can't run and I sure can't hide."

She let him hold her.

"I wonder where he is. If he would just call me. If we could just talk for a moment."

Even though it was hot, she made him lock every door, every window, on the first floor. Only then, exhausted, did they go upstairs to sleep.

Alec felt like he had only been asleep for minutes when he sensed her body. She was wearing nothing but the tiny gold chain on her neck, her full flesh warm and moist with perspiration.

Again she was urgent and demanding, silently set upon arousing him from slumber, coaxing him as if he were a child.

As before she spoke no clear sentences, framed no thoughts. She wanted this time, though, to be dominated, placing herself in positions of subjugation, guiding him with her hands.

He spoke only once. "It didn't drop off."

She slapped his backside. "Shush!"

She wanted her body entered by all orifices, turning and twisting to accomplish this goal, pulling and pushing, making tiny mewing sounds when gratification seemed to come. She was relentless in her desires, and more than once when Alec was sure that this must be the end, she would begin again.

Soft, late-afternoon sunlight filled the room. She was lying spread-eagled on her stomach, in a heavy sleep. Her body showed marks of his passion, and a tiny rivulet of blood and moisture traced itself across one giant buttock.

He looked at her in silence. He was being pulled into that body, as helpless in her flesh as he would have been in a swamp.

In bed there was no missing child, no Noah, no confused and frightened mother. In bed there was someone else, a woman of great power.

He finally fell asleep again, next to her, one arm over her bare back.

When he awoke the second time, he was alone. He could smell Chinese food.

It was dark, the harbor glittering and inky. When he got to the bottom of the stairs, Alec watched Lee for a moment at the kitchen table. She didn't realize he was up. He restrained an enormous desire to slip his hand inside the robe she was wearing and touch her body.

"I was starved," she said, opening a large brown bag with grease stains on the bottom. "So I ordered some Chinese. We've got enough for a battalion. Unless you hurry, I plan to eat it all."

They loaded all the food on a tray and took it to the enclosed porch, eating right out of the cartons. The tide was in and the water lapped at the seawall, little spurts of wave occasionally dancing up over the stones.

"Where do we go from here?" Lee finally started when they had had their fill.

"Right to the police."

Ignoring his statement, she followed her own train of thought. "Do you think the police will put the two together? I mean, the break-in and Noah missing?"

"I noticed you didn't volunteer it."

"I was too stunned," she said defensively. "I didn't know what to do."

"They might. This is a small city, the detectives probably read a day report on everything."

"Lee." He suddenly stopped, looking hard at her. "Don't go on with this. Take everything to the police. Your kid is involved in some serious business."

She looked stricken, as though someone had told her of a great sadness.

"People have searched your house," he continued. "For all we know they're watching us right now."

She looked out into the darkness toward the seawall as though she expected to see the watchers.

"What will happen to Noah if I go to the police?"

Alec thought for a long time. "If it's what I think, he'll be prosecuted."

"Would you defend him?"

"I could . . ." He hesitated. He could see a partners meeting in his mind's eye. Trowbridge lawyers don't do drug cases.

". . . assist in his defense," he continued.

"What if we find Noah first and get him to go to the police?"

"That would help, of course. But you and I aren't equipped to do that, we can't —"

Lee cut him off.

"Please. Alec. Don't. Help me find him. I want to find him and talk to him. Help him. Please help me find him first."

She was crying now, softly sobbing, her face turned down away from him. After a few seconds, she jumped up and he heard her run upstairs.

He sat there for a long time.

When he went upstairs, she was sitting on the bed in the guest room. She was fully dressed, sitting primly, her eyes red and filled with tears and fingering a tissue wadded with moisture.

She started to speak as he came in.

"Whatever has happened to Noah, whatever he's involved in, is my fault, my fault and John's. We had this beautiful child. High I.Q. Did I tell you that? He had a one hundred sixty I.Q. He was beautiful and brilliant and in fourteen years we scarred him. . . .

"Now I know I can't turn time back. I could have done something years ago when I left John, but it was so hard. You don't know. I should have done something when he went to college. Last year! Any year!"

Alec sat down next to her, but he did not try to talk.

"Alec, don't you see," she said taking his left hand and rubbing it gently with both of hers. "I can't leave this to the police. I'm stuck with this. This is my child. I can't leave Noah to police, or school officials, or doctors, or somebody else.

"Give me a week. Just a week. Maybe we can find where he is or he'll call and we can talk to him. Talk to him together. He'll listen to you. Maybe he can explain. Maybe he didn't know about the Ochoas. Nobody ever said anything at the school. They were very influential. Maybe there are different sides to the family."

He finally stopped her, holding up a palm like a traffic cop.

"Okay, okay. A week."

People are funny when they get what they want, he thought. Lee almost cooed, leaning over and kissing him. It was the wrong move. He felt more uneasy. He wished she had done nothing.

Suddenly her attention drifted on. "Why did whoever searched the house leave without searching the kitchen or the bathrooms?"

"Perhaps they found what they were looking for." Alec was unconvinced even after he said it.

"Were they looking for the money I found," she asked, "or the passport?"

"Well we know some things about the search," he said. "Whatever they were searching for is small and they know what it is."

She looked puzzled.

"If it was a suitcase full of money, they wouldn't be pulling apart cushions. Right? If it was enough narcotics to be valuable, they wouldn't be slashing cushions either. Right?" He wasn't giving her enough time to answer.

"It would be my guess it's small, a paper or a book, a key, maybe jewels, money, and they think he hid it quickly, or didn't hide it at all, but left it in his stuff. If they didn't know what they were looking for they'd have taken stuff away just to examine it.

"Just where did you find the passport?" Alec asked.

"I found it in his underwear. It was at the back of his dresser drawer, behind his underwear. Only this was some old underwear. It was probably too small because his college clothes were either in the car or he took them with him."

"The things you found were not really hidden." Alec doodled on a yellow pad. "I mean they were hidden from you. They were hidden from somebody idly coming across them. But in the underwear and behind pictures are the first places people would search. I don't think either the passport or the money was very important to Noah. He didn't need them to go to Europe. He just didn't want to explain them to you." Alec paused.

"You've really done all the obvious things to find Noah. Let's do the not so obvious. What about the girl Noah was talking about? Do you know her?"

"No. He mentioned her name; maybe I can find it in the yearbook."

Lee took a page of his paper and wrote a note to herself.

"I'm going to talk to your ex-husband."

Her face flushed. "Why, in God's name?"

"Because maybe he can help."

8

JOHN Hastings looked like a military officer. He had the sort of perfect handsomeness, Alec thought, that William Westmoreland possessed, an advertising agency's concept of what an officer should look like.

His office contributed, presumably intentionally, to this impression. It was the office of a field grade officer, of a commander.

Behind the desk were two flags hung from poles set in floor mountings. To the right of Hastings was the American flag, to the left was a blue flag with a lightning flash that Alec realized was a corporate banner skillfully designed to look quite like the Special Forces insignia.

The desk was absolutely clear except for a manila folder and a single sheet of a paper in front of Hastings. It was adorned only with a handsome set of leather-bound accoutrements, inkwell, blotter, and so forth, and a brass nameplate that faced the visitor with "John Hastings" engraved in block letters between the two eagle insignias of a full colonel.

On the office's left wall was a series of photographs, framed in beautifully turned-out teak. Hastings on parade at West Point. Hastings being decorated by General Westmoreland on a landing strip in Vietnam. Hastings in full Special Forces uniform, his solemn face looking out from under the green beret. There were shots of Hastings in jungle fatigues talking with Montagnard tribesmen half his size and a picture of a group of Americans in the black pajama dress of the Vietnamese peasant squatting for a picture alongside a Huey helicopter that bore no U.S. insignia.

Along the right wall as Alec entered were a couch and several deep club chairs, grouped in a conversation circle around a large coffee table that was a display case for pistols. There were black automatics, silver-mounted commemorative revolvers, a small machine pistol with a folding stock, and a pistol fitted with a silencer kit.

Hastings rose as Alec entered. His manner made Alec unconsciously feel as though he should march to the center of the room before the desk and report himself, "Captain Anton, sir," but he didn't.

Hastings was lean and leathered. Every muscle cord of the neck group seemed delineated, and the skin of his face was pulled tight over the skull without appearing gaunt. He was dressed in a dark gray suit of London cut with box vents and tailored shirt with a monogram on a corner of the breast pocket that was exposed as he gestured Alec toward a seat on the couch.

Picking up the paper from in front of him, Hastings came around the desk with a firm gait, poised, unhurried but not ambling. He still walked like a West Pointer, with his shoulders thrown back.

He took a chair facing Alec, folding his legs.

"May I offer you coffee?" he asked.

"No thanks," Alec answered.

"So you were in the marines." Hastings was consulting the sheet in front of him.

"Four unforgettable years," Alec answered.

"Now you're with one of the most expensive law firms in the country and my former wife who claims she never has any money has retained you to find Noah, our beloved son. She is, of course, paying you in an ancient currency, a currency she has so often dispensed to get her way."

"I beg your pardon," Alec tried to break in, but Hastings was not finished.

"Sometime, even before I met her, Lee discovered that she had a craving, that she needed to satisfy that thing between her legs. I have seen her do it with fingers, with bananas, with electric vibrators, with my fellow officers, with my best friend, and in at least one incident I knew of, with my best friend's wife."

Hastings never raised his voice. He was speaking in conversational tones, almost gently, as though he was recounting a rather sad story.

"She has a disease. I have no name for it because I could never get her to seek medical help. It is not nymphomania, my army doctor friends told me, because she can be satisfied and nymphomania implies unsatisfied sexual desire in the woman. They suspected it was a condition like alcoholism, that she simply could not control her desire for sexual gratification and would do anything to obtain it."

Alec was spellbound. Here was why he did not take divorce cases. This man and this woman had not lived together for nearly a decade. Had hardly, if Lee was correct, even seen one another. One of their children is missing and could be dead or injured and this man spends the first few moments with a complete stranger accusing his former wife of a sexual disease. No wonder Lee had not wanted him to see Hastings.

He let Hastings continue.

"This disease in an unattractive woman would quickly be distasteful, but in Lee it is the epitome of man's erotic dreams. How often did you and your men in the marines sit around talking about finding a woman who would fuck your brains out without one ounce of love and affection being demanded in return?"

Hastings stopped. He was looking at Alec in sort of a friendly inquisitive way, as though he had asked him how he liked living on Long Island Sound.

Alec did not answer right away. He steeled himself to silence, a trick he had learned in a decade of interrogations and cross-examinations. "When a witness tries to provoke you, to cause an outburst," Connie Callaghan used to say, "go silent like a turtle. Let the jury see him for the irrational one, not you."

Finally Alec answered, holding his voice as steady as Hastings had. "Colonel, that was an amazing performance. It was defamatory to me, to Mrs. Hastings, to your children. I asked to see you about your son and your response is slander. This isn't going to help Noah."

"Correction, Mr. Anton. You say you're here to see me about my son. How do I know you are not in the long chain of lawyers Lee has used to separate me from my children and my money?"

"You probably won't know until you listen to me." Alec let his voice sound annoyed.

"I spent a lot of my life after the marines in law enforcement. Your son is in some kind of trouble and he needs help. Your former wife is a neighbor of mine in Norwalk, and since Noah may have disappeared abroad she wanted a lawyer whose firm has international connections." Alec found he had slipped into that lie with ease.

"I was hoping you could give me some inkling of where Noah might be, some way we could trace his whereabouts," Alec continued.

Hastings was looking at him with a half smile, as though they shared a secret. As though they shared the secret of Lee Hastings.

"You are assuming that it is good to find Noah. That he wants to be found by his mother and father and that he has simply not decided that life with us is at an end." Hastings posed a doubt that was in the back of Alec's mind.

"That is exactly what I told Mrs. Hastings when she came to my office," Alec said. "That's also the reason that law enforcement officials are probably reluctant to open a formal inquiry. Your son is an adult. He is a college graduate and there is no reason to believe he has gone against his will.

"But Mrs. Hastings has given me the information that your son was using a false name and had a large amount of unaccounted-for funds. There have been other incidents which suggest he may be involved in something sinister."

Hastings's bland expression changed, only slightly, but distinctly. Alec could tell he was now listening carefully.

"A false name?" Hastings said.

"John Grant," Alec answered.

"Never heard it."

"Do you know anyone named Grant, or are there Grants in your family?" Alec asked.

"The only Grant I know is buried in Grant's tomb." Hastings seemed pleased with his little quip.

Alec ignored it. "Since his disappearance someone has searched his car, entered her house, and searched through Noah's belongings and hers."

Alec tried to mimic the stilted language of a police report, trying to sound professional and indifferent to his client, trying to offset Hastings's assumption that his only interest was in Lee.

"I don't know anything about that. It sounds strange, but then Noah was a strange boy. I haven't been close to Noah for eight years. I really know little about him." Hastings said this matter-of-factly with no sound of remorse or sadness.

"Can you tell me a little about the last time you saw him?" Alec asked.

"I don't think it will help you," Hastings replied.

"Try me anyway," Alec shot back.

"Well, much to my surprise Noah invited us to his graduation. My wife and myself. One of those little engraved cards the schools give with a ticket. Then he called, all cheery, about reserving rooms at the inn for us. You would have never thought . . ." Hastings's voice trailed off.

"They had chosen Noah to give the class address. Quite impressive. He was very polished, all talk about challenge and commitment. But if you know Noah, you know he could have given that address at twelve. He is very glib." Hastings seemed to come to a halt.

"Did you have a chance to talk to him alone at all? To talk about his plans?" Alec asked. He had taken out a yellow legal pad and begun jotting notes, hoping to induce Hastings to talk by lending to the notion this was an impersonal debriefing.

"Ellen and I took him to dinner. He wore a suit I would venture to say cost eight hundred or a thousand dollars. He wore a gold Rolex watch. He wore an expensive class ring. His left hand alone must have been worth twenty-five hundred. He had become very smooth." Hastings's face had taken on a wry look.

"Did he tell you about the trip to Europe?" Alec asked.

"Actually, we talked quite a lot about that. Noah said he wanted to go places Lee and I had taken him to when he was a little boy. It was so strange a conversation. I felt all evening as though it were surreal, sitting there talking like normal human beings after all that had come between. . . ." Hastings was no longer looking at Alec. He was looking off into the middle distance.

"What did you do in Vietnam?" Hastings changed the subject abruptly.

"I had a platoon, later a rifle company," Alec answered. He glanced at the paper in Hastings's hand; even upside down Alec could recognize it was a biography box from Martindale and Hubble.

"Where were you?" Hastings asked.

"The An Hoa Valley. Well, Danang for a couple of weeks. The rest in the An Hoa."

"You didn't end up with a staff assignment?" Hastings seemed puzzled.

"Nope. I opted to stay in the field for my second six months. Now I cannot remember why. Bravado, I guess. It was the most incoherent decision I ever made." Alec tried to sound light.

"How long were you in the field?" asked Hastings.

"Until I was wounded," Alec answered.

"When was that?"

"Charley wasn't going to give me an inch. They got me in my last week, a week I agreed to wait until a lieutenant could come over from the two-five. Thirteen months in country." Alec realized how easily he had fallen back into the lexicon of the war. Two-five, in country, CONUS, DEROS, MACV, the words running through his mind made him shudder.

"Thirteen months in country and I could have flown right out."

"How were you hit?" Hastings leaned forward.

Alec paused. He was really hit with Marquette's head. That's what he remembered. The blast. White. Something knocked him down to the floor of a communication trench. It felt like a football had hit him in the shoulder. A football or a medicine ball. He opened his eyes. He was looking into the eyes of Lance Corporal Marquette. Marquette looked wild. His helmet was gone. His mouth open. It was then Alec realized that Marquette's body was no longer attached to his head. Only the neck remained, tendons, blood, muscles, the trachea. That was all Alec remembered.

"In the shoulder. Shrapnel. A one twenty-two. Took out our whole bunker." Soldier talk was going to do it. Alec sensed it even before Hastings spoke. Years of interrogation had taught him to sense it. Hastings would now open up. He had found a bridge to Alec. He would come across.

Alec could hear Connie saying "People want to communicate. That's what makes them people. They have language. They can express themselves. They will tell a stranger the most intimate details of their life if they can establish two things: the person is at once sympathetic and detached."

Hastings arose and walked to his desk. "Are you sure you don't want coffee?" he asked.

"I've changed my mind. Please," Alec answered.

Hastings leaned down and said something Alec couldn't hear into a white speakerphone box. A few seconds later the door opened and a small Asian came in. Alec knew he wasn't a Montagnard, but he wasn't Vietnamese either. He guessed he was Hmong, a Lao, slightly different complexion, more like the soft features of the Cambodians.

The Asian carried a stainless steel coffee set. It looked like a pack of artillery shells on a tray. The cups were German or Danish and bore the small blue initials JH. The coffee was dark, strong and European, the way coffee is made in France or Indochina. Hastings did not introduce the silent servant or even acknowledge his presence until the small man left.

"Nhim was a headman of the Mangkong tribe. They were in the mountains along the border a thousand years before what we call the Vietnamese came down from China. He once had a wife, three children.

"When the Vietnamese found he had been helping us, spotting and watching the trail, they came at night to his village. For several hours they tortured him, asking occasionally where the American infiltrators were. He did not answer."

Hastings was walking around the room, holding his cup and saucer and sipping as he talked.

"Finally they started on his family, a method that would have been instantly effective against Westerners and some Orientals. They strangled his wife and each of his children to death before his eyes. I do not know why he did not betray us. We were nearby and would have certainly been caught. But he didn't.

"He has been with me ever since. I think he has long since gone off his head in grief. What has been fascinating to me over the years is the nature of a culture where he would let his loved ones die for an intangible like honoring his word to a comrade. We have nothing like it, do we?"

Alec nodded, not wanting to break the pace of Hastings's talk.

"To tell you about Noah, I have to tell you about Lee and myself.
Is it worth it to you?"

Again Alec nodded.

"You know the greatest moment of my life was the day I graduated from West Point. Have you ever seen a West Point graduation?"

"On television," Alec answered.

"At that moment in time I had everything. I stood thirty-fifth in
my class. I had just received orders for the infantry. I was two hours
away from marrying the most beautiful girl in my hometown."

Hastings had put the coffee down and was standing, his legs
braced, his hands clasped behind his back in the classic pose of a
commanding officer addressing the troops.

"At that moment the United States Army was the most powerful
land force in the world. The United States had the most advanced
economy in the world. The highest standard of living. . . . ." He
stopped as though he realized that it was beginning to sound like he
was on a soapbox.

He sat down again, taking on the look of the urbane, international
businessman.

"If you had told me on that graduation day that within a decade
every single institution I believed in would be destroyed, that everything I loved or respected would be dirt, I wouldn't have believed
you. I couldn't have." Hastings stopped for a moment.

Alec sat quietly.

"I was obsessed by Lee. Have you ever heard the expression
'devoured,' as in love?" Hastings was looking at Alec quizzically.

"In literature, I guess," he answered.

"Lee devoured me. She used me up. My time, my energy, my
waking thoughts. I told you I graduated thirty-fifth. I think if Lee
and I had not been lovers in the final year I could have finished fifth."
Hastings was pacing again. "She was more beguiling at eighteen
than most women are at thirty-five. She had natural instincts of how
to use her sensuality.

"From the moment I was commissioned she seemed determined
to take me from the army. A young second lieutenant has to have his
wife's cooperation. Did in those days, anyway. You can't do it alone.
Lee never said anything, but after a time I realized that she was
actually working against me. She wanted me to fail out of the army."

"What do you mean?" Alec was perplexed.

"In everything. If she had to go to a tea at the battalion commander's wife's house, she was late. If she knew I had to study all night to take a test, she wanted to make love.

"She refused army doctors for Noah. Went off post to some little hick doctor in Columbus. She wanted Noah delivered there, but I put my foot down and took her to the army hospital the night he came along. Kicking and screaming, I might add." Hastings got up again.

"Just like the name Noah. Sounds Jewish. Awful goddamn name. She did it to spite my father. He wanted Noah to be called John Hastings the third."

"Isn't this sort of the same difficulties a lot of marriages get into at first?" Alec was trying to pull him back on track.

"That's what I thought. But as time went on I came to realize that it was more than that. Lee was out to destroy me. It wasn't that she hated army life. But it was me, she hated me, because I brought her to marriage on an army post."

Slowly as Hastings talked Alec began to conclude something that had bothered him with Lee as well. These people didn't talk about their son. They talked about themselves. You asked about Noah and you got answers about John and Lee.

Hastings was continuing, out ahead of Alec, moving at his own pace.

"We hadn't been married two years. Noah was just a toddler and I applied and was sent to Ranger school. Kennedy had come in and we were getting ready for Southeast Asia. Everybody knew we had to learn to fight a different kind of war. Ranger school was the hottest school in the army then.

"Lee hated the idea. Told me not to go. Wouldn't even drive me down to north Georgia. Anyway, I'm away sixteen weeks. Except for one weekend in between, back at Columbus. Lost twenty-three pounds.

"I come back and Lee was very cool to me. Very strange. Then a major I knew, from the base MP battalion, took me for a drink. Said he didn't want to interfere. Just between us. Officer to officer. But my wife had had a lot of visits from a sergeant in his patrol force. The sergeant said he was called to investigate a lost dog and went back to give her reports. . . ." Hastings paused. It was not a dramatic pause.

"We didn't have a dog."

Hastings was talking more rapidly now, more intensely, talking about a marriage disintegrating as his other life, the army, was being drawn into Vietnam. He listed infidelities in North Carolina, Germany, Lee's hometown, and finally back in North Carolina. It was like a travelogue.

There were accusations and recriminations, separations and reunions, alienations and accommodations.

"In Germany we had a German maid and a cook. The maid was a nice young girl. Maybe seventeen. One day" — Hastings now seemed to be wearying of his monologue — "I came home early in the afternoon. Noah was playing in his room. He was seven, smart as a whip, took in everything. I said 'Where's mommy?' He said 'She's playing in the shower with Gretchen. They won't let me play. They said I have to stay here.'

"I didn't know what he was talking about. I thought they must be washing clothes or something and wanted him out of the way. So I went upstairs to the bathroom. The bathroom is locked, but I can hear the German girl moaning and crying. She was having an orgasm. They were so busy they didn't even realize I was standing there.

"I fired the maid and the cook. That was a mistake. They told everyone at Bad Tölz about Lee. Though I guess by then everyone knew.

"Even in the middle of the Vietnam buildup, the regular army was a very small place, like a town. By then almost everybody in town knew. . . ." His voice trailed off.

"Do you know what it is like to walk into an officers club with your wife on your arm and not know how many men in that room have slept with her?" Hastings was not seeking an answer.

"Do you know what it's like to be chatting with a friend and hear him use the same phrase, the same idiom your wife used only the night before?

"One evening I went back to the company office to get something I forgot. My first sergeant's telling his mates a story. It is about a woman who could, as he put it, 'suck start a Harley.'

"Descriptive phrase, 'suck start a Harley.' He is crimson when I enter. As soon as I left you could hear the laughter.

"I was Ranger qualified, airborne trained, a Green Beret, a West Point graduate, but when Lee was finished, to most of my colleagues I was just that asshole whose wife cuckolds him every chance she gets."

"Why didn't you divorce her?" Alec asked.

Hastings looked at him a long time, without speaking. Finally he answered. "I wanted her too, I guess. I wanted her so much I was willing to endure, at least for a long time, to endure."

Alec hoped his amazement didn't show. Hastings was not a man who endured. Alec had met a dozen Hastingses in the marines, in Vietnam. They were war lovers. Where others dragged themselves to the task, weeping and quaking, these men reveled in it. These men took action. They didn't endure.

"Lee would always promise that this would be the end, you know. That she would change. Things did change for a while. Veronica had just been born. Things were better. Then they sent me back to Vietnam. I knew the moment I got the orders that things would fall apart.

"You know what made it all the more ironic?" Hastings was looking very directly and calmly at Alec.

"No," Alec answered.

"As my personal life got worse, my professional life got better. Most of my classmates bet I would be the first Green Beret general officer. They bet on it!"

"What about Noah? Where did he fit in?" Alec asked.

"He was the victim. He sensed, even when he was small, he sensed we were . . . discordant. But it was more. . . ." Hastings seemed to be groping for words. "It was stranger than that. Noah seemed to use our difficulties to enhance his power, his independence.

"Do you have children?" Hastings asked.

Alec shook his head.

"Well in the regular army, with all the separations, lots of men come home to find that a son, particularly a teenage son, has come to be the man of the house. Dozens of my friends had to come home and sort of reestablish control, move out this rival, this surrogate

husband." Hastings was talking as though he was straining to say
what he wanted the right way, the careful way.

"With Noah this seemed to come early. I now believe Lee encour-
aged it, that it was part of her plan, but then I could only see what
was happening."

"What was that?" Alec asked.

"He was in love with his mother," Hastings said.

Alec looked perplexed.

"I don't mean as a mother, but as a woman.

"They bathed together. I don't mean she bathed him. I mean they
bathed together. You ask Veronica. Ask her if her mother ever
bathed with her.

"When I was away they slept together. They had since he was
small. But they still slept together when he was eleven and twelve.
And kissed full on the mouth! Kissed full on the mouth!" Hastings's
voice was going higher. He seemed incensed by the kissing and
awkward in the telling of it.

Alec realized later that Hastings never said Lee and Noah had
sexual relations. He never said the word incest, never talked about
child abuse; he walked to the door of this thought and did not
open it.

"Noah was precocious. He was very verbal, very able to carry his
own with adults. He liked being with adults more than other children. He was very opinionated, so much so I couldn't let him around
my colleagues.

"I stopped taking him anywhere. It was sad because when he was
little we'd go out to the jump range and he'd run along with the
troopers, singing, playing with them.

"Partly I stopped because of the clothes. When I got back from
Vietnam, Lee had let him dress like a freak. He looked like an
antiwar demonstrator!"

"Was your wife against the war?" Alec asked.

Hastings laughed, a tight grunt of a laugh. "Not hardly. The
army was the greatest collection of penises she had ever found, and
the war brought in new ones. Lee let Noah act and dress the way he
did to provoke me."

"Did you try to get control of Noah?" Alec opened the door
carefully. "You don't have to lead the witness," Connie Callaghan

used to say. "Judges are right. You don't need to lead, mostly they're eager to follow."

"Certainly. How could we be expected to command troops if we couldn't even get control of our families. You know what Fort Bragg was like then?" Hastings had seated himself and was leaning toward Alec.

"It was like Vietnam. People called Fayetteville, Fayetnam. Did you know that?"

"No," Alec said.

"Twenty percent of the troops were on heroin. There were three rapes in one month on base in officers housing." Hastings was slamming out information, building a case. "When you went down along Route One at night the whores pulled their pants down on the street to make a sale. You could buy a bag of heroin or a marijuana joint right on base."

He paused as if resting. "The U.S. Army was in revolt. Americans never knew, still don't know, how close a thing it came to mutiny."

Hastings was talking rapidly now. He told of his tiny group of regular officers committed to restoring values through politics or whatever other ways they could. Staying up nights keeping on a telephone net, planning survival.

"You were trying to work with Noah at the same time?" Alec asked.

"The boy was far gone. I put him on a regimen. Like my father would have. I cut his hair, got him into decent clothes. He had his duties and they had to be performed. He had to speak to me, and, yes, to his mother, in courteous tones. No more street-talk jive, no more black-power salutes, no more nigger handshakes. He had to study at night, help in the kitchen. It's called growing up."

"How did Noah respond?" Alec asked.

"He resisted it. Sure he did. I resisted discipline when I was his age. But my father kept a strap behind the bathroom door. It was about three feet long, maybe six inches wide. I can remember that strap today. When my father said 'Jump,' you said 'How high?'

"I took Noah to the woodshed. He needed it. I set up a book, a punishment book. So many demerits, so many whacks. Pain is instructive. Pain is a lesson. Animals know that."

Hastings was leaning back now, looking at Alec, challenging Alec with his eyes to argue with the method, with his conclusion.

"Did you ever strike Mrs. Hastings?" Alec asked. This was the grenade question; this would cause trouble.

There was a pause, a long pause. Hastings was looking hard at Alec, like an artillery man taking a sighting. His eyes had narrowed.

"The famous night. You want to know about the famous night. I thought you were Lee's lawyer for Noah, not for her divorce settlement. What's that got to do with Noah?"

Hastings wore a strange look. For just a moment he looked wounded — a flash of pain — then it was gone.

"Someday maybe I'll tell you about that night."

Alec retreated, dodging back from the question as though he were in a courtroom and the judge had ruled him out of order.

"I want to know where your son is. I want to know ways to find him. You tell me."

Hastings started down a new path. "Did Lee tell you Noah was caught selling marijuana?"

Alec nodded.

"That was when I decided that I wasn't going to win this one. Fort Bragg, Fayetteville. He had to be away. Away from Fort Bragg and away from his mother.

"I had already made this decision when Lee abandoned me. Her leaving, the midnight escape, was really anticlimactic. She had won. Fourteen years after we married she had succeeded in destroying my military career, the love of my son, my chance in politics. You know something?"

Alec shook his head.

"I do a lot of thinking about those years. Sometimes they are very real, other times it seems like a different age, the nineteenth century maybe. But I think we had a poisoned generation, you and I, a lot of the people were poisoned. I think Lee was poisoned.

"Anyway, my father supported my instincts. He said we couldn't abandon Noah to Lee even though Noah was refusing to live with me. He hit upon the idea of a prep school. We started a search.

"We found a wonderful place. Noah liked it at once. Out in the San Bernardino Mountains, south of Los Angeles. It wasn't a military school, but it had . . ." Hastings paused; he was groping for words. "It had traditional values. Standards."

"Mrs. Hastings resisted this?" Alec asked.

"Oh God, yes. She fought everything. She wasn't through with me. She moved back here to Connecticut, wanted a big court-trial divorce, until her father explained that an adulteress can't win a divorce case. No money, honey. That brought her around."

"How did Noah fare at school?" Alec asked.

"Wonderfully. He liked it so much he used to stay for vacations. He would only come to see his mother twice a year. He wouldn't see me. But he would see her," Hastings said.

"Why?" Alec asked.

"That's another story." Hastings seemed to want to draw to a close now. He was mentally looking at his watch.

"You know what was interesting?" Hastings wasn't expecting an answer. "What was interesting was how Noah developed. By the time he left Mountainview he had a capture of business and finance that was just short of the Wharton School. Something incredible happened to him at that school. His teachers mentioned it. He and another youngster had put a little money they earned into stock and they were making money.

"He has done so well that he paid for his own college, you know. Lee and I didn't pay for that."

"Did it strike you as strange that a youngster could make enough on his own to pay for a fifty- or sixty-thousand-dollar college education?" Alec asked, keeping his eyes on his yellow pad.

"No. What struck me as strange is that he couldn't quite tell me how. He talked about the flower business. He said he worked for the world's largest carnation grower. I said if everyone in the country wore a carnation a day it wouldn't pay him the kind of money he seemed to have.

"Then he said, well, it wasn't all carnations. There had been some investments.

"I told him I'd let him handle some of my investments if I could make the kind of money he was. He said he'd think about it, like I was a goddamn customer. Then I realized it was probably all bullshit. He's selling drugs."

The interview was concluded. Hastings signaled it by standing up and buttoning his jacket. "I think that is really all I can tell you. I don't know about this Grant business. I don't know why somebody would be searching Lee's house, but as you may have surmised I think she is manipulative and obsessive. Maybe she made it look like her place was searched?"

He escorted Alec down the long hall to the factory building's security desk.

"Why all the security?" Alec asked.

"Foreign military sales. We have lots of small arms here. Ammunition. Sniper scopes. Night-vision equipment. Counterinsurgency weapons." Hastings made a sweeping gesture with his arm across the compound.

"We sell the weapons, the ammunition, repair and service support, and a training program. You have an insurgency. We have the counter. Mr. Nhim and I and some others conduct courses, all over the world, on how to win such wars."

Hastings smiled. "You know we won, don't you?"

Alec looked quizzical.

"In Vietnam. You and I won. The American government lost. The public riffraff lost. You and I won."

They shook hands.

Alec sensed Hastings was still standing behind him as he went out through the electronic doors. He wondered whether Lance Corporal Marquette felt like a winner. Maybe Hastings was right, Alec thought. If winning is being alive.

When he got to the rental car, he saw Mr. Nhim, the Hmong. He was standing near the corner of the wire fence, a little man in a strange country.

9

IT was dark when he got to Manhattan, and the running lights of the tugs going down the East River twinkled red and green under the Queensboro Bridge as he drove down the Franklin Delano Roosevelt. He went off at Thirty-seventh, south on Second Avenue, and west on Thirty-fourth to the garage.

Hastings had disquieted him. No question about it. The colonel was chilling, some missing link of human caring, something. Never once had Hastings expressed any concern for his son. No questions about why Noah was missing, only a long pathetic litany of his life with Lee. No offer of help to find Noah; nothing. Strange.

Alec had decided to drive to New York on impulse, to stay in the apartment. Hastings had raised questions. All kinds of questions.

Was the colonel right about his wife? Was she a woman obsessed with sex, unable to keep her hands from men, even her own son?

Jesus, what was he into? He felt entangled, what New Yorkers fear worst, he laughed mirthlessly to himself: "involved." He felt out of control, like he was hurtling down a hill on a bike.

His thoughts were so deep that he had not noticed anyone else in the garage. But there they were, standing in front of the Trans Am. They had parked halfway up the slope to the second-level exit so no other car could pass.

The smaller one was smiling. "Meester Grant. Hey, Meester Grant." Alec could not get to the exit, to the elevator, nor to the stairs without passing them.

"I'm not Mr. Grant," Alec called out. He still had maybe fifteen feet to go before the Trans Am. The big one covered the ground in less than two seconds.

Alec saw the foot coming and tried to turn, to crouch. It was too late. It hit him square in the stomach, knocking the breath from his body. He went to his knees.

The second kick hit him in the neck, rolling his head back. A third landed on his left ribs. He tried to fold into a fetal position.

When he came to, they had him down between two cars. The big one was kneeling behind him with his arms pinioned. The little one squatted in front, his face very close. He had eaten something thick with garlic and cumin.

"Let's pretend you're Meester Grant. You give us the disks and we say good-bye, right?"

Alec still could hardly breathe. "I don't know . . . know what you're talking about."

The little one winked at the big one behind Alec. There was a movement. Alec screamed. He felt as though his arms had been torn from their sockets.

"That wasn't the right answer. Julio will be like a buzzer. You give me the wrong answer and I push the buzzer. You give me the right answer and I give you the prize."

"What's the prize?" Alec tried to stall.

The little one was enjoying himself. "The prize is you' lady's tits. If I don't get the disks I'm going to operate. I ain't no doctor, but I'm going to take her tits off jus' as nice as you please." There was a mechanical clicking sound and a knife blade, possibly five inches long, sprang in front of Alec's eyes.

Just like gangs when he was a kid. New York's emblem ought to be a switchblade on a field of shit. Alec was letting his mind wander.

The little Hispanic brought it back.

"She won't be such a good lay without no tits, eh? Just big holes here." He touched his chest.

He stopped smiling. "Where's the disks?" Alec was silent. The buzzer sounded.

Alec screamed. They played buzzer scream for a while. Alec wasn't sure how long. He knew he was crying from the pain. Like in Riverside Park when he was a kid. The Aerobondos had all seen him cry. They had started laughing when he had cried.

The siren came from the Thirty-fifth Street side, the exit ramp. Julio let him go as soon as they heard it and the two sprinted for the

Trans Am. Alec couldn't see them anymore. He heard the squeal of tires and then the voices of other men.

"Here he is." It was Ralph, the desk clerk. "I saw you park on the monitor, and when you didn't come upstairs I called the cops." Ralph's thumb gestured back over his shoulder at two giant policemen.

They started to pull Alec up by his arms. He screamed. "Not my arms, God, not my arms."

Alec was begging Ralph. "I've got to call, got to call . . ."

"No, Mr. Anton, you're hurt bad. You need to go to the hospital."

"I've got to call first."

Ralph had to hold the phone. Lee's voice came on.

"Are you okay?" he asked.

Lee seemed perplexed. "Yes. Of course."

"Are the girls okay?" he panted.

"Yes. I just talked to Eileen. What is —"

"Do what I tell you and do it now. Get your car. Come down to my apartment, the Westminster, west side of Park at Thirty-fifth. The desk clerk will have the key. Don't let anybody in. Call the police if anyone tries."

The doctors treated him after the man with the gunshot wound and before the Puerto Rican woman with the punctured blood vessel.

"Whoever attacked you twisted your arms in such a way that he has stretched or torn the ligaments around your arm sockets." The intern looked about twelve years old. He was trying to grow a mustache to look older. "It will cause you intense pain over the next few hours."

No shit, kimosabe! Doctors always said the obvious.

"We'll want you to stay overnight, until we see the test results."

Alec looked at him like he was crazy. "I can't do that! I have to get home . . ." He started to say "to my wife," then stopped. "I have to get home."

The doctor looked disappointed, as though he'd lost a real chance. "I really don't advise . . . The kicks you received have seriously bruised your body. I don't find any internal bleeding, but there may be other complications."

Alec cut him off. "Okay, okay, doc. Where do I pay?"

He couldn't leave Lee alone. Even through the pain he knew he wanted to be with her.

The cops had left an hour earlier. He had given them the description of the two men and the Trans Am and the question about Mr. Grant, but he hadn't told them the whole story. He was getting a very funny feeling that he didn't know the whole story.

It took half an hour to check out of the hospital. They took American Express. He called the apartment; a nurse helped him dial. Lee was there. She sounded frightened and tired. Ralph had told her what happened. "I'll be there in twenty, twenty-five minutes. Don't open the door to anybody."

Getting in the cab without using his arms turned out to be a trick, like doing the limbo except he didn't feel so limber.

They drove over to Third Avenue and turned uptown. Even though it was nearly midnight, the Korean grocers were still going and the bars and the restaurants were taking in customers. The people made him feel safer.

This was dangerous shit. Thoughts were flashing through the murk of his mind like cue cards held up too fast to read. In a little more than forty-eight hours he had gotten himself into dangerous shit. This kid Noah was involved with really nasty people. That's why he disappeared! He took something they wanted and he knows they're bad and he split, leaving his mother holding the bag.

But why did Julio and his little friend Smiley think Alec was John Grant? Wouldn't they know what Grant looked like? They had ransacked Lee's house to get something. Disks. They didn't find them. When she came home with a man, they figured that had to be Grant. Now they were looking for him!

He had a wild desire to get out of it. Maybe go to the FBI or the police. But how could he persuade the Hispanics that he wasn't Mr. Grant?

Lee didn't speak as she opened the door. She just pulled him gently into the apartment with her fingertips on his shirt. He must have looked awful because it showed in her face.

"I know those are the same men who searched our house. I know it. I'm so sorry I got you into this." She was leaning against him, letting him lean against her as well. "What has Noah done? What's happening? Oh God! What's happening?"

"I don't know, lady. I really don't know."

She made him a Stoly's, pouring the vodka over the ice and holding the glass so he could sip it. He didn't know whether it went with Darvon, probably not. But he didn't care.

He walked into the alcove and tried to get the gun down from the shelf but his arms wouldn't go that high. "Please, help me!"

Karen had hated the gun. She wanted him to turn it in to the police. It was strange; he had found himself attached to it. Like part of his life.

It had come in the mail years before, from Sergeant Burns. "When you went out on the medevac, lieutenant," the note said, "I picked up your Colt. You know, it had been blown half out of the holster. I kept it for extra. It came in handy. Two-gun Pete! When I got ready to diddi mao CONUS, I wasn't surveyed for it. Thought you might like a souvenir."

"Get that box up there." He nodded toward the shelf. Lee put it on the dresser. "Unwrap it."

She unwrapped it from an oiled cloth. It was black and glistening. There were scratches on the chamber, and the butt was dented where he had used it as a hammer, but even unloaded it looked lethal.

He had taken it out in Connecticut and fired it a few times. Alone on a gun-club range. It would be hard to describe having affection for a firearm. Gun nuts had affection for firearms. He had no love for the M16s, the M60s or the M79s or the shotguns. The tools of the infantryman's trade.

But the M1911 Colt. He thought of Hastings. Lee hadn't understood his war and her face showed she didn't understand this. She just kept staring at the pistol.

His mind went back to Vietnam. Alec could see them tumbling down the hill, firing as they came, the satchel charges slung around their necks, the AKs chugging rounds. He had been sure he would die that night, sure he would never see the sun.

They were coming so fast the momentum carried them forward even after they had been shot with the rifle bullets.

He remembered the recoil of the Colt. He was sure he had missed, but the figure, no more than a boy, had stopped in midleap and had been thrown back as though struck by an unseen blocker.

The sapper had already pulled the lanyard on the satchel and it blew an instant after Alec fired. Only pink froth and fragments of flesh dripped from the bunker when the smoke cleared.

Now he tried to load the magazine, but his fingers could not hold the bullets, brass glinting with oil fell to the floor.

"What are you doing!" Her voice was almost a shriek.

"Help me."

He made her take the gun and the box of bullets into the living room. Her hands were shaking. "Don't tell me an infantry officer's wife hasn't seen a Colt .45 before. Put those in there." The pain made him nasty. He motioned to the magazine. "Push hard against the spring."

Her eyes filled with tears and her hands quivered as she loaded the magazine and then, smoothly, without seeking more instruction, rammed it home in the butt and pulled the slide forward, pushing a round in the chamber.

"Here!"

"I'm sorry. I didn't mean that." Alec tried to apologize.

"Don't apologize. You were right. John showed me how to use a pistol. They all did. It was their little thing. 'In case anything happens while I'm away.' Just aim, breathe, and squeeze. Isn't that right? Aim, breathe, and squeeze?"

Even with the vodka and the Darvon Alec's arms hurt. He wished he could sleep but the pain kept him awake.

"Did you and John have a nice little talk, soldier to soldier? Man to man?"

She sounded bitter and angry, no more questions about the attack, Smiley and Julio.

"Did he tell you the one about my having relations with a seventeen-year-old maid in Germany?" Lee asked.

Alec didn't answer.

"That was one of the worst things John ever did. The girl was pregnant. She had been made pregnant by an American soldier and her father had thrown her out. She could barely speak English, but finally she had told me about it. In the bathroom while we were washing clothes. She threw up and I took off her dress to help her clean up. I locked the door to keep Noah out."

"Suddenly John was there. He smashed in the door, screaming

accusations that we were making love. He threw her out of the house. The poor girl lost her home, her job, and her reputation in the same week."

Alec was having trouble focusing. His eyes wanted to close but her voice kept him awake.

"He must have also told you I screwed everybody on base. That's one he likes to tell. How the hell would he know? He wasn't around." Alec couldn't see her eyes in the dark, but he knew she must be looking at him.

"Do you want to know something?"

Alec wasn't expected to answer.

"All John ever knew about my love life was what I told him!

"Get the facts. Get them here!" She said it with a newsboy cry.

She was talking about some friend of Hastings's who had seduced her on a golf course. Or something. He wasn't sure. There were no tears, no remorse in her voice.

"It was awful and sordid. I hated it while I was doing it. We had to sneak around on his wife, on my children. It was almost ludicrous."

He realized she was like a defendant named in a sealed indictment, groping to answer the charges against her but unsure what they were.

What she didn't realize was he didn't care. He wanted her as he found her, the beautiful woman down the beach. He also wanted to sleep.

She kept on, as though a complete tale had to be offered. As though everything depended on her persuading him that whatever Hastings had said was not the truth.

Suddenly in the darkness, listening to her voice, unable to see her face or her eyes, he realized he had probably fallen in love with her. What a stupid thing to do. He laughed without sound. Like everything else Alec Anton does: Just go for it!

What was funnier was that he was stuck with her. Julio and Smiley forced them to become a couple. "You' lady's tits," Smiley had said in the garage. He was a common enemy and a shared danger. What bond could be stronger?

"Lee, be quiet." His voice stopped her. "You don't need to do this."

For the first time he could see her eyes in the half light. They looked confused. "Oh, I do. You see, you're my last chance."

His fingers touched her lips. "Don't talk," he whispered. He must have fallen asleep at that moment, sitting up, because he felt her help him to lie flat on the couch.

He could see her, in the half light, hike up her blouse then loosen and remove her brassiere, letting her breasts dangle free as she settled for bed.

He was twelve. It was in Riverside Park and the Aerobondos were all around. Wendell and Burton had made it because they could run faster, but he had stumbled and now they were kicking him. He could see Wendell and Burton up on the wall along Riverside Drive. They looked frightened. Then they disappeared.

His mother was bending over him. "Aleki, what has happened?" Burton is telling her about the Aerobondos, about how Alec turned to fight them so he and Wendell could get away. Burton doesn't know Alec had just stumbled, fell in his slowness and the Aerobondos were upon him. His mother has put him in a hot bath. "Oh, my poor Aleki, Aleki." She sponges his bruises. "You never think. You just do things."

When he awoke the room was empty. The sun from the Park Avenue side was streaming in. The chairs had been rearranged and everything was straightened up.

Alec tried to move. It was a mistake. He cried out.

"I didn't know you were awake." She looked anxious and drawn. "I think they're across the street."

"Who?"

"Those two men."

He got up slowly and painfully and walked to her side at the window.

"Where?"

She pointed. The Trans Am glistened as though it had been polished. It's distinctive shape was clear even from above. He couldn't see inside the car from this angle.

"Did you see anybody?"

"A little while ago a man came along with two coffee cups and got in."

"Why didn't you wake me?"

"I wasn't sure."

"Shit!"

He went back and got the Colt. He could hardly lift it. His arms were weaker than they'd been the night before.

"Take this."

She took the pistol from him and held it against her blouse.

"What do we do?"

"Call the police."

Lee dialed 911 and held the telephone so Alec could talk.

"I think two men who mugged me last night are parked across from my building."

The report took forever. Did he remember the name of the officers? Time? Was he injured?

Halfway through Alec was beside himself. "Do you think we ought to get around to the part where you send a police car?"

He heard the siren before they saw the car. Julio and Smiley did as well. The Trans Am lurched forward and then made a hard right onto Thirty-fifth before the police car heading down Park had passed Thirty-sixth.

The two officers took a second report. One was skeptical. "You aren't going to call us every time you see a Trans Am are you?"

Alec ignored him. They left.

"Why didn't you tell the police about Noah?" Lee asked.

"Christ no! Unless you want to be all over the *Daily News:* 'Trowbridge Lawyer Beaten in Girlfriend's Narcotics Case.' "

Lee glanced at him. "Am I your girlfriend now?" There was a faint smile on her face.

"I guess so," Alec answered. "Everybody has a girlfriend in the *Daily News.*"

"What do we do now?" she went on.

"Now? Now we get the hell out of here!"

"How can we avoid those men?" Lee asked.

"An old friend of mine claims you can't keep track of anyone in New York." Alec could hear Connie Callaghan: "When we were chasing Reds after the war, half the time the FBI agents lost them in the subway."

"I hope to hell he's right."

Alec quickly dressed in a business suit and put toiletries and the rest of the ammunition in a briefcase. He stuck the Colt in his belt in the center of his back, where he hoped the drape of his coat would hide it.

"Where did you leave your car?" he asked.

"In the garage. Your desk clerk let me put it there."

"Okay, we'll take it."

Alec called his office. He told Shirley he had been mugged, calmed her concerns, and said he was going to take some pills and stay in bed.

"Reschedule Felix and Jimmy for early next week, will you? Maybe Tuesday, and tell them I'll be in the apartment all weekend." He hoped it would be suitably misleading.

"What's that all about?" Lee asked.

"I don't know how much these guys have invested in this. But the way the FBI and a lot of private investigators keep track of people is a telephone tap. So we'll take them down the garden path."

The garage seemed as empty as it had the night before. He walked nervously toward the car, drawing Lee by one hand. She held the briefcase. He held the gun. No one accosted them.

They went up Park Avenue, across the park by the Metropolitan Museum of Art, and worked back and forth across several streets in the high seventies and eighties.

"Watch out the side mirror without turning around. Just look for the Trans Am or any other car that stays with us," Alec said.

Twice she thought she saw it. Another time they drove around and around until they lost a black panel truck that had stayed with them.

After twenty minutes, he found a parking lot on Eighty-first Street between Columbus and Central Park West.

"Are we alone?"

"I think so."

With Lee in tow, he walked south to the building where Karen lived. He chose it because the main entrance was on Central Park West, but it had a drugstore that opened onto Seventy-sixth.

The building was loaded with doctor's offices, and the desk clerk didn't bother a purposeful, well-dressed couple appearing to be on the way to a medical office. The large bluish bruise that covered Alec's lower jaw and neck supported the image of a medical patient.

They went up to the third floor by elevator. There were three doctor's offices on that floor alone. He led Lee down to the fire exit and stepped inside, leaving the door open a crack. He took the pistol out and held it by his leg. Five minutes went by and no one got off on the third floor.

They crossed the street and entered a building near Columbus, waited another five minutes, just inside the glass door. Only two people passed. One, an old Jewish-looking man, was walking a dog. He eyed them nervously.

"We're the best-dressed muggers he's ever seen," Alec whispered.

The second was a woman carrying a Henri Bendel bag and a toy poodle.

He hailed a cab on Columbus. "Take us to the Hertz Rental at the West Side terminal."

They rented the biggest, heaviest car they could get, a Chrysler New Yorker. If they were going to cover some miles, Alec wanted speed.

It was shortly after eleven when they headed North on Tenth Avenue. He turned east at Fiftieth, north on Broadway, and east again on 110th. He pulled briefly into Central Park, got out and fiddled with the hood, watching which cars followed him. In nearly three minutes only two cabs entered the park and one wasn't carrying a passenger.

His heart was beating so fast he thought Lee would be able to hear it when he got back behind the wheel.

"Are we okay?" She was still whispering.

"I think so." He started to laugh, a sort of uncontrolled giggle. "This is ridiculous. How would I know? I don't know any more about this stuff than the man in the moon. There are probably ten of them right behind us."

Lee was laughing too, almost hysterically. She looked out the rear window. "I don't think so."

A giant New York sanitation truck was right on their bumper.

He had driven for half an hour when Lee spoke.

"Where are we going?"

"To find Noah."

"Oh, Alec, no! I was wrong. Let's take this whole thing to the

police. We don't know who these people are, but we know they're
desperate."

"Jesus, Lee! I called a couple of cops this morning to snag two
muggers sitting across from the scene of the crime and it didn't work
so well.

"Last night I was sure that was what to do. But here are two
hoodlums asking me about disks I never heard of, my body covered
with bruises because I'm not Mr. Grant . . ."

"Disks?" Lee interrupted.

"That's right, disks. Does that ring a bell?"

She shook her head. "I suppose computer disks."

Noah studied computers, she said, in boarding school and college, but Lee could not remember his bringing home any disks.

"Did they say what the disks meant or anything?"

"No. You see, that's what I'm talking about. Lord knows I've
dealt with enough cops. I know how to make the system work, but in
this little deal there are too many things like the disks I don't get!"

"Can't we just tell them what we know, what's been happening?"
Lee asked. "That's what you've been telling me to do."

Alec looked cross. "I know that's what I've been telling you, but
now I've got second thoughts.

"Put yourself in the lawman's position. Two people come in and
say that a twenty-two-year-old man is missing. They say they found
a fake passport and a lot of money. They say he knows a big drug
smuggler and has been throwing money around for four, five years.
Hell, he even got his mother a big business deal.

"Their first question is, 'Why didn't you come to us four or five
years ago?'

"What they're really going to investigate is you and probably me.
You're the one with the fake passport and the thirty-two thousand
dollars.

"While the police are looking into us, Julio and Smiley are looking for me."

Lee still seemed doubtful. Alec pressed on.

"Only one person can straighten this out: Noah! One thing we
know is his drug business has blown up. He disappeared because he
knows some bad guys are after him. But shit; he's a kid. First offense.
No record. Just out of college.

"Maybe, just maybe, if I handled this right, I could get some kind of a deal for him with the feds."

"Do you really think you could?"

Jesus, Trowbridge is going to love this, he thought.

"I sure can't without him," he said doggedly.

"I'll make you the same offer you made me." He turned to look at her. "We give it a few days. See if we can get a line on him. If we don't, I'll take you to the U.S. attorney in New York. Okay? At least we can get an investigation started that won't lock us up by mistake."

She didn't answer, but she squeezed his hand. It hurt, but he didn't cry out.

10

THEY got to the two-family just after eight, bleary-eyed and nearly dead from driving straight through. It was cool and clear in Burlington, the air as crisp above Lake Champlain as it was heavy in New York.

As Alec and Lee walked toward the stairs to the girl's apartment, the door opened and a man appeared.

He was probably in his forties, stocky and wearing yellow slacks and a green summer blazer. His clothes looked rumpled, like he'd slept in them. Behind him, in the doorway, was a young woman wearing a bathrobe. The man's hand was inside the robe and the girl was giggling and drawing back into her apartment, pushing the man out with her hand.

Alec pulled Lee close enough to the side of the building that they couldn't be seen from the second-floor landing. He couldn't hear what the couple were saying, but he heard the man laugh several times and, finally, a door close. The man came skipping down the stairs whistling without noticing Alec and Lee.

He climbed into a white Cadillac Seville and drove off, tires squealing on the pavement.

Alec climbed the stairs and knocked on the door. A girl's voice called out "Freddy! I told you it's closed for today! You've had yours."

"This isn't Freddy."

She opened the door a crack. "Who are you?"

"I'm Noah's mother." Lee pushed in front of Alec. "Are you Anne Barnes? I spoke with you last night."

The girl looked sullenly at them without speaking.

"Can we come in?" Alec asked.

"Now?"

"Not tomorrow."

The two-room apartment was a shambles. The first room had a small stove, refrigerator, and sink combination built against one wall and an old-style wardrobe, instead of a closet, which left little space for two chairs, a lamp, and a table.

Double doors opened to a second room dominated by a double bed and another cabinet. There were no closets. A far door to the left of the bed, Alec guessed, led to a bathroom. Clothes, food, magazines, and cosmetics were strewn all over both rooms.

Her face was puffy, and she had not washed off the mascara and eye shadow from the night before so it was smeared in a macabre mask. Someone — presumably Freddy — had put a hickey on her neck, a gesture Alec thought had gone out in the fifties.

"Can we sit down?" He was looking for a spot.

"Can't we do this later? I just got up," the girl whined.

"Nope." Alec cut in before Lee could speak. "Things are moving too fast to fool around." He kept his voice hard.

He picked up a garter belt and a towel off of one chair and threw them on the bed.

She didn't look as well turned out as she had in the yearbook, but she was still a good-looking girl, tanned face and perfect teeth, the unmistakable sign of the upper middle class.

"Who's Freddy?" Alec asked.

"My boss." The girl pouted as she answered. "What do you want?"

For more than an hour, they questioned her.

Her story would have fit in a guide for eastern colleges. Two sophomores, a handsome young man from Connecticut and an attractive woman from Long Island, meet in the bursar's line during registration. Dates, dancing, skiing, studying together. No drugs, no strange trips, no problems. Gosh, she hadn't seen Noah since graduation.

A good yarn except for the wretched apartment and the unflattering reality of Freddy. Still the girl persisted.

When Lee pointed out the contradictions, the girl threatened to order them out, standing up several times and walking toward the door.

Lee was raising her voice and struggling to control her emotions at the same time. The words came out in a garble.

"Anne, cut it. My son's no saint. But you're no candidate for coed of the year. We know Noah's tied up in something very dangerous involving drugs. We can't find him and we think some men are looking for him. We've got to find him before they do. Help us!"

But help wasn't in her heart, it seemed. Her face twisted in hatred.

"Noah may need help, but he doesn't need yours and he doesn't need mine. Your precious little son is a big drug pusher. You didn't know shit about him, did you? Did you?"

Lee shook her head.

"Look, I don't know where Noah is. He said he was going to Europe," Anne screamed. "I asked if I could come. He just blew me off! He blew me away! He said he needed time to think. He's been balling me for three years without thinking one damn minute!"

The girl's anger was rising as she spoke.

"Something went wrong this summer. I don't know what or why. Noah and I were going to share an apartment in New York. We had it all picked out. He had a terrific job. He'd worked for the people before and he was going to go straight into securities, bonds or something. Then boom!" She paused for breath.

"You know, I don't have to answer shit for you. You can't make me. My mother never should have told you where I live. Get the hell out of here!"

Alec's voice was so loud it startled both women.

"Do you want to talk to us or do you want to talk to the cops?"

The girl backed up against the sink, startled by his tone.

"I told you I've been attacked by these men and we think you can help. You're a material witness, possibly a witness to a more serious crime, if Noah has been hurt. We don't have any time to screw around with you."

When the girl did not respond, Alec grasped Lee's arm.

"Let's go find some cops."

The girl started to say "Wait a minute," but only half the word "minute" got out.

"We're not talking about traffic charges," Alec interrupted. "We're talking about going to jail. A federal drug conspiracy charge with violence is maybe ten years, total, with a sure three years behind bars."

Alec had opened the apartment door.

"See how you like fighting off two-hundred-pound lesbians who want to stuff your head between their legs.

The girl looked stunned and pale. "You can't do this to me. You can't walk into my life and do this to me."

"Watch," said Alec. He turned to go.

"Please." The girl's face was filled with anguish. "Close the door."

She sat down on the end of the bed. "If I talk to you, will you go away?" she asked softly. "I want you to go away. I can't handle any more trouble. I have all the trouble I need."

She wasn't looking at them; she was studying the floor.

"What trouble?" said Lee quietly.

"My mother has cancer. I just can't have any more trouble right now. I've had a lot of trouble lately."

Alec sat down next to her. "What else?"

There was a long pause filled with the dry gulps of air people take when they are about to break down.

"I hit a woman with my car down near Kingsbury. In October. She wasn't badly hurt. I cut my face on the steering wheel and blacked out. But when I was in the emergency room the police had the hospital run a blood test." She stopped, her breath coming in pants. "And it came up" — she started to cry — "came up positive."

"Positive for what?" Alec asked.

"Positive for cocaine," the girl answered.

"It was right after my mother found out she had cancer. My father went spastic. He made me plead DUI. But the deal was I have to go to detox in Vermont."

"You're on probation?" Alec asked.

"Five years."

"Where did you get the cocaine?" Alec said softly. He was sure he knew the answer.

The girl looked at Lee. "From Noah."

"Did Noah use cocaine?" Lee asked.

The girl got up and walked over to the window. The sun had made Lake Champlain a shining blanket, so bright that it was hard to see the boats through the reflected light.

"Noah is so strange. He is the strangest person I ever knew. You know, like mysterious. He is so good he can do anything. Just anything.

"He can do cocaine or he can shine cocaine. He can get perfect marks without studying. He can ski down a slope perfectly the first time. He is everything I'm not. He's confident, he's cool. I never saw him even stumble. He can make money with a phone call. Just a phone call and some investment would make him money. Once he showed me a suitcase full of money. I guess it was a million dollars."

"Where did he get the money?" Alec asked. "Maybe the same place he got the cocaine?"

Anne Barnes hesitated; she did not seem reluctant now, only perplexed. "I think New York," she continued. "Once when we went to New York to deliver some flowers, he left me and went down somewhere near Chinatown, and when he came back he had some coke. We were having a party and he wanted some."

"What sort of a flower delivery?" Lee asked.

"Well, usually Noah picked up the flowers in Canada and put them on a train at Rouses Point or delivered them around here, but sometimes he had to take them to Boston or New York.

"The time he got the snow in Chinatown the delivery was to a wholesale florist down on the East Side. For some reason he was really mad about it. I remember that. We didn't stay overnight. We drove straight through."

Anne turned around. "That's what I mean mysterious. When I first met him, he didn't deliver flowers. He told me he'd worked in the flower business summers.

"Then one day, about two years ago, he shows up at my dorm one night with this crazy truck full of carnations. They were all pink. There must have been a million of them. He said he had to drive them to Boston."

"Was it his truck?"

"I guess so. He's had it ever since."

"Noah never had a truck," Lee interjected. "I never heard of that!"

"Well he has it now!" Anne was adamant. "When he first got it, it had Quebec plates, a sign on the dash said 'POOR Limited, Montreal.' He kidded about the name. 'One thing this van is, it ain't poor,' he would say.

"You know what else is strange?" She had turned back to the window. "I never saw Noah sell cocaine. Never. Not a gram. Hell! There were big hitters at Kingsbury College. You'd be surprised if I told you. But Noah never moved a gram. He gave it away, but you couldn't buy it." She threw her head back and shook her long hair as if punctuating this accomplishment.

Alec started on the van, point by point trying to find out where Noah got it, what he did with it, and where it was. The last Anne had seen of it was the week before graduation, parked behind a filling station on the road to Vergennes.

"Did you say you went to Canada with Noah?" Alec asked.

"A few times. He went there a lot, but he didn't ask for company most times."

The trips had seemed aimless to her, recreation more than anything. They always went in the van and always crossed at Philipsburg. Every time they crossed the border Noah had sternly demanded she be sure she didn't have a trace of cocaine. Once he had thrown a purse out the window because he recognized it as one she had spilled coke in. He washed and vacuumed the van before every trip.

Another time the van had been thoroughly searched as they had come back through the U.S. side. The customs officers had joked with Noah, whom they seemed to know, and one had asked whether Noah could supply corsages for a high-school dance in Stowe.

She guessed now there were four trips. Maybe five. They had been to Montreal. Noah had gone up in an office building twice and she had walked around shopping. Once he had picked up a package at Dorval airport, but she didn't know what was in the package or what happened to it. Once he had delivered hundreds of flowers to a big party at an English-speaking country club outside of Montreal.

They usually did not stay over, but he sometimes took her out for a fancy dinner, and often he gave her money to buy clothes.

They stayed in Montreal once. Noah said it would be a weekend to party. It was the weekend she met Philip Ochoa.

"He was so cute. He kissed my hand and we spoke Spanish the

whole time. I could hardly understand sometimes, but Noah was really fluent! Philip had a fantastic woman with him. Jamaican. I think she went to the university with him. It was one of the greatest times I ever had with Noah."

Noah and Philip were "like brothers," she said. "They had little jokes, you know, between themselves about Mountainview Academy. The crazy teachers and funny rules."

"Did you do coke that weekend?" Alec asked.

"Yes. It was a party. Philip had it all over. It was in candy dishes."

"Did you do anything besides party?"

"They talked business. I guess the cocaine business. Philip asked me if I would take a trip for him once in a while, but Noah got very upset. Philip dropped it."

"Did they talk much about the investments you mentioned?" Alec asked.

"Not much. We were having a good time. I got the impression there was one big guy in New York. One afternoon, they talked all the time to somebody on Wall Street. I think it was about buying something in Europe. Zurich maybe."

"Did you see Philip again?"

"No. I talked to him on the phone. Noah would call him and then say 'I'm talking to your friend Philip.' Once he put me on and we kidded in Spanish. Noah had this little joke about how I wanted to go to bed with Philip and he'd go to bed with Jemel."

"When did you see the million dollars?"

"It was just before that trip!" She said it in a surprised way as though now it fit. "That's when he showed me the suitcase."

"Where were you?" Alec asked.

"We were sitting in the van."

"Can you remember the denominations of the bills?"

"Sure. Hundreds. I remember, he said, 'Don't worry about anything. Mr. Franklin's going to take care of us.'"

"Had you ever seen the suitcase before?" Alec asked.

"No. It was just a suitcase, but it was all aluminum like a camera case or special equipment case. He had it in a special place in the van, like it fit."

"You mean a hiding place?" Alec asked.

"Sort of. A special slot behind his seat."

"You have any idea where Noah might be?" He shifted the subject fast, like a car swerving.

"If I knew where he was I'd go there." She was looking at Alec hard. "Noah's a lot nicer to do business with than Freddy."

The girl's eyes filled with tears.

"Do you want to know what I think?" the girl asked.

Lee nodded.

"I think maybe Noah went to California. I think he made up the Europe trip and went to California."

"Where in California?"

"Where he went to school."

"Why do you say that?"

"He and Philip used to talk about going back there someday, buying a cabin in the mountains, hiking. That kind of stuff. Noah told me that was the best part of his life. That he wished it would go on forever."

11

HE had completely botched the visit to Mountainview Academy, violated every rule of a good interrogator, of a good cross-examination. He had flown from New York to Los Angeles nonstop. A drink with lunch on the plane had given him a headache with the jet lag. He had rented a car, driven sixty miles across the desert to the mountains, and then spent another hour finding the right roads five thousand feet up through the giant pines to Idyllwild.

By the time he entered the school's ornate gates, he was worn out, tense, and his headache was worse.

"When you start a cross-examination," Connie Callaghan used to say, "however you feel will transmit to the witness even if you stand in the farthest corner of the room. If you're tired, nervous, angry, your peptic juices sour, this will signal something to your witness. Be sure what you signal is what you want."

Mountainview Academy's headmaster came across like Peter O'Toole playing Mr. Chips. He had an unctuous, smiling manner designed for fund-raising events.

He examined Alec's letters of introduction from Lee and John Hastings with great care, complained mildly that the visit was "so unexpected that he had had no time to prepare," and called the school's lawyer to drive up from Palm Desert.

Alec was sure that it was his own brusque, New York manner and intimidating demeanor that had resulted in the headmaster calling his lawyer.

He realized that everything had gone badly since he left Lee at her sister's a week ago. He was worn and tired from the tension of watching out for Smiley and Julio and worrying about Lee. He had carried his pistol with him in New York either tucked in his belt or in his briefcase, and he spent great care so as not to end up in isolated or out-of-the-way places.

Twice he had almost called Doherty to ask for help and to turn the case over to the federal government, but his commitment to Lee had kept his hand from the telephone.

At least she sounded okay. By setting up a code with her sister, he found a difficult but occasional way to talk to Lee. The girls, she said, were excited by the intrigue of being in hiding, and Veronica had met several strapping young local boys so her bikini was finally getting the attention she had hoped it would.

But it was really Freezetemp that hammered at him. Jimmy and Felix had opened the door to the biggest case he'd ever been involved in, but he couldn't think clearly, couldn't concentrate. Lee and Noah pervaded his every thought.

Vinny had called and pressed him on when their next meeting would be. Alec wondered if he knew more than he was saying, but if Vinny thought there was a big case here why was the deal so lousy?

Desperation had driven him to California. Maybe he could locate Noah, move on one front if not another.

Now Alec sat in a school waiting room, three thousand miles from his home, playing detective in a case his law partners would never want. He realized he longed for Lee and without her this whole venture quickly became idiotic. He had been more frightened by Julio and Smiley than he liked to admit. The notion they had followed him was farfetched, but he still felt nervous and jumpy.

Well into his wait, the headmaster had instructed his secretary to show Alec the school, making it clear by manner and tone that she was to show, not tell.

A tour with her was not hard to take. She was pure California, tall, blond, tanned, and lean as though she played tennis morning, noon, and night.

The campus was as beautiful in its way. It had been built as a mountain retreat for the University of Southern California in the 1920s and sold to the trustees of Mountainview to begin a school just before World War II. The school buildings were log cabin in style with the exception of two larger modern classroom structures, and each building was nestled in its own cluster of towering pine.

The school itself was halfway up the San Bernardino Mountains;

above it rose peaks of eight thousand feet. Unlike in the smog-shrouded valleys below, the view was spectacular.

"Did you know a student named Noah Hastings?" Alec asked as the secretary was pointing out the school's seventeen horse-riding stables, but he got a brisk "he was before my time" answer.

The students Alec met seemed to be cheerful and bright youngsters — part of the summer program that Lee said Noah liked so much — clearly wealthy and clearly allowed to display their wealth. The parking lot looked like a showroom for BMWs.

"How did you come to work at Mountainview?" Alec asked.

"Lots of townies do. There are only three things to do in Idyllwild. Work for the schools, work in the tourist business, or be a forester," she answered. "I didn't want to end up talking to trees."

"Then you'll know a good motel," he said.

"I don't know if they're good necessarily, but my aunt runs one of them and my cousin on Mother's side runs the other." She was grinning now.

"I see what you're trying to say about Idyllwild. Which do you recommend?" Alec asked, laughing.

"My aunt's is the Blue Bell. It's got color T.V."

When they went back into the office, Alec noticed the young woman's expression seemed to change to one of anxious anticipation.

The school's lawyer was casually dressed in a tan silk jacket, tan gabardine slacks, Gucci loafers, and a dark blue shirt with a yellow tie. On his left hand he wore two gold rings and a heavy gold chain-link bracelet. He clearly wasn't the little local guy who does wills.

"Mr. Anton, this is Jeremy Vale. Mr. Vale is a member of our board of trustees and also the school's legal counsel."

They shook hands. "I'm sorry you had to come up here, Mr. Vale. This really isn't a legal matter. My clients are worried about their son, Noah, and since I was in California on another matter, they asked me to see if he had come back here recently or been in touch with somebody at the school."

"My presence should not imply we thought this was a legal matter," Vale began coolly. "We don't. Enrolled in Mountainview at the present time are the sons and daughters of entertainers, the son of a prince of an important oil-producing nation, the daughter of the chief executive of the world's largest construction firm, and the son of a United States senator.

"As the Hastingses can tell you the academy has been given this responsibility because it has a reputation for good educational standards, physical safety, and great, great discretion."

The speech was so cold and formal Alec assumed that he was supposed to stand up, apologize, and leave. Instead, he called upon Connie Callaghan's admonition about silence. He smiled expectantly. No one spoke.

Finally Vale said "What do you want?"

Alec feigned surprise. "It was in the letters. We would like your cooperation."

"In what?"

"In finding one of your more successful graduates, who disappeared after an extraordinary college career in which he finished at the top of his class." Alec waited again.

"What would we know about that? Young Hastings graduated four years ago," Vale said.

"You might not know anything, Mr. Vale, but possibly some of his teachers or advisers may have heard from him. A college friend thinks he came here," Alec answered.

"I wouldn't think so," Vale said.

"Why don't we ask them?" Alec said innocently.

"The teachers at Mountainview sign a contract which specifically prohibits them from discussing students with parents or outsiders unless directed to do so by the school." Vale, Alec could see, was getting a tiny bit heated.

"Let's go back to the beginning, Mr. Vale. I arrived here as the representative of two parents who gave me letters of introduction indicating that I, and my firm, are helping them locate their son.

"They are confused and perplexed and reaching out for any assistance they can muster. I arrive at a school to which they sent their son from the time he was fourteen until he was eighteen, a school they felt was partner with them in his education. Instead of cooperation I've been treated to a lecture on how the school will not help. Is that really the image you're trying to draw?"

For the first time the headmaster started to speak, but Vale cut him off.

"The relationship between the Hastings family and Mountainview ended four years ago. They were provided, in those years, full written evaluations of their son, teacher counseling sessions, report cards, and his scores from the SATs and other tests. There is nothing more we are required to provide."

The stonewall could only succeed in arousing suspicion, and Alec guessed that Vale was not dumb enough to do this by accident. Vale clearly didn't want the wealthy parents of Mountainview youngsters to learn one honored graduate had disappeared and a lawyer was conducting a nationwide search for him.

Alec decided to show a tiny flash of the blade he had under the cape.

"While Noah was at Mountainview, he began to exhibit extraordinary amounts of money that his parents didn't give him. He told them he had made this money in investments with a classmate, Philip Ochoa. We suspect that this business venture has continued and may be important in his disappearance."

The headmaster seemed startled. "Investments?"

"Yes."

Vale cut in. "We aren't going on a question-and-answer session with our teachers about Noah's extracurricular activities. Young Ochoa comes from a prominent family in Colombia. We can't discuss his school activities with anyone but his family. Why don't you contact them?"

Alec was growing tired of the fencing. "I didn't say they were extracurricular activities. You did. Your response today suggests there's some difficulty here. I hope you think over how much help you can be to the family. I'll be here overnight at the Blue Bell; maybe you'll change your minds."

On his way to the rental car, he passed a beige Cadillac convertible almost the same color as Vale's clothes. It had a vanity plate that said "Vail" and a medallion that said "California State Magistrate."

Once in the Blue Bell, Alec lay on the bed staring at the ceiling. This visit had been important and he had completely screwed it up. He knew no more about Noah or Ochoa than he had before, and he had created such a hostile response that he doubted even private visits to members of the staff would help.

Dusk was coming from behind the mountains to the east when he went out to eat. He wasn't really hungry, but he was too tense to sleep. In the little town crossroads by the post office were three restaurants. One was quite fancy, with valet parking and a menu that said it had a Swiss chef and the cuisine of the Alps. Another was clearly a bakery and breakfast shop. But on the third quadrant, past the memorial to men from Idyllwild who had served in World War II, was a log chalet bar and hamburger joint that appeared to be crowded to the eaves.

Alec pushed his way to the bar. He could see they didn't have Stolichnaya, but there was a bottle of Finlandia and he ordered a double on the rocks. About half the crowd seemed to be one hiking group, young men and women with tanned legs and Austrian boots.

The rest looked like locals. Two waitresses weaved like dancers through the throng to avoid the roving hands of boisterous young men in work clothes.

It was only after he'd been there twenty minutes that Alec saw the secretary from Mountainview. She was in a group that included three men and another young woman, all laughing and talking animatedly, surrounded by empty bottles of Corona and piles of lime peels. Their eyes locked for a moment, but she made no sign of recognition and Alec turned back to the bar. The vodka made him feel better and he ordered a Corona and a bacon cheeseburger, "the Best in the West," the menu assured him.

When he looked across the room again the secretary and her friends were gone. When he looked back the cheeseburger had arrived.

"I wouldn't eat that burger. A living animal died for it. It's got fatty deposits, cholesterol, going to block your arteries before you even stand up."

Alec turned toward the voice. The man had sat down next to him so silently that Alec had not even sensed his presence. He looked very much like an Indian. He had dark brown hair, long enough to hang below his shoulders. His face was so lean the indents under the cheekbones showed clearly. He was wearing shorts and a faded blue work shirt open at the collar. He wore no socks and his feet were shod with worn, tattered running shoes.

Alec guessed he was six feet tall, and his skin had a leathery look from sun and exposure.

"What do you suggest?" he said.

"Not much in here. Stuff is all made with lard, animal fat of some kind. Get the guacamole salad and the fresh tacos. They buy them over at Hemet and they're made with limewater and corn."

Alec took a bite of the burger. It was not the Best in the West.

"I think I'll take you up on that."

He ordered the guacamole and offered the man a drink.

"My name's Anton," Alec said, thrusting out his hand. The man grasped his hand in a grip that was like iron and held it. "I know."

Alec firmly tried to withdraw his hand, but the man held it fast.

"What do you want?" Alec asked.

"Naww. You got the question wrong. The question is, what do you want?" The man's grip was becoming painful.

"You'll never know if you break my arm." Alec said through clenched teeth.

So maybe this was Smiley's West Coast associate. He looked to see if any police might have come into the restaurant, to gauge what would happen if he had to run. The grip did not relax.

"Buy me a Corona, will you?" the man said. "And let's find a table."

"Next time just ask for a beer if you want one," Alec said. His hand still hurt.

The hikers had left and the restaurant was beginning to clear out. Alec and the long-haired man took the beers and the guacamole over to a corner table.

"How'd you know my name?" Alec asked after they sat down.

"Half the people in town either know your name or know you're the lawyer that came around Mountainview asking questions. So many questions they had to get Mr. Vale up from Palm Desert. Right?"

Alec nodded.

He told the man a brief account of Noah's disappearance and the Hastings family's concern.

"I'm looking for people who might have heard from Noah recently. Some of his college friends think he came here and this might have accounted for his disappearance."

"Up here in the mountains things aren't as plush as they are down in Los Angeles, you know." The Indian-faced man was looking out across the smoky restaurant. "Life is better here. There's no smog, no gangs. But you've got to have a way to make a living, you know, pottery, or baking or something."

Alec could smell a hit. This guy is selling. He's asking the price for something. He let Indian Face dangle.

The man paused a long time before casting the lure. "Are the Hastingses offering any reward for Noah?" he finally ventured.

"Nope." Alec let him hang a little longer.

"If they sent you way out here they must have some money to spend. They must want help a lot, wouldn't you think?"

"They're pretty desperate. I know they want help," Alec answered.

Indian Face changed the course. "Vale is a big lawyer around here. He's also on the San Bernardino County police board and used to sit as magistrate. I don't think people will want to take the risk of making him mad."

"Do you know much about the school?" Alec slid past this line of talk. He wanted to see what Indian Face was selling.

"I used to work there, a long time ago. I have a master's degree in forestry. Taught the wilderness course."

"Did you know Noah?" Alec asked.

Indian Face looked straight into Alec's eyes. Alec recognized something in the eyes. He'd seen it before. In mental hospitals and in the gaze of an occasional witness who was a heavy drug user. Indian Face's pupils were tiny pinpricks, giving him the look of someone who slips in and out of the world. He was here now, gone tomorrow.

"Sure I knew him. I knew Philip, too. That's what you're here about. Noah and Philip."

Alec nodded.

"I need help." Indian Face looked sad to say so. "I can help. But I need help. Can the Hastingses help me?"

"How much help do you need?" Alec said it very softly.

"I need to go away from here. I need to go up to Ojai or San Luis Obispo. I can't stay here."

"How much help?"

"Ten thousand."

"That's ridiculous!" Alec said it before he could stop himself.

Indian Face looked truly hurt, as a child does who's been told there's no candy.

Alec tried to recover. "What does that get the Hastingses?"

"Everything. The story. The school records. The psychiatric record. The bank."

Alec got up very slowly and walked to the bar. He wasn't sure why he would want the psychiatric record or the bank. Indian Face clearly thought he knew more than Alec did. The price was crazy. How could he arrive at ten thousand dollars?

"Give me two Coronas and some more guacamole. Okay?" he told the barman.

The two men sipped their beers in silence for several minutes. Neither touched the new plate of guacamole. Indian Face nibbled a corn chip.

"I don't think the Hastingses can go ten. Maybe five."

"Don't bargain, man. Don't be the fool. Their kid's in serious shit. He was in serious shit six years ago. That's the price." Indian Face used an exasperated tone.

"How do I know what you've got is worth anything?" Alec played for time.

"You don't. Why don't you call your clients? Ask them."

"It's too late to call them in the East now," Alec said, stalling.

"Bullshit. You call them tonight. You have an answer by tomorrow. Otherwise the offer is history." Indian Face was trying to change his approach; he'd decided, Alec guessed, to abandon the whining tone.

He left without another word, crossing the restaurant with the long strides of someone accustomed to walking in the woods. He had never mentioned his name or how he'd get in touch with Alec.

Through the restaurant's windows Alec watched as he climbed, in the street light, into an ancient brown Porsche, maybe a late-fifties model. It glistened with care. He was gone.

The Blue Bell's phone connected through the switchboard. Alec decided to find a highway telephone. It took him nearly an hour down the winding roads to find a call box in a garage outside Hemet, the first desert town to the west.

It was 1 A.M. in the East. Lee's sister was groggy and startled but she got Lee to the telephone.

"Did you ever remember Noah mentioning a wilderness teacher? Maybe a guy with long hair, looked like an Indian?" Alec asked.

There was a long silence on the other end of the line. Finally: "There was a man. I never met him. He let the kids work on his car. It was the year Noah was obsessed with cars. Why?"

"I'll tell you in a minute. Let me ask you a couple of other things. Did the school ever mention it made psychiatric reports on students?"

"No, but there was a psychiatrist on retainer."

"Did Noah have a bank account out here?"

"Not to my knowledge. Not unless he opened it. We sent him cash or checks that could be cashed at the school. Have you found something?"

"I don't know."

He told her about the cool reception at the school and the strange meeting later.

"I'm not sure I could get ten thousand dollars quickly," Lee said plaintively.

"How much can you muster?"

"Maybe four or five thousand from some CDs my father left."

"Okay. Let me see what I can find out."

"Are you okay?" Lee was speaking in a low voice. "You sound down."

"I guess this thing wears. I guess I miss you," Alec said.

She spoke in such a tiny whisper he could hardly hear her. "I think you do love me, don't you?"

"I've fallen under your spell." Alec tried to sound lighthearted, but his fatigue was showing through.

"Get to bed, my sweet," Lee said in a normal voice.

12

HIS body still on Eastern time, Alec awoke at five. He decided to take a long run, heading out from the motel along the highway and turning up a fire road that curved off to the left about two miles along.

It was hard going. The altitude left him breathless long before he normally tired, and he had only been running three miles when he felt his heart pounding and his air coming in gasps.

As silently as the night before, Indian Face was beside him, running easily in long loping strides, his breathing as normal as if he were walking.

"It's the mountain air. Track teams come up here to train. Try to take shorter breaths."

Alec found he couldn't speak to answer him. They ran another mile. Alec tried the shorter breaths, tiny artificial pants, and it seemed to work. The road was now rising, and with the combination of the thin air and the steep climb Alec had slowed to half his normal pace.

He finally stopped, bent over trying to catch his breath. Indian Face led him to a log.

"You'll be okay. Put your head down between your legs."

The glade of woods was totally silent and through the trees Alec could see what he guessed was Riverside down in the desert, rows of tract houses, an occasional orange grove, bisected by a single rail track.

"Have we got a deal?" Indian Face spoke as he looked across the desert floor.

"We've got . . . what we lawyers call . . . an agreement in principal," Alec said, still talking slowly.

"You show me what we're buying . . . and I am empowered to pay up to, and I stress the up to, five thousand dollars. That's all the Hastingses have."

There was a long silence.

"Okay," Indian Face said.

Alec told him he couldn't get the money until late in the day. It had to be wired from the East, to a local bank.

"Don't wire it to Idyllwild," Indian Face warned.

"I wasn't planning to," Alec said. "But before I do anything, you have to show me jacks or better to open."

He waited, watching Indian Face's eyes.

"Okay." Indian Face made a gesture with his fingers as though turning up an imaginary two hole cards. "Big-time cocaine. Big-time."

"Do you know where Noah is?"

Indian Face stood up.

"Later."

In the same effortless gait he started up the mountain.

It was already midday in New York but with Shirley's help he got a vice president at Chase Manhattan to wire the cash to a bank in Hemet. Lee could pay him back later.

There were no messages at the Blue Bell, no sign of Indian Face. He walked around Idyllwild, circling the center of town three times in twenty-five minutes. Waiting around unobtrusively was going to be difficult.

When he got back to the Blue Bell, he had the distinct feeling he was being watched, the same feeling you had in Vietnam when you were in what seemed total wilderness and then a mortar round or sniper shot would come in.

At six he went to the hamburger joint and had a beer and some more guacamole. Maybe Indian Face had decided not to sell information or had lost his nerve. Maybe it was a put-on. Maybe Indian Face had set him up for a robbery. His mind jumped from one dark thought to another. The robbery was unlikely. Indian Face would have to presume he did not have the money with him, that he had left it at a bank.

It was nearly midnight when the knock came. Indian Face was at the motel room's door. He wore black Levis and a dark blue turtleneck shirt and he seemed nervous and jumpy. "Come on, let's go for a ride."

They took the Porsche. In the darkness of secondary mountain roads, Alec knew he could not easily retrace his steps, but he guessed they were heading up, deeper into the San Bernardino forest and away from Idyllwild. The last two miles or so were on a bumpy logging road, and Indian Face winced each time the Porsche took a bump or jar.

The cottage was a one-story, cinder-block and wood house probably built as somebody's summer retreat. It was incredibly messy. Dishes lay unwashed in the sink, clothes strewn about. The main room reeked of marijuana. Alec couldn't see any in the open, but he would have guessed there had been big bags of it open within hours.

As his eyes got accustomed to the dim light thrown from two wall lights over a dinette, he realized there were lots of women's clothes in evidence, a skirt one place, a blouse and underclothes piled near a giant old-fashioned washing machine that sat next to a kerosene heater.

In the center of the floor was a large pile of paper records, folders, a ledger, and a steel box. They had clearly been dumped out from a duffel bag nearby.

"You asshole. You bagged the place," Alec said to Indian Face as much as to himself.

Indian Face seemed flustered at his anger. "What the fuck did you think?"

"You jerk." Alec found himself filled with mounting rage, rage at himself, rage at this drugged-up idiot. "I don't need evidence. I want to find Noah."

"We gonna talk money?" Indian Face had regained his composure. He was back to basics.

"Let me tell you how this is going to go." Alec's fury had not abated. "You're going to tell me what you want to tell me. After. Repeat. After I hear it, I'm going to decide if it's worth anything. Then we're going to meet in Hemet and I'm going to pay you."

Indian Face started to speak. Alec cut him off. "If you don't like that deal I am starting back. It's a long walk."

Indian Face sat down on the floor without looking at Alec and began to rummage furiously through the papers. Alec sat on the edge of a ratty couch. He was trying to remember if he had touched the doorknob or anything in the room. He put his hands in his lap as though he had to watch them.

Finally Indian Face selected one manila folder from a group and tried to hand it to Alec. Alec kept his hands in his lap.

"Just tell me about it. Okay?"

Indian Face kept rummaging and came up with a leather-bound portfolio and set it aside on the floor by the book.

He crawled over to the refrigerator and got a beer from the bottom shelf. "You want a beer?" he asked.

"Nope."

"You ain't going to touch anything are you?" Indian Face was grinning. "What if you have to take a piss? You goin' to touch your pecker?"

"Shoot," said Alec.

"Okay." Indian Face leaned back against the refrigerator door.

"First, I don't know if Noah's been here lately, but he and Ochoa have been in and out since they graduated. That I know!" He sounded like sometimes people didn't believe him.

"Why did they come back?" Alec asked.

"I'll tell you the whole story. You'll understand."

Indian Face seemed to have his own pace.

"The first year I'm there, we're working with kids who are druggies in the main. The school didn't advertise as one of those places for curing substance abuse, but what they were doing was getting referrals from psychiatrists, so most of the kids were there because they had serious problems."

"Was Noah like that?" Alec asked.

"*Definitely.* He was like the rest. Somebody didn't love them. Mother. Father. Or both.

"I'll tell you one thing. His father had beat the living shit out of him. The nurse showed me pictures she'd taken the day he came. Pictures of his back. The headmaster had her take them to prove it hadn't happened at Mountainview."

Indian Face seemed to digress.

"You know this was a gentle place, at first. Some of the teachers blew a little marijuana, but away from the kids, in their homes. There was a little lonely rider coke around town."

"Lonely rider?"

"You know, get on a plane, go down to Bogotá, get a key and sweat out customs, and sell it to your friends.

"Then came Mr. Ochoa. He wasn't like any kid there. He didn't seem to have any emotional problems. He was cool, cheerful, spoke good English."

"How old was he?"

"Fourteen, I think." Indian Face began to ruffle through one folder. "Yeah. Fourteen going on thirty-five.

"Ochoa didn't come alone. He had a man and a woman with him. Indians from Colombia. I don't think the woman spoke a word of English. The man spoke sort of minimal stuff. They rented a small house, halfway up the road you took to the school. The man drove a Mercedes. If Ochoa went anywhere—the man, his name was Eberon—Eberon would go. I even took him out in the woods."

Alec interrupted. "Where did Ochoa live?"

"He lived in school like anybody else. He was Noah's roommate. They called us together when Ochoa came and the headmaster, Wells, said the boy had never been out of Colombia and his parents wanted two servants to be nearby, but that the Ochoa boy would be treated like anyone else."

Indian Face had gotten up now and was walking around the pile of records, his face only sometimes visible in the room's darkness.

"It didn't take me long to figure the guy Eberon was a bodyguard. When we went out on an overnight the first time, I saw a gun under his arm when he was getting ready to sleep. If you watched the cottage, you could see that the woman was awake in the daytime. She was moving about. But generally Eberon was not. Then late at night, you would see a cigarette glow on the porch. He was sitting there. I guess so he could watch the road."

Indian Face stopped and plunged into the records. "Let me show you something."

Alec drew back.

"Don't worry. You don't have to touch nothing." He spread out the records so they could read them.

"This is Noah's folder. You got psychiatric evaluations, payment records, teacher letters, the whole scheme.

"Take a look at Ochoa's."

There was a single piece of paper. It was the school application form. It gave his name in Spanish and English, an address in Bogotá and an address of what Alec guessed was a farm, Hacienda Arhuaco, and an address in a place called Medellín.

There was a physical description, a list of schools in Medellín and Bogotá, and there were three references. One was from Vale, another was from someone with an Hispanic name and an address at the Bank of Miami, and the third Alec recognized. How odd. Trumbull Oakes. Why would a Colombian boy have a New York investment banker on his application? Why list Vale for that matter? Indian Face pulled him back to the shadowy little room.

"Every semester I wrote an evaluation of Ochoa. So did everybody else. I also had a regular session where I gave him the evaluation and at the end he signed it and could write whether he thought the evaluation was correct or not. We did it for all the kids. None of them are in there."

Alec had dropped to a sitting position on the floor, and he leaned back against a chair. "So somebody has the money to smooth their son's way through school, get him a degree and on to college. This isn't the first private school that sold out."

"You're missing it, man. Philip Ochoa wasn't here to learn. He was here to do business. He already had a career in the family business."

"What'ya mean?" Alec asked.

"Cocaine. He was a transfer point for cocaine."

"How do you know?" Alec asked.

"Because Nathaniel knows all about drugs. Don't you, Nathaniel?"

The woman's voice came from behind Alec and to his right. It so frightened him that he rolled out left as though he were under fire, reaching instinctively into his belt for the .45 that was back in New York.

It startled Indian Face, who leapt up and reached into a kitchen drawer. He brought out a revolver. Alec could see it, black in the shadows, but couldn't make out the muzzle.

"You stupid bitch. I told you to stay quiet."

Alec hadn't recognized the voice, but now he could see in the entrance to a hall the blond secretary from Mountainview.

"Put that gun down!" She sat heavily down on one of the chairs.

Nathaniel slowly put the pistol back in the drawer.

She ignored Alec. "You fool. You're going to tell him the whole story and he hasn't even shown you a thin dime. That's why I couldn't stay in there."

Nathaniel turned back to Alec appealingly. "What's our deal?"

"Our deal is that when I hear your story and evaluate its usefulness to my clients, they agree to pay you." He omitted the amount.

"When?" she asked.

"The money's down in Hemet," Alec said. This seemed to satisfy her.

In the beginning, Nathaniel said, the drugs the youngsters used had mainly been marijuana and uppers and downers. They had diet pills clipped from parents, tiny bags of marijuana bought on some L.A. street corner after a weekend home.

"Sometimes a kid would get PCP and maybe the coaches or the wrangler or I would have to help wrestle them down."

Police were never called to Mountainview. That was a strict order, and the only outward evidence of drug use was the rare occasion that a kid got stopped on the highway.

"Nathaniel had a nice little business. Didn't you, Nathaniel? Didn't you?" Her tone was caustic, accusatory.

"I ran a little grass. Local stuff from Humboldt. I made a trip down south a couple of times, but I never sold it to a kid under sixteen. Never. Teachers, forestry guys up at the fire station. Grass isn't dangerous. Even a little coke won't hurt you."

Alec kept silent.

"Cocaine wasn't much around here. Never. Then, about the same time Ochoa came to the school, cocaine began being big over in L.A., down in Palm Springs, not crazy like it is now, but you heard about it."

Nathaniel was spinning his tale with fervor, a modern historian of the cocaine trade.

"Remember, nobody's telling me nothing. But there were things you noticed. After Ochoa had been here a few months a lot of the kids were doing cocaine. The nurse gets a couple of kids who are sick on cocaine. One of the house parents finds a little in a room inspection. Kids are carrying tooters. Spoons."

"What's a tooter?" Alec asked deadpan.

"Little glass tube. Let's you snort in public. You want to see one?" The blonde started to get up like she was going to show off a family treasure.

Alec shook his head.

"Did Ochoa start to sell coke here?" Alec interjected.

"Naw." Nathaniel looked as though he was talking to a small child.

"He was sent here as a transfer point."

"Why would they choose a little mountain town where everybody knew everybody to transfer drugs when they could hide in Los Angeles?" Alec was incredulous.

"That's easy." It was clear Nathaniel had worked this through. "It gave an address, an exclusive private school for things to be shipped to from all over the world. Of course people send their kids clothes, gifts. What could be more natural?"

"You don't know that, Nathaniel. Why do you say such a thing? You don't know that." The woman was remonstrating in a quarrelsome tone. He brushed at her with his hand.

"He had more packages arrive in that first year than any five kids in school.

"It's my guess" — he stressed the word "guess" — "that at first Eberon or the woman took it to L.A. or Palm Springs. But I guess they figured that was dangerous. Even though they had passports and visiting permits, they looked like a couple of wetbacks and Ochoa or Vale must have thought a border patrol would stop them for a document check."

"What about Noah?" Alec pressed him.

"That's what I'm coming to. They needed mules. They needed people to deliver it from here to their distributors.

"So young Mr. Ochoa, he opened a business. A delivery business. Nice, white, rich little boys and girls delivered millions of dollars of cocaine for him. Every two weekends or so these kids fanned out for the richest, hottest drug markets in Southern California. Newport Beach, Beverly Hills, Thousand Oaks, Palm Springs."

"Did they know what they were doing?" Alec was now mesmerized by the story.

"Most of them. Shit! Ochoa was paying in coke or cash is what I heard. He paid what the traffic demanded."

According to Nathaniel it was only a few youngsters. Ochoa had chosen carefully, forming strong, very personal relationships with the ones he trusted.

"Where did Noah fit in?" Alec asked.

"He was his money man. They were never apart. Never. Noah screened the kids and picked up the money when they got back."

"You mean young kids delivered large amounts of cocaine around Southern California?" Alec was clearly amazed.

"Not only that, but their parents helped deliver it. Ochoa didn't want a courier of his stopped on a traffic violation, so he made his kids call their parents or a family member to pick them up. A lot of them have places down in Palm Springs anyway."

Indian Face paused, considering his tale.

"You know, a few of the parents really saw it as great improvement that the kids called them, like they were coming back into the family."

"You never saw any kids carrying this, did you?" The blonde tossed her head angrily. "You've been telling me this for years, but you've never seen it."

"Goddammit, I've seen the packages. I've seen them leave. I've seen them come back." He brushed her away again with his hand.

She continued doggedly. "He's teed off because Ochoa ended his little trade. Tell him how Ochoa closed you down." Nathaniel ignored her.

"You mentioned Vale. Where did he come in?" Alec asked.

"Don't get ahead of the story." Nathaniel was the teacher now; he had his pace. The staff, he said, in a delegation, went to the headmaster. They told him about their suspicions that cocaine was sweeping the school.

"Remember, back then we don't know about Ochoa. There are tales among the kids, but we don't know."

The headmaster appears shocked by the cocaine stories. He orders more stringent drug rules and greater surveillance of the cars and private baggage.

"He had a board meeting. No teachers attended, but the nurse told me several of the psychiatrists asked her to make plans for periodic urine tests. They weren't going to say it was for drugs. They were going to say it was for something else."

The blonde was leaning against Nathaniel now, following his words animatedly. "The nurse was giving it to you, wasn't she? She was giving it to you."

Nathaniel was annoyed. "Shut up."

"Tell him about the endowment. Tell him," the blonde said.

Nathaniel made a gesture of annoyance. "I'm getting to that."

"One day, oh, maybe two or three weeks after we met on the cocaine problem, everybody — kids and teachers — gets a notice of a big assembly. School-wide, everyone attends. Classes suspended. No excuses.

"When we get there young Ochoa is on the stage. Vale is there and a tall, swarthy man who turns out to be Philip's father. The Ochoas, the headmaster announces, have endowed Mountainview. The school has received a one-million-dollar endowment. He called it the Carnation Trust. He said there'll be another million every year Philip attends."

Nathaniel dropped to the floor and began rummaging through the paper. He pushed legal documents at Alec. They were helter-skelter, but Alec could see they looked like deeds of trust.

"Ochoa comes to the podium and he says something in Spanish and Philip translates, about how great it is for a simple flower farmer to see how wonderful an American education is for his son."

Vale was appointed to the board of trustees and would act as the Ochoa family liaison with Mountainview, Nathaniel said.

"That day the cocaine crackdown ended."

According to Nathaniel, the whole world at Mountainview be-came topsy-turvy. The nurse was fired for being late. "She'd been late every day for five years."

"Late because she slept around," the blonde was half mumbling.

One teacher who had been vocal about the cocaine was arrested by San Bernardino sheriff's investigators at a shopping center in Bannock for having two ounces of cocaine in her car. "They said they had a tip from an informant. I know the woman. She was your regular little-biddy art teacher. She had probably never even had a drink. She wouldn't have known snow from talcum."

Though the teacher avoided jail as a first offender, she was fired by Mountainview after the conviction.

"Suddenly you could get cocaine everywhere." The blonde was talking now. "I was going to UC Riverside and coming home every two weeks or so. One night I stopped in the Hamburger Chalet and a man I'd never seen in town is drinking at our table. He says to come over to his room at the Blue Bell later. They're having a party.

"I never saw so much cocaine. It was around in dishes. There were some kids I knew, but mainly people I'd never seen from L.A., Palm Springs. Some marines from over at twenty-nine Palms."

"It was like somebody marketed Idyllwild. Like somebody said 'flood that market,' " Nathaniel said with a tone of amazement.

"It was cheap. I didn't know the prices then, but later I found out it was selling for about half as much here as it was in Palm Springs," the woman said.

"They undersold Nathaniel. They were selling coke lower than Humboldt weed."

"Did you know Noah very well?" Alec was looking at Nathaniel.

"I knew him better at first, before Ochoa."

"Did he do coke?"

"I don't think much. I think he did things for love. A lotta these kids felt unloved. That was why they were at Mountainview. Somebody didn't have time for them."

"Why do Philip and Noah come back?"

"This is still the hub."

"Who runs it?"

"Vale and another Colombian kid. He's been here three years. That's why Vale couldn't let you wander around. But he's got to know where Noah is. He's got to."

"You said something about bank records," Alec began.

He had more questions, but he wanted to finish with these two. He wanted to be gone. He didn't like this at all. He didn't like Nathaniel and the girl. They were trouble.

Nathaniel began rummaging through the floor pile again.

"Ginny found this one day when she had to reorganize some old files."

He started to hand a manila envelope to Alec then drew it back. "How much are you gonna pay?"

"I haven't decided what this is worth."

The woman started to speak. Alec now presumed she must be Ginny. "We have to leave. We haven't anything left. I sold my car. I owe the bank. This is my uncle's cabin. We've sold everything good in it. He doesn't even know." She seemed like she might cry at the last thought.

Nathaniel cut in. "I think we can start a nursery in Ojai. Lots of expansion there. We went up there last month. They don't have a nursery."

Alec found himself wondering whether they were talking about a child nursery or a plant nursery. God, he hoped it wasn't a child nursery.

"Let's see the bank records." Alec pointed to a place on the floor where Nathaniel could lay them out.

The papers were the March 1977 bank statement from the Bank of Hemet for the Memorial Fund of San Andres Y Providencia Hospital. The account listed itself as care of P. Ochoa at Mountainview Academy, Idyllwild, California.

In one month, the figures showed, nearly $10 million had passed through the account. There were only two kinds of transactions. Deposits and wire transfers. He stared in amazement. That was $120 million a year, more than his law firm banked, more than half the businesses he had ever dealt with. Noah Hastings was a principal of a big, big business.

13

THE teller at the Bank of Hemet was cheerful and chubby. "Two hundred, three hundred, four hundred . . ." Her plump fingers efficiently ruffled through the hunded-dollar bills. "Five thousand, right?"

"Did you ever hear of a San Andres Y Providencia Hospital around here?" Alec was smiling as he asked.

Her brow furrowed. "Ina, what was that San Andres thing we used to have?"

Ina was as thin as the teller was fat. "Was that a hospital?"

"Yeah, some kind of a charity for a hospital."

"Is the hospital around here?"

Ina shook her head; her mouth was full of doughnut. She mumbled something Alec couldn't understand.

"The San Andres people were just like you," the teller said.

Alec looked quizzical.

"They dealt in cash, cash for deposit. Takes forever to count all this cash, and if it starts backing up the other customers, they get real ornery. Course it's not busy today." She smiled. "So you don't have to worry about that."

Ina had walked over and swallowed her doughnut. "It was some kind of charity. People mailed them cash from all over."

"Do they still have an account here?" Alec gave another of his nicest smiles.

"Oh no, not for years."

He left the five thousand dollars by a tree five miles outside of Hemet. He didn't look around. He didn't tarry a minute. He turned the rental around and floored it. He wanted to be gone.

It took him more than an hour to drive to Palm Springs. He let the radio roar rock and roll. By midmorning the heat was so intense he could see it shimmering off the car hood.

He had not called Lee. He didn't want to talk to her. There wasn't much to say. His investigation had been successful. He hadn't found her son, but he'd succeeded in getting enough evidence to convict him.

"Hi, hon, your kid is a big-time cocaine smuggler and he'll probably do at least twenty years in the can. I've got all the evidence with me."

He was talking to himself. He could hardly hear over the music, but it didn't matter, because he wasn't listening to himself either.

He had spent nearly all night in the motel sorting through Indian Face's papers. He only touched the ones he took, sifting the others with a fork. Indian Face had jail written all over him. Alec didn't want to be around when the cops came.

Half of the papers were shit. Things Indian Face and Blondie had snatched in their haste, memos about school supplies, form letters to the College Board. But in the others the story had come through; like a freighter coming out of the fog on Long Island Sound, suddenly all at once you saw its shape.

He had read them like he was back in the U.S. attorney's office. He had read them like a prosecutor. It was a case. It wasn't all of it, but it was the framework.

When Noah had come to the school he had just been another fucked-up kid.

The psychiatric reports were full of a lot of gobbledygook from a consultant to the school, but they had some nasty conclusions. He had been terrorized by a father who he thought loved him, and though the psychiatrist never said it, he implied the child was in love with his mother.

Alec didn't know how the other children were rated, but even through the clinical language, it was clear the psychiatrist thought Noah was one strange kid. He had nightmares three nights out of seven and fits of depression that lasted days at a time. He was impressed by Noah's aplomb, his command of language. He called him a leader at one point and "emotionally manipulative" at another.

"Noah has been accorded adult status in sexual and emotional relationships which have left his maturation process disjointed," the psychiatrist had written. "He sees himself as an adult in relation to his mother and as a child in relation to his father."

Then along came Philip Ochoa Oberon Restreppo. When Alec had lined up Noah's files in chronological order, they showed steady improvement in every category from the time Ochoa arrived.

A year before Noah graduated a different psychiatrist, this time a woman, found "Noah has formed a friendship with Philip that has freed him from the terrible emotional strains that his family placed on him. He has in effect resigned from his family and Philip and his family have taken their place."

If Ochoa was consuming Noah, Indian Face's records showed he was devouring the school.

According to the records, in 1976 Jeremy Vale had purchased a large segment of the school's land on behalf of a corporation based in Panama and leased it back to the board of directors.

He had also been appointed a trustee, and he appeared from one document to be managing the school's investment portfolio.

It was nearly dawn when Alec found the letter, attached, probably accidentally, to the school's 1977 budget workup. It was from Vale to the headmaster.

> Dear Wells,
> I am enclosing the paperwork necessary to shift the Ochoa family interest from Valencia, S. A., of Panama to POOR Ltd. of Montreal. This action has no direct consequences for the board or the school, but allows the Ochoas to reorganize some aspects of their business activities. Please sign and return the affidavit indicating you have been advised of the change.
> See you next month.
> Regards, Jeremy

His hands had started shaking when he found it. Partly from excitement, partly from fatigue. It had been a long night. But there it was. POOR owned the flower van that had been sold to John Grant in Vermont. It was no longer hearsay and speculation.

There was a case. A prosecutor could now link a wealthy Colombian family, the one Indian Face tapped for cocaine smuggling in Southern California, to a van owned by John Grant, the name on a false passport held by a schoolmate of Philip Ochoa. This same family fed millions of U.S. dollars through a small branch bank in Hemet, California, to a hospital charity in Colombia.

He marveled at POOR. Young Ochoa's initials. No matter how smart they were people could never resist, he thought, a little arrogance. It was like a running back's dance when he crosses into the end zone.

As witnesses, Indian Face and Blondie were not so good. Their direct knowledge was limited. The girl in Vermont was a witness of medium value; she had some direct knowledge. But to a federal prosecutor Vale would look very good.

It was as Alec was driving into Palm Springs that he realized this worked both ways. If he knew how the cocaine conspiracy worked, the cocaine conspiracy now knew that it was being investigated by Alec Anton. Julio and Smiley would know he wasn't Mr. Grant but would know who he was and where he was.

It still didn't fit. Why didn't Julio and Smiley know what Noah looked like, or how old he was? Questions and more questions. Do Smiley and Julio know where Noah is? "I need answers, not questions." He said it out loud.

He found the Federal Express office and put the Mountainview papers into four overnight envelopes with a note to Shirley to put them into the firm's safe.

The county business directory at the public library listed three addresses for Jeremy Vale. There were law offices in Palm Desert, a residence in Palm Springs, and something called "Vale of Vail, Investments." The ad had crossed skis.

Three telephone calls disclosed that "today Mr. Vale is at the investment office." It was a storefront across from the Gene Autry Hotel in a shopping center that backed up to ranch hills.

Alec entered unannounced. He could see Vale in a glassed-in office in the rear. There were three men at desks in the middle of the room and a receptionist by the door.

"My name's Anton. Tell Mr. Vale I'd like to see him."

Vale spoke into a box on his desk, but the receptionist had the phone to her ear and Alec couldn't hear what he said. She looked up, a little dismayed.

"He said your business was concluded at the school."

"Tell him I want to talk about San Andres and POOR Limited of Montreal."

Vale looked up sharply.

The receptionist smiled. "He said 'By all means ask Mr. Anton in.'"

Alec crossed the room slowly, like he was walking away from a satchel charge. The marine training manual said that no matter how tense you get don't run after planting a charge. It will increase your danger of falling and being unable to reach safety before the explosion. He'd never seen a marine who didn't run after throwing the satchel.

He walked in, a smile on his face.

Vale got up, motioned him to a chair, and closed the office door behind him. The people in the outer room were glancing at the office expectantly.

Alec looked at Vale hard in the eyes but kept a smile frozen on his face.

Vale started to speak. Alec cut him off.

"Tomorrow Federal Express will deliver to my partners in New York documents that link you to Philip Ochoa in a significant international cocaine smuggling operation."

"What the fuck . . ." Vale's smoothness slipped.

Alec kept the smile frozen on his face.

"If anything happens to me or my clients, they will immediately deliver the material to the United States attorney for the Southern District of New York and the FBI."

"What in God's name are you talking about?" Vale's face was a map of restrained rage.

"Insurance, Mr. Vale. Insurance. My clients and I have been threatened and endangered by associates of your client Mr. Ochoa, and this little visit is for insurance purposes."

Alec smiled even more widely.

"I no longer represent the Ochoas. I haven't for some months."

"Do you represent Mountainview Academy?"

"You know that."

"Then you know Mountainview is effectively owned by Philip Ochoa."

"Mountainview is controlled by a Montreal charity corporation called POOR Limited." Vale was quibbling, but halfheartedly.

Alec leaned back.

"Among the information amassed by my firm is evidence that POOR Limited has been directly involved in the distribution of cocaine in Vermont."

Alec noted a tremor in Vale's left hand as it fidgeted with a corner of the blotter on his desk.

"Can I tell you something, Mr. Anton?" Vale asked.

"Sure."

"You're getting into something which will destroy your clients. You sound as if you've got a lot of things out of whack, a lot of crazy talk. It won't help find your client's son. It will only rip to shreds his chances for the future."

"Did you know I spent a long time as a federal prosecutor?" Alec asked.

"It was in Martindale and Hubble."

"Can I talk to you from a prosecutor's viewpoint for a moment?" Alec pressed.

"You're going to anyway."

"If I was prosecuting this case, I'd look across the board right now, and what would I see? Philip Ochoa and his family may be the main perpetrators, but more than likely they're abroad and outside my immediate jurisdiction. Noah Hastings is twenty-two years old. A good deal of the charges that might be leveled at him involve acts committed when he was a juvenile. He has no prior record. Frankly, there isn't a lot of jury appeal there.

"But then I find that when these youngsters were fifteen and sixteen years old their affairs appeared to be handled by a prominent Palm Springs attorney and investment counselor. Gosh, Mr. Vale."

"What do you want?" Vale suddenly looked tired and worn.

"I want to find Noah Hastings."

"When you approached the school two days ago, I made inquiries about him in what little way I could. I don't think the people I'm in touch with know where he is. They'd like to find him too."

"I want to meet the people you're in touch with. I want to meet Mr. Ochoa. Can you set it up?"

"It'll take a while to find out. Where will you be?"

"Right across the road at the Gene Autrey. He was my favorite Saturday serial."

Four hours later Alec was sitting by the pool. He had bought trunks at the gift shop and had a swim and a nap. The nap was fitful. Threatening Vale could work or not work. He awoke sweating in the room's air-conditioning.

Outside, it was late-summer, desert, California hot. Across the pool was an aging television star. Alec couldn't place her, but she had the familiarity of someone he knew. She had once had a dynamite figure, but not so anymore. This did not restrain her from showing it in a bikini fit for a Rio beach. He wondered if the bikini could stand the strains it would face if she moved.

He saw Vale's shadow before he saw Vale; it loomed above him from the rear.

"Can we go inside? This is really awful." Vale didn't look well. Alec wondered if he partook of Ochoa's product.

They sat in a shaded area of the café where guests could come with bathing suits. Alec had scanned the lobby and the dining area nearby to make sure Vale was alone. He was sure of his insurance. A rational person would never harm someone who had evidence to send them to jail, but people were not always rational.

The café was filled with the old of Palm Springs, the wrinkled rich.

"The people I've been in touch with don't have any idea where Noah is, but someone will meet with you if you want. They don't think it will be useful."

"You mean an Ochoa will meet me?" Alec asked.

"I really don't know. They said come to Montreal. Stay at the Ritz-Carlton and they'll get in touch with you. I said I'd find out if you were going to New York first."

"I don't know. Probably depend on the flights."

"I've got a lot of clients in Canada. Palm Springs is a big snowbird place. You get out of here for LAX, transfer to Delta for Toronto and Air Canada to Montreal. You can be there by late today if you want."

Vale clearly wanted Alec to leave.

"Can I tell you something, lawyer to lawyer?"

Alec nodded.

"This is one of the biggest businesses in the U.S. You may not know that. This is big business. It has customers everywhere. Congress. Wall Street. Remember that doctor, two years ago, in the White House? This is big business.

"The Colombians are a trading people. They saw this business going to others. They saw a lot of Americans getting rich retailing their product. Now they retail it. They cut out the middleman.

"These people own banks, office buildings. I heard of one organization that owns half of Coconut Grove. Literally half. They can be wonderful people or they can be very dangerous. You ought to think about that."

He wasn't going to give Alec time to think.

"It ought to be legal. They ought to be able to choose it over the bar, like a nice Chablis."

"But it isn't." Alec felt the need to inject reality.

"It will be. The people I represent are moving in that direction. They're moving. In the meantime . . ."

Vale let the thought hang for a moment.

"You're a lawyer. When you see a new industry developing you ought to think about what it can mean to you. You ought to think about opportunity."

Alec realized Vale wasn't threatening him. He was trying to reassure himself.

"Your clients are unhappy with you?" Alec asked. He used a very pleasant voice.

"I think they think you're off to a bad start. They don't see why you would be our adversary."

Alec studied Vale. Californians are really foreigners. It's more than a three-hour time difference. People who speak the same language but come from Mars. Alec longed to be back in America.

"You want my secretary to book your flights?"

"No. I'll get there," Alec said.

"Let me ask you something. Where do you, Jeremy Vale, you personally, think Noah is?"

"I haven't got any idea. I hardly knew the kid. I know one thing though. The people I'm in contact with would like to find out."

He decided to leave by a different route than the one Vale had suggested. Insurance was okay, but you never had enough.

He stayed in the room long enough to book the flights just as Vale had wanted. Getting listed on a four o'clock out of Palm Springs with a connection at LAX. He also got himself a confirmed reservation for the Ritz-Carlton in Montreal.

When he checked out he ostentatiously asked the clerk for instructions on how to get to the airport, which was less than two miles away. He carried the map she gave him out to the car, looking around as though checking street signs.

He saw the sheriff's department car maybe a quarter of a mile down the road. Coincidence? He thought of the little teacher who got bagged with coke. Maybe.

He drove to the airport fast but saw no sheriff's car behind him on the long flat streets. He never slowed at the airport turnoff, flooring the car and roaring through undeveloped desert until he hooked up to U.S. 10.

He could make out no car that seemed to stay with him. At LAX he caught American's red-eye to La Guardia. If he was going to Montreal, it was going to be on his terms.

First class was empty. He got a vodka from the stew before takeoff and put the earphones on. Mozart. He drifted to sleep.

The summer sun was coming up over Long Island Sound, through a haze left by smog and humidity.

In the arrival concourse, the newspaper boxes stood like a silent honor guard to the weary passengers. The *Daily News* had gone to giant block type: "STUDENT BODY FOUND IN TRASH BAG."

The *Post* ran a graduation picture of Noah under a head that said "Killers Left a Carnation."

Alec passed the first headline; it meant nothing to him. He saw the second headline in a box by security. Then he saw Noah's picture.

He ran to the newsstand. Even the *Times* had put it on the front page. But in the *Times* way, it was on the lower-right-hand side of the page with a picture and a two-column headline: "Body of Kingsbury Student Found." The subhead said "Police Suspect Murder in Drug Transaction." He bought all three and sat on a bench by the men's room.

The *Times* said that the decomposed body of Noah Hastings, a Kingsbury College student who graduated in May with honors, had been found June 15, off Avenue A in New York's most notorious drug market and identified only two days before when police matched a description and artist's rendering with a missing persons report.

One of Noah's professors was quoted in the *Times* comparing him to Prince Hal, the hero of Shakespeare's *Henry IV*. Like Hal, said the professor, Noah liked the idea that he could walk between several worlds.

The police said medical examination showed the boy had been strangled to death with what they believed was a metal wire and his body placed in a green trash bag and thrown off the roof of a building near Chinatown.

The murder took place, they guessed, in early June, but the body was not identified until July 24. The only thing found on the corpse, the *Post* said, was a decayed carnation. "The coroner reports he ate a hearty Chinese meal before he died," the paper confided.

The word "carnation" stopped Alec midsentence. Ochoa. They killed him and left a trademark. It was like a movie. Gangland killing and a single carnation. He felt a rush of guilt. He had been too late. But, he told himself, the boy had been dead before Alec even started. The boy had been dead all the time.

John Hastings had identified the body. He was quoted in all three papers. He talked of his son's long fight to overcome a drug habit that had begun when he was a teenager. He said that he had done all he could to help his son and had been "heartened" — that word was in each interview — when he had seen Noah at his graduation.

Hastings had clearly been liberal in granting interviews. All three papers described the senior Hastings as a Vietnam war hero and international exporting company executive.

The *Times* had a picture of him inside with the jump of the story, talking to reporters in front of his Connecticut home. His wife was not in evidence, but the little Hmong was over in a corner of the photo.

Lee had been kissed off in every story. She couldn't be reached for comment in the *Times*, but had, it was said, reported her son missing in June. In the *Daily News*, the writer said she had "mysteriously disappeared." The *Post*, with its Australian argot, said "Mum Takes Off" in a jump headline.

It wasn't really clear, but it appeared the story had started to break late the day before and television had staked out Lee's Harborview house. One unnamed neighbor said she and a New York lawyer had left with her daughters two weeks ago.

For a long time Alec sat there. The phones were right across the concourse from the bench, a whole row. But he couldn't make himself get up. It was like his body didn't want to work. He remembered the final scene from *Twelve O'clock High* when Gregory Peck couldn't pull himself up into the bomber.

He couldn't make those muscles work.

Finally he called her sister. "She's in Harborview. We're going back down now."

Morning traffic was heading into New York and outbound was wide open. He made it in an hour. Drivers at Sebring should do as well.

There was a Stamford T.V. truck in the driveway and a Norwalk police car with two cops in it. The shades of the inland windows were drawn. Lee's brother-in-law was sitting in the living room watching the *Today* show.

Alec had dealt with death. Lee's house reminded him of a dust-off pad laid out with the body bags. Nobody ever quite looked at the body bags or spoke of death; the living comforted the living.

"She's still asleep. Eileen got her to take some Valium."

The brother-in-law didn't look so good. He had been crying; his eyes were red and they started to fill with tears when he tried to speak to Alec. "He was such a cute little boy. When he was little he came to stay all the time. We don't have kids, you know, and he was like our own."

Alec sat down. The brother-in-law stuck a cup of black coffee in his hand. The heavyset man said something else, but it was so low Alec couldn't catch it. He was looking at the television set but tears were running down his face.

For the first time, Alec thought of Noah as a human being. The thought amazed him for a moment. He realized that up to now he had been talking about a subject, like a prosecutor would.

SNOW WHITE
147

Lee had been human. Her daughters had been human. But for all he had now heard about Noah, until that very moment Noah hadn't been real. In truth he had a sad little life. Strange and sad.

As soon as he walked into Lee's room, he realized something had changed between them. She was a mother whose baby had been killed. There was a sister, there was a brother-in-law, there were children, there was the father. These were the people of Noah's life, and Alec sensed almost immediately that he was on the outside. He had not known Noah. He had only known a perverted version of Noah.

It wasn't that Lee blamed him. It wasn't that. It wasn't that he had failed to help her find her son before he was murdered. It was that in the search he had opened a window through which she did not want to look. He had shown her a vision of her little boy she did not want to see. And now that Noah was dead, it all seemed so useless.

The barrier between them was so complete that as he looked at her sitting in the bed, wrapped in a robe against the chill of the air conditioner, it was as if they had never been intimate, never kissed, never made love. He was her lawyer come up from New York for instructions.

He carried them out quietly. He arranged for the body to be released to a funeral home in Norwalk and gave Alphonse De-Nunzio, the New York detective handling the case, a truncated version of what he and Lee had learned.

It included Julio and Smiley, the search of the house and car, and the possibility of Noah being involved in cocaine, but excluded what he had developed in California and Vermont.

Those were her instructions. She had been adamant. She did not want Anne Barnes and Philip Ochoa brought out. "That was his life. Leave him his life."

It made Alec nervous, but he walked it through in his mind. He was sure that he wasn't withholding evidence. People always tell themselves what they want to hear.

He was not invited to the funeral. That had rather stunned him. It was held at her family plot near an old colonial church outside of New Canaan. The story had faded on T.V. news in New York, but was still of enough interest for a Stamford station to send a truck.

The cops had kept them off the church property, but they took a long shot.

Lee, the girls, her sister and brother-in-law, and several others stood on one side of the grave, and what he guessed was Hastings's party stood on the other. Hastings was erect as though he were in uniform; a woman Alec guessed was his wife stood at his left, and an older man, who must have been Hastings's father, to his right. There was a large bower of white and pink carnations.

The Hmong, Alec noticed, was on the fringe of the crowd.

14

AUGUST in New York is awful. Everyone is gone. They flee to the Hamptons, Martha's Vineyard, the Berkshires. Those who remain are worn by the heat and bitter about their lot. Good restaurants are closed. The better shows are on understudy casts, the galleries showing the same exhibitions that they did in the spring. Central Park wilts. Real news stops and the papers rely on rape, murder, and mayhem.

Alec ran every day in Central Park, early, just after dawn, before the worst of the heat. He would come back to the apartment drenched in perspiration, his head throbbing. He breakfasted on cold watermelon he picked up at the Korean's on Madison.

After the funeral Lee had sent him a note. It thanked him for all his help and included a check for five thousand dollars. It said she and the girls were going away for a while. It did not say where. He called her, told her she needn't have sent the money, and asked when he might see her. She was distant, cool. After she got back, time unspecified, they would see each other.

The next day her house at Harborview was empty and someone had hauled her boat up on shore and beached it over two sawhorses.

Alec hadn't been in Connecticut since. He had done New York relentlessly, like a punishment. He worked until dark. Read well into the night. He listened to Vera Lynn sing "Yours" and "As Time Goes By" and stared into the darkness of Park Avenue at night.

At first he felt pain, a nagging, center-of-the-stomach ache that left him gazing aimlessly at the harbor from his office window or reading the same sentence over and over.

Sometimes he wasn't sure what had really happened. Events had been so swift it was like watching a subway train hurtle through the station, too fast to read the destination card.

He found he wanted Lee more rather than less as the days passed. He didn't feel anger and rejection as much as grief, a loss akin to death or a long parting. The onslaught of this woman had been so swift and unexpected and now the severing so sharp that he could not shake it off.

A week after Lee's check arrived, he got another for two thousand from Hastings. A note thanked him for his help and said when Hastings had given him a letter of introduction to the school he believed this was tantamount to retaining him and hoped the enclosed paid for "the research in California."

Alec had Shirley send it back with a courteous note that Mrs. Hastings had taken care of his fee.

Two days later Hastings called.

"I sent you that fee by way of saying I was sorry. I know at our first meeting I may have appeared a little unfeeling. My son and I had a rocky life. Things seemed so hopeful at his graduation that when he disappeared I felt betrayed again."

Alec let Hastings talk. There was something about Hastings that didn't ring right. Alec concluded he didn't like war lovers.

"Do you think the police will ever find who killed Noah?"

"I'm not sure, Mr. Hastings. I know it is a well-publicized case and they tend to work harder on those. I'm going to try to help them find two men who were looking for Noah, and maybe that will help."

"What was Noah involved in?"

"I think you should talk to Mrs. Hastings about that. One reason I returned your fee was that it is hard to represent clients with divergent interests. She asked that my findings remain confidential. Since you helped open the door to his school records, I feel obligated to answer you, but I need her permission first."

"He was still involved with drugs, wasn't he?"

"That would be a fair assumption," Alec answered.

Hastings did not press.

"I want the men who killed my son found. If I can help you, call me right away." He said it with vehemence. It was a father determined to get revenge.

Alec spent one afternoon with Detective DeNunzio going over

mug books and made both Smiley and Julio after four hours of gazing at Hispanic faces. Both turned out to be Puerto Ricans. Smiley was a twenty-eight-year-old native of the Bronx who had two convictions for armed robbery and a dozen arrests for everything from wife beating to receiving stolen goods. There were no narcotics arrests.

Julio, twenty-three, had done time as a juvenile and an adult for armed robbery. He had also been convicted in a loan-sharking conspiracy case where he had supplied the muscle.

DeNunzio said the armed robberies were street muggings with knives. "These guys are cheap dates. They do minor leg breaking for a whole bunch of customers.

"I'm electing them for the boy's murder." DeNunzio grunted. "If we don't find them now, we'll find them later. But who ordered it?"

That was DeNunzio's problem. Alec no longer focused on Noah. The boy's death had been closed out of Alec's mind. The mother remained, but the boy was gone. It was a defense mechanism left over from Vietnam. Don't dwell on the dead. He could remember the men who had died in his unit better now than he could then. Then, you shut them out.

Vale had called once, two days after Alec was back in the East, asking Shirley why Alec had not attended a meeting in Montreal. But by the time Alec had called him Vale knew Noah was dead. The Palm Springs lawyer sounded frightened over the telephone. "This closes the whole thing for you?" he asked hopefully. Alec didn't give him a straight answer. He didn't call again.

Felix and Jimmy were giving him fits. He was afraid their impatience was undermining his control. A story once told is easier to tell, and who knows who they might tell. He got a reprieve when Vinny went to Hyannis, warning Alec he would have to "make a decision soon after Labor Day."

Alec laughed to himself. The FBI must be tearshit. They like to take their cases to the grand jury for indictment as soon as they complete them, not after a prosecutor spends three weeks on Cape Cod.

Moira Moran, the young associate he'd assigned to work on the Freezetemp case, had been miffed when Alec disappeared looking for Noah. She had done enough work on the case to realize that if the allegations were true, it was going to be big and she didn't want her boss distracted.

A week after he got back to work Alec took her to the Algonquin for dinner to get briefed on the case. It wasn't the fanciest place in New York by any means, but it had history and charm and he thought a new young lawyer starting out in town might like it. He had been right. She was entranced. The stories of the roundtable that his mother used to tell, of Ross and Dorothy Parker and the actors who stayed in the hotel's tiny old-fashioned rooms clearly mesmerized her.

She turned out to be quite fascinating. She had taken a minor in literature, and when he kept the conversation off the law she was filled with thoughts of writing and art, enthralled that his mother had written poetry, and shyly revealed she had written some herself.

"I guess that's part of why I chose Trowbridge. I wanted to be in New York."

They had drinks in the threadbare comfort of the lobby and then went into the dining room for a quite good Dover sole and salad. Dessert and coffee were shared back in the lobby.

She had made two important discoveries. Alec had to keep her from reaching into her briefcase to spread papers on the table, urging her just to talk them through.

One had been that sometime shortly after leaving the Nixon administration Trum Oakes had been nearly bankrupt. How nearly was unclear; why was easier to reconstruct. He had spent a small fortune to build a political and public persona, but elective office had eluded him and then association with the Nixon administration had denied him the influence and access on Wall Street that often followed government service.

"Fortunes improved," Moira said sipping her coffee, "when Dumont joined the firm."

Dumont had been a foreign banking and investment specialist for Chase Manhattan and later had his own small investment house. He had been brought into the firm to "open foreign investment opportunities," according to a brochure prepared by the Oakes firm when he became a partner.

"What is strange is that is the last time, as far as I can tell, they ever promoted or advertised his services."

Two other things had caught her eye. The main office of Oakes, Ames, where Felix and Jimmy had had their meeting, was not where Dumont operated. She had found the foreign investment offices in a nondescript building on East Forty-first. "Maybe because it was near the U.N.?" she wondered out loud.

Dumont's untimely death was no less perplexing. Indeed one of Trowbridge's insurance clients had gotten Moira a copy of the claim file. The company had paid Dumont's wife $250,000 and gotten a release. The file showed other insurance in force with accidental death clauses totaling nearly $5 million. The widow, Alec guessed, was $5 million less likely to be bitter and talkative.

The accident had happened at 11 P.M. on a dry road Dumont had traveled regularly that ran from the expressway to his home. It was a clear night and there was no mechanical failure. The police speculated he had dozed off and run head-on into the abutment. His blood alcohol level indicated he was not drunk, but he had ingested alcohol within two hours of his death.

Moira had found no disgruntled employees. There were no divorce actions, no civil suits where significant discovery had come into court records, and no tax cases.

"I'm not sure this is very helpful," she said rather timidly as they finished their second espresso. He found that time with her had driven Lee from his mind, not altogether, but for the moment. Alec found her wide-eyed direct gaze disconcerting. He realized it was time to end the dinner.

"On the contrary. Dumont doesn't ring right. You don't come into one of these small firms as a partner out of the blue. He brought them something very valuable. It may be worth finding out what."

He put her in a cab and walked home. Away from the carnival of Times Square, the streets were deserted. The night air had driven the temperature down five degrees. It wasn't pleasant, but it was bearable.

He couldn't make a deal for Felix and Jimmy on what he had now. Vinny had his case; Alec couldn't take on such a formidable target as Trumbull Oakes without more ammunition.

There had to be something to put Oakes or his firm in it solidly. There were three options. Either Felix and Jimmy had evidence and didn't know what it was; or they didn't have any; or, as he guessed, they were still holding out. He had three weeks to find out.

The next morning he ran the East River instead of Central Park, stopping at the Oakes office on Forty-first as he headed for the river. There was no trend among the tenants, law firms, travel agencies, real estate firms.

There was a travel agency on the floor above. He would come back.

Three hours later, now in a business suit, Alec got off on four and headed toward the Oakes office. It had a door that worked on a buzzer and he got through with a vague request for "Mr. Ballesca."

There was a small foyer with two chairs, a coffee table with ancient magazines, and the receptionist, who looked out through a window built into the far wall. She didn't know Ballesca, but it took her so long to check for the name that Alec knew a lot of people came and went in the office.

Behind her through the window Alec could see a roomful of young men and women sitting before computer consoles. There was a wall display of clocks on a series of international time zones and an electronic Wall Street ticker display. At another point was an ever-changing light board, which seemed to flick on and off around the room.

"We don't have a Mr. Ballesca."

"Isn't this Adventure Travel?"

The woman looked annoyed. "They're upstairs."

At the travel agency, Alec sat across from a doe-eyed brunette who had a plaque on her desk that said "Adventure Consultant."

"Where would you like to go?" She was looking intently into Alec's eyes.

"Copenhagen."

"Oh, that's very nice this time of year."

She started to reach for a set of pamphlets from a rack behind her.

"Believe me I'd love to, but I can't."

The brunette seemed perplexed.

"What do you know about the Oakes firm on the next floor?" Alec pointed down.

The brunette never asked him who he was or why he wanted to

know. She seemed to enjoy the intrigue. There weren't any customers anyway.

They had been in the building when she came to work there three
years before. She had never talked to any of the women, but she had
once talked quite a bit to one of the men. "He traveled all the time.
Investments abroad." They had only last year had a complete reno-
vation to install extensive computers. She remembered because they
had to put in a special air conditioner to keep the machinery cool. "It
keeps us cool too."

"You ever book any of their travel?" Alec asked.

"Only once. They're self-ticketing. I think they do it all."

She said once their ticketing machine had been broken and she
had written two tickets on air-travel cards for Zurich.

"Are you sure you can't get away for a trip to Copenhagen?"

"Would you come?" Alec smiled his most ingratiating smile.

Doe Eyes blushed.

When he got to the office, a temp filling in for Shirley said
anxiously "There's a Mr. Doherty in your office. I asked him to wait
in the reception area, but he was very upset. He said he was a federal
agent. I didn't know what to do."

Alec calmed her down. He got a cold chill. He had forgotten
Eddie.

"You son of a bitch," Eddie was screaming before Alec got into
the room. "You leave me checking a name that turns up dead. What
the fuck do you think this is? I'll have every internal inspector from
here to Biloxi on my ass."

It took Alec nearly half an hour of apologies to get Eddie to even
sit down.

"Counselor. This is an official visit. You better tell me the truth."

Alec left out his personal relationship with Lee and the information in his firm's safe. He skated around the details that would
indicate he had evidence to link up John Grant with cocaine and
Ochoa, but he gave Eddie the rest.

"You tell the cops all this?"

"Nope. A lot of this is hearsay. My firm developed this for Mrs.
Hastings and had Noah lived she was going to urge him to report
what he knew to the federal government. But he's dead and we have
no obligation to forward hearsay."

"You want to help us get into the case?" Eddie was still tense.

"No way. Let's be practical. Unless things have changed since I left, you've got more cases than you can handle now. Put this thing in perspective. A woman finds her son is missing and when the police aren't very helpful hires a law firm to assist in locating him. During the course of this inquiry several people say her son was involved with cocaine smuggling.

"We told the cops everything that could assist in finding his killers. They know he went to school with an Ochoa, but a lot of unsubstantiated stuff about school friends trading coke doesn't get anywhere but a slander suit."

The more often Alec made this case, the weaker it got. But Eddie seemed to buy it. He had sunk in his chair.

"By the way, did the names come up in anything?" Alec asked.

"Some. Either a real John Grant or your John Grant was a U.S. representative for a charity lottery called San Andres Y Providencia."

"A what?"

"A charity lottery. Like the Irish Sweepstakes. This one got our attention a year ago because the hospital that receives the proceeds for the lottery is on an island off Colombia." Eddie was laconic.

"How did it work?" Alec was tense now.

"Americans, Spanish Catholics, I guess, bet money on a lottery. It's drawn quarterly according to their registration. They buy lottery tickets and the proceeds go to the hospital. There's no tax deduction as a contribution because it's a cash lottery. It got into our files because they've reported cash transfers out of the country," Eddie said.

"Why would they transfer cash?" Alec tried to act nonchalant.

"You want my opinion?" Eddie asked.

"Yeah!"

"The good priests of the Providencia can buy more using greenbacks on the black market in their country than they can using a transfer through the national bank."

"Does the U.S. let them do that?" Alec asked.

"Sure. We don't care what you do with our money so long as you report its movement and pay any U.S. taxes on it."

He stopped and thought for a moment. "Oh yeah! You've got to tell the IRS if an American wins."

"What about the Ochoas?" Alec asked.

"They're trouble, like I told you in the call, but we don't get any help on them. They're the second-biggest shippers of flowers from Colombia." Eddie paused. "They've been selling flowers in the U.S. since the 1950s. We search the shit out of their loads for coke. Intelligence has always thought they are key to coke in the Northeast, but Colombian authorities say they can't make a case."

"Why do the Ochoas get a pass?"

"They're big in Colombia, rich, well known. Several have been in big government jobs."

"Oh."

Eddie had calmed down. They were back to being allies.

"Did you ever hear of a guy named Trumbull Oakes?" Alec looked out over the harbor.

"Sure. He was deputy secretary of the Treasury. Every treasury agent in the country thought he was there to dismantle treasury law enforcement."

"How so?" Alec sat forward.

"At the beginning of the Nixon administration law enforcement could do no wrong and budget requests were rolling along. I was in the Washington field then. They even moved customs headquarters up to a really nice office on Constitution Avenue.

"Oakes was the guy who stole Christmas. He was supposedly the one who trimmed law enforcement money for customs, ATF, and the IRS. I don't know how much of this is true, but it was the rumor. The story went that he had a mandate to get treasury law out of the business community. Particularly the IRS."

Eddie waited patiently to be told why the interest in Oakes, but Alec didn't volunteer it.

"Why?" Eddie finally asked.

"I'm not sure. His name has come up in a case and I'm just trying to figure out how all the pieces fit together.

After Eddie lumbered out, Alec spread Moira's findings out on a table, rearranging the pieces like a puzzle, moving the *Forbes* magazine cover here, the Dumont clips there. He was looking for a door, a door into Oakes, Ames and Dumont.

For two hours he walked around the office, pacing one way and then another, but the answer wasn't there and for most of the pacing he knew it. It wasn't until he was on the Long Island Expressway in the rental car that he admitted how dangerous it was going to be.

If the widow wasn't cooperative she could give somebody a nice shot at him through the bar association ethics committee.

At the Suffolk police headquarters he got the accident report on the grounds that his firm was doing a quiet audit of whether the insurance claim was processed properly.

The accident report showed the same information as the insurance workup. The car was first discovered by a passing motorist, no name given, who called the report from a highway phone. Alec waited around almost three hours and was allowed to talk to the officer who handled the accident when he came on duty.

He was a young cop having great difficulty sorting out Dumont's death from the dozens of other fatals and near fatals he had handled since.

"Was there anything that you can remember that seemed out of the ordinary?" Alec pressed him.

"If I'm thinking of the right one, I remember being surprised that there was no one at the scene when I got there. When we get a nine-one-one call from out there it's usually a local person and they stay around or try to render assistance to the motorist. You couldn't tell this guy was dead. The car was bad and he was pinned, but we weren't sure he was dead until the fire department pried him out."

"What does that mean?" Alec asked.

"That means somebody is pretty cold-blooded. They drive by a wreck and don't try to help the guy and call us from a highway box."

Dumont's house was one of the third generation in the Hamptons. It was built as land values forced the townships to reduce lot size and setback requirements. The Dumonts, Alec thought as he drove up, were what his mother would have called, in a particular tone she used for the distasteful, the "nouveaux riches."

The house was one of those places you find pictured in the back of the Sunday *Times* magazine where the table on the deck is set with steaming lobsters, butter, cheeses, French bread, and glasses of white wine surrounded by people so lean they couldn't possibly eat like that.

It was a very pretentious effort to be unpretentious.

He pressed a button by the door that rang oriental temple bells.

"Can you just roll that in the kitchen?" a woman's voice called out.

"Nope."

"Why?" The voice was a trifle annoyed.

"I don't have anything to roll," Alec answered.

"You didn't bring it?" Now there was real anger in the voice and it was heading fast toward the door.

He was trying to place the accent when the body appeared. He forgot the accent immediately. She was maybe forty-five, but beautifully preserved like Jane Fonda. Lean. Classic features. A bikini that left no doubt that every inch was trim. Her skin was tanned dark, like the ladies at Larnaca.

"I beg your pardon." Alec wore his most pleasing courtroom smile. "I realize you were expecting someone else."

The woman drew a wispy, lacelike beach coat around her. It didn't cover a thing.

"Who are you?" she asked.

He suspected the accent was French, definitely a Romance language, possibly Italian or Portuguese.

"I'm a lawyer and I'm looking for Mrs. Vernon Dumont."

Alec proffered his card, but she stayed behind the screen door.

"What do you want?" She had not admitted she was Mrs. Dumont, but Alec now surmised it.

"I represent two businessmen who I think knew Mr. Dumont before his death. They are in some difficulty and I'm trying to gather information that might help them. I know this is abrupt, unexpected, but it is also urgent and I felt a personal visit might be best."

"I cannot talk about Vernon." She said it as though it was physically not possible, as though her voice wouldn't.

"I know this is difficult, and I know possibly painful, but if you'll let me describe the situation I think you'll see how vital it is my clients get help."

Karen had once told him, he remembered now, that he had first "gotten into her pants," as she put it, "because to women you're really not a threatening man. You're threatening to men. But to women you're more like" — and she had groped for the word — "more like a teddy bear." He had clearly been hurt by this description and she had hurried to try to repair the damage. "Think now. Don't most little girls have a teddy bear on their beds?"

It must still work. The woman nodded quickly toward the living room.

"Sit down. I'll be right down."

The living room had the same pretentious quality of the rest of the house, as though all the furniture were new and had been placed there temporarily by an interior decorator. He sat on a small sofa in what the decorator must have called the "conversation pit"; it encircled a modern center-room fireplace.

When she came down she had put on a wraparound skirt and a blue work shirt. Her feet were bare, her face as stern and as inhospitable as it had been at the door.

She accepted his business card. She did not speak.

He took this as a cue. He described Felix and Jimmy in terms so flattering their mothers wouldn't have recognized them. Two businessmen inexplicably drawn into a maelstrom of federal persecution that might, just might, have really been caused by misplaced reliance on Oakes, Ames and Dumont.

He had to shoot in the dark because she didn't speak. It became so painful after several minutes he felt an overwhelming urge to stop his soliloquy and ask "How am I doin'?"

He resisted it. Instead he groped for Dumont's role or her knowledge of Dumont's role. Was it possible that Oakes, Ames and Dumont were involved in nefarious international financial activities? Could it be her husband had known of these?

She spoke so abruptly it startled him. "You are chattering nonsense. I know the fellows of whom you speak, Felix and the other. No one pulled the wool over their eyes. You are really silly, you know."

Alec felt like he stepped on a land mine. This was going to be the bar ethics committee, for sure. He drew himself up as though he were about to leave. Before he could speak, she interrupted him.

"I do not want to be drawn into this. It is over and done with," she said with finality.

"I can promise you, absolutely promise you, that you will not be drawn in. But I need help."

There was silence.

"What could happen to Oakes?"

"If what?"

"If it were true what you said?"

"He would be prosecuted for any crimes that might have been committed."

"Trumbull Oakes prosecuted." She said the words slowly, as though savoring it. For the first time her face had a pleasant expression. It vanished with a flash.

"My daughter is having a party here this evening. I must ask you to go. We have a lot to do." She was holding his business card in both hands in her lap, running a thumb over the raised engraving. It was as though through this braille she would find something she was looking for.

"I may call you."

By the time Alec could see the spires of New York poking over Queens he had convinced himself she would never call. He should have pressed her there.

He turned in the car at Hertz, the agency where he and Lee had gotten the car to go to Vermont. He felt the pain again. It took three vodkas to get to sleep.

The next day the Dumont woman's lawyer called.

The firm was one of those Park Avenue tax shops that help the rich stay that way. The lobby of their building was a giant multistory atrium with enough jungle in it to hide an NVA regiment.

Mrs. Dumont was beautifully attired, her arms draped with jewelry, her clothes well cut, foreign, as though fresh from the Continent. Vernon Dumont had paid off in the end.

"I am unalterably opposed to what Mrs. Dumont is about to do. I have told her that it conceivably could disturb her settlement with her husband's firm and have other long-term consequences," her lawyer began.

Alec's heart gave a leap. She was going to help him.

The lawyer, a small man impeccably tailored, kept shooting his cuffs as he talked, examining the arms of his jacket for nonexistent pieces of lint. The little speech was to limit his liability. Alec suspected that the conversation was being recorded or the phone on the desk broadcast it to a secretary. The lawyer was making a record.

Finally Mrs. Dumont interrupted him. "Can we get Mr. Anton's assurances, Harvey?"

The ground rules would be that what Mrs. Dumont said was only hearsay, things that she had learned from her late husband, and she had no direct knowledge. It was for Alec's use in preparing the case and she would resist a subpoena or any other effort to draw her into the case.

Alec agreed. That was easy. Whether the U.S. attorney and the FBI wouldn't want to talk to her was another matter. That was why her lawyer had so painstakingly sought to cover his ass.

"What Marie is talking about is a hypothetical case."

There was silence. Clearly Alec was supposed to ask questions.

"How did your husband become associated with Trumbull Oakes?"

"He hid some money for him."

"Hid money?" Alec wasn't sure what she meant.

"Certainly. Hid money. That's what Vernon did."

"How do you mean 'hid money'?"

The woman looked at her lawyer as though for translation. He did not speak.

She tried again. "He helped Americans hide their money overseas."

"How did he do that?"

"He arranged investments and accounts that tax collectors couldn't find."

"He did this for Oakes?"

"And a lot of others."

"Did he do this before he met Oakes?" Alec was confused.

"Oh yes. That was his business for many years."

"How did it work?"

"There were many ways. Vernon was very smart about money. He had many ways."

Harvey the lawyer was getting impatient. He interposed.

"Speaking hypothetically . . . ." He paused. "From what Mrs. Dumont has told me, her husband assisted his clients in different ways. Sometimes it involved getting European paperwork for a loss or an expense which allowed his clients to make deductions from their U.S. taxes. In turn the money they said they had lost abroad was in fact invested for them.

"In other instances he accepted money from American clients and others and made investments here in the United States on their behalf. He was the nominee or his firm was."

"Vernon arranged numbered accounts in Zurich, Geneva, St. Martin. He set up businesses. He made transfers," Mrs. Dumont continued in a matter-of-fact tone.

Harvey spoke up again. "He is credited with creating the Dutch Sandwich." He spoke of Dumont as though he were Thomas Alva Edison.

"The what?"

"The Dutch Sandwich. He devised a process in which Americans with large amounts of cash profits could put the money in a Rotterdam branch of a French or Swiss bank. Vernon would then set up a Rotterdam corporation for the American that was owned by a company in Netherlands Antilles. The American's name would not appear."

"How did the American get the money?"

"The Dutch company would loan it to him."

"It would loan him his own money?"

"Yes. The American businessman could also deduct the interest from current income." Harvey smiled in admiration.

"What money did he hide for Oakes?" Alec asked.

"I am not sure. It was many years ago. We were living in Zurich. He had just left Chase."

"Can you remember anything about it?" Alec asked.

"It had something to do with an election. Vernon met Trum while he was still with Chase. We had a dinner party for Trum and Helen. We still had the house on the lake so I guess it was in 1969 or 1970. I remember Vernon told me this was a very important American." She said the last bitterly.

"How did his business work then?" Alec asked.

Harvey jumped in. "Mr. Dumont apparently had recognized that a lot of his customers at Chase wanted what you might call 'additional services' to what Chase might provide.

"He decided that if some people came all the way to Switzerland looking for these services there might be a way to offer this sort of opportunity in the States to people who might not know about offshore banking. That was his idea. He was the first, I think, to really sell offshore banking."

Vernon was turning out to be quite a guy. He had decided to sell an illegal tax evasion service in the U.S. Alec was impressed.

"How did he manage to market an illegal service?"

Harvey started to cut in, to argue that it wasn't clearly illegal, when Mrs. Dumont cut him off.

"Through referrals," the comely widow answered. "He found small investment counselors and paid them a fee to refer customers that might want his services."

"How did he come to join Oakes's firm?"

Mrs. Dumont flashed an expression of distaste.

"Trum had been referring clients to Vernon. A few. Once in a while. Vernon told me that Trum realized Vernon was making more from his services than Trum was making from the clients.

"Then, I guess this was in '76, we came here on a trip. We all went to dinner. It was a very luxurious place in the East seventies. I will never forget it because it was such an awful evening. Trum insisted I order entirely in French. It was a school test, he said, to see if he and Helen could figure out what they would get before it came. It was not so nice a test. Helen was the only one who did not understand, and he derided her all night as the courses came.

"After dinner, he and Vernon were talking about Vernon's 'investments.' That's what Trum always called them, 'overseas investments.' He said to Vernon 'I want to be the first top-of-the-line banking house to offer all its clients "overseas" investments.' Vernon was incredulous. I remember he said 'How can this be done? The risks are too great.'

"Oakes became very excited. He was pounding the table. He said 'Taxes are killing investment in America.' Until the taxes are changed, he claimed, this special service would be sought after."

"So Vernon decided to join him?" Alec asked.

"The next year, I think it was, we moved here."

"How did Oakes carry it out. Do you have any idea?"

"Vernon told me that Oakes made a study of businesses which

engender large amounts of cash or income that is not recorded thoroughly with tax agencies. Firms with high retail sales, gambling institutions, firms with large foreign operations that may take in payments abroad. He went to them under the guise of setting up new stock or bond offerings at very low rates. Once he was in and had decided they were greedy enough he would sell his 'overseas investments.' "

Mrs. Dumont had stood up, putting her hands behind her as though she was the visiting professor of finance.

"It was quite fine at first. Vernon was very happy. He was glad to be back in his home, in the U.S."

"So when he had the accident . . . Things were not going well?"

Alec followed her pacing with his eyes. For the first time he saw tiny flicks of emotion. They were on the edge of her face, the tiny muscles that hold the human mask on the skull.

"Some things changed. Two or three years ago."

"Do you know what they were?" Alec asked.

"I know only what Vernon told me."

"Which was?"

"When he started, Vernon had some say in the clients. In Europe he had always been careful. He had followed our system in Switzerland." So it was a French-speaking Swiss accent, Alec smiled at his discovery.

She went on. "He never did business with the criminal element. He had always dealt with businessmen who were avoiding tax laws. He also had clients in small countries where instability and currency laws made them invest abroad."

"Why did he do this?"

"Vernon was very practical. Police agencies are relentless about criminals. Tax agencies are not."

"What happened?"

"Trum took clients Vernon didn't like."

"Who were they?"

"I don't know. I am not sure Vernon knew. Oakes handled them himself. But Vernon said they were out-and-out hoodlums.

"Do you know they were the biggest money launderers in New York?"

Alec shook his head.

"They were so big everyone used them." She paused.

"After Vernon found out about these private accounts, he and Oakes seemed always at odds. Vernon said Oakes became very paranoid. He was sure people were plotting against him. If they disagreed on something, Vernon said, Trum would be convinced it was because he was trying to push him out of the firm."

"Was he?"

"No. He couldn't. Oakes controlled the clients. Vernon did not bring in the clients. Like your Felix, they came from Oakes."

"When my clients learned they had come under a government investigation, they said that the people they had been dealing with at Oakes, Ames threatened them."

She seemed surprised.

"Threatened them?"

"Felix said they were shown clippings of businessmen who had accidents. He took it to be a warning to be silent."

She and the lawyer exchanged sharp glances. She sat down nearer Harvey. He put his hand on her arm. For the first time Alec got the idea he was not only her lawyer. In New York everybody's attorney must be getting special fees this summer. He thought of Lee. He longed for her.

His thoughts had left the room, and when Harvey started to speak he had missed part of it.

Harvey said that Dumont had told Oakes six weeks before his death that he would like to leave the firm and return to Europe. He was willing to sign a noncompetition agreement with Oakes, Ames. He was hoping to live on his earnings in Switzerland.

"What happened?"

Mrs. Dumont answered.

"They had a terrible fight. Trum said Vernon was betraying him and that the firm would go under. Vernon told me this was crazy. They were making more money than they ever had. Millions."

"Was your husband still with the firm when he had the accident?"

"It was not an accident." For the first time she raised her voice and her accent had taken over. Her words at first were almost unintelligible.

Harvey was now gripping her arm with some strength.

"Mrs. Dumont does not know that."

When he left the office, a sudden late-August shower had come, sweeping rain in sheets down Park and Madison. He ducked into an ice-cream shop at Fifty-fourth and began furiously writing notes. He had been uneasy about taking notes in the law office for fear Harvey would shut the deal down.

Felix and Jimmy's story seemed far less outlandish, even though Marie Dumont was not going to be much help. She and Harvey had dropped the bomb at the end. She was moving to Switzerland. "I want to be in my homeland," she said as Alec left.

Where the U.S. subpoenas don't work.

15

SLOWLY, with the young Moira Moran's help, Alec made progress. It was painstaking. They questioned and requestioned Felix and Jimmy, going over every single meeting they had had with either the Oakes firm or the mysterious money managers who had turned up later.

Moira had spent one weekend, in designer jeans and Boston pub T-shirts, her black hair drawn back in a ponytail, taking every letter, cable, receipt, or report that Freezetemp had received from its money advisers and putting them in chronological order.

The next weekend she did the same for every communication Freezetemp had received from Oakes, Ames and Dumont about its public stock offering.

It made a persuasive circumstantial picture. The money coming in from the stock sales and Interglobal was moving out into the secret accounts in sequence as though the money managers knew, even before Freezetemp's bookkeepers, what the cash flow would be.

It was on the second Sunday that Moira made the breakthrough. Alec had been in his apartment reading briefs when he got the call.

"Can you come down here? I've got something crazy I want to show you." Her voice was so excited he quelled his annoyance and grabbed a cab downtown.

The Battery was deserted. The harbor lay as Walt Whitman must have seen it, only the ferries and one steamer plied the waves, harried and chivied by sailboats.

"So what'ya got, kid?" Moira had been bending over the conference table and he startled her.

"God, you scared me."

"Look at this."

She handed him a dozen or more receipts and deposit cables. All of them, she said, were for fake transactions, transactions designed to siphon off funds from Freezetemp's stockholders. He looked perplexed.

"The writing. See the writing?"

"Yeah. So?"

"Valery Vennuzio's writing! She apparently would jot down the telephone number she had called when she discussed a bookkeeping entry."

"Okay. Then what?" Alec still looked perplexed.

"Look at the number."

In precise Catholic schoolgirl script, Felix's bookkeeper-mistress had written '555-6717.'

"That's a centrex subnumber for the Oakes foreign departments. The main number at offices near the U.N., where you went that day, is 555-6700, but if sixteen lines were engaged you'd get 555-6717." Her voice was triumphant. "She didn't jot that number on any routine transactions that I can find. She jotted that number solely on the foreign diversions."

He grabbed her and kissed her. She smelled like Ivory soap. Her lips were moist. She blushed nearly purple.

"You got it. God, it was so simple. I can't believe it. It was so simple." He was dancing around.

Suddenly he stopped. "How do we know that Valery Vennuzio wasn't using these for scratch paper and not talking on the phone about that transaction?"

"We don't. But we can surmise that she was discussing the transaction on the paper, because when you go through her work product you find she does that with everything that requires a call.

"Bank deposits have the bank number on them, American Express bills have American Express customer-service numbers. If the telephone number is printed on the bill she circles it in pencil. If it isn't on the document she jots it on in pencil. She's very consistent."

"Wouldn't she then know she was talking to Oakes, Ames and Dumont?" Alec asked doubtfully.

"Nope. I don't think so. I haven't tried it on a working day. But I tried it before I called you. It plays a recording that says 'You have reached International Investments. Our offices are closed now;

please call back after eight-thirty,' like it wasn't part of Oakes, Ames."

"But presumably she would testify that she was talking to someone about overseas financial transactions at that number." Alec said.

"You betcha!" Moira said gleefully.

Alec called Felix at home, verbally brushing past Sophie's desire to chatter with a curt "I need to talk to him."

Felix came on. "When the two guys who handled your offshore stuff came to see you, how did you get the telephone number to call them?"

Felix didn't speak for several seconds.

"Little cards. They had little cards like business cards except it only had their first name and a telephone number with an area code."

"Do you still have one?"

"I don't know."

"Will you look and call me back at the office?"

"What's this all about?" Felix sounded annoyed.

"I'll tell you later. Oh yeah. Let me ask you a couple of other things. Did you ever call these numbers from out of town?"

"Sure. All over the world."

"Then get any telephone bills, credit-card, office, home. Get Jimmy to do the same. Okay?

"Next question. Did Valery deal directly with these money guys?"

Felix's voice lowered an octave.

"Sure. She didn't know who or what they were. But she talked to them a lot. She had to post invoices and check amounts."

"She didn't know it was Oakes, Ames though?"

"No. She just had the number and the names of our financial advisers."

"Okay. Call me when you have the rest of the records."

Felix grunted. Alec hung up.

He had been watching Moira while he talked. She was bending over looking into temporary file boxes on the floor. She had a very nice figure, plump and well shaped.

In the week before Labor Day he and Moira were able to sort and organize every single long-distance telephone call billed to Freezetemp for five years. It had taken two law firm clerks and half of Felix's bookkeeping department.

It showed that before Felix and Jimmy were doing business with Oakes, Ames, they never called the 555-6700 sequence of numbers. After the association with Oakes, Ames there were repeated calls, and these calls, when organized on a computer, were also in sequence with the secret banking operations.

Even for the two lawyers, who were checking the organization work of others, it was tedious and mind numbing. Lots of Styrofoam cups of coffee and long nights.

As they worked they began to engage in long talks, about the law, their lives, Vietnam, and Trowbridge.

Moira told him how angry several of the law firm's senior partners had been when they discovered that he was involved in the Hastings case after Noah's death hit the papers, and that she had overheard one of the partners talking on the telephone about whether the firm really needed a criminal law capability.

"Why did you take the case?" she asked.

"Now, I don't know why. At the time I was reluctant, but this is a neighbor, a woman alone with two children trying to cope. So I helped her."

He fell far short of saying they had become lovers.

"The insurance branch of the firm has always been doubtful about handling criminal cases, but you have to take that talk with a grain of salt. With federal white-collar crime enforcement at its height the fees they're earning are astronomical." Alec tried to reassure her.

He recounted the story of his search for Noah.

"Do you know what absolutely astounded me?" The young woman shook her head. "How many people use cocaine. When I left the U.S. attorney's office the problem was heroin and to a lesser extent pills. I don't recall us even having a major cocaine case."

Moira seemed amazed at his naïveté. "Lots of people are doing coke. There are people right here." She pointed with her finger toward the floor.

"You're kidding. Who?"

"I wouldn't want to say. But I know what I see." She drew herself up defensively.

"Do they use it right in the office?" Alec asked.

"Mostly at a couple of bars over near Wall Street. I'm not trying to get anybody into trouble. But you asked. Lots of people are doing coke.

"I think people in the younger generation view cocaine like marijuana. It's a relatively harmless recreation drug," she said emphatically.

He bristled inwardly. The younger generation!

Alec was surprised at Moira's stories about cocaine. They supported Vale's view and the tales in Idyllwild about a cocaine feast.

The night before the Labor Day weekend they finished the Freezetemp presentation, a letter of proffer for Vincent Santorini, affidavits from Felix and Jimmy, evidence supporting the relationship between Oakes, Ames and Dumont, and the looting of Freezetemp's assets.

He would take the plan to his partners at the first partners meeting after Labor Day. He firmly warned Felix and Jimmy to use the holiday weekend to think through a decision to plead guilty and give evidence against Oakes in exchange for leniency. Once it was accepted, he warned, it was irrevocable.

"You can't go to the Supreme Court on a state's evidence deal," Connie Callaghan used to warn young lawyers. "Be sure your clients don't have a change of mind."

They finished after dark, the last two people in the office on a Friday night when half the staff had not come to work at all.

Moira looked worn and tired. Her navy blue suit with white blouse and manly tie made her appear crisp and efficient on the outside, but her blue eyes had fatigue in them. She was dialing for the car service when Alec suggested they have dinner. "Unless you're doing something," he said tentatively. She eagerly agreed.

They walked up along the Hudson to TriBeCa, the perspiration running off them after only a few blocks and rumpling their clothes. The young lawyer took Alec to a small bar and restaurant near her apartment, a few blocks off the river.

A lot of the young men at the bar seemed to know her and there was a flurry of hello Moiras and Irish-accent quips as they sat down for a drink. Moira had white wine and kir; Alec stuck to his vodka.

Moira hadn't eaten all day and the drinks made her gay and talkative.

"People see cocaine differently than they did heroin. Cocaine isn't addictive and lots of professional people see it as an adjunct to their lives. It makes them feel" — she paused, groping for words — "more alive and more alert."

The dinner was delicious. They had a fresh broiled salmon with a cold side dressing made with cucumbers, red peppers, and onions in light olive oil and lemon juice. Alec ate it hungrily, but Moira only pecked at it and kept to wine and chatter.

The waiter had suggested a California Riesling and before Alec knew it they had drunk two half bottles.

They seemed to have talked of everything by then. Lee. The war. Karen. Corporate versus criminal law, and Moira's desire to be a public defender. "That's why I jumped at a chance to work with you. You've done an awful lot in this business."

It was nearly midnight and the only patrons left were at the bar, but neither Alec nor Moira seemed willing to end the evening.

"Come on. I'll take you to the local disco. You can see the action in TriBeCa." Alec found himself tagging behind her.

It was still sweltering on the streets, and Moira led him down a dark row of onetime warehouses, most of which now seemed vacant. At the last one a neon sign announced they had reached "Val's."

The noise nearly knocked Alec down. A band was performing against a far wall on a rotating stage covered with tiny mirrors. The mirrors picked up crisscrossing floodlights. He had been in the room only a few seconds when he realized it was painted entirely black.

He guessed there were at least five hundred people, swirling, dancing, moving toward a long bar on one side or away from it. Smoke, heavily laden with the scent of marijuana, hung in the air.

Moira took his hand and they began to dance, twisting and twining between people who were twisting and twining. The wine and the vodka were working. Alec felt excited and alert. He let his body take him.

Twice they fought their way to the bar for drinks. As in the restaurant, she knew a lot of people in the room. Several times she swirled away to dance with some young man or another, but soon drifted back.

Once she disappeared for ten minutes and Alec had the sinking feeling he'd been ditched. He was getting ready to leave when he felt her tug at one arm. "Let's go," she whispered. Her eyes were bright and filled with mischief.

Her apartment was a tiny box, twenty stories up in a high rise with an astounding view of the Hudson. She opened a bottle of white wine and turned the lamp out so the room was lit by the lights of the giant advertising signs on the Jersey shore.

"Would you like something with your wine?" She was sitting on the floor by the coffee table. For a moment he thought she was talking about coffee, and then he saw the little bag. He watched in silence. He did not want to move and yet he wanted to leave. He felt like he was in prep school and someone had pulled out a forbidden pack of cigarettes.

Moira carefully laid out the tiny lines on a mirror. Her fingers worked as deftly as they did riffling through a legal file. Three lines, maybe two inches apiece. She took a second mirror from the cigarette box on the table and performed the same task.

She had taken off her suit jacket when they had come in and her white blouse was stuck to her moist skin, making her nipples show clear through the material of the blouse and the brassiere. Her neck was very white in the half light, and a small gold chain around it rose and fell with her breathing.

She offered the mirror. That was the test. To reach her, he would have to accept the mirror. It was late and his mind had no thoughts of Lee. He was thinking of no case, no person, no thing except this woman before him. He tried to get up, but it was no use. In his mind he knew he should. He should go. Walk to the elevator. Go downstairs. Walk home. Lock the door. Forget this had happened. Make believe he had left the office alone.

"What do I do?" He did not recognize his own voice.

"Watch." She held a tiny instrument in her hand, a white tube. The tooter. Her powder disappeared. Her head rocked.

She put it down. Her eyes were bright. He looked at her as though he expected her to fall over. She took the mirror and the tiny tube and came close to him. She fed him like a baby, close around him. "Breathe in." Her words were soft, but demanding.

They took six inches. There seemed to be a pace to this. A snort, a drink. At first it hurt his nose. Nothing happened. Wasn't it once used as a local anesthetic? Shouldn't it numb him? He had a thought that maybe he was immune. Maybe he was one of the people unaffected by the drug.

Then the rush began. He was awake, excited; his heart raced; he was anxious and serene at the same moment, his mucous membranes numb, like at the dentist's office.

There was no doubt about his reward. Moira was drawing off her clothes. She had a pink and white body still soft with teenage plumpness. They made love on the floor between the coffee table and a couch.

Neither could satisfy the other. He had never been this strong. His mind and body were like bright light bulbs. He couldn't turn them off. Sometime, he guessed it was before dawn, they snorted again and tried to open up the couch Moira used for a bed, but never accomplished it and ended up making love half in and half out of the door of the tiny kitchen.

The morning was the morning of the damned. Moira lay facedown on the floor, her back red-splotched from his fingers, her hair disheveled, as innocent-appearing in sleep as a child's picture. She was nude except for her panties, which clung to her left ankle, her legs spread, the black curly hair of her vagina wet with moisture.

He dressed quickly. His hands were shaking and he felt weak and dehydrated. He wanted to flee the room as a criminal must want to flee the scene of a crime. She did not move when he closed the door.

There were no cabs. The holiday weekend had begun. He walked through the heat all the way to City Hall before he found a cab.

"Thirty-fifth and Park." The cab driver smirked. Alec realized he must look like shit. No tie. He had left his tie. Shirt open. He found white powder on his coat and furiously began brushing it off as they drove uptown.

For an hour he stood in the shower. The phone rang insistently twice but he didn't answer it. Guilt flooded over him like the water. He had let some little twinky toes lead him into using the drug that got Noah killed. What was happening to him? He was the leader. Others didn't lead. He had already worried about his drinking, particularly after Karen left. But he had justified it. His running kept him in shape. He could handle it. What in God's name had possessed him to use coke? He was forty-one years old.

Why had he slept with a coworker? He wasn't one of those old partners who stalked the steno pool. She could get his ticket if she claimed he pressed his attentions on her. How in God's name was he going to work every day with Moira Moran? Every young associate and clerk in the office would know in an hour.

He was adrift. Ever since Lee had come into his life. The murder. The whole thing was seamy. Now cocaine. He felt like he was in a sailboat that had lost its tiller; he couldn't control his direction.

Two months ago he had one of the most enviable law practices in the city. Now he had become involved in a drug kid's murder, withholding information from police, sleeping with a client. He had underbilled the Hastings case without consulting his partners or even explaining to them. He had fallen behind on his other cases, slept with a lawyer in his own firm, and snorted cocaine with her.

The thoughts would not stop running through his mind, like blows of punishment. Each thought was a slap.

The phone rang again and again and then switched to secretarial. He called downstairs and told them to say he was out. The operator said it was a woman who would not leave her name.

In the midafternoon he took a train to Connecticut, standing all the way in the car's vestibule, watching the tracks. In Norwalk he ignored the cabs and walked to Harborview. The streets were hot and seedy and clogged with cars headed over the Norwalk River bridge to the public beach.

He knew as soon as he opened the boat-house door that somebody had bagged the place, though it wasn't like Lee's; they had not torn things or thrown them around. But somebody had gone through the house, opening books, looking under couch cushions, opening desks. Even the sail room with the boat gear had been tossed.

The search was not recent because there was a fine coating of beach sand and dust on even the things they had disturbed. All the doors were locked and the key he kept under the vase by the boat-house door seemed undisturbed, but the doors were old style and he figured even an apprentice burglar could card them.

At first he started to call the police, but he put the phone down before dialing. He didn't want to explain it all to them. He wanted Noah Hastings to be out of his life for good.

The people who owned the house on his left were launching their boat. He asked if anybody had been in his house and the woman remembered a panel truck had been there nearly three weeks before.

"Is anything wrong?" the man asked.

"No. I forgot I had the plumber in."

Lee's house looked forlorn and abandoned. The other half-moon of houses along the cove were alive with holiday activity, but he could see her boat was still beached and the windows dark.

He waded out to the Windmill. The cabin cover had been slashed with a knife and the cockpit was full of water. His friends weren't leaving anything to chance. He bailed it dry without using the pump and set the sails.

It wasn't until he was well out in the Sound that it occurred to him. The house was searched after Noah's death was all over the papers on July 25. His friends Julio and Smiley, if it was his friends Julio and Smiley, were still looking for something, something Noah didn't give them.

The timing was off as well. He knew it the day he searched pictures for DeNunzio, but he had put it out of his mind. If Noah had been killed shortly after his mother saw him leave for Europe, then why were Julio and Smiley still looking for Mr. Grant and something Mr. Grant possessed weeks later?

Presumably Noah died unable or unwilling to give up the prize and the two Hispanics didn't know Noah and Grant were one and the same. So killing Noah hadn't solved their problem and they were still working on it. That meant their interest in Lee had not abated, unless they had come to believe she didn't have it. Whatever it was.

He anchored off of Westport and slipped over the side to swim. The late-afternoon sun was blazing and he floated, staring up into it. He should race back to the house and try to call Lee, he thought, but he didn't know how to reach her except through her sister. He should race back, but suddenly all the world seemed so remote, maybe he would just float away.

Why had he thought he loved Lee when only three weeks after she had gone he was seducing a woman in his office? Or maybe the woman in his office was seducing him? Only thing wrong with that thought was that twenty-six-year-olds don't seduce forty-one-year-olds. You'll never make that stick in court.

Something had rearranged the people in his life. Lee was the wife figure away with the children and Moira was the summer love affair. This was crazy! He was crazy! Maybe that's what Karen had seen. He was crazy!

Almost on cue a voice screamed, "Are you fucking crazy?" It was not until then that he saw the speedboat or heard its outboards. The boat cut close on his left, the bow wave bowling him over, but it was the skier who had screamed, frantically trying to avoid decapitating him as he went past.

When Alec came to the surface he realized the Windmill was a hundred yards away and his body flooded with weakness. He had not eaten since the salmon. Nothing but vodka, wine, coffee, and, oh yes, cocaine. He barely made it, grabbing on to the anchor rope for five minutes before he had the strength to pull himself aboard.

There was no fresh food in the house, but he made a can of chicken soup and ate canned tuna. It took him three calls to reach Lee's sister. She was cool and precise. She would try to get a message to Lee, but she had been instructed not to give out any information to anyone.

"Look. Just tell her to be careful. I came out to my Connecticut house for the first time since she left and somebody'd searched it. It seems to me that this may mean the men who harmed Noah still want something. Just warn her! Okay?"

He was filled with mounting anger. The woman's tone had sounded as though he was at fault, as though he had meant to harm her sister. Shit! Her sister came to him! The relationship up to now had caused him nothing but grief.

16

THE conference table at Trowbridge, Wilton, Pogue and Callaghan had been made by the bonding of four pieces of teak, so that the patterns of wood ran one toward another like waves of brown and tan.

Alec concentrated on it, trying to imagine the workers sanding and polishing, stepping back to admire their handiwork, and sanding and polishing. The table cost Trowbridge $30,000 and was to the older partners a symbol of their success. They ran their hands over it as they sat down almost to reassure themselves.

Alec focused on the wood because eye contact at a partners meeting was, he had learned, to be used sparingly. It could support, challenge, or engage another partner. Looking out the window at the Manhattan skyline during a meeting was regarded as bad manners.

It was symbolic of the relationship of the criminal practice to the firm that matters involving criminal cases were taken up last unless the client was an old mainstay that gave the firm other business.

A lawyer on the window side was droning on about a leveraged buyout of an insurance company in Mason City, Iowa. He cited the economic advantages their client believed the amalgamation would hold for Mason City. Alec wondered idly whether the lawyer had ever been in the Iowa town.

Before each partner was a folder with précis on the issues to be taken up, a delicate gold-embossed coffee cup and saucer, a writing pad, and three sharpened pencils. It was never two, always three. Alec wondered if some ancient partner had broken the point on two and thereafter ordered three put on the table.

Coffee service had been copied from the Supreme Court. It was served from an urn on a cart pushed by a white-coated waiter. He left the room when matters of privilege were discussed because an opposing law firm had once considered subpoenaing a waiter at a Trowbridge meeting.

It was nearly noon before the Freezetemp case came up. Alec sketched the history of the case, the surprise in July when the U.S. attorney had discovered one of his clients had an undisclosed foreign account. He cited the damage that had been caused to the chances of concluding the case without a trial, and recited the options he felt were available to Jimmy and Felix.

"What you see before you in your folders is a proffer to the United States attorney of evidence our clients might be able to provide on a worldwide money-laundering conspiracy conducted by a well-known New York investment banking firm.

"It would be my hope that the prosecutor would agree to reduce the criminal liabilities of the Freezetemp principals in exchange for their assistance in investigating and prosecuting members of the Oakes, Ames and Dumont firm."

Later Alec realized that until the name came up most of the partners were bored with the meeting and half asleep. It was at that moment that heads went up and fingers began ruffling through the memoranda.

He sketched the evidence that Felix and Jimmy were prepared to give and the independent findings of Moira Moran and other associates that seemed to corroborate that position.

The ensuing debate was in such mild terms that only an insider would have recognized the anxiety with which Alec's proposal was met. He later realized he had underestimated the resistance.

Partners who knew Trumbull Oakes were shocked and disquieted that he was accused of these crimes and suggested that the Freezetemp officials had made up the charges to save their skin.

Alec reported his meeting with Mrs. Dumont and her lawyer and her belief that Oakes had directed her late husband in his activities.

Other partners were willing to accept that Oakes might have a criminal involvement, but were deeply concerned that Trowbridge would appear the instrument of assisting the U.S. attorney in prosecuting a Wall Street investment firm.

"We're not located in Schenectady," argued the only living heir to the Wilton family. "We're a Wall Street firm. We do business with the financial structure of this country, and they're going to be pretty nervous about a firm which got involved in prosecuting a venerable and respected investment house."

Alec wondered to himself how the only living heir to the Wilton family had concluded that Oakes's firm was venerable.

Connie Callaghan used to say that the decision-making process of legal partners was like a Quaker meeting. "Anybody can stand up and say anything they want, and then the members go forth as to their own view of God and their conscience."

Alec watched the debate almost as a spectator, but finally he stepped into play.

"I think this is one of the most important discussions we could have at this table, because it goes to the heart of our offering defense in criminal legal matters to our clients." He could feel everyone's eyes on him, but he engaged glances only with the man facing him, an aging trust lawyer who dealt mainly with the legal problems of the widows of insurance company executives.

"The Carter administration made white-collar crime a major target and increased the attention of the SEC and the FBI to this end. Now we have an activist U.S. attorney in New York. The smart money in legal circles is saying that insider trading, defense department fraud, securities fraud, tax fraud, are going to be the mainstays of criminal practice in New York in the 1980s.

"If we want to be in that business, we are going to have to be willing to operate by the rules of that field.

"Trading up is a Byzantine, but an accepted, fact of federal law enforcement. The small fish survives in some fashion by delivering a bigger fish. I didn't have to tell the Freezetemp officials that. The FBI agents told them that. The U.S. attorney told them that. The IRS told them that," Alec lectured.

Alec took a sip of coffee so his throat would remain smooth. There was absolute silence in the room. He continued.

"The question then became, are they making scurrilous, un-substantiated charges about Trumbull Oakes to save their skins, or is there a likelihood the Oakes firm is involved in nefarious practices?

"It seemed to me that the standard for Trowbridge was to make some independent assessment of the accusations before advising our clients as to whether to approach law enforcement officials with this deal.

"That assessment is included in the workup. From my experience as a prosecutor" — he paused for effect; only one other Trowbridge lawyer had been a prosecutor and his cases had been small, limited matters for the New Jersey attorney general's office — "there is evidence to suggest that the Freezetemp officials are telling the truth."

"Even if they are telling the truth" — the living heir to the Wilton family had taken the floor — "is that our job? To help them destroy Trumbull Oakes?"

Wilton, like Trumbull Oakes, was everything that Alec was not. He had taught at Yale Law after clerking for Justice White and had come to his grandfather's firm relatively late in life. He was one of what Connie Callaghan used to call "the salesmen."

"You've got to have them," Connie would lecture. "They don't have to know anything about the law. Their value is when a big client is looking for a case, they say let's give it to old so-and-so, he was at Yale with my brother."

Alec waited deferentially until Wilton had talked through his point.

"You couldn't be more right. Our job isn't to assist in the prosecution of Oakes, but our job is to give our clients the best defense possible, and, if they conclude they want to report a crime to authorities in the hope of leniency for themselves, to advise them on how to do that."

"Want to report a crime." Alec grimaced inwardly. That wasn't entirely correct. Felix and Jimmy wanted to stay out of jail. "You'll be federal witnesses," he had told them. "Trumbull Oakes is never going to mess with federal witnesses. That's not his style. He'll drown us in lawsuits."

He did not tell the partners that he thought this would be the most publicized case since Vesco. They didn't like publicity.

By twelve-thirty, Alec knew the decision would not be blocked, but he also knew it was not sitting well.

"Our real decision is not whether we advise Freezetemp how to make their proffer, our real decision was already made when we took them as clients. This is a prominent and newsworthy case. Can we tell these men we no longer will represent them in the face of it becoming an embarrassment, that we took that course because they wanted to give information to the U.S. attorney we didn't approve of?"

"The firm doesn't always have a chance to review your clients, does it, Alec?" Wilton was smiling as he said it. "I noticed in July you accepted the case of a Connecticut woman who got your name and ours in every tabloid in New York."

The nastiness of the attack stunned everyone at the table and several of Wilton's colleagues in the civil law section looked sharply at him.

Alec paused. It was like throwing a grenade. If you set the explosion timer too quickly it went off in midair and killed you, but if you set it too long, it gave Charlie time to pick it up and hurl it back. Timing is everything.

"I'm very sorry about that. Mrs. Hastings is a neighbor of mine at my Connecticut home. Her son, a quite brilliant young man, had disappeared and she was beside herself. I told her that our firm was not likely to have the legal services she wanted. But in her hysteria what she valued most of all was a lawyer whom she knew.

"It may be her failing, but she did not know her son was involved in drugs, nor could she have anticipated the tragic way his life would end. We now know he died even before she came to me. All of this took place in such a short space of time there was no chance to bring it before you in a formal way. I apologize."

There was silence. Wilton had made a mistake in the short term.

"You'll keep us up to date on the U.S. attorney's response, won't you?" Old Pogue had cast the deciding vote.

Battery Park was packed. Even in the August heat the secretaries, clerks, delivery boys, and messengers who toiled in the skyscrapers of lower Manhattan took their lunches to the park, packing the seawall and the promenade.

He and Moira found a seat facing the Statue of Liberty. They seemed instinctively to choose seating where they could talk without looking at one another.

In the office before the partners meeting they had never mentioned Friday, even by inference or inflection. They had not looked at one another's face or exchanged a pleasantry.

Throughout the weekend his remorse and fear had grown. If the young woman proved to be difficult, to think their Friday evening was more than a sexual escapade, how was he going to handle it?

He had been in the elevator heading for lunch when he realized she was behind him. She must have staked out reception and timed her leaving with his.

"Can I talk to you?" She said the words in only a whisper.

"Sure."

"When?"

"Now."

Hot dogs alfresco had been his idea. No partners of Trowbridge ate lunch in Battery Park. It could seem incidental, accidental if they were seen. Buying her lunch in a restaurant would have seemed entangling, like part of the net he was trying to cast off.

As at the disco, the park air was filled with marijuana, and the salesmen passed through the crowd silently mouthing the word "toke."

She held her hot dog, still wrapped in its paper, clasping it in both hands in her lap like a Bible, her eyes gazing out over the water.

Her voice trembled. In a terrible moment Alec realized she was going to cry.

"What did Friday night mean?"

"There was no Friday night. In fact, if you recall, last week didn't have a Friday at all." He said it firmly, without humor.

"Alec, you're wrong. We have something. You can't avoid. Friday night happened. There is something between us. You know there is."

He looked sideways. Her eyes were filled with tears.

Impulsively he put his arm around her in a quick gesture and then pulled it back.

"Bullshit."

Tears were dropping onto her hot-dog wrapper, making a little patter like a tiny rainstorm. Christ, if somebody he knew passed by they'd be sure she had just told him she was pregnant. God! The thought chilled him. Not that too.

"Two consenting adults went out after work." Alec appeared to be talking to a pigeon. "They were overly tired and they should have gone home. They had too much to drink and behaved stupidly. It embarrassed them both. One adult, the older, certainly should have known better. There was no excuse. He has been reminding himself for four days that there was no excuse. This was unacceptable behavior for a mature man, or, for that matter, for a mature lawyer."

The rain was still falling on her hot dog.

"I can't face you all the time." She was sobbing as she talked. "I can't come in and work with you and, and . . . not think about you. I felt this way since I first met you." She shuddered as though chilled.

"I need you. I want you. Please don't hurt me."

He turned and looked into her eyes. She was really quite pretty, the wonderful mixture of pink and cream the complexion of Ireland.

"I don't want to hurt you. But this is what we are going to do: We are going to work together. We are going to go into the office every day and do our jobs. We are not going to think about or discuss this. That's what a professional is. This is a lesson about management of fatigue, alcohol, and personal contact. It's not about love or needs. Let's learn it and go on."

They sat in silence. Alec ate his hot dog and drank his Coke. She fed half hers to the pigeon and sipped her soda.

"Will you try?" He turned to her.

"I guess so. I have no choice."

She touched his arm. "Don't decide today. Give us a chance. You and I are drawn together, you know that. You're frightened by the thought, but it is true."

"Go fix up your face before we go back. I've got enough trouble in this firm without them thinking I make the associate members cry during lunch." He tried to be light.

She walked to a water fountain and fiddled with a napkin. He watched the Staten Island ferry making its way across the harbor.

They started back.

He stopped for a minute and they turned and faced one another.

"I can't tell you what to do with your life. But don't use coke. You may be right that it isn't harmful. But all lawyers are officers of the court. They taught you that in law school. It is hard to be an officer of the court and advise others they broke the law when every day or so you break the federal controlled narcotics act. That's the harm if there's no other."

She started to speak.

He cut her off by turning back toward Wall Street. He was trying to control a feeling of elation, the kind of joy one gets when a traffic policeman doesn't write the ticket for speeding. He was going to get away with it. He felt for the moment quite the pirate. Maybe he did have a way with women.

The feeling disappeared almost as quickly as it had come. Someday she would talk about it. She would confide in a friend or some other partner. For all he knew she had banged other partners. Or something would happen and she would cast this truth out to defend herself. Maybe she even believed there was something between them.

He realized he was getting too upset. He tried literally to stiffen himself as he walked. He realized how Felix must have felt. Moira was Valery Vennuzio; she now had something on Alec Anton.

Their minds must have been traveling the same path. As they reached the lobby she turned, now all the Catholic schoolgirl. "I'll never breathe a word of what happened. But I think you are making a mistake. Think. Think about it." She kissed him behind his ear. He looked around hoping no one had seen.

17

VINNY treated the Freezetemp proffer as gingerly as green troops handle Claymore mines. When he finished reading it, he placed it at a point so far away on his desk Alec worried that it would slip off onto the floor.

"That's a little slim, Alec." Vinny looked tanned and rested from his vacation. He was wearing a blue shirt with a white collar and gold cuff links that bore the crest of the Justice Department on them. Alec had always wondered who bought the gimcracks that were listed in lawyer mail-order catalogs.

"It's probable cause, Vinny."

"I really thought when you said you wanted to make a proffer it would be a little stronger." Vinny was being both snide and patronizing.

"What's the problem with it?"

"How can I go to the enforcement agencies with an offer of cooperation that contains very little hard evidence and ask to open an investigation against one of the most respected men on Wall Street. Are you crazy?" Vinny had pushed back his chair and crossed his legs, showing a razor-sharp pants crease and a black English shoe. Vinny was one of those people who always seem to be wearing new shoes. Alec idly wondered how he did it; the U.S. attorney made $76,000 a year.

"Vinny, my clients can testify that they were directed by an official of Interglobal that in order to get the tanker contract they had to pay kickbacks. They were instructed by this person to take their investment banking business to Oakes, Ames and Dumont. They do. They have direct meetings with Oakes. People representing a department of Oakes arrange for a series of offshore accounts to assist them in raising the capital to pay Interglobal. Oakes is on Interglobal's board!"

Vinny broke in. "It helped them loot a lot of money from their own firm."

"Okay. Granted. But let me finish," Alec said patiently.

"Your own witness, Valery Vennuzio, can testify that she was in regular contact with seemingly anonymous money managers that were actually at a division of Oakes, Ames."

Vinny raised his voice to interrupt. "Goddamn it! Trumbull Oakes is the best known investment banker in this town. He doesn't need this sort of thing. Shit, he can walk in and talk to the President without an appointment!"

Vinny's face showed actual pain, all the control learned in the seminary was going to slip away. Alec realized the notion of prosecuting Oakes had stunned Vinny. Maybe Vinny didn't want the case to go this way, after all.

"Take it easy." Alec put his hand up in a traffic-stopping gesture. "That's just what I said when these guys gave me this story. But I also know that there is probable cause for you to consider a crime may have been committed in the Oakes firm and that my clients can help you. Turn this around for a minute. How can you avoid looking into charges of a major money-laundering operation? Particularly when it involves a powerful political firm?"

Vinny swung around in his chair. He was gazing at the picture of Attorney General William French Smith as though it were the Shrine of the Immaculate Conception, as though he would receive a sign.

"Why don't you guys look at that proffer again," Alec said softly. "Talk among yourselves. I think my clients can help you open a major new investigation, maybe a whole avenue of investigations. Nobody has ever tried to take a money-laundering case back toward the clients since that Paradise Island deal in the Miami Strike Force."

Something told Alec he had scored. It was like at the ball game after you leave your seat in overtime; you can hear the crowd roar but you can't tell the score or the play. Alec could hear the crowd.

Two days went by. Nothing. Finally Vinny's secretary called. Could Alec attend a meeting at the U.S. attorney's office?

"You know what's wrong with you, Anton. You can't come in here with evidence against any goddamn Democrats."

Everybody laughed as Alec sat down in an empty chair before Vinny's desk. The office was crowded. There were two FBI agents, one who Alec knew and another who he'd seen around. Eddie was there, trying to avoid eye contact with Alec, and another customs agent, a woman Alec didn't know.

There was an SEC guy and another female, a lawyer from Justice, to his left, and a couple of guys who also looked like agents sitting against the wall.

"This august group of gentlemen, and ladies" — Vinny nodded toward the women — "is my financial crimes task force. You know most of them. They've all read your proffer. They've all given me some thoughts on it, and I ask you here to answer a couple of questions before we make our decision. Okay?"

Alec nodded. This was the old Vinny. The Democrats line was the tip. Vinny was Bensonhurst. Vinny was Jesuit trained. Vinny had streets. He wouldn't have shown these guys to Alec if he wasn't trying to send a signal that he wanted this case. He would've wanted a private meet if he was going to back off. This was a little theater. Was it for him? Was it for the SEC?

"Will your guys wear a wire?"

"One has the guts for that. One probably doesn't. But it may be too late."

"Why too late?"

"They cut these guys off quick at the beginning. They said, go take your lumps. In fact" — Alec leaned back and looked at the ceiling for a second — "in fact I think that's why my clients allowed me to make this proffer."

"It wasn't because we were going to send them to jail for a decade or so?" Everybody laughed. Good sign. Second one-liner.

Alec didn't answer. Vinny continued. "I hate it with two guys. Their objectives will start to diverge." He said it as though he was talking to himself.

"I don't think so. These guys have been partners for years. They like and respect each other and their objective is to try to live out their lives in peace. They know they've made some mistakes."

"If we want to work only with one guy, can you arrange for the other to be away under our supervision as this is going forward?"

"That depends on our deal. How long? How far? But in principle, sure."

Vinny looked around the room silently. The financial crimes team stared back, trying to keep their eyes noncommittal.

"Everybody here knows Oakes is a prominent Republican. He can call Reagan and get through. God only knows if that'll help him." Everyone laughed. "Worse, he can call Nancy." More laughter.

Vinny suddenly looked serious. "What that means is we have to have a case that's clean. We can't afford a Billy Carter deal. No con men. We have to be able to move right to Oakes. That's why the wire.

"Alec, you worked here. What does Anton the ex-prosecutor think?" Vinny was looking at him with his dark Sicilian eyes.

"There's a case in the firm. No way there isn't a case in the firm. Whether it could have operated without the head man knowing . . ." Alec shrugged, his shoulders posed the question.

He had to be careful here. If he appeared too eager, too sure his clients would deliver Mr. Big to the government, the prosecutors would become suspicious that he was desperate. That his guys were ready to fold.

"I don't know anything about investment banking." Alec's face took on a look of appropriate modesty. "But from what I read this is a small firm. Three named partners, two living, one who died recently, and all actually operated the firm. So this isn't General Motors and I would think it hard to conceive that if a systematic, illegal, offshore banking operation was going on it was not known to everyone in the firm."

Alec let that sink in. "Also you get a bonus off of Interglobal. My clients say that the shipbuilding project is a kind of giant international Ponzi game. The capital has been attracted, but the ships aren't going forward."

Vinny had already thought of that. Alec could tell from his eyes. "Most of the principals are foreign nationals. I don't want to try this in the World Court."

He stood up. "We'll let you know. Thanks for coming in." Warm

Vinny was not. Alec had been dismissed as summarily as the office boy.

It was beautiful on the Sound. Crisp whitecaps kicked over the water like little groups of running children, and Alec knew if he was out in the Windmill he would be riding high on the gunwales, holding on for dear life.

Alec had suggested Felix's boat because he knew it would make the men more at ease. Slipping away from land was to slip away from problems, to cut oneself adrift. He had once worked on a case where the FBI had arrested the subject in a small boat off of Barnegat Bay. The man had been surprised when they came alongside, as though he had not considered the FBI had boats.

The Gallaghers sat at a little table in the cabin balancing drinks against the swells and Felix sat at a helm and dashboard that looked like Mission Control in Houston.

Sophie moved her bulk between the forward cabins and her guests laden with enough good deli to block the arteries of Paul Bunyan.

Alec had broken Connie Callaghan's rule. He was drinking with his clients, his second Stolichnaya resting on a knee.

"So. Tell me again. What is this deal?" Sophie acted like she was buying dubious meat at a stetl in the Ukraine. It had occured to her to find out if this Alec Anton was selling poison to her Felix.

"We sign a letter of agreement to provide the government evidence of wrongdoing against officials of Oakes, Ames and Inter-global and to assist them in investigating those crimes. They in turn agree to allow Felix and Jimmy to plead to one felony and one misdemeanor count each. They will oppose a jail sentence in court and recommend probation. The IRS will open negotiations to settle the tax issues as a civil matter and no criminal tax charges from this investigation will be filed."

Alec stopped and took a sip. "There's a hook in there and you've got to think it through. If they find other tax evasion, other tax difficulties predating the liquid gas deal — boom! They can go criminal."

"Let's say they do; what's likely to happen?" Jimmy was leaning back against the bulkhead. Alec realized that the Irish have a problem that compounds drinking. They show booze more easily. Jimmy's ruddy complexion was already flushed dark red.

"My personal view is that they will stay civil if you guys pay. Tax prosecutions are for two reasons. One, as a deterrent and, two, because the defendant has spent the money. The IRS is in the business of recovering money. That's their objective."

Jimmy's wife had bought new glasses to look younger and they made her look like a tiny wrinkled shrew. "We can't go on like this. We have to do something."

Alec decided to slow her down. They still hadn't grappled with their decision.

"There's something else. Something that maybe Felix can understand better than others. When you make this agreement, effectively you're pleading guilty. You'll lose your independence. There is less that I can do for you and less that you do for yourself."

Sophie looked thoughtful. "If they were convicted at a trial?"

"It would be the same, only worse."

"Could we win at trial?"

"Truthfully? I don't think so. That's why I brought this deal to you."

Felix had made no comment. He had kept his hands on the helm and his eyes on the water ahead in a determined way as though to turn to the group in the cabin was to make a decision.

His question rumbled from his chest. "What do I have to do?"

"One of you" — Alec gestured with his glass — "has to try to contact guys at Interglobal and the Oakes firm and get admissions. You've got to work undercover." To Felix he said "You know the Interglobal guy better, and I think it might best be you."

Alec didn't say that he believed Jimmy would collapse and give the whole thing away.

"Who protects Felix?" Sophie looked hard into Alec's eyes. He realized that she was strikingly beautiful. Now overweight, overmade-up, and overwrought, you could still see in her face the pretty young girl she had once been.

"Government agents."

"Like they did Americans in Iran?"

"Better, I hope."

"I hope so too, Mr. Lawyer." Her steady gaze posed the unspoken — *or you will answer to me.*

The FBI, Alec had long since concluded, was an investigation agency mesmerized by technology. When he had been in the U.S. attorney's office one of his colleagues used to joke, "*Why not* use satellite surveillance, voice-stress evaluation tape, and psychiatric analysis when a simple check of city files will do?"

The bureau leased two rooms at the Barclay at Lexington and Forty-eighth and wired them for sound and video, placing the cameras and microphones in one room and a monitor and recording equipment in the other. The agents were hoping Felix could lure Oakes and others into having key conversations in the room and thereby avoid the difficulty and danger of having Felix wear a body mike into an environment the bureau couldn't control.

The first attempt was nearly a disaster. Felix had demanded Alec be nearby and so he sat with the agents, technicians, and an assistant U.S. attorney in the monitoring room while Felix tried to call Spanos Canosous, his original contact at Interglobal.

Felix was alone in the room so his conversation with Spanos would be as natural as possible, but the tension the husky executive was under could be seen on the monitors in his every move.

He knocked the telephone off the bedstand twice trying to dial and this created static in the bureau's taping connection. Perspiration streamed down his face and at first his voice quavered. Alec was sure he had made a mistake. Felix would never be able to carry this off.

Finally he got the call through to Spanos's Halifax office.

"Spanos?"

"Yeah?"

"This is Felix."

"Who?"

"Felix Schwartzberg."

"Why are you calling me?"

"We have to talk."

"What?"

"We have to talk. Jimmy and I can't hold out."

"Where are you calling from?"

"The phone's okay; don't worry." Felix was getting his pace, his voice sounded more assured.

There was a long silence. Alec wondered whether Spanos had clicked off and they hadn't heard the disconnect. The FBI technician was tinkering with the dials on his recorder.

The television monitor showed Felix staring at the receiver.

"Spanos?"

"Spanos?"

The Greek's voice came back on.

"This is over, Felix. There is nothing I can do."

Felix's voice took on a hard edge.

"We need to meet. The government is going to wipe Jimmy and me out. Wipe us out. They have more than we thought. They're asking me about you. They're asking me about Oakes."

Spanos said something unintelligible in Greek. It sounded like a curse.

"Felix, Felix. Don't be fooled by Mr. Oakes. He is not so nice. He has other clients in his business, very dangerous clients. You were told to take care of this."

Now on the television monitor, Felix even looked angry. He had been abandoned. It was clear this is what he believed anyway.

"I am not so nice either. Jimmy and I are not going down alone. I didn't work all those years in a stinking cargo hold so some goy with soft hands is going to rob me."

He hung up.

From the moment of that first call, Felix and Sophie would never have a moment alone. Either bureau or Treasury agents would be with him at all times. The surveillance would have to be as subtle as possible so that Spanos or others who might check into Felix or Freezetemp would not suspect he was working with the federal agents.

Alec had tried to tell Felix, to make him understand that until this case was over he was back living in a totalitarian land, in the hands of the government.

They went for a drink in the Barclay's lobby bar. Two FBI men sat at a nearby table and used the break to eat supper. They were on until midnight.

"Spanos mentioned something Mrs. Dumont said." Alec sipped his drink.

Felix looked quizzical.

"That Oakes had some rough clients. Did you hear that?"

Felix nodded.

"Does he mean people like Spanos?"

Felix shook his head. "Naw. Spanos is a fixer. There are rough people in the shipping business, but not Spanos."

"Got any idea who they are?"

Felix shook his head.

"Organized crime?" Alec leaned forward and spoke low.

Felix shook his head again. "I'd have known that. I've been dealing with the wops all my life. Labor. Supplies. They woulda rung my bell if I was into one of their things."

"Mrs. Dumont said Oakes took some clients her husband didn't like."

Felix was silent. He was looking at his giant hands.

"I don't know . . ." Felix's voice trailed off. "There were clients he was having trouble with. Once I remember, it was just before things blew up, he was yelling at someone on the phone. When he realized I was standing there he stopped. I had never seen Oakes raise his voice."

Felix looked tired, drawn. Alec decided to let him go. They shook hands silently.

The government had leased a limousine so it could have an agent with Felix at all times without attracting attention. As it pulled away East on Forty-eighth Alec could see him wearily lay his head back on the seat.

Alec's office was dark when he got back to the Battery; the guards admitted him to the elevator with weary nods. He pulled the Noah files from the safe and ruffled through them until he came to it.

"Trumbull Oakes, investment banker, 555 Fifth Avenue."

Philip Ochoa's application from Mountainview.

It had been at the back of his mind since California. The probabilities were that it meant nothing, that Oakes was not connected to Ochoa's cocaine operation. But hadn't another reference, Vale, been the cocaine lawyer? Maybe there was an axis here.

It could be material to the federal investigation, an important lead. He looked at the paper a long time, as though he thought it might speak.

If he put this in play it would reopen Noah's death, put Lee's life back on the front page, bring more pain, more unpleasantness. It probably was just a coincidence, he lied to himself.

He needed to talk to Lee. He couldn't move without her permission anyway. He couldn't involve her without her willingness.

He wondered where Lee was and what she was doing. He wondered if she would ever return.

Spanos Canosous called Felix three days later. The federal agents had been beside themselves in the interval, sure that something had scotched the operation, sure that somehow Spanos had been alerted. But when he called he wanted a meeting. He was coming to New York.

It took several more calls for Felix to lure him to the Barclay. Spanos had not seemed suspicious as much as he seemed desirous of eating well and kept insisting they go to one or another of his favorite restaurants. But Felix had prevailed with the notion that at the hotel they could talk freely.

Watching on the monitor, Alec could see as a defense lawyer how devastating video is. In a television age when everyone on the jury watches television daily, here was a way prosecutors could get an enactment of a crime in the medium most compelling to the humans they were trying to influence.

The actors could not disguise their true natures. This was an unforgiving witness stand. Spanos played fixer, as though he had read for the role.

"Felix this is nice. You have this place for a little nooky" — he made a gesture, with his right hand, of copulation — "a little getaway from Sophie?"

Felix winked.

"I would have thought after Miss Vennuzio that your taste for nooky would have cooled. She still gonna testify?"

Felix grimaced. "The most expensive pair of tits I ever sucked."

Spanos and Felix laughed, the rich laugh of big heavy men who have done real work in their lives.

Spanos seemed totally at ease. He made a drink from the mini bar, opened pretzels and potato chips, and turned on the television. "How did the Jets do?"

"They lost."

"I couldn't watch the game. I was flying."

Felix walked to the window and was looking out. "You miss living in the U.S.?"

"Only sports. You know, if I could live where I want" — Spanos looked wistful — "I'd live in the village where I grew up. Can you image that? I get homesick for a place so bad, in the civil war nobody wanted it."

Both men laughed.

"Someday. Maybe."

Suddenly his whole demeanor changed. It was if a storm had come over the Mediterranean, quickly and from the sea.

"Felix. I put you in the tankers because I knew I could rely on you. You made enough money to get out. Now you come threatening us because you got caught. We didn't get you caught."

Felix started to speak. Spanos put up his hand.

"You're thing was just a little thing. There are lots of people in the tanker deal, people all over the world. Oakes has a lot of other clients. These people won't go for this."

Felix spoke slowly, unflustered.

"Spanos, I'm fifty-six years old. Jimmy is sixty next year. We can't go to jail. No way. It is too late."

Spanos interrupted. "What is your fucking lawyer doing?"

"He's doing okay. But this new U.S. attorney, he's out to make a name for himself. Anton says we're being used as an example on white-collar crime. No matter what we offer they want a jail sentence. No way."

The two men sat in glum silence as though thinking of solutions.

Felix stared at the flickering images on the silent television.

"I want to live abroad. Israel. Italy. Greece maybe. Maybe your village."

Spanos spoke through a mouthful of potato chips. "What do you want from us?"

Felix turned his whole body to face Spanos.

"Jimmy and I have some assets, some things the government

doesn't know about or can't get if we move fast. I want to meet with
Oakes. Get set up to disappear."

Spanos did not look pleased. "If you do a Vesco, the government
is going to be pissed off. This will get to be a big case. It could start to
unravel other things."

"Jimmy and I are not going to jail." Felix said it with finality.

"These guys can be bad, Felix, very bad." Spanos shook his head
in sadness, as though Felix was beyond rescue.

Felix looked as mournful. "Don't threaten. That is over. Don't
dance. Do what I ask."

Spanos got up abruptly. "So we'll see what we shall see." He took
a bag of pretzels as he left.

Within the next two days the FBI surveillance cars picked up a panel
truck staking out Felix's Long Island house. Its two occupants, males
of undetermined ethnicity, never attempted to enter the property,
but seemed intent on watching who came in and out.

In the next two weeks all contact with federal agents was funneled
through the leased limousine. Felix could call the U.S. attorney's
office over a secure line or by giving the driver information. Tail cars
were kept few and distant.

The bureau ran the plates on the van and came up with a Ryder
rental in a false name. It let the two men alone. Everyone waited.

Alec's office became a secondary meeting place between Felix and
the feds. The building was so large, with bank upon bank of eleva-
tors, that it was easy for the government men to get quietly to
Trowbridge and natural for Felix to visit his lawyer from time to
time.

Spanos had not recontacted and both the agents and Alec guessed
the Greek was having Felix carefully checked out before going further. Eddie Doherty had the more chilling notion: They were staking Felix to kill him. Security was increased.

Alec became more and more anxious about what he had in
Trowbridge's safe. The longer he didn't show this to the government
the more remiss he was. At first he could have said he didn't notice
the connection or that he could not release it without his client's
permission, but as the investigation of Oakes went forward, this
became less tenable.

He started calling Lee's sister regularly. She was warming up, and one night they had talked for an hour about Lee as a little girl and her marriage to Hastings.

Each time they talked Eileen swore she was passing on Alec's messages. "She isn't ready to face anything yet. She's got something about you. You don't have to say anything. I can tell. But I told her to be careful. She can't stand much more."

The last week of September the bureau let Felix go on ice for a break. The strain of his waiting and watching for Spanos had taken its toll. He needed to rest. The agents let him take his boat out with Sophie. The bureau trailed with a small cabin cruiser and got surveillance assistance from coast guard helicopters.

Alec took the train to Connecticut. It was a clear, chill early-fall day and when he took the Windmill out he wore a sweater and a windbreaker. With winter now more than a hint, the wind was brisk on the Sound and he spent the three hours in a rugged battle with the sail and the tiller, hanging out half the time, his hands rubbed raw in the wind.

When he got back the tide was up and he took the Windmill to the seawall. Several of the summer residents had already boarded up their houses, and the island was putting on its winter cloak. The marshes had turned from green to brown and the trees on tiny Peach Island were showing red and gold leaves.

It was Alec's favorite time. The mist hung low by the rocks at Wilton Point and the first Canada geese began their landings on the trip south.

He pulled his sailing jacket around him and started off down the beach. The sun was low over the housetops in the west and it made every mast of every sailboat a golden lance.

For all the love and companionship he had had in his life, he realized that he really relished solitude, and the sense of being on his own, unfettered, gave him a lift as he walked along.

He walked as far as Lee's house, the point where the half-moon of sand ended and the rocks of Wilton Point began. He peered in the window but the house was as empty and silent as the beach at night. Noah's Porsche sat on the macadam, covered by a tarp, and the Lightning now had the look of abandonment, its hull brown with dust and sand.

He wondered if Lee would ever accept Noah's death, would ever be able to have a life again, to love him or anyone, to have hope or desire. You could survive the death of parents, he knew that. You could survive the death of dear companions; indeed, you could watch them die and survive it. But a child? A child you bore?

It was dark when he got back to the house. He had walked the whole island, the beach, the marshes, the causeway. Except for a couple of kids on the leeward side, he had met no one, uttered no words to another human since he had gotten to Harborview.

He drove down to Donnelly's in the old VW and got a bowl of chili and a beer. The waitress who had run the marathon with him last year sat down and they talked about winter races. The Saturday-night singles had not come in and Alec had another beer.

Noah was on his brain. He could see the kid kneeling, the wire around his neck. Julio was holding the wire, the way Julio had held Alec, and Smiley was asking him questions. Maybe Julio wasn't a rocket scientist after all. Maybe he just pulled too tight. He could see Smiley rage at Julio, scream that the big goof had made a mistake.

Or maybe they meant to kill the kid. Maybe Noah was begging, telling them he would help them, he would do what they wanted, and Smiley said "snuff him." Being Smiley he said it with a smile. The kid had gone forward, his brain now robbed of oxygen for so long that even if he had lived it would have been on public welfare in the nut ward.

He wondered how Noah met death. Did he know it was coming and think about his mother? Was he surprised? Sometimes in Vietnam it was the surprise that amazed Alec. Why would someone be surprised they had been mortally shot in a place where hundreds of thousands of men and women were running around trying to kill each other?

Maybe Noah was like that. So convinced of the immortality of childhood that it was not until the last breath of life was going that he realized his time was up.

Alec called Eileen from the bar.

She seemed surprised he was in Connecticut.

"Something's come up. Some important information. Can I come up tonight or tomorrow and tell you about it?" It was contrived. He knew it.

There was a long silence. He could hear Eileen had moved away from the telephone.

Finally he heard her voice again. "Maybe tomorrow, for late breakfast. Okay? Eleven o'clock."

When he got to Eileen's house it was ten forty-five and there were no cars out front. He rang the chimes. For a long time no one answered and he turned to look at the town square when he heard her voice.

"You're early."

Lee looked quite different, really. She had drawn her hair up on her head and she wore more makeup than he had remembered. Her blouse was a sort of cossack affair with a broad belt, and she wore tight, washed-out Levis that looked like they had faded from time, not chemicals.

He did not attempt to embrace her. They both stood silent for a moment.

"Come in."

She seemed to be alone and there was no sign of Eileen or the girls. The sun room had been set for breakfast.

He sat down looking out at the garden. Eileen must be good with flowers, he thought, because it was an almost perfect replica of a garden of colonial times, with herbs and vegetables neatly set out amid flowers and shrubs.

Lee talked, pensively stirring her tea as it grew cold in the cup.

At first they had simply been in Guilford. Eileen had let no calls through and they had not gone out. Even Veronica had seemed willing to sit and stare for hours at a time.

In the past weeks they had been on Block Island in the home of one of Eileen's friends.

"I've walked two thousand miles on that island," Lee said.

"Sometimes now I think Noah is simply away at school. Safe, happy, in good hands. All the justifications I once told myself.

"He will be home for vacations. He will come in the door any minute. Tell me all about Zurich and what he did in the Alps. Any minute.

"That is now.

"Then sometimes he is a little boy, running to keep up with his dad's long strides. Making cocoa and playing checkers. Hiding in the attic. Dressing up in his father's cadet uniform with a stick for a gun. That is sometimes.

"I have this dream. Noah has called from school. He needs little things. Shirts. A new toothbrush. He tells me about school. About the mountains and the long hikes. When he starts to hang up I say 'Honey. Please don't hang up.' But he always hangs up. I can't stop him. He always hangs up."

She had begun to cry, great wrenching sobs that shook her whole body. She was holding on to the table edge so hard her fingers had made indents in the tablecloth.

Alec was afraid to touch her. He was afraid to move.

Afterward she got up and cooked the breakfast. She moved mechanically. Alec sensed she was using her concentration and energy on eggs and sausage, on meticulous grapefruit preparation and careful toast buttering.

He talked about the sailing at Harborview and how the fall birds had arrived, waddling up and down the beach as though they owned it.

He told her about the Freezetemp case and what was going on in New York. Chatter. A constant chatter. If he stopped chattering, Alec realized, he would open the door to her grief.

"You told Eileen you had something important to tell me?" Lee had eaten almost nothing. He realized she had lost weight since he had last seen her. Her face was angular, the muscle on her neck stood out more clearly.

"This is not the time. Another time perhaps."

"No. This is the time. I want to hear it. This is the time."

She said it almost fiercely, as though she had to hear it, as though it was necessary like a bitter medicine.

He avoided being graphic. He told it like a police report: that Ochoa was sent as a distributor of cocaine by his Colombian family, that the evidence showed Noah had become some sort of factotum in this operation and that his role in it had continued through college until his death. He told her about the strange coincidence of Trumbull Oakes's name being involved in both his cases, but she didn't recognize the name or the firm.

"Could that have been the job Noah had in investments?"

Lee shook her head. "I don't know. I just don't know."

Alec said he doubted that Noah was killed in a drug purchase, but more likely died as an outgrowth of the Ochoa conspiracy.

"We know that Julio and Smiley have been looking for something. One working hypothesis is that it was something Noah had and when he wouldn't or couldn't produce, they killed him."

"No, that's not right!" She interrupted angrily.

"John and I killed him. We killed him when he was fourteen years old!"

"I don't go for that either," Alec said softly. "As a lawyer I can see that's not a good working hypothesis.

"Noah goes to Mountainview, a lonely, rejected young kid. He happens to make friends with a boy whose family is from another culture. They're exporting a deadly substance and he gets in the family business with his friend. I'm not clear he really is hooked on cocaine. In fact I think he isn't.

"What he's really found is something he does well. It happens to be illegal. But even that may not be clear to him. Lawyers, school-teachers, other role models are in the same business."

There was a long silence.

"What should I do?" Lee was staring into her cup.

"Go on living. You have two daughters, a life."

"I can't seem to get it started."

"It's very soon. Time will do it."

"Where will I go? What will I do?"

"Go away. Start again. Change your name. I'll help you." Alec looked into her eyes; even in grief she was an extraordinarily beautiful woman. "Start part two of your life. Sure you'll have memories. You can't block them out. But someplace new, someplace different won't throw memory into your face each day."

Eileen came back, ostentatiously closing the car door with a bang and stamping up the walk as though she expected them to be entangled in love's embrace and in need of fair warning.

As he watched the two sisters he realized that Eileen was an ally. She seemed to take his part on, putting her hand on his arm, and gently teasing her sister about her New York lawyer.

It was late afternoon when he left, nursing the old VW down the ot open Noah's story. Please. Not yet. I have to decide. I have to decide how to live."

He started to speak, but she spoke first. "Good night, darling."

He found himself elated, unexpectedly happy. He had not gotten her permission to turn the Mountainview materials over to Vinny. But he didn't care. He knew it had been a pretext anyway; a pretext to Lee.

Lee Hastings was in his life again.

18

EDDIE Doherty's voice hit him hard with its urgency.

"There's a meet."

"When?"

"Now."

He looked at his watch. It was five minutes after midnight.

"They're obviously putting the rush on him." Eddie sounded tired. "They want it at two A.M. and they want him to drive himself. They figure he can't set them up."

"Are you going to stall?" Alec was sitting up now in his darkened apartment. He could hear the cars on Park Avenue and their lights played shadows across the ceiling.

"Vinny says no. Go. The FBI wants to too. Me, I'm a little nervous."

Alec trusted Eddie. Eddie had been a New York cop before being a fed. He'd been a narc. Narcs really shoot their guns. Most of the FBI only get to fire on the range.

"What does Felix want?"

"He told Vinny he'd go if you'd go."

Shit! Alec sat in the dark. It was like a bunker with the lights of flares playing shadows. For the first time in ten years he wished he had a cigarette. A cigarette was a stall. He could hear them in the dark, their nineteen-year-old voices. "Hey, lieutenant, can we finish the smoke?" Sure. Prolong life. Pray you were smoking Herbert Tarletons. Pray you were smoking something that took forever.

"How're they going to wire him if the house is under surveillance?"

"They already wired him. He got the call in Periso's. He was eating with his old lady and another couple and he gets a telephone

call. Smooth. But he was smart too. He never left the booth. He had
his back to the room, so he says nobody saw him dial."

Alec was still confused.

"How did they wire him?"

"In the car going home. They got a team to the parking lot while
he was still eating. They hid in the back and wired him. It works too.
That's how we've been talking to him."

Alec cursed to himself again. If they've been talking to him,
somebody with a scanner could have been listening. Fuck all. Even if
the jerks in the panel truck were just playing the radio, the FBI
transmitter would click like a code.

Eddie was getting impatient. "You coming?"

"Should I?"

"I think they'll push him even if you don't. He's a tough old guy.
He keeps telling the agents that if God wanted him dead he would
have let the SS do it."

"Okay."

"Go down to your garage. Don't go out the front. There's a car in
your garage. They'll take you to the command post. Okay?"

"Okay."

It was chill. October had come in cold. He put on his old field
jacket, slacks, and a sweater. The .45 was lying in with his shirts. He
laughed to himself. There'd be enough firepower out there tonight
to relieve Khe Sanh. For guys who didn't use them, the FBI loved
guns.

The customs agents had their adrenaline up. They were young.
Maybe twenty-eight or thirty. They kept calling in and talking radio
talk. Kids. This was their first deal. He could tell.

"Mr. Doherty told us to fill you in." Alec nodded.

"The subject —"

Alec cut him off. "His name is Felix."

The kid looked hurt.

"Felix is supposed to take his own car. Not the limo. Take the LIE
to the Van Wyck to the Belt. No speeding. Get off at Fort Hamilton
and go to the booth by the access ramp."

That gave them, Alec guessed, twenty miles of predawn parkway
to see if Felix had a tail.

"The Feebees got a plug on the car and they told Felix to hum or something once in a while, but they also got the coast guard at Floyd Bennett to make one pass up the beach as though they were going to Islip." The kid was reading his notes from a clipboard.

The helicopter was a mistake. The coast guard copters didn't fly unless there was a rescue, but what the hell, it might be covered by flights on the pattern to Kennedy.

The command post was in a park department maintenance shed underneath the Verrazano. The FBI was there en masse with a van radio transmitter–monitor and a half dozen cars. Eddie and the customs team were there and a guy from the U.S. attorney's office that Alec only slightly knew.

Somebody handed him a container of coffee. Two New York cops were unloading coffee from a Blue and White.

One of the FBI men asked peevishly "What are they doing here?" Eddie patiently explained that without them little old ladies in apartments on Shore Road would be sending cops down all night.

An FBI man who said his name was Capper or Tapper shook hands with Alec.

"You know how this works. We can't talk to him. We can hear everything he says and we can monitor where his vehicle goes." He nodded to a guy at the console. A switch was flicked and the steady homing drone of the car transmitter came on.

"He left his house at one-o-six. Barring traffic he ought to go off at Fort Hamilton at about one-fifty."

Suddenly one of the receivers crackled. There was heavy static, but Alec could hear a faint humming. It sounded for all the world like "Ain't She Sweet."

"Is it going to be clearer?" He looked at the agent.

"Yeh, when he gets into range."

"What if they drive him somewhere?"

"Naw. Then we take it down."

Alec must have looked pensive because Eddie cut in.

"The deal is they give him a location. Oakes, alone or with Spanos, is supposed to be there. Oakes and Spanos come over and sit in his car. Or they talk outside, but he doesn't leave his car and he leaves the motor running."

Alec was sweating inside his jacket. This was a very nervous deal. He should have stopped this thing when he first heard about it.

"Where's the panel truck that's been on his house?"

"It's about four miles behind him," the FBI man said.

The hum from the car transmitter got steadily stronger. Felix must be nearing Fort Hamilton, thought Alec.

"I hope to shit that telephone works." Eddie was nervous. "How these guys found a phone box that ain't been stripped beats the shit outta me."

Everybody was silent.

The hum was really strong and now it was steady. He must have stopped.

Suddenly Felix's voice came through the crackle. It was quite clear.

"So I'm getting out. The booth is a block away; you can hardly see it from here.

"So I'm walking alone. I'm not seeing nobody. I'm walking and I'm not seeing nobody. Can you hear me?

"The booth ain't lit. So I'm waiting."

The waiting was interminable. Alec finished a second container of coffee.

Surveillance said the panel truck exited the Belt at Coney Island.

Twenty minutes went by.

The FBI man looked disappointed. "Let's pull it in. They spotted something."

He had just started to turn to the cars behind him when the ring came. It was very faint over Felix's radio.

"Hello. Where the hell you been?

"Where?

"The sanitation wharf?

"Where?

"Twenty-third and the East River.

"Okay."

Eddie grabbed Alec and they jumped into the customs car.

The FBI were already rolling. Only the cops remained, the lights of the van casting across a little stage of littered cups and cigarette butts.

No sirens, but they flew.

"If he walks back to his car slow, like we told him, we'll have plenty of time." Eddie was still tense. Alec could feel it in the darkened car.

The bureau cars went off the FDR an exit early and they pulled into a parking area of the Peter Cooper apartments.

The sanitation wharf loomed across the road three hundred yards away. Behind it the water of the East River looked like ink. A fuel barge with its running lights twinkling was passing, the two figures in the wheelhouse as clear as if in a lit apartment window.

When the FBI van lumbered in, they kept the back closed and entered through the step door.

The steady hum of the car monitor grew stronger and stronger. Felix's voice cut in. "I'm going off on Twenty-third."

They could see the lights of his car go down the ramp and then make a wide arc as he turned south. Now they were only headlights, so bright they couldn't see him or the windshield. He parked directly in front of the giant rolling doors of the wharf.

It was desolate again. A *Daily News* truck roared south, a cab with a lone passenger came up the river and went up the ramp to the FDR. Nothing.

It was several seconds before they saw the Chrysler LeBaron. It came straight across Twenty-third, but the driver turned the lights off before he made a left, and when it pulled in behind Felix's car it was shadowed from their vision in the glare of the headlights on Felix's car.

"I wish he'd turn those fucking lights off!" the FBI man said to no one in particular. He had binoculars trained on the cars through the van's windshield.

"Somebody got out of the Chrysler. He's walking up to the car." The bureau man was reporting like a track announcer.

The radio static crackled.

"Spanos?" Felix sounded tense.

"Where's —"

The explosion roared, smashing the van back five feet and momentarily blinding all of them.

Pieces of metal like hot shrapnel were falling all along the street and the flames were leaping up along the wharf doors like demons on a stage.

The FBI man screamed. He had a high-pitched voice girlish in fear. "Shiiiiiit."

The men in the van were like gerbils in a cage. Two were trying to get out the door. Eddie was furiously screaming into a microphone for fire equipment and an ambulance. The FBI technician was angrily jiggling the dials of the monitor as though it had betrayed him.

Alec had worn old running shoes and he was streaking, as if in the middle of a marathon, outstripping the men on either side.

"Watch the Chrysler." He thought it was Eddie's voice. "It's on fire."

Felix had been blown out the driver's door. His giant body was engulfed in flames and he looked like a creature from a horror movie.

An FBI man pushed past Alec and fired a small hand extinguisher at the driver's side, but it had too little foam to arrest the blaze. The Chrysler was fully engaged, some chemical in its seat covers roaring green and blue.

Alec ran forward reaching out for the old man. It seemed like Felix was reaching back. Alec knew his own face was burning and his clothes seemed to be on fire. He could smell burning hair. It was his.

The Chrysler's gas tank went. Alec only half heard it.

The *Daily News* head simply splashed "CAR BOMB." They gave it the front page over a picture of smoldering wreckage of the two cars. Their photographer must have gotten there within ten minutes of the blast.

One morning newscaster said Beirut had come to New York. "Channel Seven has learned that one of the victims may have been an Israeli agent."

The *Times* never made the story at all the first day.

On the second day it carried a detailed report under the byline of one of its best reporters. It said Felix Schwartzberg, an executive of a refrigeration firm that had been under federal investigation for several years, had been killed in a car blast. Police and federal officials said that a second man killed in the blast had been tentatively identified as Spanos Canosous, an executive of an international tanker company. The story speculated on organized crime and labor racketeering.

No news report said the explosion had been watched by fifteen federal agents, an assistant U.S. attorney, and the victim's lawyer. There wasn't a word about that. An unnamed source in the *Times* coyly noted the FBI was assisting local authorities.

Alec read the *Times* as Eddie drove him out to Felix's. He could only see out of one eye, which was disconcerting. The bandages covered part of his face, his head, and his other eye. Both hands were bandaged and a portion of his neck was covered by ointment and gauze.

"You shoulda stayed in the hospital," Eddie was grumbling. "She has her family there. You ain't responsible. You didn't make Felix and Jimmy into crooks."

Alec read in silence. He was trying to find a theme in his mind. There was a theme here. The war had been a failure. The war had been his first real job. He had been a platoon leader. But as time went on there was no platoon. There were the dead and the replacements. They had depended on him.

Karen had saved him from the war. She had put his mind together. Got him on a track. But he had failed at that as well. It was funny because as the marriage sank, he knew it was sinking. But he couldn't right it. She said he was a risk taker. "But I am not! Don't you see!" That's what she had screamed.

Now he had failed as a lawyer. The theme was judgment. He didn't have good judgment. He had passion. He had arrogance. But he had no judgment. He should have pled them both. A simple charge. Jail time. They would have bitched and gone to Eglin Field. Sophie would have sat it out on Sanibel Island and come up on visiting days.

No deals, no undercover. Vinny would have continued his political career with a nice win. So Alec would have lost. So what?

The same as with Lee. He should have said no. No, I don't handle missing kids. Go to the police. Go to the FBI. Tell them everything. They can help. But he entangled her, involved her in something he didn't understand, probably never would understand, and all the time her kid was already dead, which was what he should have suspected in the first place.

Eddie was talking again. "We figure that they rigged the bomb when Felix was in the phone booth at Fort Hamilton. That's why the

Feebees didn't see it when they put the plug on his car. It was a straight radio-controlled device. We got pieces of the receiver. Looks like it came out of a hardware store. Industrial magnet. The explosive was industrial dynamite."

"Where's the panel truck?" Alec turned painfully to look at the heavy Irishman.

"Ducked surveillance in Seagate. As impossible as it may seem, the FBI managed to lose a truck on a peninsula that runs into the Atlantic Ocean," Eddie said bitterly.

"You get it, don't you?" He glanced sideways at Alec, taking his eyes from the road.

"Get what?"

"Felix's friends gave him the story when Freezetemp ran into trouble. They said take a hike. He was dead when he came back on them. They canceled him and Spanos. Just like a stamp."

Sophie looked awful. She wore no makeup and her skin had a gray wrinkled texture without it. The roots of her hair showed and her face was puffy from crying. The house was crowded. Alec didn't know who the people were. One was an Hasidic rabbi, another was a man who said he was Felix's cousin.

At first Sophie would not look at him. He told her of his sadness and the shock of Felix's death. He asked her if he could help in any way. He must have talked for five minutes. The room had fallen silent.

She never answered him.

He and Eddie stood by the door. Nobody had to ask them to sit down or enter farther into the house. Eddie was ill at ease and turned to start out.

Her voice startled him, it was so raspy.

"He trusted you. He used to say, 'That is a good boy. A mensch! Too bad he isn't Jewish.' He was sure you knew the right thing. I said 'Felix, this is crazy.' But he said 'Alec knows the right thing.' "

For all time he would remember one thing about Sophie. Sophie had timing. She let it drop right there. No remonstration. No screams. Just the indictment. Just what he had to live with.

The Gallaghers fired him the next week. They got a courthouse lawyer over in Brooklyn who pled Jimmy to one charge, no jail time, and a settlement with the IRS. The government was embarrassed. It didn't want to hear any more about the Freezetemp case.

Alec had an acrimonious meeting with Vinny. Just the two of them, no bullshit.

Vinny started very official.

"We've been reviewing this in financial crimes and we think it has to go on the back burner." He was shuffling papers across the desk. "Without Schwartzberg, we really can't go forward on Oakes. Gallagher can't carry it. It only went to Canosous anyway. The FBI says that Oakes has closed the Forty-first Street office. Moved out lock, stock, and barrel. We presume record destruction. Putting anything together is going to be very hard."

Alec listened in silence. His burns had begun to itch and he was very uncomfortable.

He spoke in a very low voice.

"You know, Vinny, you guys couldn't manage a two-car parade. You take a straight businessman with a minor-league problem who's going to deliver possibly the biggest financial case you've ever had and you so fuck it up he gets killed in the first ten minutes."

Vinny was out of his chair. "Who the hell are you to talk to me that way?" Ethnics scream. Vinny was no preppy.

Alec roared even louder. "I'll tell you who I am. I'm the guy who's going to sit down with the *New York Times* and tell them how the strange car blast over on the East River was a fucked-up fare-thee-well to a U.S. attorney–FBI operation."

"You do and I'll lock you up and take your ticket. . . ." Vinny had come around the desk. "That's grand jury. That's rule six-E. When I'm done with you, you won't be able to write wills in Massapequa."

Alec went silent. Vinny stopped roaring in the sudden quiet.

When Alec spoke next his voice had a dead quality that clearly stunned Vinny.

"When you were staying out of the draft in the seminary, Vinny, I was killing people. I killed men so close up I could smell the fish sauce from their food. I killed them with a gun. I killed them with a knife. I blew them up so there innards dripped down my face. Do you think you're going to scare me? Do you really?"

Vinny looked ashen. "Karen said you were crazy when you came back. She said you were crazy. I didn't believe her."

"You know what? I wasn't smart enough to get out of Vietnam. I'm not as smart as you are. I'm just not smart enough to see why we shouldn't make this case.

"Your people haven't talked to the widow of Dumont, they haven't run the financials out, and they haven't found out why a witness under government protection can get killed like that!" Alec snapped his fingers.

He stood up. "The Oakes case is open. Isn't it, Mr. U.S. attorney? It's not on the back burner."

19

FOR two days he sat in the apartment alone. He put the telephone on secretarial. Shirley was calling incessantly. Lee called twice or three times. Karen called. Moira called. Vinny called twice. Eddie called. When he didn't come down, the desk sent the messages up and slid them under the door.

The pile of messages was like a little white flood slowly spread out into the room from the front door.

The first day he drank until he threw up. He had hardly eaten since Felix died and the raw vodka made his stomach burn. He slept part of the night. The next day he sent out for beer. He made the guy leave it in the hall and pushed a twenty under the door. The guy hooked the change.

Beer was really better. It didn't make him sick.

He wondered if Oakes told his wife he had killed Felix. He could see them at breakfast. Reading the *New York Times*.

"Took care of that pesky Yid the other night."

He could see the woman smiling. "Oh! Good, dear. They're such a bother."

But it didn't ring true. He was having trouble visualizing Trumbull Oakes as evil. Smiley, Julio were evil. But Oakes was remote. Distant.

Alec realized that he couldn't conceive of the rich being evil. They were bumbling, pantywaists, effete. It was a bias, a stupid bias. They could be evil like anybody else.

Death surrounded Oakes. Dumont died in an auto wreck. Felix's car was blown up. Spanos was dead. He had underestimated Oakes. Richard Nixon got impeached because he was unpleasant. Oakes was going to get away with it because nobody could visualize him as evil. It was that simple.

By nightfall Alec couldn't tell what thoughts had been dreams and which had come to him awake. But he had made a decision. There was no equivocation now. He had decided.

Ochoa was Oakes's muscle. The Colombians were the bad guys Spanos was talking about. When Oakes ran into trouble, the Colombians took out the garbage for him. They did the heavy lifting. He had misjudged Oakes because he hadn't put Oakes and the Colombians together in his mind fast enough.

He went to the office early the next day. He stopped at a clinic on Thirty-fourth and had his bandages changed. The doctor suggested the bandages on his face be removed so the burns would heal more quickly. He looked in the mirror when the doctor left. It was not pretty. His eyebrows were gone and the first two or three inches of his hair had been singed back. His face, though free of bandages, was covered with ointment over puffy blisters.

Shirley confirmed his diagnosis. She gasped as he entered. "Oh my God! Look at your face."

Alec gave her no explanation.

"See if you can get me that guy Jeremy Vale in Palm Springs. Try to get a home number."

"It's six A.M. in California." Shirley looked perplexed.

"I know."

It took her nearly an hour to track down Vale. He was at the investment office.

"Hey there." Vale sounded cheery. "I thought this matter was closed."

"You thought wrong.

"Tell Mr. Ochoa to get in touch with me, or the papers go to the U.S. attorney at the close of business today. Tell him not to get confused. If anything happens to me, the papers get there even faster."

There was silence.

"Look, Mr. Anton." Vale did not sound so cheery. "That's not the right way to go at this. You can't operate with these guys like that."

"Mr. Vale. There are three murders in New York connected to this deal. Don't stall me."

Vale said one more word.

"Okay."

Alec had no more than hung up when Eddie Doherty called.

"Jesus, I've been trying to get you for two days. Vinny is pissed. He said government cooperation with you is off. A secretary said he pulled your personnel file. He told her he was looking to see if you had psychiatric treatment."

Eddie waited, as though Alec were supposed to faint.

"The only thing he's going to find is I was underpaid. Is the Oakes matter still alive?"

"Barely. The bureau's running a pretty thorough investigation of the bombing, though. They got a description of the two guys who rented the Ryder truck."

Alec was momentarily confused. "Which truck?"

"The one that was watching Felix's house."

"Yeah. So?"

"So it's two spics." Eddie started rattling off a description. He was only halfway into it when Alec recognized Smiley and Julio.

"Tell the FBI to talk to a cop in Manhattan South named De-Nunzio. He's made these two guys for killing that kid I was looking for. The Hastings boy. If they don't believe DeNunzio, take a look at the description I gave the police of two guys that mugged me in July."

"I can't do that. I'm not supposed to talk to you."

"Tell them I called you and blurted it out," Alec said impatiently.

"Okay, counselor. But I smell withholding evidence. Let me say only one thing: Vinny is seriously mad. If he got embarrassed in the papers it would end some political hopes he has. Do I make myself clear?"

"Fuck him." Alec hung up.

He walked down to the records room. Secretaries gasped as he went buy. He realized that his face was now flaming. Fresh blood must have rushed in behind the blisters, bloating them and giving him a crimson and white mask.

It hurt like hell and his arms itched.

"Let me have the Freezetemp file wagon."

The clerk looked perplexed. "We're boxing it up. One of the

clients' new lawyers called and said they wanted the files. Mr. Wilton said it was okay."

Alec went berserk. They could hear him screaming all over the firm.

Old Pogue ran in gasping for breath. He was not used to running.

Alec had just told the clerk he would "personally, fucking, cut his balls off" if that file wasn't restored. The clerk looked like he was going to cry.

Pogue reassured Alec and took him back to his office.

"I'm sure there was a mistake. I'm sure this can be done after you're finished."

Alec sat sulking in his office. He couldn't even drink coffee because the blisters around his lips hurt.

Moira called interoffice. "I saw you in the hall. Oh, your poor face. Let me take you home. Alec, you ought to be in bed."

"Leave me alone!" He hung up.

He pored over the files as though a search would develop something. Shirley was holding back all calls except one. "I don't know who it will be, but it will be for me and you won't recognize it."

It didn't come until nearly five.

"Would it be a Mr. Ochoa long-distance from Canada?" Shirley said it timidly. This was not the Alec she had known for five years, and the new Alec frightened her.

"Absolutely!"

"Mr. Anton?"

"Yes."

"My name is Philip Ochoa. You wanted to see me?"

"Yes."

It was a young voice, very self-assured, very North American. A young businessman, surprised at Mr. Anton's interest.

"Can you come to Canada?"

"When?"

"Right now if you like. It is late today. Possibly lunch tomorrow?"

"Where?"

"My family has an apartment in Montreal. When you get to Montreal call 239-5571. All right?"

"Okay."

He and Shirley took the materials out of the safe and he spent the next two hours preparing a detailed memorandum of everything he knew about the drug smuggling, Noah's death, Vale, Mountainview, and Trumbull Oakes. They had asked the firm's notary to stay and notarize the affidavit.

Shirley was anxious to leave. Her kids were with her sister. Dinner was late. He pressed her to stay, carefully going through the instructions. "If anything happens to me. Accident. Disappearance. Anything. Get this packet to the U.S. attorney's office. Call Eddie Doherty to help you. Don't give it to anyone else. No one. Not even a partner. Okay?"

She nodded. Alec could see she was scared.

Alec took a second copy of everything, the memorandum, the Mountainview papers, and sent them, Federal Express, to Lee. Shirley had finally gone. He typed a note for the Federal Express package.

I couldn't talk to you after Felix. I just couldn't. I have done everything wrong. I'm a lawyer. I know what I can and cannot do in that realm. A lawyer is a third party. His judgment is detached. When he mixes it with love or ego it doesn't work. I do love you. But people who relied on me are dead. Now I must act. I only hope you can bear the consequences. If anything should happen to me, send this material to the U.S. attorney for the Southern District of New York.

He signed it "Alec." His arms now hurt so badly he could hardly hold the pen.

There was one sleeper left on the Montrealer. It left Penn Station at eleven. He barely made it. He had a bourbon with milk and sugar in the club car. The train was packed with well-dressed old people on a fall foliage special. They were playing the piano and singing college songs. One look at Alec and they stopped singing. He went back to the Pullman. He was asleep by New Haven, a heavy sleep of near exhaustion. He had chosen a train so he could take the .45. It made a hard lump against his waist.

When he awoke, Canadian immigration and customs were coming through. It must be Rouses Point, he thought. He put the pistol in the washroom up with the water tank and filled out the customs form. He marked no to the question of whether he was bringing firearms or explosives into Canada.

He didn't know why he had brought the gun. He didn't know what he'd do with it. Maybe it was a gesture. Maybe a gun suited rage. He had rage, all right.

He took a cab from the station to the Ritz-Carlton and got a room. Some of the blisters had burst and he needed new bandages and ointment. The hotel sent him to a doctor two blocks away. His face looked a little better than the day before, but the pain in his hands had not subsided.

It was cold in Montreal, a sharp wind was cutting in off the St. Lawrence, and it seemed to awaken Alec. He ate the first real meal he'd had in a week: eggs, toast, and potatoes. He didn't call the Ochoa number; instead he lay down in the hotel room and dozed, letting the meal settle. Even after the sleep on the train he felt sluggish and exhausted.

The phone startled him.

"Mr. Anton. Welcome to Montreal."

Young Ochoa's voice sounded close by.

"Would lunch around one be okay?"

Alec groggily agreed.

"I'll send a car."

The apartment was a penthouse in one of those new buildings overlooking Boucherville. It had been done in all-white leather and glass with a deep white rug and a set of moderns that were tasteful and well hung.

The artists painted in the Spanish school, slashing reds and greens, rich dark colors that gave the room life.

Ochoa was handsome in the way of male models. It was a handsomeness to such perfection that it did not at first seem real. His skin was the color of teak, smooth and flawless, his face lean with an angular Castillian appearance rather than the thick features of Andean Indians. He had black eyes, wavy glistening black hair drawn back in a tiny bun, and a set of teeth from a movie screen. He wore a loose-knit sailor sweater and pressed blue jeans set off with boots made of what had been a large snake.

He had not risen to greet Alec, forcing the lawyer to stand before him, like a supplicant.

"My chauffeur said our car monitor shows you are carrying a dense mass of metal at your waist." He was smiling, but his voice was not solicitous. "I hope it is a belt buckle."

Alec did not smile. He had found in the morning that smiling hurt. The skin over the dried blisters had contracted. It felt like his face was covered by Saran Wrap.

"It's an old military Colt. I have an unusual fear of muggers."

"The Canadian police are very strict about guns. I hope you don't get arrested."

"That would be the least of my problems."

Ochoa was seated on an enormous circular sofa before the north bank of windows. Behind his head, the vista seemed to go on for miles. Alec could see the St. Lawrence winding through brown and multicolored country. In the distance was the skyline of another city. Three Rivers or Quebec.

Ochoa gestured toward a chair facing the windows.

A waiter in a white coat had silently entered from behind Alec and looked expectantly at Ochoa. The young Colombian examined Alec's face with evident distaste.

"Are you in pain?"

Alec shook his head.

"Maybe a glass of wine? My father owns a vineyard near Medellín. Someday he is hoping to export it."

Alec nodded.

The waiter disappeared and reappeared without a sound.

The wine was a Riesling. It was good. Not great, but good.

"So you threatened Vale. You said you will get us for murder." Ochoa was leaning back, his arms thrown across the pillows of the couch.

"This is the second time you've scared that buffoon. You must be a very scary man."

"Why did you kill Noah Hastings?"

Ochoa came to a sitting position. It was such a startling move that someone started in the room behind Alec. He guessed it was the chauffeur or the bodyguard.

"Vale said you were stupid." The young man's face was filled with anger and the good-host front was slipping fast, but he seemed to be struggling to hold it.

"I didn't kill Noah. Hombre. You talk like a crazy cowboy."

Ochoa was looking fiercely into Alec's eyes. He spat out his words like a series of orders.

"The only reason you're not lying in a ditch in Palm Springs is Noah. He was my best friend. Maybe you know something. Maybe you don't. You're alive until I find out."

Instead of fear, Alec found his rage mounting. This fucking overdressed parrot was threatening him. His hands were shaking in anger. He wondered if Ochoa would misread the movement as fear.

"Then we are going to have an understanding, aren't we? I want to know who killed Noah. I want to know who left the carnation pinned nicely to his sweater. Was that a family carnation?"

Ochoa leapt up. It was clearly to get the dominance of height. The person behind Alec moved abruptly. Alec forced himself not to turn around.

"You want to give me shit? I give you shit." The private schools and colleges were slipping away fast. Even a Spanish accent was beginning to appear. "Maybe we whack you and forget you." He said something in Spanish and Alec felt a gun muzzle at the base of his neck.

He looked up at the youth. Ochoa was moving back and forth on his toes in a barely perceptible way, as though he were a snake quivering before striking. His eyes lent to the image; they glistened darkly and without expression, like a snake's.

But he knew Ochoa and his bodyguard had already made a mistake. They had let an armed man into their midst.

"You didn't let me come all the way to your apartment in Montreal to whack me. Like you say, I could be in a ditch in Palm Springs."

Just as suddenly as he had stood up, Ochoa sat down. It was as though someone unseen was speaking to him.

"I don't know who assassinated Noah. My family doesn't know. It is important to protecting ourselves, and our product, that we find out.

"At first we thought it might be another cartel. Lehder or Gecha.

"There is a war in my country. In Medellín or Calo people get killed every day. At first we thought it was part of that. But nobody has claimed it."

He was staring into the distance as though he was trying to work through a problem.

"Why would people in Colombia want to kill an American college student on his graduation trip?" Alec's voice was caustic.

"He worked for my father. In the family business."

"The business?"

"Flowers."

"Who else could have killed him?"

"Maybe the blacks. Where he was killed is run by the blacks. We supply them. We collect. But the blacks and the Puerto Ricans run it."

Ochoa paused for a minute. He seemed to be trying to decide how much information to render.

"Can the gun be moved?" Alec had been sitting motionless since the pistol was pressed against his neck. He could now feel the body heat of the man behind him.

"We leave it for a while."

Ochoa went on, looking neither at Alec nor the bodyguard.

"Noah didn't have to be on the East Side. That used to be a stop for him, but not for a long time. We don't know why he was there. At first, we spread a lot of money around and a lot of juice to find out. We got shit!"

Alec shivered. He realized the glass walls of the penthouse weren't very good insulation against the cold, and a low overcast now filled the sky.

"You mean to tell me that you can't find out who did a murder in a drug market?"

Ochoa was sitting back now.

"Yes."

"What do you, Philip Ochoa, think?"

"I don't know."

"Maybe personal? A girl?" Alec groped for a word to describe a sexual relation. He didn't even know why he was trying to be delicate.

"I don't think so, and I think I knew everything about him."

"Does the carnation mean anything?" Alec asked.

"He loved them, yes, dark red ones. Even when they weren't ours he bought them. Anywhere. He loved them."

The bodyguard moved his position slightly and the pistol shifted to behind Alec's left ear.

"*Bastardo!*"

The pistol was removed.

"Put your gun on the table. It will make Ricardo happy."

Alec removed the Colt and put it on the table. He still didn't even know why he had brought it.

Lunch was served in a dining room that faced south. Large crystal bowls of carnations stood around the room. From the table Alec could see the planes lifting off from Dorval, circling as they made altitude, and the interchanging waterways that stretched from the city toward the U.S. border.

The affair was very European. A first course of shrimp done in what Alec guessed was a garlic and white-wine sauce.

They walked into the room as two businessmen, as though the anger and violence of the past minutes had not existed.

Ochoa had started talking about Noah.

"When I got to Mountainview Noah was already there. He was so different from the others. He was cool, you know? Cool.

"He used to say" — he laughed to himself at the memory — "that his father hated him and his mother had abandoned him. Then he would laugh. 'Parents do the best they can,' he'd say. 'Being a daddy and mommy is a thankless task.' "

"Did you room together the whole time?"

"Yes, except when I went to my servant's house to sleep.

"At first, you know, he had terrible dreams sometimes about his father. Awful dreams. He would cry and scream and wake me up.

"In the morning, he would not remember a thing."

"So he became your lieutenant in the drug business? Your helper?" Alec didn't feel like fencing. He was tired of fencing with people.

"He became my friend." Ochoa did not seem to take offense.

"Where does Trumbull Oakes come in?"

The waiter was taking Alec's plate and bringing new wineglasses for a red that was open and breathing on the sideboard. The white wine with the shrimp had also been from California, a Chardonnay. It was fitting. This was a California story.

Ochoa's face had a look of distaste.

"He has been associated with Father for some years."

"How do you mean associated?" The Saran Wrap was tightening on Alec's face.

"Are you investigating our business?" Ochoa snapped defensively.

"I don't give a shit about your business. I wish I never heard about your business. But three people are dead. An old Jew who made it through the death camps and a twenty-two-year-old kid. As far as I can tell they should be alive."

The tone of the voices brought Ricardo into the room. Even if he didn't have English, he didn't like the sound.

Ochoa waved him away.

"Who else is dead?"

Ochoa seemed genuinely confused.

Alec told him of Felix and Spanos.

"You are trying to tell me you don't know?"

"Those names I don't know." Ochoa took another sip of wine and studied the glass. "Is that what happened to your face?"

Alec nodded.

"I want to find out who killed Noah and the old man. Right now you and your family are high on the list."

"That is ridiculous. All the time you read in the American press about cocaine wars. Colombians kill this person, Colombians kill that person. Do you know what?"

Alec shook his head.

"That's business. The *Wall Street Journal* would say we are an industry that is shaking itself out. Small, poorly financed operations are disappearing. Larger well-organized, well-capitalized firms are coming to dominate the industry. That is what the *Wall Street Journal* would say." Ochoa leaned back. He was not smiling. "We don't waste killings."

The waiter brought in tiny fillets of beef; they had been done in a French style with a little crust of dough, lightly flavored with onion. There were thin, crisp beans crystallized in a light salt and a potato-and-onion dish.

Ochoa ate hungrily, gesturing for Alec to do the same. "This man cooks for my father in Madrid. He is here to see his aunt. I am so lucky."

The food was good. The wine was good as well.

Ochoa drank the wine in tiny sips.

"We don't know why Noah died." He stopped midphrase; for just a second he looked stricken, then it passed. "But we are working on it. It is a peculiar problem.

"I let you come here because you may be of use to us. Is that possible?"

"Everything is possible." The wine was working on Alec, softening his thought line. "What would I do?"

"You would help us" — he paused — "get information. You must have sources who can tell you about the investigation of Noah."

Ochoa left Alec no time to interrupt.

"How much do you know about our business?"

"I used to prosecute smuggling cases for the government. I know a little."

"Well you know then the problem is the money. This is a business that creates an enormous amount of cash in small bills. To render the cash useful it has to be removed from the country or converted into legal assets."

Ochoa seemed to enjoy the notion that he distilled the cocaine trade to business terms.

"Noah had a sort of natural sense for how to do this. When we were still at Mountainview he got this brilliant idea. The kids were rich and their parents were always sending them money, but few of them had Social Security numbers or tax identification numbers. The banks didn't care because mostly the amounts were low.

"So Noah suggested that we take names of kids at school and open bank accounts for them here in Canada. My father got very excited. He liked Noah a lot. That was the year he took Noah to Colombia for vacation." Ochoa seemed pleased by the memory.

"In the end we opened twenty-one accounts. Associates of my father acted as the guardians for these minors' accounts. The cash went into the Canadian accounts and in turn those accounts bought assets in the U.S."

"Was this legal?"

"These were legal assets held by the Canadian bank accounts of minor children. Later they sold the assets to entities that represent my family. Of course the sales were fictitious; no money passed hands."

Ochoa settled back and sipped his wine. He seemed to want to allow the beauty of this creation to sink in before he went on.

"What happened when the kids whose names you were using grew up?"

"Aren't you smart! No wonder you're a good lawyer." Ochoa seemed genuinely pleased at the question.

"Of course the little tykes grew up and got Social Security numbers!

"So we decided to create our own minor children so to speak. We found some twenty-six, now it is thirty-two, real persons who had died in the U.S. as infants but who would remain minors for at least ten years."

"Like John Grant?"

Ochoa seemed surprised. "You know that name?"

"Didn't Noah use it?"

"Yes, but how did you know?"

"He left his passport with his mother."

"Oh. Oh." Ochoa appeared to file that information.

"Why did you send men to search his mother's house? For the passport?"

"I sent no one."

"You sent no one to rough me up searching for computer disks?"

"Never. I know nothing of computer disks."

"Do you have a man working for you named Julio, a big man, an American of Puerto Rican descent?"

"We have no Puerto Ricans. None. That is how we stay in business. This is a family business. A Colombian business. Noah was the only person in our business who was not of Colombia. He had become like my father's son."

"What about San Andres Y Providencia?"

Ochoa gave a delighted laugh.

"You know that too. Vale said you knew a lot. The good fathers. They are such bandits.

"When we first started, back at Mountainview, we were encountering persistent questions at the moment of deposit. Whether we used mail or personal visits, banking officers would ask about the amounts. In one case the banking officer is now working for us, but that course could not always be followed.

"Noah and I thought and thought. For days. What could explain a lot of cash, a lot of small American bills, that would provoke no questions?

"Noah remembered that his aunt always had bought the Irish Sweepstakes and each year she sent cash in an envelope to Ireland even though everyone said her money would be lost.

"We decided right there" — Ochoa pointed to the living room — "to have a sweepstakes of our own."

"So what do you do now?"

"We deposit the large amounts of cash in an account for the San Andres hospital. From there it is transferred to our thirty-two asset holders or abroad."

"Is there a hospital?"

"Oh yes! Oh yes there is! It is on the most godforsaken little island not far from Nicaragua."

"Don't they have to know about this?"

"The priests who ran that hospital are living better than they ever did in their lives. They fly to Madrid, they spend weeks on my father's farm. They go to Rome. Once a year one of them comes here and validates the charity papers for the Canadian authorities. He sometimes serves mass right out there."

Ochoa pointed to a westerly portion of Montreal.

"Where does Oakes come into this?"

"I'm coming to that," Ochoa said impatiently.

"When we went to college, Noah became the collection point for the Northeast money. Before, Colombians brought it across. That was dangerous. The Canadians were suspicious. But an American. No way.

"Noah did a little business — a little flower business."

Alec could see the truck in his mind's eye.

"We shifted one planeload of flowers from Bogotá to Dorval instead of everything transshipping from Miami. Noah picked up the flowers here and took them to the U.S.

"At first we had to throw them away, but later he actually sold them."

"They were just a cover?" Alec sipped the wine.

"Yes, a deception.

"Noah went across once or twice a week. Entering the U.S. he carried only flowers. Customs searched each time. Coming back Noah carried the money. He was never searched coming into Canada. Never."

Ochoa was gazing toward the U.S. as though he could see the little truck coming over the border.

"But he was getting scared. He didn't want to do it. He wanted to do something else. He was sure one day he'd go down.

"My father finally said okay, he would help him get a job. Noah wanted a legitimate job. He wanted to work on Wall Street. Oakes handled our investments. Investments for the Canadian accounts and other investments. It seemed natural."

"You mean you invest the money right back in the U.S.?"

"Sure. Where else?"

"Wouldn't it be easier in Panama or the Bahamas or somewhere?"

"Easier. But they take a share. Men like Noriega. They take a big piece. They know too much about your business."

"What was Noah going to do with Oakes?"

"He would become a sort of account executive for our accounts. He was liaison for me."

"You said Noah's death left you a peculiar problem. Why?"

"Noah and I suspected Oakes was stealing from us. We did not know how. We didn't dare ask Oakes for a detailed accounting. My father had rejected these suspicions. It is impossible for him to believe he was wrong. You see?"

"No." Alec was having trouble following.

"Oakes didn't want Noah, but my father made him hire Noah. He kept resisting the idea of bringing Noah in. Even when my father agreed that his first year's earnings would be deducted from our dividends.

"As soon as Noah began going to the firm he found funny things."

"Like what things?"

"He said he wasn't sure. He thought maybe Oakes was accelerat-

ing our trades. Eating up money on commissions. The week before
he graduated he spent the whole time in New York. He called me
from campus. He said there was something wrong. He thought
some of the assets might be double leveraged."

"Double leveraged?"

"Put up for loans more than once. Used as collateral for Oakes or
someone else. After graduation he wanted to go to Europe and check
it out."

"What happened?"

"That was the last time I heard from him."

"Did you ask Oakes?" Alec pressed.

"My father did."

"What did he say?"

"Oakes was very upset. He said he too was mystified. Noah had
just walked out. Oakes flew down to Bogotá in July. He brought all
his records. He persuaded my father our investments were intact.
He said Noah told him he wanted to start his own investment
company and take over the Ochoa business."

"Was that true?"

"Down the line. We talked about that."

"With your father?"

"No, no. Noah wanted to learn the business first."

"What's at stake?"

"I would guess nearly a billion dollars. Maybe more."

Alec whistled softly. Commissions on that had to be half of
Oakes's total earnings. Then along comes a twenty-two-year-old kid
just out of college who's going to eat his lunch. A twenty-two-year-
old who's strangled to death.

"You said only Colombians were in your business. What about
Oakes?"

"Oakes is not in the business. He only knows that we have a lot of
money and that it is not reported to Colombian or American revenue
services. That is how he could steal from us, because he knows we
cannot make an audit."

"Why was Oakes able to explain away Noah's questions?" Alec
sensed he was not hearing the full story.

"My father feels in his debt. In the beginning Wall Street houses
were not eager to handle accounts like ours. Oakes helped my father

when he was in government. He even arranged a visit for our president to see Ford."

"So Oakes may have killed Noah?" Alec looked hard at Ochoa.

"Maybe, maybe not. But I must know who and how." To Alec's ear the "must" sounded personal.

"What am I supposed to do?" Alec was sipping coffee. It was delicious. An espresso.

"I want to hire you as my lawyer. I want to retain you. My father has given me permission."

"I don't want to be your lawyer."

"You don't approve of cocaine?"

"I never thought of it one way or another."

Ochoa laughed.

"Be our lawyer for other interests."

"What services would you want me to perform?"

"Information. That's all. We have lawyers for criminal matters."

"Why should I want to work for you, beyond money?"

"Trumbull Oakes. We both believe he killed somebody. You believe he killed Felix and I suspect he killed Noah."

"You are in a violent business. Can't you get to the truth more easily?"

"I can do nothing so long as my father has regard for Oakes. Nothing."

"How will I be retained?"

"By POOR Limited of Canada. All on paper. Fees by check on the Bank of Nova Scotia. No connection to cocaine. Okay?"

Ochoa seemed to be almost pleading now. Hiring Alec seemed important to him. It was the first time he had mentioned obtaining his father's permission.

"Okay. So I'm your lawyer."

"We need to know what you learn about Oakes on a daily basis. What the police are doing."

"Your father really doesn't know you've hired me. Does he?"

"No."

"What if I tell you I've changed my mind and I don't want this case?"

"I will have you killed." The wine was making Ochoa slur a little.

20

IT was nearly midnight when he got back to the apartment. He was stiff and his face and arms hurt. He had trouble opening the door. Suddenly it gave way. His heart froze. She was standing just inside and caught him as he stumbled. They fell into each other's arms.

"How did you get in?"

"The clerk let me in. He remembered me from the night you were attacked. Are you all right?" Her voice was filled with fear and concern.

"I brought the file. If I hadn't heard by tomorrow I was going to take it to the U.S. attorney." She pointed to a manila folder on the table.

"Close. I should have called." Alec's eyes were trying to get accustomed to the dim light. "I was going to call you tomorrow. But I'm not feeling too well. Where are the girls?"

"With Eileen."

Suddenly she saw his face full for the first time in the lamplight.

"Oh my Lord God!" She drew both hands over her mouth. Then, very softly, she took one hand and let the fingertips brush a blistered cheek.

"Can you get me a drink?" He sank into a chair.

She poured two vodkas and started to get ice from the kitchen. "No ice."

"Tell me about the explosion." She sat on the chair arm and the warmth of her thigh came through his jacket sleeve like a comforter.

He told her. He realized well into the tale that he was crying.

"Felix was reaching for me."

"I don't think so, Alec," she said very softly. "He was just trying to get out." She had begun to pet him very softly, like a dog or a child.

Gently she was undressing him. She helped him into the bed.

She stood over him holding a glass of juice. The sun was streaming in the windows, catching little particles of dust like silver powder in the air.

"Well, I'll tell you one thing." She was smiling, the first smile he had seen since Noah died. "You're not just another pretty face."

He had slept without dreams, for what seemed like days, and for the first time since the explosion he felt rested.

Lee took a chair across from the bed.

"Where have you been? I was so worried. Your secretary was worried too. She said you received a call from Canada and left. I supposed it had to do with Noah."

"You're partly right. I met Philip. That's where I've been. Montreal. I was sure he or his people killed Felix, maybe Noah too. Now I don't know. He says he didn't. I think he was telling the truth, part of it anyway."

The smile had left her face.

"Do you want to know more?"

She nodded.

He told her of the meeting with Ochoa, Philip's business with Noah, and his suspicions of Oakes. It took an hour in the telling. He did not tell her he had agreed to represent Ochoa. He did not know why he didn't.

"Something still nags me. Why did Julio and Smiley give up?" Alec wondered aloud. "They were still searching for something well after Noah died, and then they stopped."

"Maybe they found the disks or whatever they were looking for?" Lee said, offering the obvious.

"Maybe." Alec didn't sound convinced. "One thing we know. Even with Noah's death, Oakes wasn't sure he was safe. He still didn't have the disks or something that was dangerous to him because Julio and Smiley kept at it."

"Maybe Oakes just became convinced that we didn't have what they were looking for," Lee said.

"Ochoa claims Oakes went to Bogotá in July to explain himself.

"That was his deadline. He had to have his act in order to talk to this most dangerous client. If Julio and Smiley were working for Oakes that would explain why they were under pressure. For Oakes to face the Ochoas in Bogotá, he would have to be fairly sure he wouldn't be contradicted. That was why Julio and Smiley took the risk of rousting me in the garage. That was the deadline."

"But you said Ochoa told you Oakes got through with the meeting and persuaded his father that he has not finagled the accounts." Lee now looked as perplexed as Alec.

"If Julio and Smiley killed Noah for Oakes then Oakes knew in the first week of June that Noah wasn't going to upset his apple-cart," she said. "But their breaking into my house weeks later, their calling you Mr. Grant . . . as though they didn't know who Mr. Grant was . . ."

"Something is disconnecting here and I don't know what it is," Alec agreed.

"What is so strange here is Oakes." Lee's face wore a quizzical look. "I've seen him on T.V. From what you tell me it's hard to believe he's involved in this at all."

"Maybe Oakes was into cocaine?"

Alec had moved around to face the sun of Park Avenue. His face hurt.

"I can't believe that." Lee seemed doubtful. "I can understand better what happened to Noah. Young people experiment. Life is experimenting. Touching to find hot stoves. But I don't see why somebody as wealthy and accomplished as Oakes would use cocaine. I don't see it."

Alec shuddered. His mind was filled with the vision of Moira lying nude on the floor. In a painful flash he could see the whole evening.

"I don't know." He didn't look at Lee as he said it. "Maybe it did something for him."

It had done something for Alec. He had wanted Moira and cocaine had provided her. Maybe Oakes wanted something, something that money and clubs and country houses didn't provide.

"What are you going to do?" Lee was walking around the room now, roaming, touching furniture, restless.

"I am going to find out who killed Noah and Felix."

"To what end?"

"Justice. Law. Fairness. Sanity. Completeness. God, I don't know." His voice had begun to rise. "You really shouldn't be able to have people killed anytime you want. You shouldn't be able to just snuff them out."

"Why not let it rest?" She was very calm, very serious. "The authorities will deal with this. Restore yourself. Leave this alone."

"Don't you care about Noah?"

For the first time her voice rose. "The point is I do. If we leave him alone, he will be a boy who died too young. It will be like an auto accident or a fall. If it goes on, Noah's life takes on no new meaning. Less. All it will do is make it worse. I already know more than I wanted to. He is dead. Let my little boy rest." Her face had begun to twist with grief.

"I can't do that. I can't. It's not Noah alone. It's Felix. He trusted me. I misjudged the entire affair. I misjudged Oakes. Until the moment that bomb went off I would not believe we were dealing with dangerous people. I thought it was all talk. These were men in the money-laundering business!"

He softened his tone, but it was determined.

Lee stood up very slowly. She picked up her purse and her jacket. "Alec, you are doing this for yourself. Not for Felix. Not for Noah. Not for me. Lord knows, not for the law. You are doing this out of arrogance." She sounded tired and resigned.

Women always address you by name when they're serious. He knew this was serious. Lee looked very sad as she left. He struggled to get up, to go after her, but he was too weak. The file she would have taken to the U.S. attorney lay on the desk.

At the Tuesday partners meeting everyone was solicitous. Old Pogue said it wasn't public knowledge, but Alec had been burned trying to save the life of Felix Schwartzberg, and that it was a tragedy the case had turned out that way.

The assembled partners had all been studying Alec's burns as surreptitiously as possible. The facial skin had begun to peel and some of the blisters were oozing liquid. It was not a pretty sight. They seemed glad to turn away.

As the meeting got under way, Alec had the distinct feeling of apartness. It was as though there was a private joke and he didn't know the punch line. He had never been one of them, never close, but something more had changed. He could feel it in the room.

One lawyer gave a long detailed analysis of a case Alec worked that was coming to trial. One thing Alec noticed. He never turned to Alec once.

When new business was discussed, Alec reported dutifully that he had been retained by a Canadian export firm, POOR Ltd., to suggest ways to ease U.S. laws and regulations regarding importation of flowers and plants and that a $100,000 retainer had been placed on account at the Bank of Nova Scotia.

Brows furrowed at several seats, and Pogue asked Alec to send him a memorandum on POOR and its business interests.

Next Wilton started to speak. "I have been in touch with Trumbull Oakes over the past few days." He was looking right at Alec. "And under the circumstances he is being quite magnanimous. In fact, he had learned that clients of our firm had set out to wrongfully accuse him, but he said he realized Trowbridge only did what it must as a responsible law firm.

"As some of you may know he has been selected to handle a municipal bond issue for Raleigh, North Carolina. If you look at your memoranda for April you'll see I mentioned we should be trying to get involved in that."

No wonder Wilton's concern for Oakes. It wasn't all family, breeding, and long thin fingers. Oakes had the key to the Raleigh bonds. Alec smiled inwardly. Mr. Wilton's motives were not so different after all.

"Raleigh is a three-billion-dollar issue for the modernization of the airport and the adjoining municipal services center. Two of our clients, Indemnities and Varnum, are bonds and construction insurers and Trum has agreed to bring us in as the principal law firm."

Wilton was managing to keep what could have been a rather pompous address in the tone of reasonable conversation at the dinner table.

"I hope you can approve this. To my knowledge it no longer conflicts with any case we have. Now it is clear the charges against Oakes were trumped up and unfounded, he hopes we can do more business together."

Alec was on his feet so fast his coffee cup spilled and began to run across the treasured conference table in tiny rivulets.

He was shaking with fury. "Somebody took the trouble to fry a fat old man down on the East River after he made those charges against Oakes. If they were unfounded why isn't Felix sitting in my office right now? There is a federal investigation of Oakes. Why don't we at least wait until the ashes cool before we sign on as Oakes's lawyers?"

Few of the partners seemed to be listening to Alec. They were all out with handkerchiefs and napkins trying to stem the flow of the coffee. Wilton was the only one who remained transfixed. He looked like a bridge player who has the trump.

"I think Alec is misinformed. Oakes tells me that his counsel in the Freezetemp matter obtained a letter from the U.S. attorney saying that Oakes is not a target of a federal grand jury. I have copies of it here." Wilton began passing the letter around the table.

Alec sat down. Vinny was a smooth son of a bitch. The letter wasn't worth shit. It didn't mean the matter was closed. In the criminal business it was a nuance; the grand jury could be looking at Oakes's records right now. But it was a nice cheap way for Vinny to remain politic. All those Republican fund-raisers had paid off.

Pogue, one of those men who easily bore the description "kindly," did not look that way. "Alec, have you anything else?"

Alec shook his head. He set about drying his notes and legal pad. The coffee had run off the table onto his trousers.

The partners voted unanimously to accept the Raleigh matter. Alec abstained.

Over the following week he reorganized the Freezetemp records on matters involving Oakes. He made complete copies and turned the originals over to a Nassau lawyer who was representing Mrs. Schwartzberg and Freezetemp.

He had asked for the aid of an associate, but got a note back from Pogue indicating they were all deeply involved in other cases and suggesting paralegals might help.

Shirley, a barometer of the secretaries' lunchroom, seemed to grow more and more tense. One night she asked to see Alec.

"Are you leaving?"

"Not to my knowledge. Why?"

"Everyone says you are."

"Who is everyone?"

"Oh, you know, the secretaries."

"That's just gossip. Take it easy." Alec put his hand on her arm; he had bristled when she first walked in, but he realized she really cared about him. She was in the minority.

"Do you want to move to another partner? Is that it?"

"Oh no!"

"I wouldn't be hurt. You've been a terrific help to me. I want what's best for you."

"No, I'll stay."

The following day Carl Michael, another lawyer, came in. "I just want to be sure you really . . . want to take on the Monarch trial with me . . . with your face and everything. . . ." Alec assured him he did. Michael seemed like he was going to say something else, but left in silence.

On Friday the FBI came to interview Alec about the car bombing. Their questions made it sound as though Felix's death was an unpremeditated act of violence and Alec a passerby. At least they had followed up with DeNunzio. Alec told them about Noah Hastings's death and Julio and Smiley.

The taller of the agents handed Alec a photo. It was a surveillance picture, gray and grainy. Julio was in the driver's seat of the panel truck. He was picking his nose. Smiley was there too, but he was harder to recognize; a shadow blocked that side of the cab.

"That's Julio, the same man I picked out of the mug book."

Alec traced the story of Mr. Grant. He included the passport. The agents perked up; the tall one sat forward. "Do you have the passport?"

Alec got it from the file and gave it to him.

"Why didn't you mention this earlier?"

"I saw no significance to it. Noah was dead."

He did not mention the Mountainview papers, Jeremy Vale, or Ochoa. For all he knew they were the only reason he was still alive.

"Do you think you'll be able to find these two men?" Alec gestured toward the picture.

The tall agent looked dubious. "They're long gone. We'll pick them up in the end, but it will be for something else, somewhere else.

"By the way, we would like to talk to Mrs. Hastings." The tall agent was folding his clipboard writing folder.

Alec looked sorrowful. "She is still very upset about her son's death. I don't think she can tell you more than I did."

"Will you ask her?"

"Certainly."

They left.

It occurred to Alec they might need help. He called DeNunzio and got the full names and descriptions of Julio and Smiley.

"It's for my final report to Mrs. Hastings."

DeNunzio sounded no more hopeful of finding the suspects than he had the day Alec identified them.

"The D.A. has the case."

Alec commiserated with him. "What do lawyers know?"

DeNunzio chuckled. It was not a friendly chuckle.

The harbor out Alec's window was bathed in a fall sun that glinted off the windows of the ferries and painted the old buildings of Governors Island in gold. He turned to study the water as he dialed Ochoa.

"Do you know when exactly Oakes was in Bogotá this past July?"

"Late in the month. I think it was the nineteenth or twentieth. Why?"

"I'm not sure why, but it might be important."

"By the way, I thought you might want the full names and last known addresses of the men who attacked me. The Puerto Ricans?"

Ochoa sounded interested. Alec read him the descriptions.

"Good hunting!" he said.

"We always have good hunting," Ochoa answered.

On Saturday morning Karen called him at the apartment. She sounded happy and relaxed. Her chirpiness made him feel glum. She said she was calling to find out if he was all right, if his burns had healed, if she could help in any way. The more he listened to her, the more he realized that wasn't why she called.

"Karen, Karen. Enough Florence Nightingale. What's going on?"

Her voice dropped to its most conspiratorial octave.

"I didn't want to tell you all this. I know you must still be rocky. But I feel I must. You're the talk of this office. I think Vinny may have ordered a surveillance of you. I can't be sure, but everybody on the financial task force seems to know you're sleeping with one of your clients, the Hastings woman."

Karen said "the Hastings woman" as though she were reading from *The Scarlet Letter.*

"How would they know that unless they have a surveillance going on? Believe me I'm not asking you questions. I just wanted to tell you. This is not a question."

Alec started to say something, but Karen was already galloping forward.

"Then two days ago Vinny asked me on an official basis what I knew of your wounds in Vietnam. He said he was inquiring as the U.S. attorney. It was very strange. He had his secretary in with him when he asked. He said he wanted to know if there was concussion. I told him I didn't know. I said why didn't he ask you! He said he was having trouble getting your hospital records from the marines. He wouldn't tell me why he was looking for them.

"Eddie came by my office. He says he can't call you anymore. He looked worried, and you know you can't worry Eddie. He said the bureau is operating on the theory your client was bombed because somebody leaked they had a meeting set up. Eddie said that was crazy, but it would suit the bureau. He said it would also suit Vinny to have you suspected of the leak."

As she chattered on, Alec was getting a cold feeling.

Vinny was making a serious attempt to neutralize him. He was preparing for the day Alec went to the *New York Times.* He could see Vinny at the news conference, explaining sadly that Alec Anton, a former government prosecutor, was a Vietnam veteran who had had continuing psychiatric problems. Vinny then would regretfully reveal that Alec himself was under investigation in connection with the bombing. As a result, Vinny would regretfully suggest to the reporters, he couldn't comment on the accusations made in the *Times.* Very neat. There was no question Vinny had studied under the Jesuits.

"Another story around is that you're out at Trowbridge. People here are talking to people there. I know that. They say the firm is planning to take you off the Monarch case. Is that true?"

Finally she ran out of gas. Alec could hear her breathing through the receiver. He could see her, probably sitting on her bed, waiting for his response. She loved gossip.

For the first time since he had kissed her in the law library lo those many years ago she frightened him. Had Vinny gotten her to call? Was the phone bugged? Had she been assigned to step up the pressure?

He tried to be light. "Sweetheart, that's quite a load of innuendo, half-truths, and pure bullshit."

She seemed hurt. "I said it was just the talk around here."

"Your friend the U.S. attorney and his boys screwed up a major case. He knows that. I can't discuss it further because it's a matter before the grand jury" — he allowed his voice to take on a righteous tone — "but Vinny also should know that slandering me isn't a wise course.

"Who I sleep with is my business. I used to sleep with you in and out of wedlock. It wasn't so bad. Was it?" That would sound nice on the FBI tape.

Karen giggled. "Listen, when I heard about you and the famous Mrs. Hastings, I was happy for you. I can remember her in a bathing suit. Wow!

"Anyway, you were getting pretty lonely. I know the signs. When I saw you in the hall last summer you were taking my clothes off with your eyes. I'm glad you're relieving that awful little tension," she teased.

"My tension wasn't that little was it?"

She burst into laughter again.

"Tell me about Trumbull Oakes." Alec's tone had changed slightly.

"Is that who you guys were —"

"I didn't say that.

"Just tell me about him." He pressed. If the FBI wanted a tape, here it was.

"I don't know a lot. I see him at Guggenheim board meetings. He's very pompous. He reminds me every time I see him that Reagan will be asking him about Justice Department appointments, as though I give a shit."

Karen went silent as though she was thinking.

"He's no joke though. I heard that when D'Amato wanted his guy for Treasury enforcement secretary last year, Oakes marched right over his head and put Chatham there. I'd be surprised if Vinny wanted to go after him. He's where you have to go to get the money."

"What's the rap on him personally?"

"Personally? Personally everybody thinks he's a shit. I heard a story that a woman broker in his office named him in a sexual harassment suit. Nothing came of it. She was in a major auto accident right after that and then she left New York."

"Major auto accident?"

"Something like that. I don't know if she was hurt or what!"

"What kind of harassment?"

"She says he put the arm on her for sex. When she wouldn't do it, he took her off one of the best accounts. The only reason I know the story is she went to a friend of mine for advice."

He kept up a calm, assured chatter for ten minutes. If nothing else it would leave Karen reporting that her ex-husband seemed pretty confident, that all the rumors about his difficulties were exaggerated.

It would buy him a little time. But Karen was right, the federal bar in New York was a small town. He was getting more isolated every hour.

It was mid-Sunday when he decided he ought to fire a round back. This wasn't a static defense. He was in a fight.

It took him four calls from a pay phone to get the right Benjamin Stein.

He had wrapped the phone in his handkerchief and the *Times* reporter was clearly having difficulty hearing.

"Who are you?"

"You don't know me, Benny, but I can help you on a story."

"Which story?"

"You know the bombing of the guys in the Freezetemp case?"

"Sure."

"Check with the NYPD homicide. You'll find the FBI is looking at the same suspects in the bombing case as the cops are in the murder of a college kid on the Lower East Side."

"You mean the Kingsbury kid who got strangled?"

"Yeah."

"Who are the suspects?"

"A couple of spics."

That was far enough. Alec clicked off. His only hope was that Benny wasn't totally lazy.

It took three days. On Thursday morning the *Times* carried a story in the lower-right-hand corner. "Bronx Men Linked to Three Murders." The headline explained the pair was sought in a bombing and a strangulation case.

The U.S. attorney's office was silent, as was the FBI. But the NYPD confirmed the link and an apparently eager assistant in the district attorney's office said that a grand jury was considering charges against Julio and Smiley in both matters.

Alec smiled. Robert Morgenthau had been U.S. attorney. He didn't like being upstaged by Vinny. Everyone was saying Vinny was a young Bob Morgenthau. Bless his heart. Human nature had won out. Morgenthau still thought of himself as a young Bob Morgenthau. Even better, Stein had written it as though the tip had come from the police or the New York D.A. He probably thought it had. Alec's using the word "spics" had been a nice touch. It sounded like cop talk.

The *Times* story set off a minor media blitz. Julio's former wife told Channel 7 that her husband beat her often and was quite dangerous. His mother told Channel 9 that his ex-wife hated him and that he had never adjusted to living in New York.

"I should have never brought him from Puerto Rico," she said.

All the T.V. stations used lots of film of the car wreckage, college pictures of Noah, and reports of unnamed police officials who described Julio and Smiley as killers for hire.

Two local call-in shows devoted their entire programs to organized-crime killings. Most of the callers seemed confused about whether Julio and Smiley were Italian, except for the Italians who called in to complain about being associated with organized crime.

It was the following Sunday that Stein surpassed himself. According to unnamed police sources, the *Times* said, Felix Schwartzberg was working undercover with authorities when he died and the explosion was witnessed by federal agents.

Again the U.S. attorney's office had no official comment, but an unnamed federal agent was quoted as saying "You don't kill an FBI witness and get away with it. We're trying to find how the killers knew when and where the meeting was to take place." So Vinny too was not without contacts in the media.

It was Monday morning when Morgenthau's office called. They wanted Alec and the Hastingses before a grand jury. Did he still represent them? He said he presumed he did and would call them back.

John Hastings readily agreed. He said he would be glad to have Alec handle the matter and would certainly come to New York "if it will help punish those who killed Noah." It sounded to Alec as though Hastings was practicing what he would say to news reporters.

Lee was a far different matter. She was reluctant to come to the phone and angry when he told her about the request.

"You've caused all this. You simply have become obsessed. I can't go through with it. I just can't." She was gulping air so hard in her anger she couldn't speak.

Finally he got her to call her sister to the telephone. Eileen was eager to help and listened to him carefully.

"I didn't cause this," Alec explained. "This was going forward anyway. Tell Lee if she wants I will try to get them to use the police reports as evidence or to accept an affidavit. They only want to know about when she last saw Noah and the house burglary."

Eileen said she would try to reason with her.

"You know, she can get a new lawyer. Either one here or there. That might be better."

Eileen said she would call back.

On Tuesday he explained to Morgenthau's office that he would not be able to fully testify about the Freezetemp killings unless something could be worked out with the U.S. attorney's office over grand jury secrecy. "The U.S. attorney has advised me I'm privy to grand jury matters."

Two hours later, Morgenthau's office called back. "Your appearance Thursday will be limited by stipulation to the death of Noah Hastings. We'll give you a letter." The letter, which arrived by messenger, left the door open for Alec to be subpoenaed on the Schwartzberg bombing at a later time.

Later Tuesday Lee called. Her voice sounded lifeless and weary.

"I'll come to New York and testify. Can you handle it for me?" He started to explain her options. "Just take care of it, please!"

Morgenthau's office scheduled them all Thursday as a courtesy. Lee first, John Hastings second, and Alec third.

"Can I ask you a question?"

The young assistant D.A. paused on the phone as though considering that request.

"Sure."

"Do you really expect to get an indictment without a witness placing them at the scene?"

"I can't tell you much about this, Mr. Anton. But the police have made headway there."

"Thank you." Alec hung up. DeNunzio shouldn't have been so depressed. He was making progress.

On Thursday he met Lee and John at a restaurant across from the criminal courts building. It was crowded and noisy.

"You people must have been up before dawn to get here." Alec smiled.

Facing them he realized they were a handsome couple. They looked like they had come into New York for a shopping day. The Connecticut couple, out for a lunch and a matinee. He was floored at how suitable they seemed, as though God in his heaven had willed them to be a matched pair.

"I stayed at the University Club," Hastings answered. Lee was silent. There was an awkward pause.

"Well, let me tell you what to expect." Alec took out a yellow legal pad as though he was going to conduct a meeting.

"This is a New York State grand jury. You will be testifying under oath and naturally you can be held accountable for your answers."

Hastings cleared his throat. "If we lie we can be prosecuted?"

"Sure." Alec smiled his most lawyerly smile.

"I don't think that's a factor in your case. I only stressed that you will be under oath so that you'll want to tell the truth, the whole truth, but I wouldn't volunteer opinions or things you don't have direct knowledge of. Let the D.A. and the members of the jury ask the questions."

"Will you be there?" Lee's voice sounded timid.

"No. You can ask to leave the room to consult me at any time. But I won't be there with you."

"What will happen when we go in?" Lee pressed.

"They'll ask you to sit at a table on a dais. On your left will be the D.A. Maybe more than one. The jury will be seated on a kind of bleachers right in front of you and a court reporter will be in the well between."

"What do they want to know?" Lee asked.

"This is a record-making session. They want to establish when Noah was last seen, by whom, and establish his activities leading up to the time of his death.

"They'll also want to know about things that happened after his death. The search of his car, that sort of thing.

"It's not likely to come up, but let me mention one other thing to you. I am not going to testify about anything you told me as a client or I learned from you in my search for Noah. If they determine that's vital, and I can't see why they would, there is a procedure for you to release me to answer. Let's not bring it up unless we have to.

"By the way, colonel, did Noah ever mention Trumbull Oakes to you?"

"No."

"Did he tell you much about his job in New York?"

"Well, he did say it was an investment banking firm. Do you mean he was going to work for Oakes?"

"I don't know," Alec said.

Hastings thought for a moment.

"In fact I asked him several times about his job. He said he was going to join this one firm, but he might not be there too long. It was a little mysterious.

"Will they ask me about Oakes in the grand jury?"

"I don't think so," Alec said. "It was just a thought I had."

"I'll just be asked about the last time I saw Noah, the dinner he, Ellen, and I had?"

"Right."

"But I told the police all that last summer."

"That's what I said. This session makes a record for planning a trial. They'll probably ask you whether Noah seemed afraid or worried during the last meeting. Maybe the men who killed him had threatened him."

The witness room in the courts building exemplified the condition of the New York State legal system. There were four chairs. One was broken. The telephone had been ripped out of the wall without the benefit of anesthesia, and only one bulb burned in the heavy wall sconces.

Previous guests had written thoughts both scatological and obscene in Spanish and English. One had offered to "suck off every motherfucking judge in the state." Alec wondered how the members of the bench would go about establishing their qualifications.

DeNunzio sat in one seat, holding a plastic briefcase on his knees. He was wearing a three-piece he had bought when he was at least two sizes smaller.

Behind him stood two officers from the Department of Corrections. One had a set of leg irons in his hand.

Alec introduced the Hastingses to the detective. The couple took the two good seats, leaving Alec the broken one.

After ten minutes of silence, the door to the grand jury room opened and a manacled black man was led out and ushered to the two correctional guards. They silently fitted his leg irons.

Lee stared in what Alec guessed was horror. She had not seen the nation's nineteenth-century jail system close up before. The black and DeNunzio did not look at one another, but Alec had the sense they were avoiding glances. This must be DeNunzio's witness.

"Alphonse DeNunzio." The detective followed the clerk into the jury room. Forty-five minutes passed before he left.

Lee and John each took twenty minutes. Both said it was as Alec predicted, perfunctory.

"Why don't you go ahead? Don't wait for me," Alec said.

The assistant D.A. looked very young and Alec didn't know him. The grand jury, he could see, was weary and kept glancing at the clock.

The D.A. outlined Alec's role, noting at one point, "Mr. Anton is a former United States prosecutor and has great familiarity with how grand juries work."

They walked through his knowledge of Noah's death. He suspected he would be finished in ten minutes. The jury members had asked no questions. It was the black man in the corner of the second row who signaled he was wrong.

"Did you go to California looking for Mr. Hastings?"

"Yes."

"What did you find there?"

He hesitated a millionth of a second, but he knew it was enough to signal the prosecutor that he was selecting information.

"I did not find him."

"What did you find out about him?"

"I found that some people believed he was involved in cocaine."

"In using it or selling it?"

"Both."

"Was he involved with his roommate?" The black man looked down at a paper. "Philip Ochoa."

"That was what I was told."

"Did you report this to police investigating his death?"

"No."

"Why not?" The prosecutor had taken up the question.

"It was hearsay of people who had not seen Noah in years. I judged it not to be factual information."

"Did you contact Philip Ochoa?"

Alec tried not to move, but it was difficult. This was where it was going to hurt.

"Yes."

"When?"

"Earlier this month."

"To what purpose?"

"To ask him about Noah's death."

"Did he have any material information on Hastings's death?"

"He said he didn't."

"Did he say whether they were in the cocaine business together?"

"He said they were not."

In his mind Alec counted the words. "He said they were not." Five words. Up until now he could have danced between the raindrops. Reporting crimes you didn't witness had always been a gray area. Criminal lawyers deal with criminals who tell them about crimes. It was a thin line.

But perjury, perjury is clear. "He said they were not." But of course Ochoa had said they were.

Now it was a record, a transcript, a report. A year from now men Alec had never seen or heard of, in a room somewhere, without his knowledge, could begin to compare, to analyze. There were the words. He couldn't rub them out.

"Did you report your conversation with Mr. Ochoa to the police?"

"No."

"Why?"

"I didn't think it was material."

"Where is Mr. Ochoa?"

"I think he is in Montreal."

"How did you reach him?"

"I obtained a telephone number."

"Where?"

Again the millisecond. If he started on Vale he had to go all the way.

"From school records."

Second lie.

"Do you recognize the name of the firm POOR Limited of Canada?"

Alec felt pain rise in his neck muscles. Somebody had dropped a dime on him. He idly wondered who. Wilton. Pogue. Ochoa. Shirley. Anybody at the partners meeting. Anybody who had seen the records in the firm's safe.

Another millionth of a second.

"Yes."

"Is that firm controlled by Philip Ochoa?"

"I believe so."

"Are you retained by that firm?"

Definitely somebody at Trowbridge. He had the sinking feeling of a man running through a mine field when he realizes he doesn't understand the enemy's pattern.

Another millisecond.

"Yes."

"In what matter?"

"Research on importation of agricultural products from Colombia."

"How much have you been paid?"

"One hundred thousand dollars has been placed at the disposal of my firm towards a retainer."

"Do you represent Mrs. Hastings?"

"Yes."

"Do you represent Mr. Hastings?"

"Yes."

"Did you tell them Ochoa had retained you?"

"No."

"Did you advise members of your firm that POOR Limited was controlled by a man who was under investigation in the Noah Hastings death?"

"I didn't know he was under investigation."

"I have nothing else."

The young D.A. scanned the jury.

"Does any member of the jury have any other questions for Mr. Anton?"

They were putting on their coats for lunch. None of them even looked at him.

When he reached the street he began to walk, ignoring the cabs. It was cold and gray and the lower Manhattan caverns were whipped by sharp wind gusts that whirled the leaves like dancing dervishes in front of City Hall.

He wondered how fast the transcript would be in the U.S. attorney's hands; how quickly Vinny would get the Drug Enforcement files on Ochoa. He wondered how much the DEA really knew about Ochoa.

He tried to put himself back into the other side. He could see the files before him. Here was a private lawyer accepting a whopping retainer for legal work a clerk could do from a man who he has testified is a drug smuggler. It would have to make the feds wonder what Alec was doing for the fee.

It was all legal, he reassured himself. He had no real proof the money he received was from drug sales. He hadn't done anything but give Ochoa information that had now been published all over New York.

What bullshit! This was nice ammunition for Vinny. It was a real start.

He wondered if Vinny had really ordered the bureau to open an investigation on him. They knew a leak about the bombing was nonsense. The appointment was made by a man killed in the blast. All the suspects would have known where the meeting was even before the FBI.

Was this nonsense a gambit? Was it just to freeze Alec Anton? Or did it let Vinny start an investigation to get evidence of wrongdoing by Alec Anton? The tension caused the tendrils of pain to widen their attack, down along his shoulders and across the top of his back.

Vinny was becoming a pain in the neck.

Shirley had gone to lunch and the pink telephone notes were laid out in a row on a folder carrying his day schedule. Connie Callaghan's call lay on top.

He tried to remember if he'd forgotten to do something for the old man. He had addressed a Fordham law seminar in June. He couldn't think of anything else.

He dialed the number. Connie's voice was still strong, firm and rich with the tones that he used to slip a jury off into a world where the facts had been rearranged.

"Hi. This is Alec. How are you?"

"Considering I'm seventy-eight years old and can't dance the polka, I'm fine."

"What did I do, forget your birthday?"

"Oh no! I want to have lunch or a drink."

Alec began thumbing through his calendar for November. "I'm looking at tough times until mid-November. Have you got a date in mind?" He started to read several letters Shirley had opened and organized.

"Today or tomorrow?"

A bell went off in Alec's brain.

"This is business?"

"This is business."

"Tomorrow?"

"Twelve-thirty at the Century Club."

"Sure. I'll be there."

Connie had taken him to the Century Club the first time they had met. It seemed like a hundred years ago. He had worn his best suit. Karen had ironed a fresh shirt before she went to work, and he had

shined his own shoes. They had spent the night before sitting in bed
trying to guess why Connie wanted to have lunch with Alec.

"One of my professors told me that aside from Edward Bennett
Williams, he's the best courtroom strategist in America," Karen had
gushed. "He said Callaghan virtually created jury analysis."

That first lunch had led Alec to private practice, to Trowbridge.
It seemed in another era.

This time Connie had gotten there first and he was standing by
the large old table that dominated the first-floor entranceway. He
looked hardly changed from the day Alec had first seen him. He was
not a tall man, but he carried himself in such an erect fashion that he
always looked taller than he was. His hair had been a pure white for
three decades and it was always beautifully combed and brushed.
Connie had an absentminded gesture of touching the back of his
head with a hand as he talked, as though to be sure no single hair had
dared to move.

Karen once said she thought Connie was so neat "his wife must
dress him, mount him on a skateboard, and roll him downtown."

The club had once been one of the Whitney mansions, and across
this same floor had trod the robber barons, the Morgans, the Van-
derbilts, Harrimans, the men who built the American industrial
empire.

The first floor was done in pure white marble, gray with age and
polishing, like a giant sparkling cavern, its north side a double
staircase to ballrooms and dining rooms above.

They shook hands and marched up in unison. Connie inquired as
to whether Alec's face caused him pain. Alec said it did not. They
reached the top. Connie's rate of breathing never changed. Alec was
puffing.

"Hello, William."

"Hello, Mr. Callaghan."

"Do you have a nook or cranny left?"

"Of course."

William, who looked eighty, led them through one luncheon
room to a tiny alcove on the far side that had only enough room for a
table and four chairs.

"Thank you." The two old men smiled. To Alec the smile seemed to say "As long as I am here to eat and you are here to serve, we are both still here."

"Do you know why I like this club?"

Alec shook his head.

"It was formed by the publishing industry. I'm one of the few lawyers on the board. Ross was a member. The Sulzbergers. Cerf. It was a club where talent and achievement won you membership."

"Plus a little money," Alec said wryly.

"Plus a little money." Connie nodded. "But for those of us like you and me whose families didn't get here in the first migration, it was more than hospitable."

They had Dover sole with a white wine, endive salad, and little turnip casseroles.

Callaghan did not talk business over food. It took a while for others to understand that. Opposing attorneys would find that their attempt to start talking about the case before dessert brought them relentless stories about Callaghan's grandchildren or golfing in Westchester.

"Did you read the story in the *Times* about the man who beat that goose to death in Larchmont?" Alec shook his head. A murder he had missed.

"I play that club from time to time. The damn geese like it for the same reasons we do. The club seeds the green regularly, which is like serving an open buffet; it has pleasant little lakes and hollows and predators are kept off the property.

"But the geese leave their droppings all over and stand right by the hole when you're trying to putt. I nearly beat one to death myself."

"What happened to this geese beater?"

"He's run into a lot of trouble from bird lovers. The club is talking of asking him to leave. I wrote him a note and offered to take the case — pro bono, mind you — to the highest court. A man in America ought to have the right to beat to death any silly goose that messes up a good putt."

It came over coffee, as bitter as the espresso. Underneath the Irish charm, Connie Callaghan was a very tough man. Age had not softened him.

"You are in deep trouble."

"How so?"

"At Trowbridge."

Alec started to talk about the Oakes disagreement with Wilton. Connie stopped him.

"Do you know a young associate named Moira Moran?"

"Yes. She worked on the Freezetemp matter for me."

"She has given the firm an affidavit."

Connie was watching Alec's face. Feigning surprise wasn't going to help.

"Saying what?"

"Saying you seduced her. She says you promised her a chance to work on major cases if she would have sex with you. She said she resisted your advances, but that you used a business dinner to lure her into a compromising position. She said you gave her cocaine and when she tried to extricate herself, you threatened to expose her."

Alec could see it all quite clearly. Wilton.

"Who did she go to with this story? Pogue?"

"No. Wilton."

"Wilton took it to Pogue."

"Yes."

"What happens now?"

"I really don't know." Callaghan did not look as though he didn't know. "I've made some calls. My smell is they want to get you out."

"Can I tell you the real story, or are you representing the firm?" Alec found himself plagued by a disconcerting vision of Moira lying nude in her apartment.

"I represent no one. Pogue called me for advice."

Alec told him about the past months. He omitted his relationship with Lee, but gave him a full description of the night with Moira and the Hastings and Oakes cases.

Callaghan occasionally interrupted with technical questions. He never asked Alec if he regularly used cocaine, whether he had ever had another affair at the firm, and he made no moral observations.

"Do you know what I think?"

Callaghan nodded his interest.

"I think I am being punished for letting my clients try to trade Trumbull Oakes for a no-jail deal."

Callaghan looked at him as one would look at someone who has decided that daylight is associated with the sun.

"Of course."

"How could I have done differently? I owed it to my clients to give them the best defense."

"Is that really what's going on here?" Callaghan had leaned forward and was studying Alec's scarred face.

"Schwartzberg and Gallagher were out of luck. The government had a clear looting case. They really didn't have anything to trade up. You just sat there and told me yourself that you and that Moira woman had to find enough circumstantial links to make a proffer. They had no evidence to give. They had to go out and work undercover to make a deal. These are two men in their late fifties. What in God's name made you think they were going to be able to carry it off?"

The two men sat in silence. The dining room had largely cleared and Alec realized it was midafternoon.

"Why did Vinny take the proffer?" he asked defensively.

"You know why he took it. You knew he was going to take it. He's ambitious. More than most. You knew he was looking for a case with national proportions. Vinny isn't the first man to see the Southern District as a starting point. My dear friend Mr. Dewey saw it that way as well. Tom would have taken this case in a minute. He would have loved to prosecute some prominent person in his own party. You knew Vinny would go for it.

"Furthermore he couldn't pass it up. You knew that too! He couldn't afford ever to have it come out that he wouldn't look into charges about a powerful Republican."

"Why doesn't he want it now?"

"Why? Because it isn't easy now. Now its a real investigation. Now its big trouble for Vinny. Now the telephone calls have started. Bush, old Judge Tyler, Stone. What's this about Trum Oakes? they're asking.

"The only answer to those calls is an indictment. A nice clean case, Oakes on tape, and Vinny could have taken his time about amassing financial records and all that stuff. With good tapes and your man's testimony, he knew he'd get a plea. Nothing heavy, but Oakes is gone."

Callaghan slowed as though thinking through his next sentence.

"Vinny would have been known in song and story as a tough, no compromise prosecutor who brought down possibly the second or third most powerful Republican in New York. For Vinny that is better than ten Democrats."

"But what if even now I could show Oakes makes millions laundering money for drug smugglers, that he's their money man?" Alec said.

"You've got this all wrong. You're not a prosecutor anymore. That's what's really going wrong for you at Trowbridge. You've got to grow up. The fees in the Freezetemp case have stopped. That's it. This is a business. You go on to something else." Callaghan was looking at Alec as though seeing him through new eyes.

"Private law practice is a business. If you wanted to be a prosecutor, you could have told me to go to hell in that dining room right out there." Callaghan nodded toward the room. "You and Karen wanted the private cars picking you up, the vacations, the Connecticut house, the first-class airfares, the private clubs. I noticed you and Karen are on the board of the Guggenheim. How many assistant U.S. attorneys are?"

Alec shook his head dumbly.

"What did you make last year?"

Alec paused. "One-eighty, maybe two hundred, plus deferred fees."

"What is your projection after ten years at Trowbridge?"

"Six-fifty." Alec said it in a small voice.

"Six hundred and fifty thousand dollars, a stock purchase program, complete free financial planning, investment advice, medical care.

"It isn't this Moira what's-her-name. God, we've had those things before. Lawyers are human. I once had to extricate one of the old names from a Haitian orphanage arrangement where he'd bought two little boys. Bought them! I said 'What were you going to do with them?' 'Oh!' he said, 'I was planning to keep them in a house on Long Island.'

"I'll tell you what is happening here. You. You've got to find out who you are and get on with real life."

Alec was completely subdued.

"I have to fight this, Connie. I can't go out of the firm now! Everybody on the street will know something's wrong. I won't be able to get on with another large firm. You know that."

"You haven't got much to fight with." Callaghan seemed resigned.

"Trowbridge won't want this all in a lawsuit. They don't want to be the cover story in *American Lawyer* week upon week," Alec said defiantly.

Callaghan fixed him with a gaze. "You're right, of course. But they'll survive it. You won't."

Callaghan smiled at William as they left the dining room. It too, Alec realized, was a message: I will be back tomorrow. I hope you will too.

"I'll call you." Callaghan stepped into the limousine that Trowbridge afforded him as part of his retirement settlement.

21

THE grand jury returned an indictment the second week of November. Alec had no advance warning. He first knew it when Julio and Smiley's mug shots stared out from the eleven o'clock news. The announcer said they were indicted in the slaying of Noah Hastings, "the young Kingsbury student." Alec wondered if there were such a thing as an "old Kingsbury student."

The pair were also charged, the announcer said, with assaulting Manhattan attorney Alec Anton, and Connecticut authorities were seeking them in the burglary of Noah Hastings's home and car.

Julio's mother again made local T.V. She said she hadn't seen Julio in months and didn't know where he was. The video caught her in the hallway of a project in the Bronx. Alec guessed the hallway alone would be pretty good evidence Julio had a deprived childhood.

Morgenthau announced the indictments. He said the police expected to make an arrest shortly and that his office was also investigating the pair in the bomb deaths of two business executives. Alec could see DeNunzio's bulky form hovering in the second row of officials behind Morgenthau.

The news conference was a nice touch. Morgenthau could teach Vinny a thing or two. He had taken the high ground. Now he was leading an investigation in which the FBI and the U.S. attorney appeared to have faded to the wings.

One reporter, Alec couldn't see which one, kept asking Morgenthau who Smiley and Julio were working for in these killings. It was like watching a bullfighter. Each time the reporter's question charged in, Morgenthau would brush it aside with his cape, letting the questioner's own momentum carry it away.

"Is this a Mafia hit?" the voice persisted.

"We believe these killings are the work of professional criminals."

"Who was paying for it?"

"I think that's the sort of thing we ought to wait to develop at a trial. I don't want to try this case in the media."

Morgenthau also did not divulge how his office had linked Julio and Smiley to Noah's death. But the *Times* the next morning quoted unnamed sources in the district attorney's office who said the police had a witness who placed the pair in the Avenue A drug market at the time of the killing.

The witness, the *Times* said, was a convicted drug dealer who had come forth with information after he had been arrested in a separate case. Sitting at his kitchen table reading the paper over coffee, Alec nearly spit it all over the room.

No wonder DeNunzio hadn't been eager to advertise his big break. The key witness who would testify he saw Julio and Smiley at the scene of a killing where even the day of death could only be guessed at by the coroner was a drug dealer facing new charges.

Detective DeNunzio had clearly chosen the course of least resistance. He was betting on the come. He was betting Julio and Smiley would never come to trial in Noah's death. He was betting his "witness" would never sit on the witness stand.

The criminal justice system was working flawlessly, Alec thought wryly. The State of New York cleared up one murder and avoided a trial in a drug case. To testify in a well-publicized murder case the D.A. must have given the drug dealer a pass. He whistled.

Again Leland Hastings could not be reached for comment. Her house was described by the *Daily News* as "the family's Long Island Sound home," and the tabloid reminded its readers that she had "disappeared soon after Noah's murder."

No news account seemed to have much information about a motive for the murder. John Hastings was quoted as saying authorities told him it "was a drug sale gone bad" and Jimmy Breslin chose Hastings as the subject of a column about how a "Vietnam hero came home to fight a different war."

"He has lost his son," the column said, "but he thinks the war for other kids can be won."

The *Post* blew up Noah's college yearbook picture. He looked like he was going to laugh any minute. He must have found the world a funny place. By the time many Americans his age were thinking of their first job, he was involved in a successful international business.

If the product had been toys, there would have been a feature in *Business Week* about how two young boys started marketing toys in high school and had their own business by the time they graduated from college.

Maybe that was the joke Noah had in mind.

Alec had not tried to call Lee after the late news. But early the next day he tried to reach her at her sister's in Guilford. Eileen seemed perplexed. "I thought she had been in touch with you. She's back at Harborview with the girls. She moved down two weeks ago."

"She may have forgotten to call me," Alec said.

Eileen gave him the unlisted number. "I hope she wanted me to do this."

Veronica answered guardedly and brought Lee to the telephone.

"Hi. I just wanted to be sure you were aware that those two men were charged in Noah's death."

"Thank you. A television truck was out early but we closed the curtains and turned the lights off and they went away."

"You can always refer them to me for comment if you like."

"That's all right."

Her voice had a weary and lifeless quality to it.

"Alec, I've been meaning to call you. Can we meet at your office or somewhere? In the next few days. Tomorrow?"

"Okay. But I'd rather not meet at my office. Do you want me to come to Connecticut?"

"If you want."

He went up that night. There were lights on in Lee's house, but the shades were drawn and he didn't try to stop by. His house was cold and damp. He had forgotten to put on the furnace and it took three hours to warm the rooms.

It was funny. He knew that night what the next day would be about. He had known all day. But somehow he couldn't move to change the course of events. He ordered no flowers, planned no speeches, sought no new promises. Several times he reached for the telephone, determined to take direction in his own hands, profess his love, ask her to marry him, promise a new life for the four of them.

But something stayed his hand each time. It was as though Lee were a sailboat, loose from its moorings, that was drifting away. He made no move to stop her. He would keep her if the tides and currents drove her back toward him, but he would not lift a hand to change her course.

He had run ten miles, starting well before dawn and circling the entire harbor as the sun broke above the waters of the Sound. It was cold. A sharp wind cut in hard across the water unimpeded by trees or hills. When he passed Lee's on the way back the house still showed no sign of life.

But now he could see her walking down the beach. She had on a silver ski parka and Levis and she was bent against the wind.

She started for the back door, but he called out and she came up along the beach side.

"Good morning."

She was an extravagantly good-looking woman, he thought. She wasn't wearing makeup, her hair was combed back in a quick ponytail, but she was even more beautiful than if she had been turned out for a dinner party.

Inside the porch, she sat down, putting her feet up on the bookcases that lined the sea side of the porch wall. Even though the porch was enclosed in glass and heated it was chill, and she left the parka on but unzipped. He could see one breast pressing out against a blue sailor's jersey.

He felt enormous longing. He did not want to have weighty discussions. He did not want to have a serious talk. He did not want to make a life decision. He wanted to make believe it was just some normal morning. He wanted to chatter and flirt, make Bloody Marys and putter. And, finally, he would draw her to him and they would make love.

He felt as he had at the end with Karen. He wanted to reach out, to hold her, to do small incidental things. But Karen had been bent on resolving a crisis. There was nothing Karen liked better than dealing with what she perceived as a difficulty. She liked to "settle matters, to meet them head on." She had been enraged when he wouldn't acknowledge their marriage was in jeopardy. He could see her sitting on that same porch, animatedly punching the air with her hand.

"Alec, you live in a world by yourself. No one else matters. No one. No thing," Karen had said that day. He wondered if that was true. Women must require recommitment. They bring their loves and marriages to the brink of disaster to test commitment.

Lee had called this meeting. She began to speak.

She wouldn't or couldn't look at him as she talked.

"I am going away."

"Where?"

"I don't know. I think Seattle."

"It rains all the time in Seattle."

"I know, but I have a cousin in Seattle."

"How can I help you?"

"There's nothing I need."

"When are you moving?"

"Next week."

"Can I come out with you? Help you get things set up?"

"No. I can handle it."

"The girls are going to miss school."

"They've already lost the term."

"Does this mean we're not going to get married and live happily ever after?"

He tried to sound lighthearted.

He realized he was crying. His Slavic heritage was betraying him. Tears. His mother, who was German and never cried, used to say "Russians cry at the drop of a hat. You mustn't take it too seriously."

Her gaze across the water never wavered.

"That's what it means."

"Can you tell me why?"

She paused.

"Two horrible things have happened in my life. My marriage to John and Noah's murder. Between these events it was boring, humdrum, and lonely."

She paused again.

"But I realized since Noah's death that actually, that is life. My daughters were safe and happy. I was making things go. In my fashion I was happy.

"You and I were brought together because of tragedy. That was what we had."

"No." He said it hoarsely.

"Your life is filled with things like this. The war. Drug investigations. Criminals. You can't change it. That's your life."

She kept her gaze fixed firmly on a lighthouse three miles out over the water. She was steering by that vector.

"I don't want that. I want to live like other people do. I want to go to the grocery. Take two days to pick out a movie. Wash the kitchen floor."

Alec could feel the tears were coursing down his cheeks.

"Maybe that's what I want too. Is that possible?"

"No. You say that now, but that is not true. You like your life. You may think you don't but I can tell: you do."

He was sobbing now. He knew it had to do with fatigue, fear, tension. He knew it was not solely Lee. He had spent the last month of nights and days trying to absorb Felix's death, the troubles at Trowbridge, and fencing with Ochoa. It had taken its toll. He could not cope with one more thing.

He wondered if he could get a continuance, like in court.

"I can't continue this matter at the present time, your honor. My client Alec Anton has had enormous difficulties in his personal and professional life in the past few months. He has been beaten and later seriously burned. He may lose his job. He is under investigation by the U.S. attorney and is fearful of an indictment for perjury by the New York D.A. He would like a continuance. He wants this woman, but he just doesn't have the energy to fight for her right now."

He was not in court. The chill of the Sound seeped into the porch. It made his shoulders ache.

Lee was still talking. He had lost track of what she said.

"What?"

"I said please don't act this way. Don't. You're not thinking clearly."

Men crying disconcerted women. He was embarrassed. He wiped his face.

"I think you will someday agree this was best. If we had met in a different way. If . . ." She couldn't say if Noah hadn't been killed. "If nothing had happened. It might have been different."

For the first time she looked at him directly. Her gaze was devoid of affection. She had not shed a tear. He looked into her eyes. There was nothing for him there. It was strange how final it was. One look.

He took the late-morning train back to New York. It was nearly empty and in its emptiness the car was all the more shabby and bleak. He huddled down in the seat. All told this was turning out to be a very lousy year.

Two days later Lee called and asked him to handle the legal aspects of the sale of her house.

He held the telephone in dumbfounded silence.

"Do you mind? I know it is an imposition."

"No, of course not."

She executed a power of attorney and his office picked it up by messenger.

The house was sold the weekend before Thanksgiving. She didn't call him. He got a note with a Seattle address. It reminded him that he could deduct the money he had advanced for the Mountainview records purchase from the sale price.

"Have a nice holiday" was the last line.

He worked until midevening the night before Thanksgiving. Trowbridge's offices were deserted by six on the holiday eve. He had passed Moira Moran twice during the day. She had averted her eyes. She had a new office on the civil litigation corridor and a secretary. She was moving up fast.

The week had been spent writing POOR Ltd. a long and detailed account of customs laws, bonded warehouse regulations, transshipment and export rules. It was impressive. He billed $52,000 in fees, only a modest $2,000 over half the retainer on account. Despite the wrinkled brows at the partners meeting, Trowbridge accepted the billing.

The report was detailed enough so he could defend himself in court or before a bar ethics panel. He had been retained to handle a civil research matter and had done so.

Ochoa had been surprised by the report. "What in God's name do I need this for?"

"You don't need it. I do." Alec didn't spell it out.

Ochoa's sources confirmed Alec's suspicions. Al DeNunzio's witness had been a longtime snitch for police narcs. He was looking at a third sales conviction with a mandatory sentence when his lawyer called DeNunzio about Noah's murder.

"Opportunity didn't have to knock twice," Ochoa had said.

Ochoa's sources were less sure about Smiley and Julio.

"We are told they are no longer in New York. Some say San Juan. Some say Miami. Don't worry, we'll find them."

According to Ochoa, Oakes was keeping Ochoa's father up to date on developments in the case. He had told him about the indictments, reiterating his sadness at losing Noah.

"He did not tell him about your friend Felix or the explosion. He made no connection there.

"I tried to tell my father, if Oakes gets swept up in Freezetemp we lose too, but he doesn't understand."

If Oakes had told the Ochoas only one half the story, he had told Wilton the other half.

Alec knew Oakes must know that Alec was the link between the cases; that Alec was his nemesis. Oakes was moving to alleviate that problem. He was the energy behind the effort to force Alec from the firm. There was no question about that.

But Oakes apparently didn't understand that Alec had a line to Ochoa, that he was in touch with Philip.

It was slim, but it was an advantage.

There were few others.

Callaghan said it was going to be hard to turn Trowbridge's decision to force Alec out.

"The first thing you have to do is drop the Oakes matter entirely. Just forget it. If Vinny doesn't call you, don't call him.

"I want to get you with Pogue as soon as I can, but it has to be with Pogue and not Wilton.

"Right now Pogue is being difficult. Your outburst in the file room really scared him. That's not the kind of lawyer he likes."

Alec did not argue with Callaghan.

"Connie, it was an obsession. You know how it is. You get into a case. Maybe it gets into you. That's over."

He wondered if he sounded sincere. He could hear the old man breathing on the phone. He tried to read the breaths. It was impossible.

In a way Connie was right. If Lee didn't want to find out who killed her son, and Sophie didn't want to find out who killed her husband, why should he end his career over it?

Alec worked furiously on other things, on POOR, on the Monarch case and two minor SEC cases he had been carrying. He sat quietly in partners meetings, ate lunch at his desk, and never left the office until midevening.

He ran at night as well as in the morning, loping along the park paths as late as midnight and then hitting them again just after dawn.

It was a nuclear life. The late twentieth century. A man, wealthy by world standards, who lived in a small box high in a Manhattan skyscraper. He had everything, but nothing. He could go entire days without a personal conversation. His matrix of friends dissolved with Karen. Now Lee left him emotionally numb, unable to even make the overtures to new human contacts.

No one in the office had invited him for Thanksgiving. Shirley was concerned. "Are you going to Connecticut for the holiday?" she had asked. He only nodded.

He had not planned to. He had planned to stay in New York, go to a gallery perhaps, take in a movie. But when he got to the apartment it seemed so dismal he was not sure he could stay in it for four days.

He made the midnight train. It was packed with a late business crowd that had stayed in Manhattan for a couple of pre-Thanksgiving drinks. He felt like a small child watching an adult party he had not been invited to.

Thanksgiving morning he ran for nearly two hours around Norwalk Harbor and the shore road to Westport, weaving in and around the marshes and the big estates. It was cold and overcast, the low clouds like rolling dark gray smoke from a giant furnace.

On the way back he stopped at Lee's and peered in the window. The house was clear, every stick of furniture gone, every picture, every sign of family or life. He could see a giant pile of trash in the kitchen.

He spent the day cleaning his house. It was a furious endeavor, a kind of catharsis. He scrubbed every inch of the floor, dusted, vacuumed, stowed sailing gear for the winter, chopped firewood, and secured storm windows. He ate nothing, drank prodigious amounts of club soda, and kept Mama Cass roaring out of the phonograph.

He went down to Donnelly's late in the afternoon, sat at the long dark wood bar, ate chili washed down with two Molsons, and listened to the bartender's marital history. He was on the difficulties of his third wife when Alec paid and left.

Alec had brought Lee's keys and stopped to haul her trash out to the curb. Night gripped Harborview and there was the smell of roasting turkeys and firewood in the air. He could see the family gatherings in year-round houses, children running, people standing around, and steamed up windows.

The overhead bulb in Lee's kitchen cast a barren and dismal light on the trash. Someone had swept down the whole house and left the remains bagged or piled in the kitchen. One bag was unopened junk mail.

He was combining the mail with a packing box of old wire coat hangers when he saw the Pan American letter. It was unopened, addressed to Noah Hastings.

He broke the seal.

It was a form letter. In pen someone had written Noah's name under "addressee."

The letter said that two pieces of luggage — the two was a handwritten figure — were held at "JFK unclaimed baggage" and would be disposed of in thirty days unless claimed. It was dated October 15.

He stared at it a long time.

Lee must not have seen the letter, or thought it was an ad. He went through the entire trash looking for other mail addressed to Noah, but the remainder were advertisements or addressed simply to "occupant."

He drove to Kennedy early Friday morning, the old VW straining and clanking as he crossed the Triborough Bridge into Queens.

"This letter expired." The clerk pointed to the date with an incredibly dirty index finger.

"Yes, I know. But Mr. Hastings has been seriously ill for some time. We're trying to help him. Could you check anyways?"

Even on the Thanksgiving weekend, the clerk seemed unmoved by this appeal.

"Do you know what the bags look like?"

"One is a carryon and one a sort of duffel."

Alec wasn't sure about the duffel, but he could remember Lee saying they had packed two bags.

Finally, seeing himself unable to remove Alec from his counter, the baggage man shuffled back into the gloom of his empire.

Once he reemerged with an orange backpack marked "Cheryl." Alec shook his head.

He came back a second time to ask when the flight left.

"June third."

"June!" the clerk exclaimed, and carefully pronounced each syllable of "motherfucker."

Twenty minutes later he had found them: a dark green duffel and matching carryon. There was a half-torn luggage check on one, nothing on the other.

"You have the checks?"

"Mr. Hastings couldn't find them."

"Uh! Uh!" The clerk drew his breath in as though he might be having some difficulty in his nasal passage.

"He thought the letter would be sufficient."

"You'll have to sign for them," the baggage man said darkly.

He pulled a giant ledger book from under the counter and laboriously wrote out the long numbers from each bag. Alec signed. It seemed the least he could do. He signed "Noah Hastings."

He opened the bags in the parking lot. There were clothes, mainly outdoor clothes, but a full business suit had been folded into the carryon. Alec found boots, two books, maps, and a shaving kit. The toothpaste was toothpaste, the talcum powder, talcum. But inside a nail-file case Noah had folded a roll of hundred-dollar bills. Alec didn't stop to count it. He guessed there were forty or fifty one hundreds.

A gift wrapped in lavender paper was at the bottom of the duffel. He tore open the wrapping.

There they were. What Noah Hastings had died for. Four IBM, double-sided computer diskettes, wrapped in tissue and placed in a plastic holder.

He wondered if Noah would now think protecting these insignificant pieces of plastic had been worth it. They had sat in this luggage for nearly six months. Had the luggage been returned, they might have changed the entire course of Lee's search and the police investigation.

He looked around, half expecting to see Julio and Smiley coming at him across the macadam. But the lot was filled with anxious travelers trying to wrestle large suitcases into small cars.

Why hadn't he thought of the bags? Why hadn't he or Lee ever wondered what happened to Noah's luggage? The bags had been checked in for a flight. God only knew where they had been. Alec wasn't about to ask for details. Right now all he wanted was to find out what was on the disks. On the drive back to his office his mind raced to find the meaning of his new discovery.

Noah must have had a baggage check on his person. Alec wondered where the ticket and baggage checks were. The police had said the body was stripped of any identification. Nothing but a carnation. Smiley and Julio must have taken the ticket and the baggage claim check when they went through Noah's pockets. Why didn't they get the bags?

It took two telephone calls of cajoling to get Shirley to come in. She had planned on a four-day weekend and had to find a baby-sitter.

At Trowbridge she made two copies of the disks and set up a place for Alec at the IBM terminal. When she arrived he had given her an embarrassed kiss and an envelope with two hundred dollars. "Don't argue. That's for the kids to go to the zoo. We'll pay you double time for today as well."

He closed and locked the door. They started through the disks. The computer glowed eerily in the dark, overcast day.

The first disk was the balance and activity of hundreds of investment portfolios as of May 15, 1981. The company names were all strange to Alec, but the addresses for the most part were postal boxes in Montreal or Toronto. Interspersed there were the accounts of thirty-two individuals, with different banks in Canada listed as their addresses. John Grant, the name on Noah's fake passport, had what appeared to be $10 million or so in investments, from stock to Krugerrands.

They raced through the files on the disk. It seemed to be made up of sections taken from other records, as though Noah had gone through vast computer banks and selected out certain accounts or names at random. There was no alphabetical sequence, no numerical sequence.

The second disk had real estate transactions, rental records, and performance reports for properties both in the United States and abroad. The owners of the properties or the principals seemed to be many of the same Canadian-based firms or individuals.

In some transactions, Alec found assets from the securities and currency investments had been posted as security in the real estate purchases.

The final phase of the second disk seemed to come from a totally different set of files. It documented positions for some of the same companies and individuals in the management of businesses. What Alec guessed was the winery Ochoa had boasted about was owned by a firm called Construcciones Cuadros and there were several Ochoas listed in the winery files.

The third disk was made up of a hodgepodge of transaction records, trades, and sales in haphazard order from January through May. The assets being traded, bought, or sold seemed to come from the portfolios of the same firms or individuals listed on the first disk, and Alec guessed that Noah had copied these to establish unnecessary trading by Oakes.

The last disk too seemed a hodgepodge. It contained the portfolios of two dozen or so European companies. Some were located in Zurich, some in Geneva, two in Liechtenstein, several in Austria and Germany.

At first Alec could see no connection to the other files. "Is there a way we can compare these portfolios with the ones on the first three disks?"

Shirley's plump fingers manipulated the machine and a split screen appeared for comparison. Some of the securities held by the

Canadian firms in the first portfolio were held in the same amounts by the European firms.

There were other strange similarities. Gold, dollar, deutsche mark, and yen investments in the same dollar amount during the same time period showed up under two different owners. Securities bought on the same day at the same price and in the same number were listed to different firms. Oakes's firm had created identical portfolios on paper; one represented the Ochoa family holdings, others listed the same holdings attributed to someone else.

The message was at the end of the last disk. Shirley gave a startled little cry.

"Come see this." She pointed at the glowing screen.

Jefe,

It is 4 a.m. and I'm about done. This is eery. One of Oakes' guys came in at 8 and said 'what are you doing working late already?' I told him I was trying to learn portfolio histories, but he went away shaking his head. That's the third time somebody's noticed I was working the computer after hours. I think I've got enough. It is like I said on the phone, I'll go to Zurich at the end of the week and see what I can see.

As soon as I'm finished making notes from the disks I'll send them. I would rather you have them than me. I ran into Oakes on Monday. He acted different. Maybe I'm getting paranoid, but there is something going on. It gives me the creeps.

I'm thinking of coming back through Montreal. We have to talk. Encararse con! Pronto! It is crazy but I miss Annie. Fucking little broad. I told her no more! She was so crazy. She wanted to carry! "En el conjo!" I blew her off! Now I heard she's working in Burlington just to be with a connection.

This is a bummer. I've got to talk to you. I'm too young to be as nervous as this shit makes me. I feel like I'm running scared forever. I want to kick back! Get with Annie and kick back!

Anyway now I've got to get out of here. So Adios, Amigo.

Alec wasn't sure he understood the end of the note. It sounded like Noah was fed up or scared. He realized he would never know.

Shirley looked beat, her eyes glazed with fatigue. They had been working nonstop for four hours. They both stared at the screen.

"What is this Alec?" She said it in a small voice.

"This is a death warrant."

"Whose?"

"Noah Hastings's."

"Who killed him?"

"Oakes."

"But I thought . . . The police said two Puerto Ricans did it. The ones who attacked you."

"They work for Oakes."

Alec took one copy of the disks and added it to his folder in Trowbridge's safe. He resealed it and logged it in the administrative partner's ledger.

He prepared a Federal Express delivery and sent a set of the computer disks to his bank in care of the assistant manager who handled his account with a note asking they be held until he could come place them in his safe-deposit box.

Every nerve ending tingled. His heart was beating fast. He felt as he did when a helicopter was going into a hot LZ. Fear and adrenaline, those were the real drugs, cocaine was no match for them.

It was funny, he never doubted his course. He was going to take the records to Vinny. It would be a hell of a case. Virtually all Vinny had to do was to start subpoenaing the Ochoa investment records and try to contact principals of the firms, or the individuals. They would be exposed by a telephone call.

Oakes could argue that he could not know whether every one of his customers was who he said he was, but this wouldn't wash with hundreds of millions in investments and dozens of companies. It wouldn't wash with 25 percent of Oakes's business.

Once the pressure was on it would tease out evidence in the killings.

When members of Oakes's firm knew, they would give Oakes up. If Oakes dealt with Julio and Smiley direct, paid them, they too could nail him. If there was a cutout, the cutout would nail him.

He took the *Forbes* magazine with Oakes's picture out. He wondered whether Oakes designed the deaths of Noah and Felix or whether he left it up to the mechanics.

Trumbull Oakes didn't look like he was going to enjoy being

stripped nude and given a delousing shower at the Metropolitan Correctional Center.

Handling Ochoa was going to be risky. The disks were what he had hired Alec to find. He must have concluded that Noah had them somewhere. He had needed somebody close to Lee, somebody who would have access to Noah's things.

If Ochoa ever got the disks Oakes was dead. If he found out Alec gave the disks to the government instead of him, Alec was dead. The thought got his attention. Hiding from Colombian gunmen in New York wasn't a pleasant prospect.

He would have to get a major secrecy commitment from Vinny — no investigators, no files, no nothing. The disks just fell into government hands. His only real hope was to persuade Ochoa he never found anything, that the government uncovered the records on its own.

He wasn't so sure about Callaghan and Trowbridge. Once the case was rolling on Oakes, maybe they would see he had saved the firm from a dangerous and embarrassing entanglement. Even though they voted to accept the Raleigh-Oakes investment representation, if they snipped it early they would look honorable and judicious.

By rights the disks were Lee's. These were the last words of her son and it should be she who turned them over to the law. But Alec knew that she would not. She wanted to forget the whole thing.

Shirley was putting on her coat; he gave her another buss on the cheek. She blushed.

"What's going to happen, Alec?"

"It means I'm going to put Oakes's big fat ass right into the slammer." He was grinning. "Pardon my French."

22

HE worked on his approach to Vinny as carefully as though he were planning an assault on an NVA position. He could hear Sergeant Burns's Virginia twang. "Lieutenant, the trick ain't going to be getting in. The trick is going to be getting out."

He cleaned a set of disks of fingerprints, handling them with rubber gloves as he packed them in a box and wrapped it with plain brown paper and plain tape.

He took a second set to the IBM technical center in Manhattan. They said that it was possible to match the disk material with the computer upon which the original information had been stored. They found coding symbols for a common business accounting software system. But there was no way, they assured Alec, of following a trail of who had opened a disk and read it.

Shirley had used a standard IBM disk to make copies and it bore no real way to trace when it was made, who made it, who sold it, or who bought it. It was anonymous.

He called Karen from a pay phone in Grand Central. Christmas had arrived. Even though the holiday was nearly a month off, the station was already decorated. As he stood by the open phone he could remember Karen staggering through the crowds, her arms laden with gifts as they headed to Connecticut. Karen loved shopping. She loved buying things, maybe more than having them.

"Hello." Her voice sounded strained.

"Have you got someone with you?" Alec asked.

"That's right."

"Okay. Quick question. Does Vinny still run from the Athletic Club?"

"I think so."

"Noon? One o'clock?"

"Early afternoon. Why?"

"I'm worried about his health."

"Really! Why!"

"I need to talk to him unofficially."

"Don't do anything stupid." Karen's voice sounded concerned.

"I won't."

It took three days to spot Vinny. When Alec finally saw him, he was cutting across Central Park South in an Athletic Club sweat suit and a red knit ski cap.

Vinny ran west up the park. He was in good shape and he had a scurrying running style that didn't look fast.

Alec made his move just past the Tavern-on-the-Green.

"Hey, Vinny."

The dark-haired lawyer looked around startled.

"I need to talk to you."

"Hello, Alec." Vinny looked a little scared. He had probably come to believe his own rumor that Alec was a crazed Vietnam veteran.

"Call my office. We'll set something up."

"No. I mean now. I have something for you."

Now Vinny looked really scared. He started to slow.

"What is this, Alec?"

"I have some evidence in the Freezetemp case. But it's dynamite. I have to be protected."

"It isn't proper for you to approach me like this."

"Fuck proper, Vinny. You want a big case or not?"

Vinny stopped. They were by the little stone bridge at the north end of the Lake.

He was looking into Alec's eyes.

"Can we talk running?"

"Yeah, but slow down. You're faster than I am."

They had made four miles and were coming down the east side of the park before Alec had even finished sketching the basics.

"You have any money on you?" Vinny was looking skeptically at Alec.

Alec nodded.

"Let's get a drink at the boat house."

They went into the boat house snack bar. It was full of kids with skates.

Alec smiled. He could remember his mother buying him hot chocolate there.

"Aleki, your cheeks are like little apples." She would pinch both cheeks and smile at him. He wished he could look up and she would be there now.

"Are you trying to tell me that Oakes was hiding money for a narcotics trafficker?" Vinny looked sharply at Alec.

"Yep."

"Why didn't you come to me when you knew the Hastings kid was in cocaine?"

"We were trying to find him to get him to go to you. All his mother and I had was hearsay. School friends. Teachers."

Another lie. Alec was getting in deep. If Vinny rolled up Vale or Philip Ochoa this was going to get sticky.

But the bigger case would cover it. Nobody would want a little withholding-evidence charge when one of the nation's most prominent investment bankers was going down on money laundering for cocaine smugglers.

"What's the deal?"

"The deal is that I'm invisible."

Alec was looking out over the Lake.

"These are bad guys. You and I already know that. They strangled a twenty-two-year-old kid with a piano wire and they blew up an old man."

"We could arrange protection." Even Vinny didn't sound convinced.

"Don't be ridiculous. I want to practice law. I don't want to be in a witness program working as a clerk in Pierre, South Dakota.

"This evidence comes to you unmarked, unsigned, unsourced. I don't want to hear from you on this case. Ever. You just do it."

Vinny was silent for a long time. Little girls with sweaters that said "Brearly" were taking off their skates. Alec thought of Elise McCormack. They had held hands. She was a better skater. "I'll lead," she'd said. He'd been letting women lead ever since.

"Okay. Unless you come up big in this case. You're anonymous."

Alec looked at him.

What the fuck am I doing trusting a Sicilian? He didn't say it out loud. But it was like a premonition. He handed Vinny the package.

Christmas wasn't really that bad. It was either get drunk or go to church. He did both.

On Christmas Eve he went to St. John the Divine. It was very cold. No snow but cold. He could remember holding his father's hand as they would walk up the center aisle. His father would tell him what it was like in the Ukrainian churches when he was a little boy.

Those Christmas Eves were the best memories of his childhood. They would walk home and have hot chocolate and scrambled eggs. He would be watching for Santa Claus but he could never stay awake. Never. He wondered how Santa got into everybody's apartment. His father said he took the elevator like anybody would. Alec was sure he came down the fire escape.

Alec prayed for his parents' souls. He wondered if they were together in heaven. He could see them sitting together watching him the way they had at football games. His mother would be glad he had gone to church.

He took a cab back downtown. The driver said he was heading home. This was his last fare. He had a big pink plastic doll in the front seat.

"Somebody's going to be very happy." Alec pointed at the doll.

"I hope she's asleep." The driver looked cold and tired.

"Feliz Navidad," he said as he let Alec off. The ten-dollar tip had pleased him.

He walked around to Toby's. A bunch of doctors and nurses from Bellevue were having a Christmas Eve drink. The barmaid with the bombers wasn't working.

He drank, silently and purposefully, until the bar closed.

On Christmas Day he ran Central Park, the same route he'd taken with Vinny. The hangover slowed him at first, but the cold air offset it.

When he got back he could hear the telephone ringing.

He got it on the last ring.

"Alec." It was Connie.

"I called you to tell you that I can no longer help you at Trowbridge."

Callaghan sounded enraged, his voice cold and unrelenting.

"What are you talking about?" Alec felt dazed.

"I told you to let the Oakes matter go. You chose not to follow my advice."

"Connie. Connie. You're crazy. I haven't had a thing to do with it."

There was silence on the line.

"Lying doesn't suit you, Alec. You don't do it well."

"Connie, I swear to you that I have done nothing about Oakes."

Again there was silence.

"I'm not going to debate you. Our association is at an end." He hung up.

Alec dialed him back.

"The Callaghan residence."

"Let me speak to Mr. Callaghan."

"Who may I say is calling?"

"Alec Anton."

Silence.

"He is not at home."

The rich are so insulated.

He sat dumbfounded. Maybe federal subpoenas had landed the week before. Maybe Oakes was guessing that Alec was the cause and had complained to Wilton. But why would Connie wait until Christmas. No. He had just learned something. Something he was sure of.

It gave Alec a chill.

All the following week he tried to get Eddie Doherty. He didn't want to call Vinny. If he called Vinny he would abrogate the deal. He would be opening contact, and he wasn't sure he'd been compromised.

Eddie was on leave, but his home phone didn't answer either.

He didn't try Callaghan back. He wanted to learn more before he called Connie.

He finally reached Eddie on New Year's.

"I've been at my mother-in-law's. Only advantage of being the SAC is getting Christmas week off. What's up?"

"I need a little off-the-record help."

"Like what?"

"Is there some movement on the Oakes-Freezetemp case?"

"Nada."

"Are you sure?"

"Not unless it was in the past eight days."

"Are you still on the case?"

"Sure, such as it is."

"Could financial crimes be working on something without you knowing it?"

"Sure they could. But not likely. I'm working with the same people on a different matter. I see them all the time."

"You didn't hear of new evidence on Oakes coming in about three weeks ago, huh?"

"No. What is this?"

"I'm just checking on something."

"When I get back to work tomorrow I'll check around and call you."

"Thanks."

Vinny had probably turned the stuff over to the FBI as a special for security. He wouldn't want everybody involved or it would be in the newspapers in a week. Eddie just wasn't in the loop.

Two days later Eddie called back.

"I did a scan for you. The Feebees tell me they boxed the whole thing. Even the bombing investigation when Morgenthau indicted. They say he isn't expected to charge in Felix's death, but the feeling is they've got the same guys in Hastings and that's good enough."

"What about money laundering?"

"There's nothing on that. The IRS guys are totally off and the FBI reps on financial crimes are working on the same thing I am. It's not connected."

Alec had a bad feeling in the pit of his stomach.

"Eddie, could it be possible that a whole raft of financial records on Oakes could come in, major international stuff, and be worked on without you knowing?"

He could hear Eddie's breathing over the receiver. It had picked up its pace. Eddie was worried now that somebody was spinning him around. Alec knew the feeling. Candor on the federal investigator grapevine was expected. Eddie wasn't going to like it if he was being spun.

"I'll be back to you."

Another two days went by.

"Alec. Listen, I don't know what you've been told but this office is clean. Maybe Morgenthau got a dump, but I don't think so. But there's nothing here. Nothing."

"Could Vinny be doing something in the U.S. attorney's office alone?"

"I don't want to name names over the phone, but I got that covered. I doubt it."

Alec asked after Eddie's family. There was nothing else to do.

Alec didn't want to face it. He was being had. But it was easier to let it drift.

He flew to L.A. with Carl Michael. Michael seemed to accept the fact Alec was still on the case. He was pleasant and Alec kept his mouth shut. They did pretrial on the Monarch case. Michael came back East right away, on a Friday. Alec went down to San Diego.

It was hot. New York was freezing. He stayed on Coronado, running the beach in the early morning, swimming in the heat of the day, and drinking in the funky little bars off the waterfront. Mostly he thought. He thought of going to Seattle. But after a while he thought better of it.

He went back on the red-eye Tuesday. It took a week of staking out the Athletic Club this time to catch Vinny. Vinny had been busy. He was getting lots of T.V. time and ink with Mafia drug cases, the Pizza Connection, the *Daily News* called it. It was an old FBI case. Alec remembered when it started he was still an AUSA.

Vinny was rolling up a bunch of Italians nobody ever heard of. Capo this and capo that. He liked it better than fooling around with one of the best fund-raisers the Republicans ever had.

Alec stopped Vinny just as he entered the park.

The Sicilian's eyes flashed. He was pissed off.

"I thought you were going to be invisible."

"What's going on with the case, Vinny?"

"Things take time."

"Vinny, how come I don't hear any noise at all?"

"The records have to be organized. It takes time and manpower."

"Come on. My dog could do that case. He could take the subpoenas over in his mouth." Alec didn't have a dog. Vinny seemed to be working that out in his mind.

"Let's run." Vinny started off up a path to the Sheep Meadow. Their breaths made plumes of mist that trailed out behind them like long wispy beards. They did not talk until the Reservoir.

Vinny was panting.

"You don't get it. Do you?"

"What?"

"You're not in the U.S. attorney's office." Vinny paused to breathe.

"Huh? . . . I've got my own agenda. I'll do this case when I get ready or not at all."

Alec stopped. "That's a stall. You're going to take care of this guy."

Vinny had stopped and turned to face Alec.

"I told you once not to talk to me that way. I don't want your case. I don't want your help. Stay away from me." He was shouting and jogging away.

Alec ran after him.

"You'll read about it. It'll wipe your pizza connections right off the front page. You're going to look like the biggest cover-up since Watergate."

Vinny stopped and turned back toward him.

He came very close to Alec's face.

"I have the Morgenthau transcript. I got a pretty good copy of an affidavit by one Ms. Moira Moran. So what I got here is a cocaine lawyer for a big-time cocaine smuggler who seduces women by giving them cocaine. What I got here is an indictment for perjury, for obstruction of justice. I may even be able to peg you on trafficking. I'm going to cover your ass with so many DEA agents, you won't be able to take a piss without surveillance."

It wasn't a long speech. Vinny said it very slowly and his tone brooked no interruption.

Suddenly Alec found himself remembering a Connie Callaghan lesson from long ago.

"There is nothing more dangerous than a federal investigation. In the right hands it makes the Spanish Inquisition look like a school test. If you don't believe me take a look at the Rosenberg case. By the time they went to the electric chair they were grateful."

Vinny started back down toward Fifty-ninth. Alec let him go.

The surveillance began the next morning. It was more harassment than watching. The car sat in the no-parking zone in front of the building with a portable red emergency light on the dash and the motor running. It made the doorman bring the cabs in four feet from the curb.

When Alec got in a cab, the agents pulled out so close they almost hit the bumper.

The cabby looked nervous. "You got friends in that car?"

"Security. Ignore them."

They followed him to the door of Trowbridge. They followed him to lunch, to a meeting with a Securities and Exchange lawyer, and they followed him home.

He put on his running gear and took off up Park for Fifty-ninth. The agents were right with him. It was a different car. When they got to the park, they went right around the no traffic barriers, put on the emergency light, and followed him up the road.

"At least I'm not going to get mugged." He said it out loud.

After three days everybody at Trowbridge knew. Even his closest circle of contacts were silent.

Shirley finally asked for a transfer to Carl Michael.

"Alec, we've got kids. We have to have this paycheck."

He gave her a kiss and a long squeeze.

From then on he got a different temp every day.

Vinny shut him down.

His bank notified him that a federal subpoena had arrived for his checking account, savings, and loan records. The administrative partner at Trowbridge said she had a subpoena for records of all fees and expenses for 1980 and 1981.

His credit-card companies and the telephone companies also reported they had received subpoenas.

Eddie wouldn't take his calls. Karen wouldn't either. The SEC lawyers he was dealing with grew more and more nervous with each contact. Alec felt like the three-foot-tall white hunter from the old vaudeville line: he'd told the witch doctor to go to hell.

The DEA guys really scared him. He hadn't liked them when he was in the government. If they got pushed hard enough, his apartment would turn up with two grams of coke in a closet. He taped the door every day when he left, a tiny piece on the outside at the very top. He made sure that every time he left or returned that he told the desk. He warned the clerks to admit no one to his apartment under the guise of repairs or anything else without calling him. The DEA car was out front even as Alec talked to them.

Three times Ochoa tried to call him. Once from Montreal and twice from Bogotá. He took the third call.

"So, *compadre*, I don't hear from you anymore?"

Ochoa still sneered when he talked; it was a bad habit.

"Philip, I wouldn't be too detailed on this telephone. Since we last talked I have acquired surveillance by the DE —" Suddenly there was silence on the line, then a dial tone. He had been disconnected.

Two weeks after Vinny's threat, Alec was worn out. He couldn't sleep. When he went to Connecticut he was sure the house had been searched though there was no sign of entry. His neighbor said a telephone company truck sat in the driveway one day for several hours.

That night in Connecticut, a DEA car had parked down on the causeway, its motor running. A second car brought sandwiches and relief shortly after midnight. Everybody on Harborview knew they were watching Alec's house.

It was that night he decided enough was enough.

Oakes's personal offices were on the forty-fourth floor of the Socony-Mobil Building. The reception area had a breathtaking view of the west of Manhattan from the Plaza Hotel to the Hudson.

Alec sat transfixed with the beauty. A bleak January sun and a slight haze softened the edges of the buildings. It had the softness of a watercolor.

The reception area would have rivaled a good art gallery in a smaller city. There were two fine pieces of Greek sculpture, set in boxes, and the walls held sketches, including one that must have been a Picasso original in charcoal.

Oakes's secretary had come out, a tall businesslike-looking woman in her mid-forties. "Mr. Oakes said your visit is an unexpected pleasure and he's trying to rearrange some time. Can you wait?"

Alec nodded. He didn't know what he was going to say. He didn't even know why he was here. He had to do something. It was like the old line about marine corps battle tactics. "High diddle diddle, straight up the middle."

It was twenty minutes before he was ushered into Oakes's office.

Oakes was a salesman of trust. He was asking his customers to invest millions of dollars with him and his office had been designed to assure them they had come to the right place.

It was stark in its simplicity. There was heavy use of steel, of Norwegian woods, of glass. To talk to Oakes, the visitor had to face east, and the view was a panorama of the river as far as La Guardia, where planes lifted off and arced upward over Oakes's head. Alec wondered if the symbolism of an investment taking off had entered the designer's mind.

Oakes sat at a writing table totally in contrast to the room. Where it was steel and teak, twenty-first century designs, the desk was sixteenth-century, probably from Florence or Venice. The inlay work was extraordinary, and Alec could see the tiny changes of gold or tortoise that indicated it had been repaired. He did not doubt it was original.

"Isn't this wonderful?" Oakes ran his hand along one side. "It was made for a merchant called Tolla Desupio. Before the Pilgrims had settled at Plymouth Rock he was trading with China and the Philippines."

He shook hands with Alec. His grip, like his skin, was soft and delicate.

"History remembers soldiers and statesmen, forgets merchants. For all of George Washington and von Steuben and the Continental Army, they would have been nowhere without my family. We were merchants. We made guns."

Oakes had managed to say that without sounding pompous. It was a polished line to remind his investors that they were as honored in pursuit of wealth as Jonas Salk had been in the pursuit of the polio vaccine.

"Why are you here?" He turned abruptly and took the chair behind the desk.

"To find out how I get myself out of a predicament."

"What predicament is that?"

"I am under federal investigation on drug charges and my law firm wants to force me out. My career is disintegrating."

"Why do you come to me?"

"Because I think you put me there."

"No. Mr. Anton, you put yourself there."

"How so?"

"Because you chose at random to destroy me to save your clients and not incidentally benefit yourself."

"But you were giving them illegal services. Why should they be prosecuted and not you?"

"The point is you selected me at random. Felix could have told you many other things. Maybe he did, but you saw in me a valuable prize, so valuable you thought it was worth the risk."

Oakes paused. He had been speaking matter-of-factly, as though discussing a good investment choice for Alec.

"I uckily, I was able to protect myself."

"By having Felix killed!" Alec found his voice rising. He had not meant it to.

"There you go, you see?" Oakes looked sad. "You don't know that. But for some reason I have become a target for you."

"Did you order Noah Hastings killed?"

"Please, please, Mr. Anton. Why did you come here, to hurl accusations?"

Alec paused.

"No."

"Good. I thought not. My lawyer said not to see you. I said 'How can I make a suitable arrangement without seeing Mr. Anton?'

"Six months ago I never heard of you, Mr. Anton. Then suddenly you have become the most dangerous figure in my life. I have served five presidents and twice the Court of Saint James. I can say with some modesty that it was my planning that rescued the City of New York from debt. And yet here I am in danger of disgrace from you.

"I don't know why. You say you have a predicament. But I too have a predicament. My predicament is you."

Oakes wrinkled his brow as though studying a very serious problem for which he hoped to find a solution.

"Of course I knew Noah. He was a very bright young man. I was hoping to bring him into the firm." Oakes looked suitably sad.

"He was, you know, involved with cocaine." Alec felt like he was setting a record straight.

"Yes, I know. I think that it was that involvement that killed him," Oakes said.

"Are you not involved with cocaine?"

"No."

"You handle the investments for the Ochoas. How do you see that?"

"I have known Marco Ochoa since the 1960s. He has made many investments through me. I presume the money comes from flowers. It may come from other things." Oakes had taken to toying with a letter opener.

"Noah seemed to believe you were stealing from Ochoa."

"Ah, so you mean the computer records. I was very saddened. A young man who is coming into my firm should not steal its records."

"I've seen those records. They show you are diverting money from the Ochoa investments to others."

"I too have recently seen them. They are an artful construction by young Hastings. Computers are still a mysterious device to me. You see something flickering on the screen. It is a record of a transaction, but then again it is not a record. It is only what somebody has entered as the record. The real record is where the assets exist, in whose hands and for what purpose."

This was how Oakes had dealt with the disks. It was smooth. He played upon twentieth-century humanity's doubt about technology.

"Suppose" — he was going further — "you had a computer with the record of your assets in it. There is probably one at your bank. And suppose somebody lifted those little electronic impulses, those few lines, copied them, and moved them inside the computer to my account?"

Alec nodded. It was a stellar performance.

"They are still your assets. They are listed in your name, maybe issued to you or your nominee directly. In my account they are simply a listing. I cannot do anything with them."

Alec shifted in his chair to signal his desire to speak.

Oakes paused expectantly.

"But if you sought to borrow money and the bank was asked for a credit listing, wouldn't the bank report those assets as yours?" Alec said.

Oakes smiled indulgently. "You're right! For me it would be of temporary assistance at best. At some point they would have to be checked and counted as collateral."

"Are you suggesting that Noah faked the records on the disks to discredit you?"

"Of course not. Wasn't I clear about that? But he contrived to choose records that did not show the real world. He chose a temporary snapshot of the Ochoa portfolio. It was done to mislead."

Oakes was using a matter-of-fact tone; it sounded purposefully controlled. Maybe this was an out-of-town tryout for a far harder show — Marco Ochoa.

"He wanted my business. He and young Ochoa. They thought they could supply Philip's family better investment services than I could for less. Marco hasn't seen it that way and the computer disks were a last desperate attempt."

"So you had Noah killed. The Ochoa accounts have to be twenty-five percent of your business."

"Don't play the fool, Mr. Anton. The Colombians are some of the most violent people in this hemisphere. If you've followed their history since 1948, they make the death squads in El Salvador look like Cub Scouts.

"The fact is the family supplies thirty-two percent of my business. Nevertheless I wouldn't have thought to harm him. The Ochoas would never stand for that. They can be very unpleasant. The reason I let Noah into the firm was in hopes of deflecting his drive. Make him part of my operation and serve the Ochoas even better."

Oakes was silent for quite a time. Alec watched his face. It was a good face for an investment counselor. It had a cheerful visage and direct gaze, almost like a baby's.

"I have wondered since his death whether it was the Ochoas who decided to end his career. Maybe the family grew tired of an outsider in their midst."

"Why did Felix and Spanos die?" Alec found Oakes's manner frustrating. He had not known what reaction to expect. This one annoyed him.

"I don't know. These were very common people, very crude. Maybe it was a gambling debt, a woman, labor trouble."

"Maybe it was because you didn't want your offshore banking service department exposed."

Oakes sat forward. He turned the letter opener point-first at Alec.

"The twentieth century will be known as a century of violent death. Seventy-five million people died in two world wars alone. Untold millions since. I am told you have actually killed people. I never have. But we are surrounded by murderous death. We accept some killings, condemn others. It has become so accepted, it is but a flicker on your television set. You see it and you say 'Glad that wasn't me.'

"Your Mr. Schwartzberg and your Mr. Gallagher had been cheating all their lives. They cheated the IRS, their employees, their wives, their customers. We did not provide them a service they did not want. This was their universe. They were criminals. They were guilty."

For several seconds he stared into Alec's face.

"You know, you should have worked out a suitable arrangement for them with the government. That's why we steered the case to you. Not to Trowbridge, but to you, personally. You were supposed to make a good, quick plea agreement. Wasn't that clear?"

Alec sat back. His face must have shown his amazement.

"It is my fault Felix died?"

"Oh yes. You took them beyond their universe. They went into outer space and were lost."

Alec was filled with loathing.

Oakes smiled. It was a smile of weariness and patience.

"My lawyer said you would handle it. He said this will be 'a simple plea bargain.' I remember his exact words. He said 'they do it every day.'"

"Who told you that? Wilton?"

"No. No. Wilton only handles the Raleigh matter. Connie Callaghan. He has handled things like this for me for thirty years."

Alec found it hard to breathe. He had never hyperventilated, but he thought he would now. He had been steeled in court not to show surprise but instead to look at his papers or reach down to his briefcase to hide his feelings.

Now he turned carefully in his chair, as though adjusting his position. But his pulse was racing and he felt a constriction in his chest. Could someone who jogged a lot have a heart attack? he wondered. He wished he had a yellow pad so that he could scribble furiously. He did not.

"You didn't know that?" Oakes seemed truthfully surprised. "I met Connie when I worked for Dewey. I was only a kid then, but he had known my father."

"Why wasn't there an Oakes file at Trowbridge?"

"Connie has given me private advice. He took what little files there were."

"Why was he so sure Freezetemp could be bargained?"

"He said you weren't a courtroom lawyer. He said you were a hallway lawyer. He said you'd work it out with your friends in the U.S. attorney's office. He said you and Santorini started together."

The summation saddened him. Connie should have thought more of him.

"How does this end?" Alec asked it quizzically. He found himself interested, as a bystander.

"This hypothetical case?" Oakes said.

"In this hypothetical case."

"The young lawyer moves away from New York, far away. He gets a nice settlement from Trowbridge. He enters a practice in San Francisco. He is never heard from again."

When Alec got to the street he let the January cold sweep over him. He walked down Fifth Avenue. He didn't know where he was going at first.

He loved the section from the Plaza to Bryant Park. When he was a little boy, his mother would take him on the double-decker buses and they would sit at the front seat on the top and ride all the way to Washington Square and back. Sometimes they would get off at Bryant Park and talk to the lions at the library.

His rage mounted as he walked. Maybe it showed in his face, for he realized people parted in front of him. He had been defeated, again. His side was losing. Three dead, two wounded. Noah, Felix, Spanos dead, Lee and Sophie wounded, and he was having to withdraw, give up ground and scatter.

It took forty-nine blocks to make a decision. Later he could not remember the walk in any detail. He suddenly looked up and he was at Tenth. He couldn't feel the cold. He stood by the graveyard of an old church.

Again he thought of his mother. She would not like what he was going to do. He hoped she and his father weren't sitting in heaven watching him after all.

Oakes was right. Alec knew more about killing than many did. It was funny but he could not remember a single day in Vietnam in which he had thought "today I am going to kill somebody."

Before every patrol they polished and prepared their murder weapons. They taped the magazines together so they could fire the most bullets, sharpened the knives so they would enter the flesh of another human quickly and easily, set the grenades to go off at their most devastating moment, loaded and oiled pistols so they would fire without jamming.

But he never thought of it as setting out to kill someone. Alec thought of it as saving his own life. Killing was incidental to that overwhelming goal.

Preservation. That he was walking down Fifth Avenue today was a monument to self-preservation in Vietnam.

Maybe he wasn't so different from Oakes, after all. Now he was setting out to destroy. Self-preservation or revenge?

The plane to Montreal was crowded, skiers going to the Laurentians and business travelers. He had to sit in Smoking next to a man puffing Gauloises, and by the time he got to Dorval he felt woozy.

There were two DEA men on the plane. They had no baggage and had been caught by surprise by his trip. He had seen one of them desperately arranging to carry their pistols through security.

At Dorval they were met by what he presumed were Montreal police or Mounties. They were taken through immigration ahead of him. He ignored them.

He got a room at the Ritz-Carlton and called Ochoa. He wasn't in. The man who answered had a heavy Spanish accent. Alec could

not tell whether he meant Ochoa was not in the apartment or not in
Canada.

He had supper sent up by room service and watched television. It
was nearly ten when the phone rang.

"Did you come here to bring me the DEA?" Ochoa sounded
angry and suspicious.

"I came to bring you a letter from Noah."

"*Qué pasa?*"

"It is what you want."

"Do you also have the DEA?"

"Yes."

"Be in the lobby in twenty minutes."

Alec left his suitcase and briefcase in the room. He unwrapped
the disks and put them in his side pockets, two in each. He put on his
overcoat but left his shirt collar open as though he were planning a
midevening walk.

The man who picked him up was not the same as had met Alec
before. He was a Colombian, but older and with a hard face that had
been burned with an acid or a hot substance when he was a child.
The skin had grown differently in a circle on his cheek than it had on
his chin, giving him a strange patchwork appearance.

He did not speak. But he eyed two men in the corner of the lobby
that Alec did not recognize and hustled Alec into a red Oldsmobile
with Quebec plates.

"Mounties," he said.

"What?"

"They were Mounties."

The man began to drive at a steady medium speed, looking in the
mirror. For thirty minutes they drove around Montreal. Up side
streets, down main courses, along the river, and across to the islands.
Alec was totally lost. It started to snow and slush from earlier snows
had covered the windows with grime. He could not have said where
he was even if he knew the city.

Suddenly the car sped up, lurching and hurtling through a seedy
residential neighborhood and then breaking into open country. It
came to a halt at a desolate crossroads. The driver watched the
rearview mirror for what seemed like five minutes. Then wordlessly
he turned around and headed back to the city.

At last they drove through a portico into the courtyard of an old-style apartment complex. It was not as grand as Ochoa's high rise.

Alec got out and stood in the snow. The man backed the car out of the courtyard, its headlights glistening through the snowflakes. For several minutes the courtyard was dark and deserted. Then one of the apartment doors, number eighteen in the light, opened and a man beckoned Alec in.

"Raise your arms."

He raised them. The man searched him carefully. He rubbed his torso up and down.

"Do you want him to strip?" the man said to someone in back.

Alec heard Ochoa's voice.

"No, let him come in."

It was a shabby apartment. Children's toys and trash littered the floor. Ochoa sat on a worn couch. There were only two lamps burning. It gave the apartment a dim glow.

"I have no gun this time."

"We don't care about a gun. We were looking for a DEA transmitter."

Alec nodded.

"Why is the DEA looking at you?" Ochoa said.

"They think I may be trafficking for you."

Ochoa laughed. It was dry and without mirth.

"What is this you have got?"

He handed Ochoa the disks.

"What is on them?"

"It was what you and Noah thought. There is also a letter from Noah. It is on one of the disks."

"What do you want?"

"Nothing."

"You did not take all your fee."

"I don't want the fee. We will return the $52,000 as well."

"You want nothing else?" Ochoa seemed amazed.

"I will get what I want."

The American customs at Dorval searched Alec. It was the first time he had ever been given a border search. The customs men were deferential. "This is just routine." They read him the law that allowed them to make a body search. The other passengers had shifted nervously as he was pulled out of the customs line. This must have been the way it was in Nazi Germany. He did not protest. They did not protest. He was taken to a small room.

"You have nothing to declare?"

"Nothing."

"What was the purpose of your visit to Canada?"

"Business."

"What was that?"

"I visited a client."

"Who?"

"I am not required to tell you that."

He was asked to strip. They searched his body. They searched his rectum. Vinny was showing him how nasty this could get.

He missed the flight. The customs men were apologetic.

"You have to arrive at an international airport with sufficient time to complete the procedures," the Eastern ticket agent said. "We can't hold planes."

She booked him on the next flight. He stayed in the waiting lounge and read the signs. There were fourteen signs on one wall and seven on the other.

23

THEY killed Oakes in the way they would have killed him in Medellín: in the open, in daylight on a crowded street. A Medellín assassination is an art form. It has the flavor of the bull ring. The assassins, mounted on a motorcycle, ride down their prey as picadors would a bull.

So it was with Oakes. The two men on the motorcycle, so the police account went, had chased him down Second Avenue for twenty blocks, weaving in and out of lanes to stay with his black Jaguar.

The grenades blew his body into four main pieces. The legs stayed on the car's pedals, as though still operating the vehicle. His head and part of a shoulder were blown into the backseat and survived in such completeness that the first firemen who arrived told the newspapers they thought there were two people in the car, one in front and another in the back.

A third body section, the right side, landed against the right front door. The remainder, quite destroyed, stayed upon the seat where Oakes had been when the grenades landed.

Alec read every account with care, underlining key details. The grenades were in a bag that had been dropped in Oakes's lap as his car sat at the light at Fifty-second. The police said there were two grenades, which exploded a fraction of a moment apart. Alec guessed the assassins chose to give themselves absolute certainty.

Why the window was open on a cold winter's day was unclear. One passerby said she thought the motorcyclist rapped on the window and the driver of the car rolled it down.

Police said they were looking for two young men with dark

complexions. The descriptions weren't very good and the license plate of the motorcycle had been obscured by dirt.

Killing him by explosive had been a nice touch. The tradition of Medellín was a MAC-10 submachine gun at full automatic. Alec wondered whether Ochoa had ordered it as an artistic device, a nod to Felix and Spanos, or whether it had been the most sure and practical method for the assassins. Sureness and practicality seemed the more likely.

He had thought, on the plane back from Montreal, that he would feel remorse or guilt. He had been a lawyer for the Department of Justice, he had sworn an oath to uphold the laws of the United States.

But the morning the remains of Oakes's highly polished Jaguar flashed on the *Today* show, he felt a strange sense of exhilaration and relief. This was justice, after all.

He read the accounts over a mammoth breakfast, two eggs, bacon, the works, his appetite undeterred, indeed, he admitted, enhanced by the end of Oakes.

He found he had an overwhelming desire to call someone, to talk about what happened, to claim victory. Was it gloating? He couldn't tell. He walked around the apartment thinking he should be saddened and subdued, but instead he had a growing sense of freedom and excitement.

It was strange. In the war his greatest single feeling after battle was one of relief. The enemy dead appeared as little piles of rags and flesh, so departed from the living, so disconnected from reality that it was hard to have an emotion about them. It was hard to tell which one you had killed. There was no moral certainty. That was a loophole. Soldiers had a loophole.

In Oakes's death, he had moral certainty. He had no guilt. He wondered if his soul had deteriorated. Maybe one's conscience wears out as one grows older, sandpapered away by compromise.

He called Lee, dialing the number from the real estate papers.

"I think the man who was responsible for Noah's death may have been killed in New York today."

"What?"

"Well, it's all in the papers. That man Oakes was blown up in his car."

"How horrible."

"Yes."

"I thought you would want to know."

"I see."

It was only after he had started speaking that he realized it was 5 A.M. in Seattle. The call to her must have seemed grotesque.

"Are you and the girls all right?"

"Oh yes."

"Settling in?"

"In a way."

"What happened again? I'm half asleep."

"I can't tell you much on the telephone. The police said two men put a grenade in his car."

"Oh. God!"

She still sounded drugged with sleep.

"What does this mean?"

"I think it means it is all over."

When he hung up he was sorry he had called. The call would only frighten her. To tell her of the death must have made him sound bloodthirsty and unfeeling. Her voice awakened longing. He thought about her as he dressed. He wondered if she thought of him.

When he got downstairs the DEA car was gone. The doorman got him a cab.

"What happened to those men who wait here every day?" he asked Alec.

"They've got better things to do, George."

The doorman smiled.

In the office he chatted it up with secretaries in the snack room. His change of demeanor seemed to startle his coworkers. The file supervisor positively backed away when Alec asked him how the Knicks game had come out.

For two days the Oakes killing was a media firestorm. At first the rich and the powerful fell into line with statements of grave concern about lawlessness and terrorism that should end the life of such a prominent man.

In Washington a Justice Department spokesman said the President had asked the FBI to cooperate with local authorities in finding the perpetrators of this shocking act. Television news accounts speculated on everything from the PLO to the Mafia.

CIA director William Casey denied Oakes was working on a secret government mission. Vice President Bush honored him as a man "who made us understand modern economics." Unnamed aides at the investment firm said they were planning a major funeral from the Fifth Avenue Presbyterian Church.

Suddenly it all stopped. It was as though somebody had turned off a spigot. Helen Oakes said through a spokesman that her husband would be buried in private, in Connecticut at the family church.

Federal law enforcement sources told the *Wall Street Journal* that Oakes's death may have resulted from a feud between drug cartels. The story did not make it clear how Oakes would have been involved with drug cartels.

The following day the *Journal* reported that the firm had recently lost "several major clients" and the volume of investments it managed had dropped "over 30 percent" in a matter of days after Oakes died. A little item in the *Journal of Commerce* said the IRS was considering an audit of the Oakes accounts.

At the weekend, Ames, the surviving partner, announced the investment house would be dissolved. "Without the driving force of Trum's vision, we cannot go on."

As required by law, the U.S. attorney notified Alec that a court-ordered wiretap of his residence telephone had been in place for sixty days and that it was discontinued at the conclusion of the investigation.

Alec laughed out loud when it came. Vinny didn't even say he was sorry.

Alec took two weeks off. It was the first time he had taken a vacation since he and Karen split up. He went to San Diego, renting a little beach apartment on Coronado. The water was too cold to swim, but the running along the beach was great and the drinking was terrific.

After a week, he met a woman whose ex-husband had been a marine officer. For several days he tried to seduce her, but she wanted a meaningful relationship and needed, she said, to "put her life on an even keel."

He gave up. "I only wanted to put your life on an even bed." She laughed so hard she almost fell out of her chair. They had been drinking Salty Dogs for four hours and everything seemed funny.

He caught the night plane for Seattle. There was no one in first class, so he drank all the way, chatting up a stew with fantastic thighs. He arrived drunk.

The rental car woman was a little reluctant to give him a car, but his double row of major credit cards reassured her.

It took an hour to find Lee's house. He stopped twice for a drink and once for directions. Even in his bleary state of mind he knew he needed the drinks for courage.

The house was one of those 1920s bungalows between the university and Lake Washington. He fell over the antique milk box going up the steps and crashed against the door as Lee opened it.

"Who —"

"It's me."

"What are you doing here?"

"I don't know."

He tried to grab her but she darted back into the room and he fell against the entranceway wall for support.

"You're drunk."

"Yes. I think so."

"What are you doing here?"

"I love you."

"Oh God, Alec."

She let him come in and sit down.

"You really look awful."

"Thanks."

He reached for her and she did not move away. He held her very hard.

"Ah no," she said, quite softly.

They held each other on the couch for a long time.

When he tried to take her clothes off, she demurred. "The girls."

He finally fell asleep.

It was such a crushing hangover that he could hardly move his head and lay, at first motionless, surveying the room from a horizontal perspective.

He could see the back of Lee's bare calves through a kitchen door,

moving back and forth in a silent ballet. For a long time he couldn't
sort through just what she was doing. He finally concluded it was
preparing food. The thought sickened him.

It was well into daylight and the room was too bright to open his
eyes wide.

He closed his eyes. When he opened them again her knees were
directly in front of him.

"Are you awake?"

"Yes."

"Would you like some coffee?"

"Oh God, yes!"

She crouched down by his face holding the cup. She was so
beautiful he groaned.

"Do you want me to hold the cup?"

"No. I can take it."

His hands were quivering and he held the mug with both hands
as he sat up.

She watched him drink.

He sat silently for a long time, letting the caffeine do its work.

"Did you have any bags?" she asked.

"I think so. They're in the car."

She went to the window.

"Is it a red car?"

"Yes."

"It's on the next-door neighbors' lawn."

"Oh shit."

He tried to get up.

"Give me the keys."

She put a raincoat around her shoulders and went out holding his
keys.

He lay back down.

When she came back she was trundling his old B-4 bag. She put it
by the stairs.

She got them both coffee.

"What about Oakes and Noah?"

He told her how Noah and Philip had hoped to start an investment house with the Ochoa millions. How Noah suspected
Oakes was cheating. He told her about the disks, the luggage, the

note her son had left. He didn't tell her he had given the disks to
Philip.

"Oakes must have concluded that Noah made computer copies of
his records and sent Julio and Smiley to get them."

"They killed Noah?"

"Yes. By mistake, I suspect. Probably because he couldn't give
them the disks. Maybe Oakes just wanted him dead."

"But when did they get Noah? I saw him off at the airport," Lee
said.

"They must have somehow forced or lured him out of Kennedy
before the flight, taken him back into New York. . . ." He didn't
finish. He didn't say "to the place where they killed him."

"When he didn't show, the bags were pulled off and ended up in
unclaimed. Since Noah didn't use his ticket, Pan Am's computer
didn't show him on any flight."

"Why did they have to kill him?"

"I'm not sure that was in the plan. It may have been because the
men Oakes hired were clumsy or maybe Oakes feared Noah would
disclose what the firm had been doing to the Colombians. That
meant sure assassination. You can see that now. Oakes may have
thought it was kill Noah or die himself."

She was very quiet for a while, not emotional.

"What was the connection with your man Felix?"

"None really. Felix, like Noah, was just another cat that was
getting out of the bag. I don't think Oakes realized that Felix had
already made a deal with the feds. I think he was trying to prevent
that. He either didn't understand what my law partners were se-
cretly telling him or he didn't react fast enough. I really don't think
he would have had Felix killed surrounded by federal agents. But at
first it worked out for him anyway. The U.S. attorney wouldn't
continue."

"Who killed Oakes?"

"The Colombians."

"Because he was cheating them?"

"Yes."

"How would they know Noah . . ." She didn't say "was dead."

Lee didn't seem to notice that Alec had to think for some seconds
before answering.

"Maybe somebody who worked for Oakes told them."

She sat for a while digesting what he had said.

"You think Noah was trying to change his life?"

"The note on the disk certainly sounded that way. He wanted to get back with the girl we talked to in Vermont."

"Can I get his note?"

"It would be hard. The feds have the disks. If I were you, I'd leave it alone."

"Why did a man like Oakes get into this?"

"I suppose for money. Six or seven years ago he became convinced his wealth wasn't great enough. He found a way he could accelerate it. You look back in his family, the money had been made in the early nineteen-hundreds. Maybe he wanted to be known as an Oakes who became a financial baron on his own."

"Your son made a fortune as well."

"How so?"

"The records showed he had an account of ten million dollars under the Grant name."

"Ten million!" Lee was startled. "Incredible."

"He was in an incredible business. Millions of customers, growing popularity, no advertising, low production costs, low labor costs, no taxes. It is the American dream."

She sipped her coffee in silence.

It was an hour before he felt strong enough to move around. Lee showed him where to take a shower and change.

"Where are the girls?"

"I sent them to my cousin's."

He stayed in the shower for half an hour trying to steam out the booze. His hands were still shaking when he shaved, but he took little short strokes and managed to do it without cutting himself.

When he dressed and came out, Lee had changed her clothes and had a raincoat on.

"I was going for a walk. Would you like to come?"

They walked the lake shore. The Cascades were shrouded in fog and a light drizzle fell, misting their faces with moisture.

He found himself for the first time talking with her about himself. He told her about Moira Moran, about the crazy night with cocaine and the recriminations. He told her how he found out about Callaghan and of the sense of betrayal and isolation.

"It was as though I looked around and I was standing on a hill by myself. Everything in my life structure since Vietnam has disappeared. People like Vinny, Callaghan despise me as a fool who cannot adjust to their ecosystem. For all I know they're right.

"Even worse, all I have is being a lawyer. That's my life, and if it isn't going then I might as well shut down. I have no one to love, no children to care for, no aging parents, nothing in life but myself and my job."

They walked on, up the streets by the university and back down toward the Sound. Lee kept absolutely silent. She wasn't going to help him at all. He was going to have to ask. He realized suddenly how inarticulate he really was.

"You're making a mistake, you know, letting me get by you." He looked at her intensely. "I'm ready, willing, and able."

Lee started to speak, but Alec kept going.

"I can tell from your eyes that you don't know whether you love me. You may even know that you don't love me. But life isn't so far from those lawyer's yellow pads. It's a tote sheet. You tote up the good and balance with the bad.

"I bet if you tote me up again, you'd get a better reading."

She put her arm through his and squeezed it to her side.

"It isn't that I know or don't know I love you. I don't know about love anymore. I'm not sure about love between men and women. About love at all, really. I'm not sure I will survive Noah. Every minute I feel something. Guilt. Longing to see him. Or just a sudden memory will come along."

They walked for a time in silence.

"How can we have a life of love and affection when every time we look at one another we remember such violence? When I think of Noah . . ." She said it sadly and, he thought, not so firmly as before.

"When you are here without me you think of Noah every day."

Lee nodded.

"So then the real question is whether we can give each other more love and strength together than we can apart."

This proposition seemed to silence her.

"Do you believe in fate?" Alec asked.

"No, not really."

"Fate may not be the right word. But things are ordained. Noah is in trouble. You come to me. You've told me that you thought of me before Noah, when I was married. I have told you I thought of you."

He was working this out as he went. This wasn't as easy as a jury summation.

"So something led you to me in this crisis and something made me respond. So turn what has happened around. It may be that you were not distracted by an unexpected affection when your son needed you. What really happened was that some unseen force led you to someone who would give you aid and strength when you most needed it."

She seemed stunned by the clarity of this analysis, looking at him quizzically, gripping his arm more tightly.

He shifted the direction.

"You know, no person really controls where they're going. Look at these little houses." He took hold of her shoulders and turned her toward the bungalows that bordered the park walk. "People in them live in Seattle. Maybe they think they know that they will grow up, get married, and grow old in Seattle. But they don't know if they'll have cancer or an auto accident, whether the husband or wife they choose will love them, whether they'll get drafted or the Russians will drop a bomb on them. They move forward, by instinct. They just — live."

For a while Lee said nothing.

"Alec, I know some things are different than they were. I know from just the short time we have been here that isolation is not right, if not for me, certainly not for Mindy and Veronica.

"I know, or I guess I know, that I can't change Noah's life now, nor alter the memories except within myself. But don't you see? I am afraid of myself, not you. Something poisoned John Hastings and me. Something poisoned our child. Maybe it's like bad genes. There are things I cannot even bear to remember, things I did. Maybe I can't deal with a man. Maybe I am one of those women who cannot deal with sexuality. Maybe something's wrong with me."

She had screwed up her face in thought. She was about to say something else when he grabbed her.

"Don't fucking argue with me! I can't stand to be argued with when I have a hangover." He was smothering her face with kisses and his arms held her so tightly she couldn't escape. She didn't. He felt her hands inside his jacket rubbing his back.

They stood there a long time.

When they got back to the house she called her cousin, then locked the house, front and back.

She had taken the little attic room and given the girls the bedrooms on the second floor. There was one wide window that faced the Cascades and she had set the bed so you could lie in it and watch the mountains.

The lovemaking was like the great dark clouds and rolling fog that passed over the distant mountains. It was dark and turbulent and then gentle and soft, on and on with no sleep, food, or drink. They knocked over the bedstand and loosened the headboard.

She handled him as a woman would a child, gently, firmly controlling his every sense.

It was not over until night had fallen.

When she had finished she pushed him aside.

"That should keep you quiet for some time."

"I can't walk," he said.

"Most men can't when I'm finished."

They broke into gales of laughter.

They went down to a fish place on Elliott Bay. They picked giant swordfish steaks and had them broiled and drank Chilean rosé.

"When I was in college" — he was thinking back a thousand years — "rosé was the only wine anybody knew. I can see myself now solemnly tasting a rosé while the waiter stood by. Neither the girl or I would have known the difference, but the ritual, no self-respecting sophomore didn't know the wine-tasting ritual."

Lee was giggling. "Oh God, yes! Lancer's! When you went to an officers club in the sixties for the Saturday-night dinner. Lancer's was on every table."

The wine ended the hangover. He felt wonderful. He couldn't remember when he had felt so good. He looked at her. Her eyes were sparkling and her hands moved animatedly as she talked. She was happy. He knew it. It was the first time he had ever seen her happy. She was quite a nice woman. He found himself marveling at his good fortune.

They talked of food and wine and movies they had seen and songs and rock and roll. They didn't talk about Noah or death or drugs or the future.

The next day they had a family council. He was very nervous. He never had done anything like this.

"Alec and I" — Lee was talking with great seriousness — "don't know where things are going, but we do know that we have come to be very . . ." She paused. "Very close.

"We think we might want to be together more. Maybe for a long time."

She stopped short of saying "Is that all right?"

Veronica and Mindy seemed unsure of what they were supposed to do.

Finally Mindy said "That's very nice."

There was no jumping up and hugging Alec or anything like that. It wasn't like T.V. He wasn't sure if that was bad or good, but later Mindy asked if she could go with him when he went down to buy some things at the market, and he took it as a good sign.

He got a room at a hotel downtown and they spent three days just being together with the girls. They rode the ferries and hiked mountain trails. Nobody talked about anything but the day ahead and not much about that.

They went over to Bainbridge Island on the ferry alone one afternoon. Lee opened the bidding.

"Could you practice law here?"

"Sure. I'm not a member of the bar here, but I can get a transfer."

"Is that what you should do? Should you cast off?" She said it in a very small voice.

"Why not?"

"Well. Won't you have to give up a lot in income and everything?"

"I haven't a lot left to give up. When I get here I'll have enough."

"When you get here?"

"Oh sure. It's decided. Two conditions."

"What are those?" she said.

"You give us all the time and patience that you can. There's no deadline on our lives. Let's just live."

"The second condition?"

"You tell John Hastings you won't need any further financial support. I've got a little money and I'll have more from the house and my fee-share and savings programs at Trowbridge. I'll put it in trust for the girls if you'll do that."

"So I have to cast off as well." She said it slowly and thoughtfully as somebody who has just learned the price of something they want and has to decide if it is worth the cost.

The ferry was approaching the island. "Maybe someday we can afford a house over here." She had tucked herself into his shoulder. Then, realizing that she seemed to have decided, seemed to have made a commitment, she shifted, coming hard about like a sailboat with the boom swinging free.

"But we have to take it day to day. A day at a time."

They flew back to New York together. The girls stayed with Lee's cousin.

He began to dismantle his life. Pogue could hardly contain his pleasure when Alec told him he was leaving Trowbridge. It was clear the old man had thought, with Oakes's murder confirming his criminal connections, that Alec's influence in the firm would rescue him from banishment. He bore the look of a man who has pulled on a rope he thought was tied only to find it loose.

Shirley was the only one Alec believed was truly saddened by his leaving. They hugged a long time. She brought in her famous carrot cake and they ate in his office. "So you're going with the lady with the legs," Shirley chuckled to herself. "At least you're not as dumb as I thought."

He put the apartment and the Connecticut house on the market. And while they waited, they lived. They did the galleries and the shows, skated in Central Park, and walked through rain and sleet in Greenwich Village.

Eddie came by one night and he and Alec had a drink near the office. Vinny never talked about the case after Oakes's death, Eddie said. "He was quiet as a mouse."

"His office had some information, like you said. It was a bunch of computer disks. They turned it over to the DEA and the IRS. This guy Oakes was big in money laundering. But now he's dead it's only a recovery case."

Eddie was fishing for information. Alec didn't bite.

"I'm moving to Seattle."

"No shit?"

"No shit."

"*Cherchez la femme.*" Eddie gave him a wink.

"Absolutely. Hell of a femme."

"Good luck, counselor."

24

THE call from London came a week before they were scheduled to leave. It was like a chill wind.

"Mr. Anton, do you recognize my voice?"

He could see Philip Ochoa before him, the soft teak-colored skin
and the delicate snakelike movements.

"Sure."

"How are you?"

"Fine."

"I have some information for you."

"I thought our association was at an end in Montreal."

"It will end when I want it to."

"What do you want now?"

"Do not be hostile, Mr. Anton. I only want to give you a post-
script."

"What is that?"

"We had a long talk with the two Puerto Rican gentlemen you
met in your garage last year. It was a very hard talk. We asked about
the Jew Felix. Yes. We asked about the Greek. Yes. We ask about
Noah. No. They didn't do Noah."

"That's impossible!"

"Trust me, Mr. Anton. We know how to get accurate information. These men didn't lie to us."

"Who did kill Noah?"

"I do not know."

"Are you sure he would not have been down there that night on
business for you?"

"I cannot think why. Local people there say they did not see him.
That is why we knew the police informant was lying."

"What do you want me to do?"

"Nothing, Mr. Anton. I only wanted you to know this."

Alec sat for a long time just staring out the window. He had known, really in his heart known, that it didn't add up. If Noah was dead on June 3, why were Julio and Smiley still looking for Mr. Grant and the disks weeks later?

Alec knew why he wanted it to add up. He wanted it finished. He wasn't going to think about who killed Noah. He knew he was not going to tell Lee about Ochoa's call. Noah was dead. That was the end.

But the call had made him jumpy and tense. He took the .45 with him to Connecticut and put it in a bedroom drawer without Lee seeing. He wanted to go to Seattle, be out of New York, be gone.

Two days later the New York police announced that the two suspects in the Noah Hastings murder had been found dead in Puerto Rico.

The tabloids and television went heavy. The recession produced few good stories, this gave them "Gangland-Style Killings."

Alec called DeNunzio.

"There isn't much more than you read in the papers. These guys were hit. No question. Both were killed with a shot behind the ear. Both had been tortured. Both had their testicles cut off. I wouldn't even want to guess who did them. Anyway, it isn't my problem."

"How were they tortured?"

"Electrical batteries or cattle prods. I've only seen the pictures. You wouldn't want to."

"Does this close the investigation into young Hastings's death?"

"As far as I'm concerned."

For a week the stories cast a pall over Lee. It was like water on the tiny flame of her emotional renewal. She receded into herself. He tried to help, to distract, to nurture, but it was very hard. The timing had been bad; Noah had arisen to cast her down just as she had begun to adjust to his loss.

Alec suggested they put the final real estate arrangements in the hands of others and get back to Seattle.

But as time grew nigh, Lee seemed paralyzed. She did not want to leave without confronting Hastings about the child support, but she did not want to see him either. She seemed emotionally suspended.

"Why don't you simply send him a registered letter, tell him you are moving permanently to Seattle, work out a visitation for the girls," Alec offered. She didn't like that idea.

Lee seemed determined to deal with Hastings herself, as though that was a trial she must bear. "I cannot put this in a letter."

She didn't tell Alec when she was going, only saying, one day, "I did that yesterday." At breakfast on Saturday he finally asked her about it.

"It was very strange. He wasn't angry or abusive. He said that he didn't care whether I took the money or not. He said he wasn't going to abandon his daughters and would help them. Now that Noah was dead, he said, they were 'our heritage.'

"We talked a lot about our lives, about Noah. He reminisced a lot. Then he said something very odd."

Lee paused, as though considering his words.

"He said he had a dream that we were back together. He said he had the dream so often now that he took it as an omen."

"When I said 'John, that's crazy. We've been apart ten years. Our marriage was filled with agony,' he just smiled. 'Are you going away with someone?' he asked. I said yes. He said 'Anton?' I said yes. And that was it. I left."

It took a week to pack Alec's things. They stopped the paper, left the television set off by unspoken agreement, and didn't listen to the radio. They played a lot of music on the stereo, made simple meals, watched the winter scene of the Sound.

When she had learned of Noah's death she had drawn away from him in her grief; now she seemed drawn to him. He found she would follow him from room to room rather than stay alone; suddenly she would be at his side when he did not expect it, and at night she fell asleep holding him. If he drew away she came closer, cupping her body around him like a spoon.

Alec didn't remember when he first saw the Herreshoff. It was a beautiful one, not new but very well cared for and winter-rigged with a North Sea wind canvass over the cabin and cockpit and a life raft double lashed to the stern.

They both admired it. "That's the boat I always wanted." Lee followed the Herreshoff with her eyes as it made a tack up the channel to Cove Marine. "I sailed one once."

Three days later it was sitting off Peach Island at dusk. He thought that odd in winter. He had presumed it came to Cove for storage or fittings. Maybe the work was done. He sat until dark that night watching the vessel. For some reason it made him anxious. Jesus, what this thing had done to him! A goddamn sailboat scared him!

When he got up the next morning it was gone. He felt like a fool. Bad weather struck at midday. Rain and sleet sweeping in across the Sound, hammering the water over the seawall at high tide and rattling the windows. That explained the Herreshoff. If he'd been listening to the weather report he'd have known the Herreshoff was anchored close-in for the shelter of the island.

For two days the storm hardly abated. It seemed to fit Lee's mood, cold and dark. On the third night, Alec made rum toddies and a hot stew and the combination seemed to ease Lee. They made love in the room above the roses, finally falling to sleep in each other's arms.

Alec smelled *nuoc nam*. He could smell the fermented fish sauce so strongly he knew Charlie must be inside the bunker. It was mixed with the odor of perspiration and lubricating oil. He lay silent in the darkness groping for his pistol. Charlie was very close.

The muzzle pressing against his nose awoke him. He did not know where he was. He started up, but the muzzle, cold and steely, jammed hard into his face.

He cried out and pushed hard upward. Someone fell backward, his pistol flying up. Lee screamed. Alec was trying to remember where the Colt was. He grabbed at his side. It should be in the holster. But he was naked. He realized this was not a bunker. Someone was scrambling to stand up nearby. He grabbed for the night-table drawer. He could see the gun in his mind's eye. Just where he had left it.

The drawer was half open when he was hit. The blow cut across his face. Something tore his skin and the warmth of blood was on his cheek. He slipped away. Now he was in the bunker.

When he came to he was lying against the bed's headboard. They had already packed the lamp shades and the bare bulb of the night-table lamp cast the room in a harsh and awful light.

Lee was naked. She was panting with fear; it caused a tiny gurgle

of noise. Her torn nightgown lay before her, but she made no move
to draw it over her nakedness.

She was motionless and staring into the darkness beyond the rim
of the lamp's light. He followed her gaze. They were in the shadows.
One was tall, the other small and wiry.

They wore black wet suits, both had their faces painted with
camouflage grease. Alec thought idly that the colors were wrong.
The colors were jungle greens and blacks. They should have used all
black for a night operation. The large one had a pistol pointed at
him. He could see the muzzle of an army Colt.

The bed was wet. He or Lee must have wet the sheets with fear,
and there was blood. He didn't know where the blood had come
from. Then he remembered his face.

"Who are you?" Alec found his voice. It broke with fear.

"Hello, captain. Collecting some of your legal fees?"

Hastings moved out into the edge of the light.

He was dressed as though on a commando mission. No skin
showed, black rubber gloves, black rubber shoes, and a black-
rimmed scuba mask tilted over his forehead. Only his eyes appeared,
white and wild in his painted face.

"What are you doing here?"

"I came to say good-bye to my wife."

"This is crazy. Why have you hurt us?"

"It is normal security, captain. You know that. We've secured the
position. Secured the personnel."

The Hmong moved so fast that Alec didn't realize he was next to
him until he felt the wire around his neck. It was piano wire, strong
and sharp.

He looped Lee's neck as well, joining the ends around a piece of
wood. It was like a leash, a dog's leash.

"Move!"

Alec could see his Colt on the end of the bed. He wondered if
there was a chance. As though to answer this thought, Hastings
scooped up Alec's .45 and stuck it in his belt.

Outside it was so cold that it took Alec's breath away. A sleety rain
drummed against his bare skin.

"Please let us put something on!"

"Silence!"

Hastings struck him across the mouth. He felt a new cut and the warm taste of his own blood.

The Hmong pulled them through the seawall breach and down along the beach. The tide was out and Alec couldn't see a boat. Only one house even had a light on; it was six hundred yards away by the old bridge and Alec knew that even if the neighbors looked out the window they probably wouldn't notice anything.

Lee was crying in pain and fear, the sand under their feet had given way to harbor bottom, shells, rocks, and glass.

"Please slow down!" she begged.

Alec heard the sound of a blow striking flesh but it was not the gun; it was something rubber or leather. Lee grunted.

At the edge of the water, camouflaged as scrupulously as if in a military operation, was a rubber boat. The Hmong pulled it into the water and pointed for Alec and Lee to climb in the middle.

The Hmong took the prow and Hastings pushed off, only cranking the outboard when they were in total darkness. Alec could hear Lee's teeth chattering and then realized his were drumming as well.

He did not know how long they pitched through the water, and he could tell they had stopped when he felt the rubber boat hit up against a hull.

The Hmong drew Lee on board first. Her bare buttocks glistened in the dim cockpit light as she dropped like a limp white fish on the Herreshoff's deck.

The cabin at least was warm.

Neither Hastings nor the Hmong made any effort to cover them or give them something to dry off with. They crouched on the cabin floor like two animals, their leashes now separate.

"We need tactical information."

"You need what?"

"Tactical intelligence. I questioned Noah. Now I must question you."

"You questioned Noah?" Lee's eyes had a wild look.

"Oh yes. You didn't know. Noah and I had quite a session."

"Hastings, do you know where you are?" Alec asked.

Alec realized Hastings was hallucinating. He thought he was in combat. Maybe he could be shaken to reality.

"Silence." His gaze returned to Lee.

"Your son was so grand. He bought me dinner. Me and Mr. Nhim. Quite nice wasn't it, Mr. Nhim?" The Hmong gave no sign he understood.

"A nice Chinese dinner and then a nice walk through Noah's place of business."

"His what?" Lee was still shivering even in the cabin. The boat was making sickening rolls in the swells, having swung broadside to the waves.

"His offices, my dear, his offices. The place where he sells poor benighted people cocaine."

"What were you doing with Noah. What?"

"Noah was going to handle my investments. He was going to make me as rich as he was, but first, first we had to talk about that last night so many years ago. The night he told me you wanted him more than me. I beat him then because I didn't believe it. I thought it was the talk of an evil child."

Alec could see from Lee's face that now she knew what happened to her son.

"God no, John!" She tried to struggle up to reach Hastings.

Hastings said something in what Alec guessed was Lao. It was quick and sharp like Vietnamese, but he caught no word.

The Hmong's hands grasped Lee, little brown hands on white flesh.

Hastings made another quick sound.

There was a flash of light on metal. It was so fast Alec could not follow it. Then he saw the wire draw tight. It now encircled her neck like a necklace.

"The question is fornication." Hastings was talking to Lee. Her whole body was trembling.

"Noah said he has fornicated with you."

Lee tried to say "no" but it came out "nuh."

Hastings's eyes moved perceptibly. The Hmong tightened the wire.

Alec had seen this questioning before. The Vietnamese Rangers favored it. It had its downside. If the victim ran out of air he couldn't answer anyway.

Alec said "Don't."

Hastings swung with his gun muzzle. It grazed Alec's forehead.

"How many times?"

"I never . . ."

Hastings nodded to the Hmong.

The wire was now making a purplish welt on Lee's throat.

"She has slept with him. She has told me of this." Alec lied. He had to stop the wire.

"What has she told you?"

Lee now understood through her fear.

"Yennnng . . ."

"What?"

"Yes."

"Noah said ten times."

She nodded.

"When he was twelve?" Hastings had put his face close to his subject.

She nodded.

He looked at the Hmong. The wire tightened. Her eyes bulged slightly and her hands grabbed upward. The question was a snare.

"Try again."

"Seven."

Hastings looked at the Hmong and the wire relaxed.

"Seven what?"

"I started at seven."

"To do what?"

Lee was crying now, sobbing deep internal sobs.

"I only did it to help him sleep."

"What did you do?"

"I rubbed his . . ."

"You rubbed his penis!" The interrogator was triumphant. He had tactical intelligence.

"Yes. It made him sleep, that was all. It made him sleep."

"What else?"

"Nothing."

Hastings nodded. The Hmong's hands moved.

"I put it in."

"Put it in what?"

"I put it in me."

"When he was seven?"

"No. No. Older."

"When he was twelve?"

"Yes."

There is a funny thing about torture. It begets truth as well as fiction.

"Colonel, is this how Noah died?" Alec said it in a low voice.

Hastings turned slowly to Alec.

"Noah died during interrogation."

"But you said he had answered your question."

"He had answered some questions. We were continuing. You know this, captain. There must be verification. Parallel questions. Contradiction techniques."

"Did he live until you had verification?"

"On the main point, yes."

"What was the main point?"

"Incest. He fornicated with his mother."

"What didn't you know?"

"Truth. He said he seduced her. I did not believe him."

"What did you believe?"

"She seduced him."

"Isn't that a moot point?"

"Oh no! No! No!"

Hastings became upset. The pistol had shifted.

"It is vital. Did Noah destroy his parents? That is the question I could not verify. Did he destroy us?"

"Or?"

"Or did Leland lure a child, in violation of everything holy, to destroy me?"

Alec knew they were going to die.

Hastings would kill them in the end. Even deranged Hastings knew they could not live. He wondered what fraction of a second he had to reach the gun.

"Do you know what Noah liked?" Hastings had knelt before Lee and put his face close to hers again.

The boat heeled and righted, with a creak of rigging.

She could not speak or look into his eyes.

Her lips had a froth of spittle and vomit.

He grasped her chin and moved her head so she could not evade his gaze.

"He liked it when you took it in your mouth!"

Hastings's eyes were riveted on Lee.

"So you killed him on purpose. It was not under interrogation?" Alec wanted to distract, to draw attention to himself.

Hastings let go of her face.

"Because he hated me."

"You killed him because he hated you?" Alec could not hide incredulity.

"He should have hated her." Hastings's eyes had filled with sadness.

"I did the right things. She did horrible things. I never hurt him. She destroyed him. Why did he hate me?"

Alec shifted his eyes to the Hmong; the Asian's eyes had not wavered. Alec wondered if he understood English.

"So you ordered Mr. Nhim to kill him."

"No! Of course not!" Hastings seemed shocked and insulted by the thought.

"I realized I had to end his life. He could not go on. We had perverted him, destroyed him. It was really best. I kept the breath from him, as though he was a baby. I simply ended his breathing. He didn't suffer. He slipped away. I should have done it long ago."

Hastings was looking at Lee.

"There are things a man can only do himself, that he can't order others to do."

He drew his M1911 Colt and held it forward in a formal execution position, one hand cupping the butt, the other grasping the trigger.

The boat gave its most violent lurch.

There was an incredible explosion.

Alec had one thought: How extraordinarily loud, the blast of a pistol fired indoors.

His ears were ringing.

The Hmong's body slammed back against the bulkhead as though someone had picked him up and thrown him.

The cabin was filled with smoke and the smell of cordite.

Lee lurched forward. She somehow had Alec's Colt from Hastings's waistband. The colonel had stumbled backwards.

She seemed to concentrate as though listening to unseen instructions.

Her finger squeezed.

Another incredible explosion. The bullet entered Hastings's side and blew out his stomach, showering the map table with blood and entrails.

Hastings went forward. He looked very surprised, as though finally to be shot was amazing.

Lee was shaking and the muzzle of the pistol quivered. But she steadied it with her other hand and brought the muzzle up for a second shot.

It took all of Alec's strength to wrest the pistol from her grip.

Her naked body was covered with Hastings's blood and the neck wire hung down between her breasts.

He gently took the wire from her neck and threw it into the sea.

He threw the one from around his own neck after it.

"What?" she said.

"They're gone," he answered.

Alec found a blanket forward and covered her. He put on a yellow storm suit that was hanging near the bulkhead and covered Hastings's and the Hmong's bodies with the cockpit tarp.

He fired all the flares he could find and they hung above the Herreshoff, bathing the deck in red and green reflections like Christmas lights.

Epilogue

BALTIMORE

AT first he dwelt on himself, on how fast his life had been swept away. It was as though a wave came ashore and all trace of Alec Anton was gone.

One day Maurice at the India House knows what you like for lunch and the next day all the cards in your wallet are useless. The apartment, the Connecticut house, the reserved parking space, the health club membership, all those little pieces of existence that seemed so solid disappeared within weeks.

Alec Anton's passing might have been complete, but it was not quiet.

Newsweek ran his picture as the center of what it called a "Wheel of Death," surrounded by scenes from the killings. Grainy photos, "never before released," of Noah's body being removed from the New York tenement, pictures of Felix's car, and shots of the shrouded body of John Hastings on a coast guard stretcher coming ashore in Westport. Trumbull Oakes's death was mentioned only as an aside in the body of the story.

The *National Enquirer* said it would be the "sex-love-drug killing of the decade." Somewhere it bought a picture of Lee in a bikini for the cover and used an inset of Hastings in Vietnam battle dress. *People* wrote a story about women who killed their husbands and got away with it.

Every television station in the New York metropolitan area had a go. The coroner's inquest was a circus. The tabloids, already in a circulation war in New York, went crazy. One even sent reporters to follow Lee's children to school in Seattle. Moira Moran's name did not surface.

Strangely none of them really ever put the whole story together. It was just as well.

Alec later realized that from the night on the boat he had never exchanged a private word with Leland Hastings. Maybe that too was just as well.

They were questioned by coast guardsmen and police, by the state's attorney, and by their own lawyers and a coroner's jury. Alec would relate the story and Lee would nod and agree.

Two weeks after Hastings died, the jury ruled Lee fired in self-defense. The record showed that Hastings, a Vietnam veteran who may have had emotional problems from the war, devastated when his son was murdered in a drug transaction, launched a plot to keep his former wife from marrying.

Alec testified Lee's shot killed Hastings after Hastings killed the Asian by mistake. Strangely no authorities asked about the neck cuts and Alec volunteered nothing.

Lee was gone the day after the ruling.

Alec left the following week.

Pogue made a very generous settlement, based on the agreement that Alec would no longer say he had been a Trowbridge partner. "You can't hide it, but don't advertise it" were his exact words. Alec agreed never to enter the law offices again, and never to give interviews.

He quietly set up the trust he had promised for Lee's children, Mindy and Veronica. There wasn't as much as he had thought. The legal fees were horrendous. Lee's new lawyer said she was very grateful; she was having a hard time getting started in Seattle.

It took nearly a year to find a law practice. Alec went in with a guy he'd known in the marines. They agreed they'd try it. If Alec's notoriety got in the way, they'd have to cut it off. It wasn't very glamorous: auto accidents mainly, some real estate settlements, legal services for small businesses, a little divorce, a little criminal. No drugs, he tells the clients. I don't do drug cases. He and his partner were the first firm in Baltimore to use television ads.

Nobody makes the connection much anymore. At first some people would say "Alec Anton. Aren't you . . ." and he would either have to tell the whole story or walk away. He walked away a lot. Finally he changed his name back to his father's real name, Antofski.

How his father would have laughed at that! He went through hell trying to assimilate in America and his kid surrenders it in the Baltimore city clerk's office.

Baltimore really isn't bad at all. Of course, it's not New York. Alec took his first earnings and bought a house on Federal Hill. It was a shambles, but he worked on it mornings, nights, and weekends. He got a dog from the pound they said was half Labrador. It turned out the other half was wolf. They have sort of a mutual respect; affection would be too strong a word.

And every day he runs through Baltimore, just at dawn, around the Inner Harbor restoration down to Broadway to the old market and back by the power plant.

It is not correct to say he thinks of Lee every day, but most. It is not desire or longing; it is curiosity. What in God's name happened?

Some days it is clearer than others. He wandered into a Greek tragedy, an incidental character in a classical play. Noah, the girl in Germany, the other men were all victims. The night on the Herreshoff was ordained, as surely as the sun rises. It was the violent end of John and Leland Hastings. Alec Anton was hit in the crossfire.